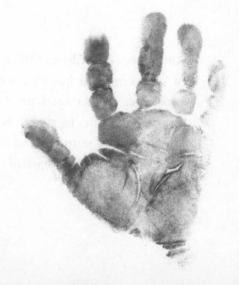

Anne Buist is the Chair of Women's Mental Health at the University of Melbourne. She has over twenty-five years' clinical and research experience in perinatal psychiatry, and works with protective services and the legal system in cases of abuse, kidnapping, infanticide and murder. *Medea's Curse* is her first thriller.

Professor Buist is married to novelist Graeme Simsion and has two children.

ANNE BUIST
MEDEA'S CURSE

WITHDRAWN

TEXT PUBLISHING MELBOURNE AUSTRALIA

textpublishing.com.au

The Text Publishing Company
Swann House
22 William Street
Melbourne Victoria 3000
Australia

First published in 2015 by The Text Publishing Company
Reprinted 2015

Book design by Text
Typeset by J&M Typesetting

Printed and bound in Australia by Griffin Press, an Accredited ISO AS/NZS 14001:2004 Environmental Management System printer

National Library of Australia Cataloguing-in-Publication entry:
Creator: Buist, Anne, author.
Title: Medea's curse : Natalie King, forensic psychiatrist.
ISBN: 9781922182647 (paperback)
            9781925095586 (ebook)
Subjects: Forensic psychiatrists—Fiction.
            Forensic psychiatry—Fiction.
            Stalking—Fiction.
            Violent offenders—Fiction.
            Suspense fiction.
Dewey Number: A823.4

This book is printed on paper certified against the Forest Stewardship Council® Standards. Griffin Press holds FSC chain-of-custody certification SGS-COC-005088. FSC promotes environmentally responsible, socially beneficial and economically viable management of the world's forests.

FSC
www.fsc.org
MIX
Paper from
responsible sources
FSC® C009448

For my parents, Greg and Jean Buist,
who are so much more than 'good enough'.

And for Graeme:
it couldn't have happened without you.

The curse of children's blood be on you.

EURIPIDES: *Medea*
(Trans. Philip Vellacott)

AUTHOR'S NOTE

Over the last twenty-five years, working as a perinatal psychiatrist, I have seen thousands of women suffering from postpartum depression, an illness that affects around fourteen per cent of women having children. It can be a debilitating disorder that affects not just the woman but her partner and child also. Fortunately, it generally responds well to treatment. These women love their children and try to be the best parents they can be. This is not their story.

In the same time period I have also seen hundreds of women whose transition to parenthood has been complicated by a range of problems including drugs and alcohol, domestic violence, poor parenting models and lack of a 'village' to support them. Many of them I have seen because they have come to the attention of child protection agencies and/or the courts. Most of these women are also trying their best but are ill-equipped to be 'good enough' parents and struggle to rise above the intergenerational trauma; sometimes the result is child abuse, removal, and more rarely and tragically, the death of their child. It is the struggles of these families that inspired this story.

As the protagonist, Natalie King, notes in this book, psychiatrists are bound by a code of ethics taken seriously by the RANZCP (and myself). Any of Natalie's breaches, decisions or opinions belong to her character, and are not necessarily endorsed by her creator.

No real patient or other person is depicted in this work of fiction. Where real cases have been referred to, they are not cases I was involved with professionally: I had access only to publicly available material.

There is a moment as she comes into frame when she hesitates. Just before the anger takes over, there is a glimpse of something else. Then she takes the stairs two at a time, headed towards the man with the wispy goatee standing halfway up. Mid-twenties, wearing a suit that looks to be borrowed from his dad, puffing nervously on a cigarette.

She turns and in the movement there's that fierce energy. Her eyes are shining like a cat's, brown pools in kohl rings. She shouldn't wear kohl, it makes her look cheap. Her legs are bare, her knees knobbly over heavy black boots. The scar at the top of her right thigh is visible as her index finger drums against the chest of the man. She has taken a position two steps above him but he is still taller.

Goatee-man looks surprised at what she is saying. It's impossible to hear her words over the standard-issue blonde reporter at centre frame reporting for Channel 7 from the Supreme Court. He tosses his cigarette away, narrowly missing Blondie, and looks around for help.

A curl of red-brown hair escapes the clasp on the top of her head and falls over an ear studded with metal. She

I

ignores it and pushes her hand into goatee-man's chest. He pulls back, grabs the banister and leans against the bluestone wall.

The Crown Prosecutor arrives—pin-striped suit, blue tie, cocky—and Blondie intercepts him. Will you be asking for the five-year maximum? He ignores her, not even breaking stride as the camera tracks him. He reaches the arguing couple and puts his hand on the woman's arm.

Bad move. Her leg swings, with a flash of white inner thigh, then with a look of cartoon astonishment the Crown Prosecutor staggers backwards. His arm catches the banister and breaks his fall. But his Armani-ed arse still hits the concrete. She puts one hand on her hip, a naughty-girl giggle on the edge of her lips. Goatee-man smirks as Blondie races into frame, her microphone thrust forward.

Another lawyer, shambolic and aghast, descends with gown billowing. The microphone catches him saying, 'Dr King...' He grabs her arm, whispers in her ear. Whatever he says pulls her up. The intensity collapses and suddenly she looks young. Her face is a perfect oval. There is a tiny heart-shaped birthmark on her cheek that would be easy to miss. Like the faint scar where she used to wear a nose stud.

Unless you knew her. Really knew her.

The frame freezes and he rewinds to the moment of hesitancy that reveals her vulnerability; no, more than that. He knows this expression: shame. His own reflection is on the plasma screen, next to hers, as if they were joined in the same world. He leans forward, and his fingers trace over her image, tongue running over the edge of his teeth.

He replays the footage. Again.

Natalie gunned the bike through the gap in the morning traffic, then braked hard before she hit the driveway. She would have missed Liam O'Shea, standing just inside the wrought-iron gate, but he sidestepped into the flower bed anyway. She parked her bike, pulled off her helmet and shook out her hair.

He was wiping his muddied feet on the brickwork border as she walked back. 'Fan*tah*stic.'

She had forgotten his Irish brogue. And the bedroom eyes.

'Didn't anyone tell you motorbikes are dangerous?'

'Yes.' Her stepfather, most Sundays. She walked past O'Shea, towards the building.

'I need to speak to you, Dr King.'

Over her shoulder she said, 'You *want* to speak to me. I don't need to speak to you.'

'I'd only be wantin' five minutes.' The Irish accent was laid on with a trowel.

Natalie, halfway up the staircase to the Victorian mansion where she saw private patients, turned back to look at him. 'Give me one good reason why I should waste my time.'

'A chance to get Amber Hardy out of gaol?'

Reasons didn't come any better than that, but O'Shea was expecting opposition and she'd have hated to disappoint. 'You got her in there on your own didn't you? I imagine you can get her out as well.'

'Five minutes?'

She could think of a more enjoyable way of spending five minutes with him; but that would have been almost as problematic as reopening Amber's case. He followed her up the stairs, across the balcony and into the dimly lit corridor. Natalie nodded good morning to Beverley, the office secretary, whose smile was directed at Liam as he followed Natalie to the coffee room. They had the space to themselves.

'I'm here about Amber's ex-husband,' Liam said.

Natalie turned towards the espresso machine and tamped the coffee down hard.

'Travis?'

'Him and his new partner. Did you know about her?'

She knew. Where was he going with this?

He continued. 'She was pregnant pretty damn quickly.'

Amber had been her patient until just after the plea hearing, and was devastated to discover that Travis had found a new partner so quickly. At that time she was still coming to terms with the charges, with incarceration and life without her infant daughter. 'Didn't he love us?' she had asked, bewildered.

Natalie handed Liam the coffee. If he took it any other way than short and black he didn't say. She studied him for signs he was leading her into a trap. 'And?'

He had the grace to look away briefly. 'Look, we all knew she did it. She confessed.'

4

'There were extenuating circumstances I could have raised if I'd been allowed to take the stand.' She felt a surge of guilt and squashed it. She couldn't afford to feel vulnerable in front of Liam.

'Defence's call, not mine. Anyway the judge, he wasn't going to buy anything you said. The media would have crucified him.'

'She shouldn't have got a custodial sentence.'

Liam drank his coffee, watching her. 'Your testimony wouldn't have made any difference.'

'Just given you a chance to destroy my credibility and bolster your own ego?'

'It wouldn't have helped her. She'd already refused to request bail. The expert witness was good but Tanner wasn't going to accept the dissociation line. Nor anything else you came up with.'

Natalie put her cup down. A trail of black liquid slopped down its sides.

Liam placed a photo on the table next to her coffee cup. A blonde-haired girl of about a year old looked up at the camera. The photographer had caught her in a moment of delight, blue eyes shining and hands coming towards her mouth as if to suppress a giggle. She looked vaguely familiar.

'Chloe. Travis's daughter with the new partner.'

'And?'

'She's missing.'

'Missing?'

'Disappeared two weeks ago.'

That was where she'd seen the girl's photo before: in the newspaper. She hadn't paid much attention. Certainly hadn't connected it to Amber. The article had been more

5

about the subculture of chaos and irresponsibility in their regional town than about the child.

'I'd love to hear your thoughts.' Liam was watching her intently.

'On?'

'Could Travis have got Amber to take the rap for him?' He added his heartbreaker smile to the accent.

Natalie stared at him. 'You think you got it wrong?'

'I want to know the truth. Which could take a wee while—and I've already used my five minutes. Can we do it over lunch?'

'How about we leave it at coffee and you finish telling me now?'

'We're talking about a child here. She may still be alive. To say nothing of Amber. You surely want to hear the full story?' He paused. 'Dinner?'

Natalie narrowed her eyes. He was using Amber as bait. 'As in a date?' She made a point of looking hard at his wedding ring.

'Call it what you like.'

'Let me guess. She's got cancer. She doesn't understand you. You'll leave as soon as the kids are grown up.'

'I'm thinking we're as happy as most and my kids like things the way they are.'

She didn't believe him but at least his position was clear. 'Okay, tomorrow night then. But I don't discuss wives.'

'That'd be just on first dates?'

'Don't expect to make it any further.'

She watched him leave. If Liam's suspicions about Travis were right, there might be a chance of getting Amber out of prison—a chance to rectify an injustice that Natalie was partly responsible for. There were just three problems.

After the incident on the Supreme Court steps she had been forbidden by her supervisor to see Amber and Travis. Permanently.

She'd just agreed to have dinner with someone who had an axe to grind with her and whom she loathed. And wanted to sleep with.

And Bella-Kaye, Amber and Travis's baby, was still dead.

Natalie's first patient didn't turn up. No surprise there. At least one patient a day failed to show, without bothering to call, apologise or explain. Half the women who saw Natalie existed in a permanent state of chaos.

Monday was the hardest day of the week. At times she felt like she was on a treadmill for months with her psychotherapy patients, listening to similar stories of abuse and its aftermath of anger, pain and despair. And each patient had to play out the same scenarios many times before the endings changed. The process was slow, and it was repetitive. She often wondered if she was doing any good at all.

Jessie Pryor, the new patient, arrived five minutes late. The one-line referral she had brought was over a year old and said nothing about why she might need to see a psychiatrist. Natalie didn't know the referring GP, and there was nothing to indicate why Jessie had decided to see her now.

Jessie was exactly twenty-two. 'Happy Birthday to me,' she said, rolling her eyes. She was wearing a Misfits T-shirt, cut off at the shoulders to reveal heavily tattooed rolls of flesh. The upper part of her left upper arm was a mess of anime cartoons inked onto her skin, overlapping with other figures that had been partly removed. Black roots were showing in her short blonde hair. Her demeanour communicated a succinct message: 'I hate you and I hate the world, but I hate myself even more'. Natalie had been in this space at sixteen, minus the weight and with piercings instead of tatts. Probably with a lot less cause.

Grist for the treadmill.

'What do you ride?' asked Jessie as she threw herself into the corner armchair rather than the upright one opposite Natalie.

Liam's arrival had interrupted Natalie's routine and she hadn't had time to change out of her leather trousers. An analyst would have said, 'Why do you ask?' Natalie was happy just to have the connection.

'Ducati 1200.'

'Big bike.'

'You ride too?'

'Nah, my brother. Used to take me on the back.' Her look suggested bike riders were cool, but that she wasn't sure what to make of a psychiatrist who rode to work.

Natalie smiled in response. 'How old were you?'

'Twelve. Me and Dad had just moved in with Jay and his mum. His real name's Jesse, can you believe? We had to call him Jay to stop the confusion.' One of the more benign problems of blended families.

It had been a turning point, after two years alone with her father. Jessie denied he was abusive, just said that 'he drank too much' after her mother died. But she had all the hallmarks of abuse: poor sense of self, inner emptiness, suspicion about people's motives and instability in her relationships. The marks of self-harm on her arms, half-hidden by the tattoos, were testimony to the times these things had overwhelmed her. Textbook borderline personality disorder.

The fifty minutes were nearly up before they got to why she was there. Jessie's life was spinning out of control and she was having thoughts of self-harm. Again.

'What's changed?'

Jessie shrugged.

Natalie began to outline the rules of therapy. Turn up on time, no suicide attempts, use the crisis line...

Jessie was grinning. There was the hint of a twinkle in her eye and dimples that negated the tattoo artillery as Natalie walked her out to the waiting room and watched her leave.

'Did you forget your change of clothes?' Beverley scanned Natalie's attire with a *what were you thinking?* expression.

Natalie let the comment go. Since her divorce, Beverley's mission had been to find a man. Her latest outfit was a canary coloured skirt and jacket that screamed out a refusal to disappear at forty-five.

Beverley handed Natalie a red envelope. Her name was printed in neat capitals, but there was no address or sender's details. 'Someone gave this to one of Dr Miller's patients as she came in and told her to give it to you,' she said. Her tone made it clear that this was both weird and interesting.

Natalie opened the envelope. A plain white filing card with a handwritten message: *Breaking the rules has consequences.* It sounded like something Declan would say but he was hardly going to send an anonymous note to remind her. He was her supervisor; he got to tell her in person on a weekly basis. What rule was the note referring to? Some perceived breach of ethics? The duties of patient confidentiality and mandatory reporting of risk were sometimes in conflict.

Confidentiality? She didn't discuss patients with anyone

except Declan so it was unlikely to be anything she had said.

Risk? She flipped mentally through her current patients. No apparent danger to any of their children. The two in domestically violent relationships were already well known to police and Natalie had done nothing to incur either partner's anger. Maybe it was something she had yet to be told or figure out. Apart from child abuse, the only thing that mandatory reporting covered was the risk of serious harm to someone. As far as she knew, none of her patients was planning a murder any time soon.

Shit, this had to happen to forensic shrinks all the time. In any event, the note was just stating the obvious. It wasn't like there was any real threat. She'd better get used to it. She turned the card in her hand, considering her options, but in the end dropped it in the paper shredder pile as she headed out the door.

'Could have been the star!'

Natalie hit the punching bag again, harder.

Bob danced from foot to foot on his perch, screeching periodically. When Natalie continued to punch, ignoring his butchered version of Dylan's ode to Rubin Carter, he raised his yellow crest and screeched at the top of his voice, 'You're a complete unknown!'

Natalie paused for breath and wiped the sweat trickling down her face. 'Bob, you really know how to make a girl feel good.'

Bob strutted, looking pleased with himself. He flew after her, up the stairs from the makeshift gym in the garage below her warehouse apartment, where she let him fly free. He regaled her from the curtain rail.

'Shit there and you're parrot au vin,' Natalie warned him. She filled his seed container to give him time to reconsider.

A patient had asked her to care for Bob while he was incarcerated. The patient had a well-demarcated delusional system that revolved around a belief that Bob Dylan had stolen and changed his lyrics; the cockatoo had picked up a few lines from his owner's versions of 'Hurricane' and 'Like a Rolling Stone'.

'You're a complete unknown,' Bob reiterated before flying to his stand. Natalie clipped his chain on and went to get showered and changed for work.

From her warehouse, Natalie cycled between the Housing Commission towers. The grounds were empty apart from a tall Sudanese woman and a dog scurrying to get out of her way. Zigzagging through the back streets of Abbotsford, she joined the bike path that ran past Yarra Bend, the forensic psychiatric hospital where she worked Tuesdays and Thursdays. Clouds of mist rose in patches from the river, and she ducked as she passed trees wet with the previous night's rain. A few cyclists were headed into town in the opposite direction. The winding route made for a longer trip but she was convinced that the physical regime kept her well, at least as much as the medication did.

The forensic hospital facility was on prime real estate. The tree-lined river path opened out onto lush parklands and a back road to the hospital gates. It was all the same to the inmates. They couldn't see out from behind the red-brick walls topped with wire any more than passers-by could see in.

Natalie greeted the security team, eyeballed the iris scanner and was let into the main yard. On the way to her ward, she stuck her head into the administrative section. The hospital manager had, as usual, arrived before the office staff. Only the top of her grey hair, pulled back into a bun, was visible as she checked her emails. She looked up over half-rim glasses. 'Good morning, Natalie.'

'Do you have a moment, Corinne?'

Corinne hesitated, then indicated the vacant chair opposite.

'Wadhwa is being unreasonable,' said Natalie.

'Professor Wadhwa has considerable experience.'

'*Associate* Professor Wadhwa'—she leaned a little on the title, awarded by some minor university without a medical faculty—'is being sucked in.'

'Because?'

'Georgia is attractive, and doesn't wear tracksuits. She's a very good liar.' Georgia Latimer had been transferred to Yarra Bend from the Dame Phyllis Frost Centre for an assessment. It was nearly complete, and she was due to return to prison to await the bail hearing at the end of next week. Natalie and Wadhwa were no closer to agreement about her than when she arrived.

'This case, it is Dissociative Identity Disorder,' he had pronounced after their joint assessment a week earlier.

'On what evidence?'

'We are not lawyers, Dr King. Not evidence—*history* and *mental state examination.*'

'All right then, on what history and mental state findings?'

'Her postings on Facebook. This is most certainly dissociation. The vagueness and memory lapses, these, they are classical.'

'Maybe. I don't see two or more distinct personalities.'

Wadhwa waved his hand dismissively. 'We have the middle-class wife and mother and the regressed child. The details will come out over time. When you have seen as many as I have, Dr King, you will know the signs.'

Natalie had gritted her teeth then and remained unconvinced now.

'I'm not saying Georgia doesn't dissociate,' she told Corinne. 'But if you're asking me to make a call, then she's putting on an act. It's a gift for Wadhwa's research project. If he didn't need the numbers, he'd be saying she had a personality disorder. Which is what she has.'

'I know what you think of his research but the project has been good for the hospital. The board of directors like us to be on the leading edge and Professor Wadhwa is helping us meet our KPIs.'

Natalie raised an eyebrow.

'Look,' said Corinne, leaning forward on her desk. 'Hear me clearly: you have to find a way of working with him. It won't look good in court if you contradict each other and you know how much media coverage he gets.' She rested her chin on her hand. 'Natalie, he's in here complaining to me as often as you are. In the end if I have to choose between an Associate Professor and a junior consultant…' she shrugged. 'And I'm not just talking about this specific case. Am I being clear enough?'

Natalie was still fuming when she squeezed into the ward office for handover.

'Most kind of you to join us, Dr King.'

Jesus, she was only five minutes late. 'Always a privilege, *Associate* Professor Wadhwa.'

Kirsty, the unit manager, winked as she handed Natalie the patient summary sheet. They had shared more than one drink reviewing Wadhwa's esoteric diagnoses, treatment disasters and lack of bedside manner. Any time anyone criticised him he would whip out a pre-written resignation from his leather compendium and storm into Corinne's office, confident she would never accept it.

'For those who have come in late,' said Wadhwa, 'we had just heard that Celeste has deteriorated.'

'Did anything happen over the weekend?' said Natalie.

'Just her brother visiting as usual,' said Kirsty.

Wadhwa looked at his list. 'She is married. Why did her husband not visit?'

Natalie tried not to smirk. 'He's probably still upset about her cutting his dick off.'

In the absence of any response, Kirsty continued handover. 'Susie has been slashing up again.'

'How?' said Wadhwa.

'Her own toenails,' Kirsty said.

Wadhwa's nodded. 'Perhaps her medication needs review.'

'Does she need suturing?' Natalie addressed Kirsty.

'No; she's so scarred you wouldn't be able to is my guess.'

'Consider lamotrigine,' Wadhwa said.

'Last time I looked at the College guidelines there wasn't a medication likely to cure severe borderline personality disorder.'

Wadhwa was shaking his head, giving up. 'So,' he paused and Natalie knew what was coming. 'Along with your other patients there will be sufficient to keep you busy, I should think?'

'Busy enough,' said Natalie. 'But don't worry, I can still squeeze Georgia in.'

'She's completing my assessment forms.'

'I'll be sure to ask if she needs them explained.'

'She has D.I.D., Dr King.'

'Well then, Associate Professor Wadhwa, I imagine that's what my diagnosis will be, don't you?'

Natalie started her rounds, mindful of the research meeting she was meant to attend. She was going to make time to see Georgia and had no intention of kowtowing to Wadhwa, or Corinne for that matter.

Celeste was back to the state she had been in at admission: rocking and pleading with her dead mother to stop yelling at her. Natalie pulled the treatment sheet from the file.

'Besides her brother, anything different? Could she have been putting the pills under her tongue?' Natalie asked Kirsty.

'Doubt it; we watch her after the pile we found under her mattress. Saturday she was playing table tennis with a few of the others and she seemed fine.'

'Spending time with anyone in particular?'

'Not really. Georgia's the only patient that seeks out company, and she prefers the nurses.'

'Good morning, Georgia.'

'Good morning, Dr King.' Unlike the other women in the unit, Georgia was well groomed—hair and makeup nicely done, clothes casual. She gave no indication that she was there for anything more serious than a chat with a girlfriend over coffee; in fact, she had a mug in her hand. In her late thirties, slim, with pale blue eyes and bobbed blonde hair, she looked younger than her years. Natalie wondered if her appearance had contributed to Wadhwa's rejection of borderline as a diagnosis. She was a qualified nurse and halfway through an online arts course. Until her arrest Georgia had been married and middle class: a gym membership and a first-name relationship with her hairdresser.

Natalie decided to deviate from her focus on building a

trusting relationship. Right now she needed some hard facts and time was short. Georgia would be returning to the main prison soon.

'How are you finding Professor Wadhwa's forms?'

'Interesting. A lot of very unusual questions. They pass the time.'

Natalie made a mental note to check them out. She knew one was a personality inventory. Georgia was too smart not to know what the forms were looking for. In any case, Wadhwa had already shared his opinions with her lawyer.

'What do you think of his diagnosis?' Natalie asked.

Georgia gave an exaggerated sigh. 'I don't really know. It doesn't make much sense to me.'

'Have you had periods where you lose time?' Natalie had already been through many of these questions, but one of the hallmarks of Dissociative Identity Disorder was that memories changed according to which 'personality' was present. Natalie hadn't seen any sign of this, though. She only ever saw the same woman—sometimes agitated, sometimes calmer. No more fragmented than her other patients with borderline personality disorder. Wadhwa might need Georgia to have D.I.D., and so might her lawyer. It didn't mean she had it.

'There are events I don't remember very well.'

'Tell me about those.'

'I've told you before. When the ambulance and police first arrived.'

A time when memory impairment was to be expected. 'What about sleep walking? Ever find yourself somewhere and not recall how you got there?'

'Would you count the time when I drank most of a bottle of vodka?'

17

No, Natalie wouldn't. It had been in response to stress and was not repeated. Wadhwa was an idiot.

'Tell me about your mother.'

'I was two when she went to prison. I don't remember her.'

'But you've thought a lot about her.'

'Of course. She was the sort of mother I wasn't going to be.'

'What about your aunt? The one who raised you. What sort of mother was she?'

'She prided herself on being tough.'

Natalie was aware that she was seeing an act and was conscious of how gullible psychiatrists could be, how ready to believe what they were told. It was a reasonable starting point—if you weren't working with criminals. Georgia had a lot at stake. Everything in this interaction was admissible in court.

'So what sort of mother were you, Georgia?'

'Caring, devoted.' She paused. 'Not perfect. My children were good kids, but they got sick. Have you ever looked after children, Dr King? Being woken up every night for a week at a time. Hourly at times. I think I did quite well under the circumstances.'

Georgia looked down. Probably not wanting to appear confrontational. She might be using the conversation as practice for the bail hearing. She had been denied bail the first time because she was pregnant and the unborn child was deemed to be at risk from a woman facing three murder charges—all her own children. The fourth child, a girl, had been born in custody.

'What about your youngest child? Do you miss her?'

Georgia looked up, ice-blue eyes unwavering. 'Three

of my children died tragically, doctor. Then Miranda was taken from me. She was taken from me in the labour ward. What do you think?'

It was a good question: one Natalie wished she had an answer to.

She brought the interview to a close and watched Georgia leave, watched her turn in the doorway to look back and smile before closing the door softly. A half-smile that Natalie was left to wonder about: carefully staged or secretive? Or merely friendly and hopeful; nothing that would be pondered on, had it been given by anyone else?

The interview had been inconclusive. Natalie understood this woman no better than she had at the start. She couldn't tell whether she had been talking to Wadhwa's fragmented, disorganised soul or a cold-hearted monster.

W hat the hell had possessed her, agreeing to have dinner with Liam O'Shea?

She read the online newspaper stories about Liam's case to pass time before they were due to meet. She was irritable and it didn't help that she knew why. She didn't do dinner dates; particularly with married men she fancied fucking. She had caved in instantly, and why? Because of an Irish accent and blue eyes?

Vow number one: no matter what, she was not bringing him home after their dinner meeting. He was already too cocksure and there was far too much of a payback element involved.

She couldn't even console herself that the evening would be worthwhile because of what Liam ostensibly wanted to discuss. She wanted desperately to know more about Travis and the little blonde girl, and to help Amber, but she had to leave it alone, or there'd be hell to pay with Declan, her supervisor.

Vow number two: she'd help him as far as she could over dinner. For Chloe and Amber's sake. Then no more Liam and no more involvement with Amber's ex-husband Travis.

The internet search didn't provide much information. No one seemed to think anything more than bad parenting was involved in Chloe's disappearance. The story had only warranted brief mentions in the metropolitan papers, but it had made the front page of the *Welbury Leader*. One picture included Travis but Natalie wouldn't have recognised him. Only his eyes were the same as she remembered, a slightly puppy-dog look. More self-assured now, in a fuller face with the goatee neatly trimmed. His chin was thrust towards the photographer, meaning business in a way that had been absent on the steps of the Supreme Court. Tiphanie, the baby's mother, had her head turned, avoiding the camera. Didn't she want her fifteen minutes of fame? Chloe looked sweet, vulnerable and innocent. In this photo she was holding a small soft toy.

Natalie arrived at the pub early after a short walk in fine rain through the backstreets, her neighbourhood of factories closing down for the night as she passed. Liam had suggested a city bar, likely to be full of lawyers and stockbrokers, but she had insisted on her local. She could free up her mind talking to the bar staff and be ready for Liam when he arrived.

The Halfpenny was one of those Collingwood classics named for an old-school union leader. In contrast to the tapas bars and cocktail lounges of Smith and Gertrude streets only a block away, it was a seventies throwback with faded floral carpets, walls crowded with photos and a *No thongs or shorts* notice over the doorway.

Vince, the owner, wasn't there. His son Benny, with his red Mohawk reverting to frizz in the damp air, nodded in acknowledgment. Maggie behind the bar had opened a

Corona and put a lime wedge in place before Natalie had even made it across the room.

'He's waiting for you in the corner,' said Maggie, tilting her head to her left.

Natalie took the beer. 'Come again?'

Maggie shrugged with a smile that suggested approval. Vince wouldn't have been as easily persuaded, Natalie thought as she glanced where Maggie had indicated. The lighting was dim but she could make out Liam in the corner watching her, sitting in front of a picture of Vince with a footballer in Collingwood black and white.

'Casing the joint?' Natalie asked as she joined him.

'I like to be knowing the lie of the land.' He was drinking a Guinness. Of course.

'Does the leprechaun impression usually work for you?' she asked, trying not to grin as she sat down at the table. She put her feet up on the third chair and took a slug of the Corona, looking him over as she did. With his curling black hair, only slightly grey at the temples, and an open-neck shirt and leather jacket, Liam could have passed as something other than a lawyer. Almost. 'So tell me about Travis.'

'Over dinner.' He took a sip from his glass, eyes never leaving her. 'Do you live around here?'

Natalie pushed the lime into the bottle. 'I like Collingwood.' Was he testing her out or trying to show he hadn't done a background check? 'I thought there was a lot to talk about. The case. Now seems a good time to start.'

Liam waved for another drink. 'Winding down from a hard day at the office first. Helps focus my attention.'

Yeah, right. Focus it on what?

'So how did someone like you end up a forensic shrink?'

'Someone like me? What does that mean?' Natalie inwardly cursed herself. She'd let him draw her away from the main issue.

'Well...' Liam lay back against the picture of Nathan Buckley and finished his drink as Maggie brought another. 'Not—shall we say—mainstream?'

'That good or bad?'

'More earrings than I can count? Motorbike that's too big for you? I'd lay bets on a tattoo somewhere. Right? Interesting.'

He was right. Annoyingly. Safer to answer his original question. 'Why forensic psych? Amber's case, in part. Plus a run-in with a motorcycle club; their psychopathology intrigued me.'

'I'm guessing that all makes you too tough for relationships?'

'I said I didn't want to talk about your wife. Same goes for men in my life, okay?'

'Not after specifics. Just wondering if you spit them out after one night or whether they occasionally last a few.'

'One's a lot more fun.'

'No care, no responsibility?'

Natalie grinned despite her best intentions. 'Something like that. Now, back to Travis—'

Liam stood up. 'Do you know what you want to eat?'

Natalie wondered if the sudden need for food was to avoid talking about Travis and Chloe because he didn't actually have any need for her input, or to streamline the pathway to the after-dinner possibilities. She went with him to the window into the kitchen and ordered her usual: steak, salad and chips.

'Same,' said Liam. 'Rare.'

'I ended up in the Office of the Public Prosecutor because I couldn't shake the idealised view of justice I'd had as kid,' Liam told her as they waited for dinner. She'd agreed to listen if he'd get to Travis as soon as the food arrived. The truth was, he was good company.

'And what was that about?'

'My da'. I guess you'd tell me that it was because I couldn't stop him beating up my ma, right? That I'm compensating now for what I couldn't do then, by going after the bad guys. Does that answer your question?'

'Do you think it does?' Natalie grinned. One point to her.

'Well it's working; little while ago I put a drug boss behind bars for a ten-year minimum. Ice was scarce on the street for weeks. I have to confess that felt good. I'd have done anything to get his brother as well.'

'Anything?' It sounded flirtatious and Natalie cursed herself silently. It wasn't as if he needed encouragement.

'Almost. As long as no one innocent gets hurt.'

Natalie looked at him sceptically.

'I had a case when I was green,' he said. 'Guy named Tim Hadden; alcoholic, wife beater, record as long as your arm. He always maintained his innocence.'

'Don't they all?'

'Mostly, but in this case he was. DNA testing came in and we had another look. And I'll never be sure that when I first prosecuted him I didn't let my dislike of the man interfere with the facts.'

'He got out?'

Liam paused, and she found she couldn't read him. Anger? Regret?

'He was killed in gaol while they stuffed around with the paperwork.'

It shed light on why he was open to reviewing Amber's case.

'My da',' he concluded, 'was a walking Irish stereotype; the bad one, unfortunately.'

'You think your father got in the way of your objectivity when you prosecuted Tim Hadden?' Natalie had put her observation into words before she remembered she was out socially, not in her office.

Liam drained his glass. 'Same again?' he asked as he headed to the bar. He returned just as the food arrived. Natalie brought him back to the reason for the dinner.

'So what happened to Travis's daughter, this one with the new girlfriend?'

'If I knew that I wouldn't be asking for your help. Not that there aren't other attractions...'

It occurred to Natalie that he worked his sex appeal without thinking. A habit. 'You think I can help because...?'

'The first priority is finding the child. We wouldn't normally be involved this early in a case but ever since the Leskie debacle we want to make sure we get everything right from the beginning. They may not find the child. The police don't have enough points of proof for a charge. No forensic evidence, all hearsay. No one's talking, probably everyone's lying about something and the obvious answer isn't falling into our laps.'

'You make it sound like a Mafia hit rather than a missing child.'

Liam shrugged. 'Nothing that well organised. Stupid eejits behaving badly.'

'Smart enough to keep you guys running in circles.'

'Which is why I'd be wantin' you running around with me.'

Was it her imagination or did the brogue thicken when he was spinning a line?

'So take me back to the beginning.'

Liam cut his steak and it bled on the plate. 'Travis and Amber broke up straight after the plea hearing. Poor hard-done-by man: tries to stand by the bitch who murdered his daughter, but in the end he has to put the love of his surviving child first.'

Natalie tried picturing Travis in the role of hero. Some women found him cute. But the poor-me attitude that appeared by the second interview had alienated her long before Amber had started to reveal the level of domestic abuse. Which was more psychological than physical, but every bit as effective. Travis had been a clear factor in Amber's depression. Had he been supportive, their daughter would probably still be alive. Which was the primary reason for Natalie's avenging-angel moment on the Supreme Court steps.

The memory of putting Liam on his backside was still sweet. She suppressed a grin.

'What's she like?' she said. 'Travis's new woman?'

'Tiphanie Murchison. First name spelt T.I.P.H.A.N.I.E.' His look suggested that the quirky spelling said it all.

'Let me guess. Small, vulnerable and a bit plain. Maybe an abusive background, if not at home then in the schoolyard.'

Liam looked impressed. 'Why doesn't he go for the pretty ones? He's not a bad looking bloke.'

'Because he needs to dominate and doesn't want to share the limelight. Pretty girls have too much self-esteem.' She thought about Amber: ordinary looking, eyes too small, facial features a bit asymmetrical. In the first police video she had been flushed and flustered. Subsequently she had looked bewildered, disappearing into clothes too big for her, hiding behind long, lank brown hair that fell over her eyes. Her family had been supportive but anxious and overprotective.

Liam rested his cutlery against the plate. 'Tiphanie looks average in the photo I saw but she's only nineteen. Police describe her as timid. Not bright, I guess, given who she ended up with. A little dumpy.' Liam looked directly at her. 'But then I like my women petite.'

Natalie stopped herself responding, but couldn't prevent a flutter rippling through her stomach. Damn it.

'Family?' So far Tiphanie fitted the profile Natalie had constructed.

'Prior to hooking up with Travis she lived with her parents. Not known to police.'

Natalie wondered what it was about Tiphanie's home life that made Travis a better option. 'Job?'

'She was working on the checkout at the supermarket where Travis was doing some building work.'

She would have known who he was, that he was married, that his wife had murdered their baby. Welbury wasn't that big. Had Tiphanie felt sorry for him? Was it a celebrity thing?

'So all seems to be going well,' Liam continued after another mouthful of steak. 'Maternal health centre nurse reports she was an exemplary mother.'

Was. The child would be dead, of course. Missing just sounded better.

'Chloe was nearly one when she disappeared. Eleven and a half months. The nurse hadn't seen her for a while. Tiphanie and her mother had had a falling out, so her parents hadn't seen them for a couple of months either. Travis's father left

27

when he was a kid and his mother was in Melbourne.'

'Neighbours? Friends? Was Chloe in childcare?'

Liam shook his head. 'Tiphanie was unemployed. She didn't go back to the supermarket after the birth. The last sighting of the child—other than by Travis and Tiphanie—was earlier the day before. By a neighbour. She only heard her playing in the backyard, she didn't actually see her.'

'What's Tiphanie's story?'

'That she'd got the child breakfast and left her watching cartoons, then went back to bed.'

'As exemplary mothers do.' Natalie remembered a home visit she'd done in another satellite town, closer to Melbourne. The mother ordered groceries online and never left the house. Her child spent all day in front of the television.

She didn't notice Liam leaning forward until his hand brushed her hair out of her eye. She had no time to suppress her sharp intake of breath. They briefly made eye contact and he looked amused. Half-ready to defend himself. She reminded herself of her two vows.

'So what happened next?'

'When Tiphanie got up at eleven o'clock, Chloe had vanished.'

Natalie wondered how a child of less than a year old had become accustomed to entertaining herself for that long. Some babies who were left to cry for long periods all but gave up. What looked like compliance was actually depression, or some infant version of it. 'Travis was at work?'

'Yes. With witnesses. Impossible for him to have got home and back without being noticed.'

Natalie thought for a moment. 'What was his reaction, his explanation?'

'Blaming anyone and everyone.'

'Including Tiphanie?'

'Not yet. The cracks have started to show but his anger is still mainly at the police.'

'And the cops think what?'

'At first they thought she might have wandered off but no one's seen her. They're on a new estate—bit desolate but it's not Siberia.'

'Could she have been kidnapped?'

'Possible. Unlikely. This is a small rural town, remember. The police are checking the paedophile registry, but she's very young. Even if the door was unlocked, how would anyone know unless they'd been watching and planning? Same for those women who kidnap because they're desperate for a child.'

'So the next theory?'

'An accident that the mother covered up. She looked spaced—vacant—but we haven't found a body and she hasn't cracked.'

'Next theory?'

'My favourite.'

Natalie looked at him expectantly. He leaned closer.

'Travis kills the kid in a fit of rage the night before. He has Tiphanie under his thumb, beats her, threatens her, whatever. He does the cover-up and keeps her in the dark about it so she doesn't have anything to tell us. Maybe he gave her some pills. Would account for her looking spaced. Maybe she was out of it when he killed Chloe.'

'So if this theory fits—if it's Travis—you'd have to question the previous child's death.'

Liam smiled grimly. 'Exactly. One child dying might be bad luck, but two, both under suspicious circumstances, to two different women? Travis is the only thing tying it together.'

'Maybe he has poor taste in women.'

'Maybe. Neither woman looks like a killer to me.'

Nor to Natalie. It didn't mean they didn't do it. 'Amber confessed,' she reminded Liam, 'and went to gaol, as you may remember?'

'If Travis had been found guilty he would have gone to gaol for murder. He'd have got a much longer sentence and he wouldn't have had an easy time. If he survived.'

'Amber hasn't exactly had it easy,' said Natalie. 'She was spending most of her time in isolation last I heard.'

'They might reasonably have expected that she'd get a suspended sentence.'

'They didn't split until after the hearing,' Natalie murmured, talking to herself rather than to Liam. Could she have got it wrong? Had Travis been directly to blame for Bella-Kaye's death and now for Chloe's, or had he driven two women to the point of infanticide?

'Is it possible? That Travis murdered both his children?' said Liam.

'Much as I'd like to see him locked up, the circumstances are different.' Natalie moved around some chips on her plate. 'Still possible, but the child was nearly a year old for one thing; out of that sleepless-night stage and too young for full-blown tantrums. Men tend to kill children in anger. Where's the body? Even if he killed her accidentally he'd have to get rid of the body, and Travis isn't a great planner.'

'Still. Will you take a look at Travis and see what you think?'

'He'd never agree to talk to me,' said Natalie. To say nothing of the apoplexy Declan would have. She was *not*

30

going to get involved. She thought of the child in the picture with her soft toy and sparkling eyes.

Liam looked like he'd expected this answer. 'He doesn't have to. He's being called in for a formal interview next week. Decide what questions you want asked and watch from the other side of the screen.'

Natalie put her napkin on the plate, leaving the remaining chips. She was tempted. Not just because of Chloe, but because of Amber, whom she owed. She drained her Corona. She wouldn't be going back on her word if Travis couldn't see her, if she didn't directly talk to him. Liam grinned, knowing he had her.

'Text me and tell me when and where.' She stood up.

'No dessert?'

'Nope, and no coffee at my place either. I have a conference to prepare for.'

Liam laughed. 'You've got tickets on yourself. What about a second date then?'

'This wasn't a first date. Just work.' Which was the only reason she was going to let him get the bill.

Not even saying goodbye to Maggie, she walked into the cool night air and slipped into the shapeless shadows of the Collingwood streets.

Keeping one vow out of two wasn't bad.

'Georgia's asking to see you.' Kirsty didn't bother looking up as Natalie entered the ward office.

'Any reason?'

'You're the doctor.'

'Wadhwa about?'

'With Corinne.'

What was he complaining about this time?

'Don't worry, not you,' said Kirsty, not taking her eyes off the computer screen. 'He sent Tania into lithium toxicity and her family are complaining. I gather he's threatening to resign again.'

They shared a look.

'Do you know if the psychologist has seen Georgia's MMPI test?'

'In the patient record.'

Natalie grabbed Georgia's file and sank into the chair in the corner. There was nothing in the notes to give any hint of why Georgia was asking to be seen, which she would have known was a regular Thursday event anyway. Wanted to be first? To feel important? Natalie found the MMPI, the personality inventory. She smiled as she read it.

'So how are you, Georgia?'

She looked serene; Natalie couldn't help thinking she had no right to seem so untroubled. She was in a high-security forensic psychiatric hospital, for God's sake.

'Getting by. Thank you so much for seeing me.' She paused and looked down at a pile of papers in her lap that had a pencil balanced on top. 'Paul's lawyers will be working hard to keep me locked up.'

'Because he hates you? Or fears for Miranda?'

'I don't think he hates me, not really.'

'Why wouldn't he?'

Georgia looked at her, pale blue eyes never wavering. 'He loves me.'

She thought about Myra Hindley and Ian Brady, the infamous Moors murderers in the sixties, responsible for the deaths of five children, and let herself wonder.

'Tell me about your relationship with him.' Natalie had little history about Paul. Her focus had been on Georgia's diagnosis.

'I met him at a party. He's an engineer. He was working for his father, in his recycling business.'

'How old were you?'

'Twenty-three. He was three years older. We clicked from the start. He was good looking and kind and I hadn't had much of that.'

'Why do you think he was attracted to you?'

'He was very quiet, shy. I wasn't. I think he liked that. I did the talking for him.'

'Is he like that with other people?'

'Not once you know him.' Georgia looked away, fidgeting with the pencil.

Natalie sat and waited. Like most people, Georgia was quick to fill the space rather than deal with the awkwardness silence induced.

'He saw himself as the provider and was happy that I wanted to be a stay-at-home mother.'

'Did having children come between you?'

'He loves me.' The pencil in Georgia's hand snapped. 'Ask any of our friends. He adored me.'

Natalie let *adore* echo in her head. It suggested a scenario in which Georgia killed her children in an act of jealousy. 'Sometimes mothers tell me that they feel pushed into the background, that their children drive a wedge between them and their partner. Did you ever feel that?'

'Of course not.' She now seemed less measured, more defensive, scatty. Would Wadhwa have called this a personality change? Natalie saw it as a response to getting too close to something painful. Which of course was what dissociation was—the question was whether Georgia was aware of the process, and if it was within her control or not. And how deep it went.

'So he spent time with his children?'

'Yes, of course, Olivia in particular as she got older. She was a good baby, even easier as a toddler. Paul was amused by her.'

'"Amused". That seems an odd choice of words.'

'She was an amusing child. She would wait by the door for him to come home and pretend she was hiding. She loved games.'

Natalie had a sense that Georgia was talking about someone else's child. An image of Amber in the acute stages of grief flashed into her thoughts. Time hopefully had helped her move on from that level of pain. Had Georgia ever felt

34

pain in the way Amber had? Georgia's children hadn't died recently. It was more than twelve years since the death of Genevieve, nearly ten years since Olivia, and five since her son Jonah had been found dead in his cot.

'You must have had less time for each other when the children were around.'

'I suppose so. But Paul is a very attentive man. Mothers' Day, thanking me for giving him such beautiful girls, looking after me when...' She paused, submerged in memories for a moment. Sad for her loss of the children, or of the adoring Paul? And why 'girls'? What about the son?

'You had some difficult times to get through. How did they affect your relationship?'

Natalie let her talk, steering her towards their sex life.

'It was fine for both of us, nothing out of the ordinary.'

There was a knock on the door and a nurse put her head in: Georgia's lawyer was waiting.

Georgia stood, smiling. 'My lawyer, she...I...wondered about, well, do you think I'll get bail?'

'It won't be up to me.' Natalie looked at Georgia's apple-pie smile and wondered where she was going with this.

'I know.' Georgia looked down, playing with the two pencil pieces. Then: 'I'm not a danger to anyone.'

'It's a court decision.'

'If I do, I would need to see a psychiatrist while I was out, right? Do you see people privately?'

Natalie looked at her, certain she already knew the answer. At the door Georgia turned and said, 'Paul could be...difficult of course, when...things didn't go his way.'

Now Natalie had two more questions to ponder: what did Paul being 'difficult' mean, and why was Georgia so keen on seeing her?

The work day turned out longer than expected. Beverley had left a text message: *Booked in old patient. Emergency 6 p.m. Can't find her file.*

The 'emergency' slot was meant to be just that. On Thursday nights, her room was free but it was not a time she liked working. Tonight it would mean a long cycle ride in the dark. The *Can't find her file* was irritating. It was Beverley's way of saying she'd stuffed up, that it wasn't really an old patient and she'd fallen for it.

Beverley had already left. She had at least organised the referral letter to be faxed, and it was on her desk. Natalie read it twice to make sure she understood.

Thank you for seeing Kay Long, who I believe you know. She has been struggling with anxiety and depression for the last year since her daughter's incarceration and her husband's sudden death. She requests to see you re management.

The doctor had included a list of her medications: the only psychotropic was sertraline, consistent with the depression diagnosis.

Natalie did know her, but there was a reason Beverley had not found a file. The patient had not been Kay, but her daughter: Amber. After a second read she fell back in the chair and tried to organise her thoughts. Kay's contact so soon after Liam had asked her to be involved in Travis's case was surely no coincidence, but how could they be connected?

There was another problem; Declan wouldn't want her seeing Kay because of the connection with Amber, the case he had told her she was over-involved in. If Kay still lived several hours drive away, perhaps this was a once-off.

Kay arrived early, in faded blue trousers and a white blouse, sensible shoes and a fawn coat with a mended pocket. Her mousy hair was tied back in a ponytail: practicality rather than fashion. The weight loss that had been steady in the early weeks of Amber's incarceration had plateaued, but the lines had continued to form and she looked closer to sixty than the mid-forties she had to be; she had been sixteen when she became pregnant with Amber. Despite the hasty wedding, and a son, Cameron, born shortly after Amber, the marriage had endured.

'Kay.' Natalie extended her hand and Kay hesitated before taking it. Her nervous smile broadened in response to the warmth in Natalie's greeting.

'Dr King...thank you so much for seeing me at such short notice.'

Natalie led her into the consulting room and they sat opposite each other in the armchairs near the window. Natalie, referral in hand, spoke as soon as the older woman was settled. 'I'm so sorry about Glen. When...?' Amber's father, the stoic farmer, hadn't ever said much, but had been steadfast in his support.

'He never recovered from Amber being charged. Heart attack. He made it to hospital but...' She shrugged.

'It's been a tough year for you.'

'Yes, but not much choice but to keep going is there? Glen's mother, and Cam and his wife help with the farm. Amber will be out soon. She'll need me.'

'You've been anxious? Depressed?'

'Wasn't sleeping for a long time. But the Zoloft seems to have solved that, more or less.'

Natalie frowned, and glanced at the referral. Kay caught the look.

'Actually, I think that's all fine.' She paused. 'You heard about Travis's second baby?'

Natalie nodded slowly, alarm bells starting to ring.

'Are you seeing Tiphanie?' The words came out in a rush.

'You know I can't tell you that Kay, I'm sorry.'

'Of course.' Kay quickly pulled herself together. 'It doesn't matter anyway. You can't tell anyone about what I tell you either, can you?'

Which meant this was about Travis.

'I need to tell you something.'

'I'm not involved in this case, Kay. If you know something, go to the police.'

'I can't.' Her tone had a steeliness that Amber's had never had. 'They won't believe me. I don't have proof.'

'What do you expect me to do with it then?'

'He did it.' Her hands were holding each other as if to stop herself hitting out.

'Did what?' Natalie cursed herself silently. Even if Amber was no longer her patient, this was dangerous territory. A lesson in why therapists shouldn't see members of the same family.

'Killed Bella-Kaye.'

'He might have failed to support her,' said Natalie carefully, 'but Amber confessed.'

'He told Glen.'

Natalie stared at her, trying to work out how to get out of the interview pretending it had never happened.

'However much of a shit Travis is,' Kay continued, 'he didn't want Glen dying thinking his daughter killed little Bella.' There were tears in her eyes. 'He came to see Glen in hospital, soon as he heard. Glen told me...but then he died and...what could I do?'

'And now?'

'Now,' said Kay, 'there's another child gone. If you do see Tiphanie, if you are involved in any way, I want you to remember what I've told you.'

The doorbell rang as Natalie was returning to the kitchen from the external staircase that led to her bedroom. She had been planning an early night. Since Liam had alerted her to Chloe's disappearance, her sleep had been disturbed by dreams about Amber and Bella-Kaye. Now with Kay Long's confession it was likely to be worse.

She had bought her converted warehouse when she qualified as a psychiatrist two years earlier, getting a good price because the renovation had been abandoned before completion. Showering in a concrete square was a long way off what the previous owner must have envisaged but Natalie liked it as it was. From the outside it looked like the other two and three level factories that surrounded her, a motley assortment of red and painted brickwork adorned with graffiti, set back from bluestone gutters.

The distinguishing feature was a corrugated-iron clad walkway on the first level that spanned the narrow lane and connected her with the fire stairwell in the building opposite. The real estate agent had described the anomaly as a Bridge of Sighs, and it was the one thing she had changed. The enclosed bridge was now lined with bookshelves, and at the end, instead of a flimsy connecting door, there was an electronically controlled sliding panel, unrecognisable on either side as an entrance or exit. No one apart from the other building's owner and the security company that installed it knew it was there, and even if they did, they couldn't get in.

Finding the doorbell required dedication. You had to know that a wrought-iron version of Munch's *Scream* was hiding it, and be prepared to lift it up in all its agony. Visitors were a rarity.

It was Tom, who lived locally, a six pack of Coronas in hand. Stocky and broad shouldered, he had shaved the beard a few years earlier. He was the drummer in her band but still looked more balding ex-biker than Charlie Watts. She kissed him chastely on the cheek.

Tom rubbed Bob's head on the way to the fridge. The bird bit him. 'Ouch.' He sucked his finger. 'Ever thought of getting a normal pet? You know, a cat or dog that likes to cuddle up?'

Natalie didn't bother answering. Bob suited her fine.

'Anything to eat?' He helped himself to a beer and tossed one to Natalie.

'Nup.' She joined him on the sofa. 'I'll call for pizza.' She added, 'And then I'm sending you home.'

There was a moment of disappointment, but Tom recovered quickly. 'Was someone just here?' he asked.

'No. Why?'

'Guy looked like he was checking the place out.'

'Maybe going to make me an offer.' Tom didn't generally make a nuisance of himself but he could be annoyingly territorial.

'Check your locks.'

Friday night she arrived half an hour early at the Halfpenny to have a burger with the band. She'd been singing with The Styx since her early twenties and they had a semi-residency there. The songs—both the ones she and Shaun wrote, and the favourites they covered—were on the sexually explicit side. It wasn't a persona she wanted her patients to see. The wig she wore on stage, short blonde and spiked, and the heavy makeup were only partly stagecraft.

It was 9.30; the kitchen was technically closed, but Vince had a soft spot for Natalie and would whip up burgers himself if he had to. There were a few upcoming gigs to discuss, including some country ones.

Shaun, the keyboard player, juggled his beer, burger and pen. The blue band of his straw hat matched the blue of his glasses and the flowers of his shirt. 'So how about Welbury? They need a fill-in Friday after next.'

Welbury. Travis and Tiphanie territory. Natalie felt as if fate was pushing; she pushed back. 'It's a dump.'

'I'm not driving,' said Tom. 'Someone coined my car last time we were up there.'

Shaun looked to Gil.

'I guess I can do one night away.' Gil, the plumber-cum-bass player, sounded less reluctant than he should have been to leave his pregnant wife.

'They pay okay,' said Shaun. 'Beats doing another wedding.'

Two all. Shaun's pen hovered. 'Welbury crowd too tough for you Nat?'

Natalie glared at him. She knew what he was trying to do.

'I can take your drums in the van,' Shaun continued, looking at Tom now.

Tom hesitated, looked at Natalie and shrugged. She knew she'd lost, but wasn't sure that at the end of the day she hadn't wanted to.

The first bracket was always a warm-up but it took longer than usual to settle in. Groups of people hovered around the bar, leaving the dance floor empty. By the end of the set, though, the crowd was having as much fun as the band and Natalie recognised a few of the regulars. Beer slopping from glasses had hit the floor and the air was sweet and hot.

Vince brought her a Corona in the break. 'You in any trouble?' Vince had a strong fatherly streak.

'What sort of trouble?'

'The sort that's in the bar asking after you.'

Natalie looked at Vince sharply. He was the other side of sixty and, if the scar on his neck was anything to go by, knew trouble when he saw it. She thought about Tom seeing a man outside her warehouse and wondered if it was a patient stalking her. She didn't work with men anymore. Maybe a patient's partner?

'Describe him,' she said, wiping her brow. It was hot out on the stage.

'Benny told me some jerk's been asking about your band but seemed more interested in you; said he backed down as soon as Benny pressed him. Same bloke I guess. A smart arse, know what I'm saying?'

Liam. Shit. 'Where is he?'

Natalie considered going out front and telling him to bugger off. He'd probably laugh. Pubs were, after all public, and she didn't own the Halfpenny. Vince did, though, and he'd be more than happy to throw Liam out on his ear. Maybe she'd keep that favour for when she really needed it. Right now there was a definite upside to Liam's presence. Her need to expend some sexual energy was escalating and she'd rather not fall back into bad habits with Tom. Not that Liam was a good habit to start, and she had promised herself she wouldn't get involved. 'No more than the usual man trouble,' she assured Vince and turned to the band.

'Guys, can we change a number in the next bracket?'

They started with a few of their own songs. It was hard to see from the stage with the lights on her, but she picked out Liam on a bar stool along the wall, watching.

Fancy this? Shaun sketched out the opening riff of 'Because the Night' on his Roland. It was one of Natalie's favourite covers and she'd practised enough to lend it her own style; Tom called it the sex-on-a-stick mix.

She sang the opening line, voice low and husky, and imagined Liam taking her as the words left her lips. She was fairly certain it would be what he was thinking. She sang about being touched and she could all but feel his hands on her as the lights were burning on her skin. In the second she finished the song their eyes locked and it was clear he knew she'd been singing it for him.

She had the audience calling for more. Natalie was

acutely aware that the song had the same effect on her she had hoped it would have on Liam; desperate had now moved into almost uncontrollable. She reminded herself that it was a really, really bad idea to get involved with this man. He was married, problem enough. But she sensed he was bad news in other ways she couldn't put her finger on. The self-warning, the sense of danger, only accentuated her desire.

She took her time coming out front, more to get control of herself than to make him wait. He was back at the bar, a spare stool next to him and a Corona ready.

'How touching, you remembered.' Natalie handed it back to Vince who was watching closely from the other side of the bar. He exchanged it for bourbon. Neat. Liam raised an eyebrow.

'Your after-performance preference?'

'Something like that.'

'You were great, incidentally,' said Liam, his expression revealing little. The blue eyes were more used to reading others than giving anything away. 'But you know that.'

He looked less lawyer tonight and more Sinn Féin. Something about the curl over one eye and the black leather jacket. And the stubble. He smelled good. Not cologne, just male.

'So can I ask what the fuck you're doing here?'

He grinned. A man used to getting what he wanted; she wasn't overly upset that right now it was her. 'I misplaced your phone number and thought I'd deliver the message in person.'

Like that was believable. 'The message?'

'Thursday, five o'clock. Interview with Travis at Welbury police station. If Chloe is still missing.'

'You don't seriously expect me to go to Welbury?' She

44

thought of Kay's eyes on her, of Amber, of the photo of Chloe. What were the police doing in the meantime? A week off had to mean they would be putting pressure on Travis for a confession.

'I'm here to persuade you.' He sat back and looked her up and down. Tight leather low-riders, and a small black tank top. She could tell he'd already taken them off in his imagination.

'I was thinking of staying overnight after the interview and coming back in the morning. You could drive up with me.'

Natalie stared at him. She reminded herself he was serious trouble too, that all he was doing was trying to even up the scores. Did one bruised ego equal one roll in the sheets? Knowing this did nothing to stop her wanting him. But if he thought he could call the shots he was mistaken. Out of the corner of her eye she saw Vince shaking his head.

'I'll think about it.' She turned towards the door. Liam grabbed her arm. Brave...or foolish, given their history.

'Honey you're not leaving already, surely?' He slipped off the stool and was standing next to her. He might not have been tall, but even with her platform shoes on he still had more than ten centimetres on her. She could feel the power in his hand. Somewhere in his busy legal career he must have found some time for weights. Natalie could see Vince poised for action; she caught his eye. Reluctantly he eased off.

She turned back to Liam. 'I do things on my own timeline.' She shook her arm out of his grip, heart pounding, and walked away without looking back.

It was only hours later, in bed alone, she marvelled that she'd managed it. Not without help though. She'd picked Tom up on the way out of the bar and he'd only just left.

Jessie was on time, more or less: session two and still in the honeymoon phase.

'You asked me about boyfriends last week,' she said. 'And I said no.' *Shit no*, actually. 'Which is true. But there is Hannah.'

Natalie waited. The abuse history wasn't the only thing Jessie had kept from her.

'I mean I'm not with her if she's locked up, right?'

'Hannah's in prison?'

'Armed rob. One of her druggie friends must have done a deal with the cops. The robbery happened before we got together; she needed the money to pay her dealer. She's been clean since I moved in.'

'How long has she been there?'

'A year.' Jessie's tone made it sound more like a decade. 'Four more, minimum.'

A year fitted with the timing of the initial GP letter.

'Was this why you were originally referred?'

Jessie nodded. 'We'd been together six months. She wanted me to get help.'

Natalie noted the genuine warmth and sorrow for her partner, not just her own loss.

'After that, I mean Jay was around...' She shrugged.

Jay—Jesse—Cadek, Jessie's stepbrother. Perhaps he'd provided enough support for Jessie to ignore the earlier referral.

'So why come to see me now?'

'It's really hard,' said Jessie. 'I don't want to cut up. Hannah always asks how I'm doing, but she isn't there. I don't feel I can talk to her about it. I mean she's the one in prison, I've got it easy.'

'Doesn't mean it feels easy.'

By the end of the session Natalie felt there was a good base to work with, the connection a little stronger, though she still wasn't certain why after all this time the situation had reached crisis point for Jessie.

She watched Jessie leave through the car park and get into a beaten-up Commodore. A gangly man with a ponytail of mousy hair, who had been leaning against the car, tossed a cigarette into the gutter and moved into the driver's seat. Jay, she assumed.

The rest of the day dragged. Natalie didn't get her mail until she was about to leave. Beverley passed her a USB stick. Natalie frowned. 'What's this?'

'Arrived in the mail. I'd forgotten,' said Beverley. 'In a red envelope. No explanation. I thought you must have been expecting it.'

Natalie was pretty sure Beverley hadn't thought about it at all. She fingered the small red device, worried about the possibility of a virus, but curiosity won. It contained a single Word document. She opened the file.

Just one line. *I wouldn't get too close if I were you.*

She hated the adrenaline that surged through her, didn't want to believe that one stupid sentence could make her feel so vulnerable.

She took a breath, closed the file and put the USB in her top drawer.

Instead of getting on her bike and going straight home she walked to the nearest newsagents, ten minutes away. The first card had been hand delivered, and she was certain the USB came from the same author. In the back of the shop were the same red envelopes and cards, but of course the girl behind the counter had no recollection of anyone buying any the previous week. Natalie hadn't really thought she'd get any useful information. There was nothing she could report that anyone could do anything about in any case.

She just needed to be proactive in some way.

'From a diagnostic point of view,' said Natalie, 'Georgia presents some interesting possibilities. The differential diagnoses to consider are Dissociative Identity Disorder—D.I.D.—and a personality disorder, Cluster B.' She smiled at Wadhwa and clicked the mouse.

Georgia's case conference at Yarra Bend had attracted most of the hospital's forensic psychiatrists and registrars, as well as several psychologists and a few nurses. Today Corinne was also present. There were obvious similarities with the well-publicised case of Kathleen Folbigg, a New South Wales mother convicted of killing her four children, largely on the basis of her diary entries. The previous week's discussion of Celeste's treatment-resistant schizophrenia had not been such a crowd-puller.

Natalie's new slide showed a list of symptoms.

'These are the symptoms of D.I.D.,' she said, clicking again. A tick, a question mark or a cross came up against each symptom. There were only three ticks. She progressed to the next slide.

'And these are the symptoms of borderline, narcissistic and antisocial personality disorder.' The next click brought

49

up an array of ticks and a few question marks. Only two crosses. 'As you can see,' said Natalie, avoiding Wadhwa's eyes, 'there seems to be more *evidence* suggestive of a personality disorder in Georgia's case.' Catching Corinne's stern expression she added, 'At this stage.'

'Dr King,' Wadhwa interjected, 'there is no reason she cannot have both D.I.D. *and* a personality disorder. Indeed, a childhood abuse history is essential to both diagnoses. She will not have a robust personality structure; this will predispose her to a Dissociative Identity Disorder. This can be read about in my paper in the Journal of—'

'I agree,' said Natalie. Her registrar hid a giggle at Wadhwa's open-mouthed stare. 'In general. In Georgia's case though'—she clicked back to the list of D.I.D. symptoms —'this remains to be proven, don't you think? Particularly given narcissistic and antisocial traits came up on the MMPI inventory.' Unable to stop herself smiling as she said it, she added, 'As well as the high lie score.' The registrar was less successful this time, turning the giggle into a cough.

Wadhwa waved his hand dismissively. 'The lie scale is always high in criminal cases. She is trying to appear better than she is. Georgia has at least three different personalities, so that's Criterion One. They clearly have power over her— they caused her to kill her children: Criterion Two. She has periods of lack of recall: Criterion Three.'

'The lie score does suggest we need to treat what she says with a certain amount of scepticism does it not?' Natalie replied. The test was designed to catch people trying to fake symptoms. In over five hundred dull, repetitive questions, even smart fakers were caught. 'Besides, I haven't ever seen any other personality. My reading suggests that though the diagnostic criteria state there must be at least two distinct and enduring personalities that take control less than five per cent of those said to have it actually fit this description.'

There was a moment when it seemed everyone was holding their breath, but before Wadhwa could open his mouth, Corinne spoke up, glaring at Natalie as she did.

'Dr King, could it be that she decompensates and that these other personalities come out with Professor Wadhwa because he is male?' Corinne, prior to the MBA, had been a psychiatric nurse. She didn't often use this knowledge, but management-speak wasn't going to cover the current situation.

'I guess it's possible,' Natalie conceded reluctantly. Her registrar spent more time with Georgia than Natalie did, and hadn't seen any different personalities. But she was female too. 'I'm not convinced I see anything other than her putting on an act.'

'Is it possible that being a woman makes you less sympathetic?' said Corinne.

Natalie was too startled to be worried by Wadhwa's smug expression. 'Because she killed her children and the maternal part of me can't forgive her for that?'

Corinne nodded.

'Maybe.' Actually Natalie was convinced the maternal part of her was either deeply buried or had never developed. Still, dealing with women who killed their children raised a range of feelings. When she first took on Amber, she'd experienced surges of irrational anger. It had taken several sessions with Declan to work through and redirect her feelings of anger at her own mother from a long time ago.

'It might be good for you to keep working with her,' Corinne suggested to Natalie.

'I would be most happy to,' said Wadhwa. 'My research

into Dissociative identity will be most beneficial—'

'Exactly why you can't work with her,' Corinne said. 'Include her in your research by all means, Professor Wadhwa, but if she gets bail, and she may well, the condition of the court is likely to be that she continues to see a therapist. Natalie would be better placed.'

Wadhwa looked no happier about this than Natalie felt. At best, she felt ambivalence towards Georgia. There was none of the sympathy she had for Amber. At least it gave her a chance to both discredit Wadhwa's diagnosis and to understand Georgia better. Natalie could hang a label from the manual on her, but that wasn't the same as deep understanding. She had assessed other women who had killed their children; Georgia was different.

Natalie acknowledged Corinne's curt nod, a vote of confidence from the manager, even if she hadn't won all the points in the round against Wadhwa.

'You clearly have a problem with Georgia,' Declan said, crossing his legs and leaning forward.

'I think my diagnosis is spot on, even if Wadhwa—'

'You know I'm not referring to your diagnosis or your problem with Wadhwa, Natalie.'

Natalie had known Declan Ryan since she was sixteen. A long stay in the orthopaedic ward, then rehab, meant she'd been a captive audience—but determined all the same not to talk to him. She had put him into the category of 'boring old people', always immaculately dressed with a manner that bordered on ponderous. It was one of the few times that her first impressions had been proved wrong.

Early in the relationship Declan had delivered his précis of her psychopathology. 'You can spend the rest of your life punishing your mother and yourself if you want to,' he concluded. 'Your choice.'

She had been stunned. All she could say was *fuck*.

The relationship had since gone from strength to strength. He'd had two of his own teenagers at the time, so probably had lots of practice with bad behaviour. Years later, after an incident in her intern year, she had agreed, under instruction from the Medical Board, to see him again. They had been meeting weekly for nearly seven years. At least she was down to one medication now, and she no longer required blood tests. Declan had taken some convincing on this.

They were in Declan's Northcote office in the front room of a renovated workers cottage, where they met most Tuesday evenings. It was tastefully, if heavily, furnished, with rugs and original prints, a bust of Freud on a pedestal and one of Mahler on a small table. His patients used the couch; a restored antique upholstered in dark blue velvet with gold brocade and ornately carved wood at one end.

Natalie sat back in an armchair sipping a glass of wine. Sharing a drink differentiated her from his patients, but they met in his office, not in the living room at the back where he would have entertained friends. He always offered her wine, allowing her to make her own choice—in this case, drinking while taking medication. He would usually offer her a second glass: her part in the game was to refuse, showing she was in control.

Declan had become a crucial part of surviving the stress her work generated, both a sounding board and a sanity check.

Right now, she was on edge. The resurfacing of Amber's case sat between them, a reprimand waiting to happen. But for the moment they were on the relatively safe ground of her relationship with Georgia.

'So,' he said. 'Tell me about your countertransference.'

'I just don't like her,' Natalie said, aware that her reply was too superficial to address his question. Her reactions to the patient that stemmed from her own issues needed to be understood so they didn't interfere in the therapy. 'She makes my skin crawl.'

'Which Amber never did.'

'No. I was angry for a while, but I always liked her. Mostly I felt sorry for her.' And still wanted to help her if she could, not that she could share that with Declan.

'So? What's different about Georgia?'

'She's cold, distant. There's an incongruence between her words and affect, something I can't pinpoint. And she's arrogant.'

'Ah.'

Natalie tilted her head and raised her eyebrows.

'She's challenging you, refusing to play patient or fit into a slot.'

'I guess.'

'Don't you like your patients to respect you? At the very least make some acknowledgment of all those years you studied?'

'I suppose so.'

'Think about Lindy Chamberlain,' said Declan.

'Mother convicted for not crying.' When she had actually been defending against the pain. 'Okay, okay. I promise to keep an open mind. If I see her; she might not get bail.'

They talked about Jessie and then, with five minutes left, Declan leaned forward in his chair again. 'So, are you going to tell me what's worrying you?'

Shit. She shifted in the chair. Could she just tell him a part of it? The whole thing with Liam was making her tense and not just because of the link to Amber and Travis, or Kay Long's take on the events.

She gave him an edited version of the case with no mention of the connection to Amber. She had been asked by the O.P.P. for an opinion on a missing child case—and her attraction to the prosecutor was affecting her judgment. She didn't mention Liam's name in case Declan recognised it. Nor did she want the Irish interpretation that would follow.

Declan had seen her courthouse confrontation with Travis on a current affairs segment called 'Mothers Who Kill'. He had been unimpressed.

'You *assaulted the Crown Prosecutor*. You're lucky you aren't facing a charge.'

'He grabbed me before I saw who it was. Anyway, it's completely unreasonable that Amber is getting all the blame.'

Declan's facial crevices had deepened even further. He took a deep breath and ran his hand through his sparse grey hair. 'You're a psychiatrist Natalie, not a policewoman—and definitely not a vigilante. Amber is your patient, not Travis. Our job is to help our patients confront the dilemmas of their daily existence, not smash through them ourselves.'

'I just told him what Amber hadn't been able to.'

'And how was that going to help her?'

He had a point. It hadn't helped Amber; on the contrary, it disqualified Natalie from giving evidence that might have helped her.

'Your lithium level was only 0.3,' Declan had said, as he threw the test results from her GP on the table in front of her. 'You know that isn't adequate to keep your mood stable.'

She still didn't think she'd been high. Not that high anyway. Someone needed to care for the desperate and powerless people she saw; too often none of them had ever had anyone stick up for them.

'You're a good psychiatrist Natalie, but only when you're well. The Medical Board has made me responsible for that and as much as I'm on your side, you know I'll report you if you put your patients in jeopardy.'

'How can I put Amber in jeopardy when I care more about her than anyone else in her medical or legal team?'

'That's precisely why,' said Declan. 'You're too close to this; it's affecting your objectivity. You're making exceptions for her. She has her own friends; let them accost Travis. If she knows you're prepared to cross boundaries, then you're no longer someone she can respect and trust. Psychiatrists that cross boundaries get sucked into their patients' repeating traumas and risk responding how their abusers did. Your role is to reflect back their problem and see a different answer; you can't do that if you're immersed in the drama. You need to stay away from her. Am I making myself clear?'

He could report her if she didn't abide by his decision. And that would put her licence to practise at risk. It was the last time he had mentioned the issue of her medication compliance—another marker, like the single glass of wine, of their relationship. But it still sat between them.

'So,' she asked now, 'should I go to Welbury or not?'

Declan sat in silence for a moment, hands clasped together and index fingers raised at his lips. 'Let me get this clear,' he said. 'You are interested in the case, that's what you're telling me?'

Natalie nodded.

'You're available?'

More or less.

'So the downside is that you might give in to lust?'

'That's the upside, too.'

'Not concerned that he's married?'

Natalie shrugged. 'So he's a louse. If he isn't cheating with me he will be with someone else. I don't mean his wife any harm but really, that should be his problem, not mine.'

'What's *your* problem then?' Declan put a hand up to stop her speaking. 'If you listen to what you're saying, you've told me you don't want a relationship. Am I right?' His look was unwavering.

'A commitment? Absolutely not.'

'He's married, so it seems unlikely he wants that sort of relationship either. Right?'

'Definitely a screw-around type.'

'Then I say again, what's your problem?'

'So I should go for it?'

Declan laughed. 'That isn't what I said. I suggest you examine why you didn't pursue the opportunity on Saturday evening.'

Natalie was more interested in the immediate options than any reflection. A one-night stand could be fun. She needed to get him out of her system. Trouble was, she hadn't given Declan the whole story; Liam was the complication. The motivation was in part Chloe; but primarily, it was Amber.

'I'll come on two conditions.'

'And it'd be a good morning to you too, Dr King,' said Liam, laying on the accent with a laugh. God it was sexy.

'First, your office pays for a room for me.'

There was silence then a low chuckle. 'Never in question. The second condition?'

'That you ride down with me.'

The silence was longer this time. The chuckle was the same. 'Do I need to bring a helmet?'

Natalie picked him up on the corner of Gertrude and Smith, a block away from where she lived. He was out of the wind, leaning against the wall of a Turkish takeaway and wearing a leather jacket that was more about fashion than protection, a bag slung over his shoulder. She threw him her spare helmet.

'All you need in that backpack?'

'I'm sure I can lay my hands on anything else I require,' said Liam, proceeding to put his hands around her hips as he sat behind her with little space in between. Natalie opened the throttle.

The travel method made escaping Melbourne easier and more bearable. By the time they were on the Princes Highway heading southeast towards Gippsland, they'd left most of the traffic behind and she relaxed into the rhythm of the ride. She loved that there was no conversation or music, that it was just the bike, the road and the wind.

On this occasion there was also a very sexy man holding on, probably tighter than he needed to. She didn't think it was because he was scared.

After escaping the suburban sprawl, they rode through

farming country. A little more than two hours after starting out they reached the outskirts of Welbury and Liam directed her to a two-storey weatherboard guesthouse with a return veranda surrounded by a large well-kept garden. It could have been found in any Victorian country town, and gave no hint of the more rundown neighbourhoods beyond. Natalie was still wondering how to deal with her inconvenient attraction to the man; not being in a motel might be the deciding factor. Somehow screwing a married man would be seedier in a motel.

Liam took off his helmet and grinned. 'That wasn't quite what I'd imagined when I thought of getting up close and personal, but it was a great ride.'

Natalie ignored him.

'See you downstairs in fifteen minutes,' said Liam as they took separate keys. She lingered after he'd left and spoke to the owner, a man sufficiently round and full of bonhomie to play Santa Claus, even if the beard was more grey than white.

'When was this room booked?'

'Last Wednesday.'

Two days before he had even told her the time and date. Liam's confidence was irritating but predictable. 'In my name?'

He nodded. 'Yes Dr King. Here for the missing child case are you?'

Mystery solved. Natalie nodded. Small towns really were small. The rumour mill hadn't taken too many turns before it got to Kay.

The police station was a short ride from their guesthouse, past homes with a dilapidated air of unpaid rent and neglect, wide streets with angle parking and a string of takeaways.

Recent droughts, floods, bushfires and an influx of welfare recipients meant the town was busy, but troubled.

'McBride's expecting us,' Liam said. 'He's been a detective in the region for a few years and is back in uniform waiting for a promotion into Melbourne. He's been called in on this because he's more experienced than anyone else here.'

A uniformed policeman wearing the crown stripes of a senior sergeant opened the door from the foyer and nodded at Liam. He extended his hand to Natalie. 'Damian McBride.' Damian's cool look at the prosecutor suggested Liam's ambivalence was reciprocated. Taller than Liam, early thirties with the good looks of an aging schoolboy, he came across as solid and serious. Probably a good thing for a cop; too steady for her tastes. His bland expression was hard to read.

'He's out the back,' Damian said, holding the door open to the inner sanctum. His eyes flickered over Liam's hand lingering on Natalie's back. 'Do you want her to do the interview?'

Natalie bristled. She'd deal with the cop referring to her in the third person later. She turned to Liam. 'I told you...'

Liam smiled over her head. 'I'm suggesting observer only.'

'Not suggesting. I *will* be observing. Travis won't talk to me.' She moved towards Damian as she spoke. 'I treated his first wife.' She saw the edge of the sergeant's mouth tighten; he still wasn't looking at her. With some effort, she dialled back the assertiveness. 'I might be able to help.'

Damian hesitated before indicating behind him with a jerk of the head. 'Go through and I'll change interview rooms.'

Natalie walked past him and turned, waiting for Liam to follow her. He didn't move.

'I'll be meeting with Senior Sergeant McBride's boss,' said Liam. 'We're developing a strategy to deal with the media.' He tilted his head. 'I'm sure you'll be in capable hands. Catch you this evening.'

Damn the man. He could have warned her. The door closed with Liam on the other side, leaving Natalie to follow a silent Damian to a small room with a one-way screen. It must have been at least twenty minutes before he returned. She suspected he wasn't hurrying on her account.

'Instructions?' The tone was just polite enough.

'Look,' said Natalie, 'I guess you don't want me here but since I am, and as the State's paying, why don't you see if I can help you?'

'Me or the O.P.P.?'

'Don't you guys work together?'

'We interview the witnesses. It's not the prosecutors' job.'

Not their stooges' job either. He didn't say it but he may as well have.

Natalie waited. When the silence eventually forced him to look her in the eyes, she said, 'Do you think Travis might be responsible for Chloe's disappearance?'

The policeman hesitated. 'It's a line of enquiry we'll be pursuing.'

'Good. Then let's pursue it, shall we?' She pulled out a list of questions. 'You may have already asked them which is fine, but the ones with the asterisks...' She waited while Damian glanced over the two pages. 'They're the ones I really want put to him while I watch.'

The corner of his mouth twitched; she thought it was an

upward one but he was working hard on not giving anything away.

'No other instructions?'

'No, but come and check in with me before you let him go.' Same indecipherable expression. 'Please,' she added.

Damian moved to sit in a nondescript adjoining room with just a basic table and a few chairs. Natalie settled down to watch via the one-way screen that divided the rooms.

A female plainclothes officer with cropped hair led Travis in. There were several minutes of formalities for the video recording.

Travis hadn't changed as much as the press photo suggested: brown overly long hair, wide set eyes, a generous mouth. He'd shaved the goatee to reveal a weak chin. A smile that made him look trustworthy. As if. He was a little heavier than when Natalie had first met him. His fingers were nicotine stained. He was wearing a muscle shirt that showed wiry arms tattooed with *Bella-Kaye* in a heart on one arm and *Chloe* in a heart on the other. Natalie had to fight a feeling of nausea. Being inked into this man's arms was a death sentence.

'Seems like you're not holding your drink too well these days, Travis,' said Damian, consulting a wad of notes that included hers.

'Wasn't doing nothing.'

'Let me see; you drank at least ten stubbies that the barman admitted to or could remember,' replied Damian. 'Reported as saying "Cops are fucking useless, they'll never get anything on me."'

'Just bullshittin',' said Travis, unperturbed. 'Anyway, it's true. What have you got on Chloe? Fuck all.'

The woman intervened. 'On that matter, we would like

to ask you some more questions.'

'I've already told you everything a million times.'

'Yes,' said Damian, 'I'm sure you want to find Chloe. Sometimes going over it again to fresh ears can help. We appreciate your time.'

Travis looked partly mollified.

'So, the day Chloe disappeared. Let's start there.'

'Same as any other day. Tiph and Chloe were still in bed when I got up.'

'Did you see Chloe?'

'No.' Travis leaned back in the chair. 'She was asleep in her own room. This was like six in the morning.'

Damian nodded. 'Did she wake the night before?'

'No she's good like that. Sleeps right through.'

Unlike Bella-Kaye, who had woken frequently.

'So when did you last see her?'

'I already told you. Before I went out to my mate's the previous night. Tiph put her down and they were like, both asleep when I got home.'

'How was she that night?'

Travis shrugged. 'Like she always is. Happy kid. Had dinner and a bath.'

'A bath?'

Travis scowled. 'Kids have baths, okay? Chloe wasn't little like Bella-Kaye. She could sit up, play with her rubber duck.'

She could easily drown nevertheless.

'How was it for you having a kid after Bella-Kaye?' asked Damian, moving into the next stage with one of Natalie's questions. Maybe a bit soon, but then Travis's concentration span wasn't great. At least he wasn't overtly irritable. Natalie leaned forward and watched him closely.

'Great,' Travis replied. 'Always wanted kids.'

Liar. *He did it*. Kay's words rang in her ears.

'Tiph did a great job and Chloe was cute, you know?'

'Was?' The female officer playing bad cop.

'Look mate, this is your chance to be as open as possible.' Damian as good cop.

'I was talking about like when she was born and what it was like.' Irritable but not really defensive. Meaning what? That the 'was' meant nothing or that he knew he wasn't going to get caught? 'She's still cute, more so, I mean she's my kid.'

'More than Bella-Kaye?' Damian spoke so softly Natalie had to strain to hear. But Travis had caught every word.

'She's older. It's easier.'

'Did you worry about how Tiphanie would cope?'

'Nah,' said Travis. 'She isn't anything like Amber.'

'Meaning?'

'Not nuts.'

'Do you fight with her like you did Amber?' Damian's delivery of another of Natalie's questions was impeccably timed.

For a moment Travis's smirk wavered. Only for a moment. 'Everyone fights sometimes.'

Natalie felt herself tense. Arguments with Amber had meant more than just a brief retort. Holes in walls, broken plates. He threw the television at her once.

'Ever feel like hitting her?' the woman asked.

'*Feel* like it?' The smirk again. 'Maybe, but I just walk off, ask Tiph.' Who might well be too scared to say any different. Natalie sensed they'd lost him.

Damian asked a few more questions about their relationship and got no further. He went back to Chloe.

'What do you think happened?'

Travis shrugged. 'Fucked if I know. She's a smart kid; she wandered off.'

'And?'

'She's cute. Maybe got nicked.'

'So you think she's alive?'

Natalie picked the flicker of a real expression on Travis's face before he shut it down. Sorrow? Guilt? Remorse? She couldn't be sure. 'Yeah,' he said unconvincingly.

Damian asked a few more questions then called a break. Travis took the chance for a cigarette. Damian squeezed into the viewing room with the woman cop and introduced her as Detective Constable Andie Grimbank.

'Nothing much to go on. Thoughts?'

'He's understandably defensive,' said Natalie. 'You might want to try and rattle him a little more. Particularly on his competence—or rather incompetence—as a father. See how much narcissism is there and how fragile it is, or if he's just pure antisocial.'

'Does it matter?' Damian watched her closely but she couldn't work out what he was thinking.

Natalie shrugged. 'Maybe not, but he isn't that smart and he might give more away if he's on the back foot. Remember he's already had the bad father tag hung on him once.'

Would he still be feeling guilty about Bella-Kaye, if indeed he had killed her? More likely to be concentrating on not being charged with murder. He had perhaps convinced Tiphanie to lie for him, but not to take the blame.

'Pretty bad effort losing two kids,' Damian greeted Travis, deadpan, as soon as they sat down again. He was good at this.

Travis looked startled. 'It wasn't my fault. I wasn't there either time.'

'So how do you account for it then?'

'Amber was nuts, court said so.' Travis folded his arms and looked defiantly at Damian.

'What about Chloe?'

Travis looked conflicted. How much to blame Tiphanie? 'I don't know,' he said. He looked to Andie for support then seemed to remember that she had been playing bad cop as well. 'Kids do things off their own bat. She was a smart kid. She *is* a smart kid.' He hit the table with his fist. Neither Andie nor Damian reacted. 'We want her back. Why aren't you bastards out there looking for her instead of wasting your time with me? I didn't do anything. Tiph is a mess. This is wrecking everything.'

'Sounds to me like you're more pissed off about the inconvenience,' said Damian.

'More sorry for yourself than anyone else,' added Andie.

Damian leaned in, face close to Travis's. 'Not much of a father or husband, are you Travis?'

Travis flinched and edged backwards slightly. Natalie wished she could tell one of them to ease up. She wanted him rattled, yes. Too much and he'd close down completely.

'Chloe cry a lot, did she? Must have got irritating,' Andie said.

'She was a good kid,' said Travis. 'Don't think you can hang this on me!'

'Now why would we try to do that to an upstanding citizen like yourself?' Damian wasn't letting up. 'Wasn't your fault last time at all was it Travis?'

'Or was it?'

Damian was so busy swinging his dick he'd lost sight

of the objective; Andie probably felt she had to compete. Natalie knew they'd gone too far an instant before Travis stood up, knocking his chair to the ground behind him. 'I don't have to put up with this shit. Just find Chloe.'

Natalie watched Travis leave. Being a self-centred jerk didn't mean he'd killed Chloe. Didn't mean he hadn't. Natalie knew he wasn't all that smart, but he only needed a low to average IQ to keep repeating the same mantra, and no one was suggesting if he did kill Chloe that it was premeditated. He didn't look away as some people did when they lied, but then he had probably convinced himself of the truth as he wanted to believe it. He looked irritated, but nothing out of the ordinary.

Had he really killed Bella-Kaye? There would be no reason for Kay to lie now; but maybe Travis, in a moment of guilt about the domestic violence, had felt sorry for Glen and thought it was no skin off his nose to send the man to God feeling better. Maybe. It was hard to picture Travis as caring about anyone other than himself. He wasn't a psychopath though, and the guilty liked to offload their secrets. *If you are involved in any way, I want you to remember what I've told you.* Okay, but what the hell could she do with Kay's information?

After Travis left, Natalie walked to the window across the corridor. Outside the police station a young girl was waiting for him. This must be Tiphanie. She looked, as Travis had suggested, a mess, with dark circles under her eyes. She gave him a guarded smile, offering him a cigarette from a packet that had been tucked into the cuff of her jacket. She was very different from Amber in how she held herself; but then she hadn't been charged with killing her daughter.

68

Natalie stepped outside to watch them more closely and Travis caught sight of her. His eyes narrowed: he recognised her, his face twisting into a grimace of fury. Less surprise than she would have expected. She wondered whether Travis had heard the same gossip as Kay. Tiphanie turned to look at her and she caught a glimpse of an expression she couldn't quite pinpoint. Shame? Guilt, maybe?

Travis grabbed Tiphanie's arm and yanked her away. She went without protest; perhaps not so different from Amber after all. As they stood on the kerb edge, about to cross the road, a car accelerated and headed towards them. A guy and girl hanging out of windows holding beer cans jeered at them as the car swerved, narrowly missing them. Travis yelled obscenities back at them, barely aware that one of the cans had hit its mark, covering Tiphanie in beer foam. If losing a child wasn't bad enough, it seemed that she was also having to deal with hostility from the local parenting standards lobby.

'What does his mate say?' Natalie asked Damian before she left.

'That he came over, they had a few beers and watched football. His girlfriend and two other guys confirmed. He arrived before the game and left straight after.'

Natalie wondered if they were now cruising in cars heckling them. The Travis that had married Amber was a bully. She guessed his friendships weren't likely to be deep.

Damian couldn't resist a parting dig. 'Enjoy dinner.'

L iam was at the guesthouse reading the *Australian* when she returned.

Natalie flopped into an armchair opposite him. They had the living room to themselves. 'I take it you never intended to be in the interview?'

'I'm not allowed if I want to try the case. Australian law keeps things separate. I can't even be briefed by the police; one of my colleagues in the office will be.'

Natalie looked at him sharply. What game was he playing? 'But let me guess, you expect me to tell you what happened?'

'I don't want details. Impressions might be helpful.'

'Talk to Damian,' said Natalie. 'You might have paid for a room for nothing.'

Liam grinned. 'That remains to be seen. Drink?'

She watched him, wondering what the hell she was doing there. She wasn't sure anything she had seen would shed light on what happened to Chloe, or help Amber. More to the point, Liam didn't seem to care and the cops hadn't wanted her there.

The more she thought about it, the more this was

looking like an excuse for Liam to even the score for the humiliation she had inflicted on him; even if it had been Amber who had suffered most from the court steps debacle.

The fridge had only Crown Lager; she nodded when he waved a bottle in her direction.

'By the way, I like the outfit.' He levered the cap off the beer and handed it to her.

Natalie was wearing the little black dress she always travelled with. She didn't want him to think she'd gone to any trouble, and travelling by bike limited the bag size. This dress didn't take up much space.

Perhaps Liam was having second thoughts too. He poured himself a scotch and for the next half hour, directed conversation towards work, not pushing for information on Travis.

'I'm involved in another case you might be able to help me with.'

Natalie thought this unlikely.

'I'm part of an investigation into a paedophile ring.' If he noticed her lack of enthusiasm he pretended not to. 'We've got a couple of minor convictions against a few people downloading, but we want the guy behind it. Thought we had him once, but had to let him go.'

'And I can help how exactly?'

'The early stuff in particular, we are sure originated in this region. The girls would now be grown up, and from what I've been told, as victims they're going to have much higher chances of psych illnesses, as well as ending in prison. Am I right?'

'True,' Natalie agreed, 'but I don't see how that has us working together.'

71

'We need one of the victims to testify, or at the least give us some more information.'

'Uh huh.'

'You see abuse victims and prisoners...'

'You think I'd turn them over to you to have the media splash their lives all over the papers and some lawyer grill them till they break down?'

'Identities are protected. You know that. I'm just asking you to keep your eyes and ears open. Particularly for anything to do with pink bunny rabbits. Seems to be what they entice or reward the girls with. Tell me if you hear anything I might be able to use.'

She hoped her look conveyed how likely that was going to be. Her patients struggled talking to her about this type of issue, let alone to police and the O.P.P.

By the second beer she remembered why she found him so sexy. His outward respectability barely cloaked his edginess and the combination was compelling. She wondered what it was about her that was attractive to him. Just settling a score? Bored with a middle-class lifestyle? She started to wonder if he went for a certain type—if she was like other women he'd had affairs with. She stopped herself. She didn't want to know. If something happened tonight it would be a one-off.

'Dinner?' he asked as their second drink was nearly finished.

'Not hungry.' Not for food at least.

Liam raised an eyebrow.

Their eyes locked and the brief glimpse behind the surface rattled her. She was a psychiatrist for fuck's sake. Why was she letting him get to her?

*

As soon as the door closed in his room she knew why. Liam worked hard on hiding what was beneath his veneer but in the bedroom, or at least in the bedroom with her, it unleashed. There was a hunger in him that took her breath away, anger and passion that she hadn't felt in a lover before, and she knew it wasn't him she feared as much as her own response. If it had been ignited by a need to prove his dominance, the same need was continuing to fuel it.

They didn't speak.

Liam pushed her firmly against the door, his mouth hard on hers. He tasted of scotch. Natalie pulled at his shirt as his hands pushed her dress up and went under the waistband of her tights. They half-walked, half-fell across furniture, pulling at clothing, knocking the lamp to the floor, bumping against the walls. Naked in the dark on the bed, Natalie could feel his cock hard against her as his tongue was in her mouth, then her ears; then he was biting her nipples. When he had pushed her need to a level where she would have given him anything he had asked, he entered her. She came almost immediately, and Liam followed only moments later.

Her arousal had left no room to consider anything other than her own pleasure. But afterwards it was not the physical gratification that she recalled, either then or during the repeat performance in the early hours of the morning, but rather, how he held her after they were spent. In those minutes was a lingering memory of what was absent: the tension that infiltrated every part of her and had been there for as long as she could remember. Without it, she was left unsure of who she was, and for a moment believed that this was who she wanted to be.

*

73

On Monday morning, Jessie was ten minutes late. The honeymoon was over already. She slumped into the chair without speaking, still wearing her sunglasses.

'Tell me what made your week so bad.'

Jessie stared at her sullenly. She clearly wanted to talk but she'd spent a lifetime learning it was dangerous to trust.

'Everything.'

'Hannah?'

'Same stuff.'

Natalie waited.

'I got a call about my father.'

'Your father?'

'He's in hospital. Second time in a month.'

Natalie underlined this in her notes. Was this why Jessie was now turning up for therapy?

'The hospital rang me as next of kin. They thought I should take him home with me.'

'Did you?'

Jessie bit her lip, and angrily wiped a tear out of her eye. 'Why should I? Bastard preferred the bitch to me, never thought about what *I* wanted.'

'You presumed my response would be that you should have taken him home.'

'He certainly did.' Jessie was lost in her thoughts for a moment.

She was too young to shoulder adult responsibilities for the man who raised her, Natalie reflected. Particularly with so many unresolved issues between them.

'Did they tell you his prognosis?' Better to deal with the here and now.

'Yeah. Shit.' Jessie looked up at her. 'Dying. The grog's finally getting him. Just not fast enough.'

'So where is he now?'

'Jay found a nursing home. Same town we grew up in.'

Natalie processed this. Jessie might well feel alone, but there was family around to help when they had to.

'Shit place.'

Natalie wasn't sure if she meant the town or the nursing home. 'Bad memories?'

'And some.'

More silence. Her father's illness had brought up things Jessie wasn't in any rush to share, and it was too early in therapy to open them up. Natalie concentrated on helping her cope with the here and now—which for Jessie was going to be hard enough.

'Sounds like he's somewhere where he can get care and you can visit. Write down your feelings when they come to you,' said Natalie. 'Then bring them here so we can talk about them.' Where it was safe.

Some fathers, Natalie mused as the session ended, had a lot to answer for. Liam's da', whose example had been rejected. Or her own: her mother refused to tell her anything about him except he had left when she was a toddler and, Natalie could only assume, traumatised them both sufficiently to not even feature on her birth certificate.

She was certain Jessie's had been worse than both, though the details had yet to emerge.

'It's Morecombe Legal Service on the phone.'

Natalie was in her office writing a letter when Beverley called her. 'Did they say which lawyer or which client?'

'No, hold on.' A moment later Beverley was back. 'Barrister called Jacqueline Barrett. About Georgia Latimer.'

'Put her through.'

75

Ms Barrett was straight to the point. 'Your name has been suggested as someone to monitor my client if she gets bail.'

Who by? Not someone from Morecombe, because she'd never heard of them.

'Is she likely to?'

'We have an excellent case. Are you able to see her?'

'That depends,' Natalie said.

'On what?'

'Whether your client is prepared to see me.'

'Exactly the point,' the lawyer said. 'Georgia will do what the court instructs, but she is worried you are not sympathetic to her.'

'If by that she means I question what she tells me, she's right,' said Natalie. 'If she would prefer to see Professor Wadhwa—'

'No,' said Ms Barrett almost too quickly. Had Wadhwa managed to piss them off somehow? More likely they thought that Natalie, younger and less experienced, would be easier to play. Perhaps they just needed a female on side? It was no coincidence that the barrister was a woman, Natalie was sure.

'She wants you, but she wants to be certain you are open to her side of the story.'

'I'm always open to the truth,' Natalie replied. 'In all its strange presentations.'

'Good,' said Ms Barrett. 'I have to tell you, we are looking into her husband. I'll be in touch. If you can get me a report as soon as possible that would be helpful.'

With that she hung up, leaving Natalie wondering, not for the first time, about Georgia's husband.

*

When the mail came, there was another red envelope. With another USB stick.

Natalie felt a surge of adrenaline, almost immediately followed by anger. She had put the last message to the back of her mind and her preoccupation with Liam and Travis and Amber had allowed her to forget it. Stupid. What was this about? She opened it on her computer.

Getting close can be dangerous for your mental health.

Vague. A threat all the same. Her mind raced. Why had the first letter been handwritten and the subsequent ones so much more calculated? All three had arrived on one of the two days she worked at these rooms. She thought of Travis's flash of anger; wondered if he wanted to get at her for taking him on before Amber's court case. He wouldn't have enjoyed cowering before someone thirty kilos lighter than him, and a woman in particular. It was on national television news and then again in the documentary; some of his friends might have seen it.

Could he have known in advance she was going to be asked to his interview, like Kay almost certainly had? Had it reignited his anger? She needed to report this; wondered at her reluctance to do so. She reread the document. *Mental health* jumped off the page. He couldn't know she was on medication, could he? She had been a little high on the court steps but Travis wouldn't have known that. Maybe it was just referencing her being a psychiatrist.

'Drop them in,' said the policeman who answered the phone.

'Will you be able to do anything?'

'Not without the memory sticks we can't.'

'But can you trace anything from an envelope and a USB?'

'Are they actually threatening you with anything specific?' The voice was polite, but what she heard was, 'Stop wasting my time'.

She hung up.

Natalie threw her bag on the sofa, called Welbury police station and asked for the senior sergeant. He hadn't been on duty earlier in the day when she had tried.

'McBride speaking.'

'This is Dr King.' She paused to make sure he had placed her. 'I want to first thank you for letting me watch Travis's interview.'

'And second?'

'Apologise that you hadn't been pre-warned. I hadn't been fully informed either.'

There was a pause but before she could fill it, Damian spoke again.

'Is there a third?'

'Yes.' Natalie took a breath. 'I'm going to be in town on Friday. Any chance of me being able to interview Tiphanie?'

There was a longer silence. 'O'Shea put you up to this?'

'No. I haven't spoken to him.'

'I suppose it's just coincidence then that his office was on the phone asking the same thing?'

*

She set her Italian coffee maker on the stove and sat on the sofa with the file she'd brought home from work: Amber's. She took detailed notes, a habit acquired when she had been less sure of herself. In forensic psychiatry it was essential.

The triple zero transcript and the police summary report of the discovery of the baby, at least, were typed. Amber had called the emergency line when six-week-old Bella-Kaye drowned in the bath.

Natalie could still hear in her head the recording that had been played in court. It had cemented the prosecution's case.

Amber, can you just go back and get her out of the bath.
Silence.
Amber, listen to me. Just go back and get her out of the bath.
A whisper. *I can't.*
Amber. The operator was now between panic and fury. *Amber, it won't make anything worse and it might help. Please. Go. Back. Now. Get Bella-Kaye out of the bath.*
Silence.
It's too late.
A click. Amber had hung up.

Amber refused to apply for bail. She would probably have been successful: as Natalie realised later, the State of Victoria tended towards leniency in infanticide cases. Amber's lawyer managed to get the plea hearing listed earlier than it would normally have been. Women charged with infanticide usually didn't serve time, he argued. But in the meantime Amber was in prison and Natalie visited her weekly.

Natalie's notes for the first few visits suggested Amber was still in shock, saying not much at all, and nothing meaningful. Mostly she reiterated her disbelief that Bella-Kaye was dead. She walked in and out of the room in a daze, crying intermittently and sometimes barely speaking. When Natalie first saw Travis, bewildered but hugging his wife and saying all the right things, she thought him likeable enough.

A different story eventually emerged. Amber had coped poorly from the moment of the child's birth. Travis had derided her as a useless wife when his meal wasn't ready as he watched the six o'clock news and a pathetic mother when Bella-Kaye interrupted his viewing by crying. The final straw had been Travis's insistence that they go to New Zealand for a rugby match when the baby was three weeks old. Neither recognised that Amber was depressed.

'Why would I be depressed?' she wept. 'Bella-Kaye was all I ever wanted. There was nothing to be depressed about.' Amber and Travis had believed that the difficulties they were having were the same as those of any new parents.

The death of her baby and the resulting guilt had exacerbated Amber's depression. The prison terrified her. Part of her felt she deserved it, but accepting blame didn't help her deal with the fear that left her sleepless and without appetite. Natalie had prescribed antidepressants.

Amber avoided discussing events leading up to her daughter's death. Eventually, it was talking about the trauma of imprisonment that opened her up, encouraged her to talk about Travis's abuse—and enabled Natalie to feel sympathy. Before her was a vulnerable girl, barely more than a child herself, in manner if not age, who was quite simply not capable of malicious intent.

Amber had been weak perhaps, but not evil. When she described being taken to court in the prison van, separated from the other women by a mesh but still in fear of her life, her terror and bewilderment had been stark.

The defence called Dianne Fisher, then Natalie's boss, an expert on perinatal mental illness.

'In a US cohort convicted of infanticide,' Dianne told the court, 'Spinelli concluded that most had a dissociative psychosis.' She had gone on to explain, 'These women's minds briefly cut themselves off from reality, an acute stress reaction as a way of coping with something that, for them, has pushed them beyond their mental capacity. Depression, sleep deprivation, crying child—they all contribute to overwhelming women who have an underlying vulnerability.'

Amber fitted the mould: her memory of the event was categorised by panic, anxiety and a separation of emotion and thought. In the police interview she had been vague and initially seemed intellectually impaired. Natalie had thought it a reasonable defence, compatible with the forensic evidence. But it incensed her that the defence barrister wouldn't let her volunteer the information about Travis that had come out in therapy.

'Absolutely not. The prosecution will annihilate you,' he told her bluntly. 'Battered Wife Syndrome isn't a recognised psychiatric diagnosis. If it's not in DSM, we can't use it. It'll only muddy the waters.'

Natalie had fumed: too junior, too green and idealistic to understand that the complexities of motive and influence were almost irrelevant. She knew now that a successful trial was a game well played, not a revelation of the truth. Because of the incident on the courtroom steps she had never got the chance to raise it anyhow.

The real issue had been with the judge. A few weeks previously Justice Tanner had been the subject of criticism after he had accepted a sleepwalking defence in a domestic violence case. Liam O'Shea had naturally been at pains to use it to advantage the prosecution case, with repeated references to 'delivery of justice demanded by the community'.

With the judge unprepared to accept dissociation as a mitigating factor and Natalie barred from giving evidence at all, Amber was left without any real defence and had crumbled under Liam's cross-examination.

Natalie turned it over in her mind again. Maybe not testifying hadn't made any difference to Amber's case. Amber had admitted her guilt, and Liam had been certain she was wholly responsible. But if the evidence now suggested something different, he had shown he was prepared to revisit the case.

Kay Long had said *he did it*. But what exactly had Travis confessed to? Maybe abusing Amber and driving her to it rather than actually killing Bella-Kaye?

Was Tiphanie feeling the same as Amber had, or was the situation different? Feelings of guilt could add to the pain. Natalie thought she had glimpsed that mix of emotions in the brief encounter on the streets of Welbury. But what was the shame or guilt for? For going back to bed and allowing Chloe to wander? Harming her as Amber had harmed Bella-Kaye? Or for not protecting her from Travis?

'Hey Natalie, open the fucking door!' It was Tom's voice shouting from downstairs.

Immersed in the notes, Natalie hadn't heard the doorbell. Or rescued the coffee. She turned it off and went to let him in.

'Want some dinner?' Without waiting for a response he pushed past with his takeaway bags. It smelled like Chinese: Tom liked cooking as much as Natalie did.

'Didn't see anyone outside again did you?' she asked.

Tom shook his head and waited. Natalie hesitated.

'Nat, I know that look.'

She explained about the USB warnings.

'So who's behind them?'

'No idea.'

'Yeah but what type of person?'

Natalie laughed. 'I'm not a profiler, Tom.'

'You understand weird people. What sort of person would send notes like that?' He grabbed some plates and cutlery and laid out the Chinese food on the coffee table.

Natalie was more used to the history unfolding in a way that allowed her to make sense of the crime, rather than working backwards from the crime to understand the criminal. But she knew about stalkers. For the first time she let the idea incubate. She'd been wishing the problem would go away, but it apparently wasn't going to.

'Depends on what the intent is.'

'Mad or bad?' asked Tom between mouthfuls.

'Bad, which is to say personality-driven rather than a psychosis. Could be a delusional disorder but I sense he wants to enjoy the feeling of power. Sits at home and gets his jollies by imagining how uncomfortable I'm feeling.'

'Sexual?' Tom flexed his substantial biceps. He wasn't tall, but he'd done a lot of working out in his youth and had more than once appointed himself as Natalie's protector.

Natalie shrugged. The *predatory* and *resentful* stalker types came to mind. 'Not enough evidence to say. If it is sexual'—she added *incompetent suitor* and *intimacy seeking* to the list of possibilities—'then it's more about power, getting back at a dominating, critical and maybe abusive parent; mother, I would guess. He is probably still scared of her—hence the need to project his anger at someone he isn't scared of but believes he has power over in some way.'

'Sorry I asked. Just tell me, does that put you in danger?'

Natalie's immediate response was *no*. She stopped herself. Not just the content of the notes, but the fact that he had sent them over three weeks, suggested repressed anger. She'd assessed murderers who had given less warning than this. 'Yes. Potentially.'

'You want me to move in for a while?'

Natalie shook her head. 'If it escalates I'll call.'

She took some time out to eat, trying to think of anything other than her stalker.

'Shaun's asking us for a favour,' Tom said through a mouthful of sweet and sour pork.

'Let me guess. Singer in the wedding band is sick again.'

'He needs us both. Singer's got an interstate audition and she's taking the drummer with her.' Natalie raised an eyebrow and he shrugged. 'They're married. Anyway, it leaves him in the lurch for the next gig.'

Natalie finished her Chinese.

'Some sort of corporate ball. "Proud Mary" and "Brown-Eyed Girl".'

'Tom, since when did I start to look like a ball type of person?'

'He needs the money.'

Tom knew she'd agree, though three sets of seventies covers was not something to look forward to.

He gave her the date. Horribly close. Shaun owed them.

Declan was finishing a session with an emergency patient and Natalie took advantage of the time to check out his bookshelf in the waiting room. He had a predilection for

Irish poets, but it was an early edition Yeats that caught her attention. His patients must be very different from hers.

Her patients. Did one of them have a copy of John Fowles' *The Collector*? Most serial killers did.

At first Natalie thought Declan was as distracted as she was tonight. Perhaps still thinking about his last patient. But the quick glances when he thought she wasn't looking made her wonder if it was his curiosity about the trip with Liam. Natalie silently congratulated him for resisting the temptation to question her. She intended to avoid the topic. If Declan found out how Travis featured in her dalliance with Liam, he'd start questioning her judgment and they'd be back talking lithium and blood tests.

She went to the safer topic of Jessie, but it was early days and there had been little progress. It would get tougher when their alliance was stronger. Patients like Jessie tended to create havoc; testing out authority and pushing boundaries had more serious consequences as an adult than as a child. Mostly they created more trouble for themselves than anyone else.

Inevitably the conversation turned to Georgia.

'I'm trying,' said Natalie. 'It isn't easy. My gut feeling screams inauthentic; it's hard to let go of.'

'Have you given any thought to why?'

'Of course. That's all I try to do.'

Declan shook his head. His brown eyes regarded her with fatherly concern. 'You try hard,' he said, 'but you're too close; step away for a moment.' He offered her another glass of wine, which she declined.

'Meaning?' She was conscious of sounding tense.

'Tell me why you don't like her.'

'She hardly invites warmth.'

'Is it surprising? Didn't you tell me her father killed her mother when she was two?'

'It was the other way around. But probably only because her mother got to the knife first; I saw the list of prior injuries. Either way, she effectively lost both parents.'

'I know you understand that would have affected her development.'

'Of course. No stable base to form the foundations of sense of self, so she learned to manipulate in order to survive. A disorganised attachment style.'

'As is the case for Jessie, yet you have empathy for her. Tell me more about Georgia's attachment style and how it affected her personality.'

'I guess she's also avoidant. She learned to get what she wanted in part by being good.'

'So the good child smiled and achieved and got some reward from...was it an aunt that cared for her?'

Natalie nodded. 'Yes, but by doing so, Georgia didn't learn to deal with emotions.'

'So she's three years old, lost both her parents and a stranger is caring for her. How did she feel?'

'Scared. Confused.'

'So she could have developed an anxiety disorder but didn't.'

'No, she developed a personality disorder instead.'

'As did Jessie.'

'Jessie's borderline—predominantly chaotic. Georgia is predominantly narcissistic.'

'So again I ask, why the empathy for Jessie but not for Georgia?' Declan picked up the bottle and poured another splash into his own glass, a deviation from his usual routine.

Natalie shook her head. 'Because she killed three

children! Reason enough surely.'

'Our job is to understand, not judge. Or at least to understand first.'

'Then because she lies, because she's entitled. Because she won't damn well face reality.'

'Natalie, you can do better than that.'

'Okay, because her survival skills are to pretend and she believes her own story. Because she isn't interested in changing, not really.'

Declan sat back in the chair, contemplating her. 'I asked what your issue was, not Georgia's.'

Natalie had to remind herself to breathe. It was maybe a minute before she trusted herself to answer. 'She makes me feel powerless.'

'And what's that like?' Declan's tone was as gentle as she had ever heard.

'I get it.' She forced a smile. 'Scary. And I like to be in control.' Or at least have the illusion of it.

Declan leaned forward. 'Dismissing emotions comes at a cost. For you both.' He watched her struggle, then patted her hand. 'I know I'm not your therapist anymore,' he said. 'But it's inevitable that your own issues come out in your work. You are very skilled with the chaos of the borderline because ultimately your foundations are not disorganised, however much your bipolar makes you seem so at times. But you have other answers to find, and it will take time.'

Was he referring now to her sensitivity to Georgia? Her relationship with her mother? Her absent father? Or Liam?

Declan watched her carefully. 'Is there anything else you'd like to talk about? Better to talk it out with me than no one at all.'

Liam then. She wasn't sure there was anything to talk

about, but he was right about there being no one else. She and Tom didn't do personal discussion, mainly because in the past it had ended up in sex. Her two oldest friends from school were overseas and interstate, and she didn't find other women easy to deal with. More to the point, most women didn't like her much. Women her age were uneasy with a woman who enjoyed sex, liked being single—and thought a man's marital status was his problem not hers.

Natalie contemplated rolling up her sleeve to jolt Declan. There were bruises on her arms from Liam's enthusiastic grip, and over most of the rest of her from banging into the furniture. Liam hadn't escaped without damage either, including several long scratches down his back. God knew how he explained that to his wife. Presumably the lights stayed out.

'Ever heard the expression "fuck your brains out"?' Natalie said with a grin, knowing she was being badly behaved and only vaguely aware it was a push-back against Declan getting too close to her core vulnerability. She didn't wait for a response. 'I never really knew what it meant either until last Thursday night. Let's just say we didn't sleep much.'

'So what does that mean to you?' He was using his fatherly I-won't-judge-you tone.

Natalie grinned. 'Great sex. He's married. I don't want a relationship.' She saw Declan's expression and shrugged. 'It's true, okay? Maybe I'm testing types out but I can't picture myself settled down with anyone right now, so having fun in the interim seems a win–win.'

She could see Declan was sceptical. 'I don't care what you say,' she added. 'Eight years older does not make him a father figure. Now you—maybe.'

'Have you considered that maybe you're a little high? And your libido as well?'

'Just running on all cylinders.'

'It might be normal for most people to keep one cylinder in reserve.' Declan frowned. 'How much are you seeing him?'

'Not sure yet.' She wondered why she didn't just tell him it was a one-off. Because she thought Liam might be there at the Welbury gig?

'True, unless...' Declan paused. 'How are you sleeping generally?'

'It was one night only. I've slept normally ever since.'

'With medication?'

'Yes.' Which was sort of true. She'd missed on that one night with Liam, but most other nights she took her mood stabiliser like a good girl.

Declan seemed satisfied.

Outside Declan's house, Natalie paused for a minute. Then she fired up her bike and headed towards the cemetery at the eastern edge of the suburban sprawl, a forty-five minute ride.

She hadn't been there in two years. She pulled into the usual side road and waited for the white Mazda travelling behind her to go by, lighting up the road as it did. The routine of hiding the bike in the brush and scaling the wall at the back where the brickwork was crumbling was a familiar one. She hadn't brought a torch but the sky was clear and the moon high enough for her to be able to find her way through the shadows.

She had spent the night of her eighteenth birthday sleeping on the grave, celebrating her bike licence as well as the mobility she had worked hard to regain after the accident. It was a big deal that she was able to ride at all, and she'd come to promise Eoin that she would ride safely. She'd visited on the day of her thirtieth birthday, to show off her new Ducati. It was far too big for her, well deserving the label of monster. A reminder of the time she switched meds and went a bit manic, but she loved it anyway.

He was there waiting for her. She could feel him as she closed her eyes and remembered. Half a lifetime ago.

'I miss you still,' she said. She ran her hand over the letters that were carved into the stone, unable to read them in the dark, but knowing what they said.

Eoin Rearden 1980–1998
Always in our hearts.

'You don't think I should settle down, do you?' Natalie said to him. 'If you were alive would we be married with a couple of kids? Would you have moved on from our pledge never to get old and boring?' It was impossible to imagine Eoin, with his irreverent grin, as anything but a wild eighteen-year-old. If the accident hadn't killed him something else would have.

'I really don't know what I want,' Natalie said looking into the starless night sky. 'I've got the band—still a rock chick like I promised. But sometimes I'm so restless. It's like I'm waiting for you to come back and catch up with me.' She listened for a while to the sounds of the night. The wind rustled the leaves in the nearby tree, and a car backfired in the distance.

'You'd like Liam,' she said. Then laughed and sat up. 'Actually you'd hate him. Arrogant twat. Wears suits.' Natalie smiled. 'But there's a bad boy in there.'

It was after ten when she got home. She didn't take any notice of the car parked outside her warehouse, faced the wrong way on a one way street, until he turned his headlights on, and blinded her.

'Shit!' she yelled. As she turned her bike into the cul-de-sac, she heard him rev the engine and take off. Standing in the empty street as the car turned the corner, she could see only that it was small and pale coloured. No chance of reading the number plate.

A sound on the roof startled her as she came up the stairs into the kitchen. A cat most likely. She'd admitted to Tom that she might be in danger, but it wouldn't be from any stalker who was seriously mentally ill. They were unlikely to be organised enough to be anything more than a nuisance, and from the rational thinking behind the delivery of the USBs she already knew that her stalker didn't fit this category.

She liked her own company. Now she found herself wishing for the buzz of the Halfpenny. Looking out across the rooftops she reassured herself that the driver could have been anyone and that she was up to tackling the large motley coloured tom cat that was there now.

Natalie had taken to checking the *Welbury Leader* online. On Monday morning, Travis and Tiphanie were back on page one. The local journalists probably didn't have anything else interesting to report; they interviewed Tiphanie and dragged a brief quote from Travis's mother. The local maternal child health centre was reported as saying they would be running a parenting support group, as the young mothers had been 'destabilised'. Senior Sergeant Damian McBride said there were 'several lines of enquiry still being pursued'.

Chloe was still missing. And Amber, not Travis, was in gaol.

To add to Natalie's sense of disquiet from the previous night, she found an article in the mainstream paper on multiple personality disorder, quoting Wadhwa, his pudgy face beaming with insincerity. He couldn't comment on the case of Georgia Latimer, he said, since it was 'before the courts' but managed to make his thoughts abundantly clear.

Maybe someone would charge him with contempt and make Natalie's day.

Georgia was booked to see Natalie Wednesday, on the assumption that her bail appeal would be successful. When she turned up on time it was apparent the optimism had been warranted. She looked smug, and there was good enough reason, though the fear of returning to prison would be in the background. Yarra Bend was far removed from her normal life. Prison would be worse.

Georgia made only the briefest reference to the court case, and instead told Natalie about the apartment she had found, and then: 'I've been shopping. With friends.'

Georgia's demeanour was disconcerting and even with Declan's insight, Natalie had to fight hard not to judge her. Emotional distancing was the hallmark of the avoidant-attached child as an adult. But the real issue for Natalie was whether Georgia was responsible for her actions. If Wadhwa was right, she was not. Her suppressed rage was expressed in one or more separate personalities that she had no control over. Natalie still thought it more likely that she had a personality disorder, which meant that when her rage was triggered Georgia had a choice about where to channel it.

There was no simple direct way to answer the question; if Georgia had D.I.D. she couldn't have told Natalie even if she had wanted to. If she had a personality disorder—and was criminally responsible for her children's deaths—there was a good reason to conceal the truth. Either way what Natalie needed was to access Georgia's subconscious.

'I've been wondering about what you said at the end of the last session.' A patient's parting words were often significant; sometimes an attempt to prolong the interaction but at other times a way of throwing a lifeline to the therapist; *this is what is important but I'm too scared to go there.*

'Oh, I can't really remember,' said Georgia, smile still fixed in place. 'What did I say?'

'That Paul could be difficult when he didn't get his own way.'

'Did I say that?' She bit her lip. 'He...liked...well you know.'

'He liked what, exactly?'

'The intimate side of marriage.'

Oh come on. Sex might have been an issue, but Natalie didn't buy the coyness.

'I mean,' Georgia continued, 'he was my first, you know, serious boyfriend, and I was a bit of a prude. Virginia and Vernon, my aunt and uncle, were very uptight, didn't really talk about sex. So Paul thought I was a bit reluctant. But it wasn't a problem, not after we got married, at least...'

'So how was sex for you?'

'It really wasn't a problem.' Georgia smiled. 'We had our lives very sorted, it worked. For three years it all went beautifully.'

Until she had children.

'It was harder because I was tired, after Genevieve was born,' Georgia continued.

'Did that create problems?'

'Paul...well, I guess he helped with Genevieve. She was a very unsettled child, particularly around dinner time, so he'd walk her or give her a bath.'

'Unsettled?'

'Nothing serious, she just seemed to be prone to colds. I had asthma as a child and I worried she might have it too.'

95

'Did she need to have tests?'

'What? I don't think anyone ever thought it was that serious.' Natalie jotted a reminder to chase up the GP's notes. 'Paul got...impatient.'

Natalie let the silence stretch and become awkward. When Georgia filled it, she returned to the sexual relationship.

'He made it hard to say no,' said Georgia, eyes averted. 'If I didn't enjoy it, he didn't like that either.'

'Did he threaten you? Physically abuse you?'

Georgia looked down. 'Not really. I mean I just knew.'

'Knew what, Georgia?'

This time Georgia smiled into the silence, a smile that dug under Natalie's skin. Ashamed and hiding something— or an act?

'Have you spoken to Paul since your release?' Natalie asked, remembering Georgia's insistence that he still loved her.

'No, I'm not allowed to,' said Georgia. 'He sent me a card.'

'Really?' Natalie found it hard to sound anything other than incredulous. 'What did it say?'

'Nothing, it was blank. But I knew it was from him.'

'How?'

'We've been married for fifteen years. Anyway, who else could it be?'

It was possible, just. Not committing anything to writing would suggest ambivalence, perhaps the inability to believe he'd been married to a monster. Or a way of still trying to control her, keeping her on a string. As for who else could have sent it—hate mail from the public wouldn't have been surprising. But the sender surely wouldn't have left it blank. Or was the whole thing in Georgia's imagination? Who would have her new address anyway? Was this a fantasy, based on a need to bolster her self-esteem?

Natalie was still making notes after Georgia had left, when a major inconsistency occurred to her. Georgia had stated that she was sexually naive, that Paul had been her first serious boyfriend. She flicked back through the case file and found it. Prior to meeting Paul she had been pregnant— and lost a thirty-eight-week foetus.

Although it was only 4 p.m., a late winter mist was settling on Welbury as Natalie turned off the freeway into the wide streets of the town and parked her bike outside the police station. Inside Natalie watched Tiphanie being separated from Travis, over protests from him. There was not a word from her. On the day Natalie had watched Travis being interviewed, she caught a look from Tiphanie and wondered about shame and guilt, and whether she was at risk from Travis. Today, though, she still looked younger than her twenty years. She swaggered in with a bravado close to truculence, like a schoolgirl caught smoking behind the sheds.

Neither Travis nor Tiphanie had been told which psychiatrist would be conducting the interview, but given that Travis had seen Natalie on the last visit, he could have made an educated guess it would be her. The messages in the red envelopes were fresh in her mind. Had Travis had sent them? *Breaking the rules has consequences.* Was that about the way she'd confronted him over Amber more than a year earlier? And if so, were the following two notes warnings about speaking to Tiphanie? *I wouldn't get too close if I were you* and *Getting close can be dangerous for your mental health.*

Would seeing Tiphanie be, as the message suggested, dangerous? Travis certainly fitted her profile; she remembered Amber telling her that his mother was domineering.

'I've told the cops everything,' Tiphanie said to no one in particular. Natalie was sitting on the same side of the table as her in small sparsely-furnished room. Damian, on the other side, was reading his notes. He'd barely spoken to Natalie since her arrival.

Natalie pulled her chair closer.

'Not that they were listening,' Tiphanie added.

'I'll probably be asking a few questions they haven't.'

'Can't tell you anything different.' Tiphanie stared at her, lips pursed. A look of something Natalie couldn't quite pinpoint. She had spent half her school years in the principal's office, sitting in Tiphanie's position: she felt she should be able to get inside her head. On the other hand this meeting was about something a lot more serious than a bottle of vodka in her locker.

'Well, let's wait and see what the questions are, shall we?' Natalie managed to hold eye contact briefly. 'How are you doing?'

'How do you think?'

'Shit, I should imagine.'

Tiphanie looked up again. For a moment there was a connection. 'Yeah.'

'What thoughts go around your head? Mostly.'

'Thoughts? Just wondering where she is, you know. Hoping...' Tiphanie took a breath. 'Hoping she's okay.'

'It must be hard not knowing.'

Tiphanie looked downwards.

Natalie took her through the routine questions about depression and anxiety and Tiphanie told her that she had been fine until Chloe disappeared. 'Now that's all I think about,' she said.

'What do you imagine?'

'Horrible things,' Tiphanie mumbled. 'She'll be missing me. She'll be scared.'

This was a definite improvement on her partner. Tiphanie was able to think of her daughter as someone separate from herself. Someone vulnerable, and still alive. It couldn't be Travis's coaching. He wasn't up to this level.

'Sometimes children feel scared even when they're with their parents,' said Natalie carefully. 'Do you think she ever felt like that, maybe when you were asleep or when you and Travis were arguing?'

Tiphanie shook her head. 'Chloe's a happy kid. She's good, easy.'

Perhaps Natalie was hoping for too much. Georgia had also said her children were 'good' as if that was evidence of what a great mother she was. There was something else about Tiphanie that reminded her of Georgia, but she couldn't place what. Narcissism? Borderline traits?

'What do you think happened?' Natalie asked. There was another moment of eye contact but again Tiphanie didn't hold it long.

'Don't know.'

'You know your daughter,' said Natalie. 'Is she capable of getting a chair and opening the back door?'

The paediatrician that the police had consulted had thought not, but experts were not infallible. They'd got the Chamberlain case wrong. Natalie didn't know any eleven-month-old children, but from her reading she thought it was a task more for a three-year-old or an advanced two-year-old.

'Don't know. I guess.'

'Tell me about her.' On this topic Tiphanie was happy to open up, able to forget that the child was missing. Like Natalie, she probably preferred to think of Chloe being still alive.

'She loves playing with the pots and pans in the kitchen while I cook. She always goes to bed, um, like, with her two favourite toys. She likes Big Bird on TV too.'

'Does Travis play with her?'

'Sure. He sometimes reads her a book.' After a pause she added, 'And helps with her bath.' The way she said 'helps' suggested to Natalie that he was next to useless. But given what happened to Bella-Kaye, maybe neither of them was comfortable with baths.

'Did you ever leave her with anyone?' Natalie asked. 'You know, so you could go out?'

Tiphanie shook her head. 'Never.'

'What about to shop? Go to the hairdresser? Get your nails done?' From her memory of Amber these were the major pastimes of the unemployed mothers in the area, though usually at each others' houses rather than a salon. Tiphanie's short, square-cut nails and limp hair suggested beauty care wasn't a pastime she had indulged in for a while.

'She comes everywhere with me,' said Tiphanie. Tears formed in her eyes. 'I miss her.'

Natalie believed her. Trouble was, Tiphanie was not describing a child that, at less than one, was likely to go any further than a metre radius from her mother. In the stranger-anxiety period of development, Chloe was neither physically nor psychologically competent to take off alone. Tiphanie and Travis's story had so many holes it was curious the cops hadn't busted it already. Tiphanie did seem to genuinely care; as you would for a missing child—or one that you, or your partner, had accidentally killed.

Outside, Damian said, 'We'd like her to cough up Travis, but we'll get him without her co-operation if we have to.' And without your help, the look suggested.

'She's hiding something.'

Damian frowned. 'She's covering for Travis.'

Like Liam, the cops seemed firmly of the opinion that lightning didn't strike twice and their focus was on Travis. She should have been delighted. Why wasn't she? There was no doubt Tiphanie loved her daughter, but there was something else. Was the sullen bravado covering fear, and if so, of what? Natalie wasn't sure. She had said she was fine before Chloe's disappearance. Then why did she need to sleep all morning? Chloe slept through the night, so disturbed sleep couldn't explain it. 'Can you check with her GP? Get her records?' she asked Damian.

Damian was noncommittal, but he wrote something down. Maybe *fucking shrinks*.

Later, Natalie saw Tiphanie walk out to join Travis, and her expression was unmistakable. Jubilation. She thought she had got away with something.

She'd ridden down alone and was staying at the corner pub where the music was loud, the crowds spilled onto the pavement and the cops did a clean-up run after midnight. She hadn't asked Liam if he was in town, and there was no reason for him to be, particularly since the O.P.P. needed to keep their distance from the police investigation. He had a wife and the usual commitments, presumably. School functions, law practice obligations, probably a list of social shit from political party fundraising to film nights. She knew instinctively that regardless of all these things he would try to make it happen tonight. Not because he'd told her so, but because she had felt his body respond to hers and knew it had surprised him as much as it had her. She'd seen his eyes later. He was hooked. Trouble was, if she was honest with herself, so was she. And it was obvious Liam didn't care one way or another about her involvement in the case.

She helped the band set up as the early arrivals hugged the bar. Natalie's experience was that, audience-wise, drunk was better than sober. The worst gig they ever did was in the early afternoon when no one had had enough on board to loosen them up.

'How's your wife?' Natalie asked Gil.

'Fat.'

'It ain't fat,' Natalie laughed.

'Not enjoying impending fatherhood I take it?' Tom threw him a cable and they plugged in the bass amp in light that was barely bright enough to see each other.

'So guys,' said Natalie, 'feel for the crowd?'

'Eighties and nineties covers.' Tom sounded depressed.

'Could be worse.'

Most of the punters were tastefully attired in muscle shirts over beer bellies. She was certain at least a few were bikies, the outlaw kind. She hoped they weren't here on business. Tom didn't appear too concerned, but as a former enforcer, he was used to keeping his thoughts well-hidden. What the hell, they'd seen worse. Natalie's sexual energy, heightened by thoughts of the possibilities ahead, would probably help. So would the fact that she hadn't taken her meds. She knew she should; she just hated how *dull* they made her feel. On stage, high, she was invincible. She just had to manage it, not let herself go *too* high. She'd take a dose tonight, after the gig. A half dose.

From the first song she had the crowd in her hand. The choice of songs, mostly left to Shaun, was also working well—the chemistry between the two of them always clicked in these numbers. Off stage they never flirted, not even a suggestive joke. But on stage there was a gritty sexual tension. No one watching would ever guess that it was Tom who was the friend with benefits.

Backstage after the first bracket she downed a water and decided not to go out front, but Gil came back with a beer she hadn't ordered. 'You've been followed.'

Natalie raised her eyebrows.

'You reckon we didn't notice that bloke at the Halfpenny?'

Natalie's stomach did a flip. The best sort. She rubbed her arms and her legs quivered.

The second bracket was straight, solid hard rock. They included some Nirvana, Red Hot Chilli Peppers, Madonna and Pink, Natalie spitting out the words with more feeling than usual. The pub was overflowing now, and outside fights had started to break out. One more bracket and they'd be done.

Liam came backstage in the break. With a bourbon.

'Come to get the lowdown on the case?' she asked.

'If you're offering, though it wasn't exactly in the forefront of my mind.'

'Well just for the record, I rang and organised the interview before I heard from your office. And Tiphanie's hiding something.'

Liam leaned against the door frame. 'What?'

'Maybe she was in on it. I guess all I'm saying is don't dismiss her.'

'Come off it Natalie, Travis did it; remember, that's why

you wanted to be on the team?' He looked her up and down. 'You are the hottest woman I have ever seen.'

'Out there or as a shrink?'

'Both. And you know where else.'

'You in town for the night?' Maybe just one more night with him, then call it quits.

'Could be.'

Natalie raised an eyebrow.

'I want to take you for a drive first.'

'You have something that'll compete with a Ducati?' Natalie asked in disbelief.

Liam grinned. 'See you after the show.'

The finale was definitely tongue in cheek. The Stones' 'Satisfaction' was Natalie's challenge to Liam, to show she wasn't going to back off from anything he could come up with. It was hard not to smile singing the repetitive chorus, the volley of teasing 'no's. She could feel, rather than see, Liam returning her sentiment with amusement in the crowd, but he didn't come backstage. Natalie looked for him in the bar and he wasn't there. She paused only a minute before making her way out, to ribald jeers from some of the locals. She found him outside the entrance in a yellow convertible, top down, talking to one of the cops. The constable was checking out the machinery.

Natalie walked over, laughing. She wasn't much of a car person so she wasn't sure exactly what she was looking at, only that it wasn't a Porsche and it didn't look long enough to be a Ferrari. Anyway weren't they all red? It was short and square and testosterone-saturated.

'Lotus,' Liam said to her.

'I know,' she lied. 'You're having a full-on midlife crisis aren't you?' She wondered what it had cost.

Liam grinned back. The corners of his eyes creased, blue and penetrating as ever. 'Jump in.'

Once away from the pub Natalie pulled her wig off and felt the air rush through her real hair as Liam hit the sound system, turned off the highway and let the car loose.

It must have been half an hour before Liam stopped. The road had ended by a river, far from the last sign of civilisation.

'So how does it rate against the Ducati?' Liam asked, undoing his seat belt. He looked at her, hard.

'Not on the same page.' Natalie returned the stare. 'But good for a car. I can cross it off the bucket list.'

'Does that list have fucking in a Lotus on it?'

Natalie laughed, looking around her. 'There's barely enough room to sit.'

'Let's be inventive shall we?'

Inventive meant a new bruise from the gear stick, scratches from twigs on the freezing ground and a mercifully short dip in the river. After he had driven back to the Welbury pub, they showered together in her room to warm up and he stayed the night without it being discussed.

'**D**ad would have been fine if he'd stayed off the piss.'
Jessie sat down opposite her. Sunglasses off: a bonus. She was holding a scrap of paper to which she occasionally referred. Natalie had told her to write down her feelings as they had come to her through the week and it seemed she had done so.

'Never did for long though. Not after Mum killed herself.'

Jessie had been ten at the time and had been the one to find her mother's cooling body. Natalie suspected the sexual abuse had started around then. Alcohol would have lowered whatever barriers her father might have had. But abusive or not, he was the only stable person in her life and when he remarried two years later Jessie might well have felt rejected.

'It seems to me that your father coming back into your life has brought up a lot of stuff from the past.'

Jessie shrugged. Not ready to go deeper yet.

'Keep writing down anything that comes to you. And put it in this.' Natalie pulled out a white cardboard gift box, slightly smaller than a shoe box.

Jessie frowned. 'What's that?'

'A box for the bad memories,' said Natalie. 'No one else will ever look into it. Once you put the thoughts, feelings and memories into it you have a choice.'

'Choice?' Jessie looked sceptical.

'Whether to take the lid off or put it back on,' said Natalie. She had used this technique several times. In her bottom desk drawer there were two boxes that had been tied up at the end of therapy and handed over to her to keep, their owners symbolically leaving their pain behind. 'Then you can use some of the mindfulness techniques.' Natalie had outlined these at the beginning of the session.

Jessie snorted. 'How's that going to help?' But she took the box anyway.

Georgia had the appointment immediately after Jessie's. Looking out of her window to the car park as she wrote up her notes, Natalie saw them stop and talk to each other. On the face of it, the two had little in common. Underneath they were, she supposed, similarly angry. One expressed it through her physical appearance and the other used her middle-class good looks to hide it. Both damaged, but Jessie was easier to read, and to empathise with.

Georgia breezed in wearing bright colours and smiling.

'Good morning Natalie.' Natalie wondered why she didn't like Georgia using her first name. It made her feel old if her patients called her Dr King. But Georgia, she reflected, used her name the way a politician did with a radio interviewer, implying—or trying to evoke—an intimacy that didn't exist. Natalie adopted a neutral smile and invited Georgia to talk about her week.

'I'm getting to the gym daily. And I checked out the new shopping centre in the city and got—'

She could have been visiting a girlfriend. Natalie cut in. 'I was thinking, after last week,' she said. 'Something you said didn't quite make sense.'

Georgia waited for Natalie to go on.

'You implied Paul was your first sexual partner.'

Georgia frowned. 'Did I?'

Natalie waited.

Georgia shrugged and said, 'I don't really like to think about before him. It's not like any of that...well I left it all behind. I was...naive.'

'I'd like you to tell me about it.'

A tight smile. 'If I must.' After a pause she continued. 'I met Gary at a party. What can I say? I was naive, stupid. He took advantage of me.'

'How often did you see him?'

'See? You mean have sex with? Just the once,' Georgia said, laughing mirthlessly. 'More than enough, I assure you.'

'When did you know you were pregnant?'

'As soon as I missed my period.'

So not a case of pregnancy denial. 'Did you let him know?'

There was the briefest of pauses before Georgia said, 'No point. He wasn't going to play happy families.'

'Did you tell your aunt and uncle?'

'Virginia?' Georgia's face made a brief grimace; in response to Natalie's look of curiosity she added, 'My uncle told me once we were both named after states of America but I'm sure it was chosen as a good Catholic name in her case. She was as pious as the Virgin Mary so I wasn't about to go to her.'

'What about your uncle?'

'We didn't have that sort of relationship,' said Georgia,

smoothing out the crease in her dress. 'I was about to start nursing and had organised a share house. So I just moved out.'

'What was going to happen with the baby?'

'I suppose I'd have put it in childcare. Maybe adopted it out. To be honest I didn't think all that much, I just... assumed it would work out.'

Which it had. By accident or design?

'It must have been difficult.'

'I hardly put on any weight. If people thought I was pregnant they never said. I didn't feel much different. It was a very rapid labour and I panicked. I realised it was dead straight away.'

'Did you call for help?'

Georgia shook her head. 'I told you, I panicked. I know now it was a precipitous labour, not like my later ones; it happened very quickly. Suddenly there was...a lot of mess and...a baby. Only it wasn't moving or crying.'

'So what did you do?'

'Delivered the placenta. Cleaned up. Called an ambulance.'

Natalie found her clinical account chilling. The autopsy had been inconclusive and there was no follow-up at the time. Only in the light of subsequent events had Georgia's behaviour come under suspicion.

'I had never bonded, you see,' said Georgia. It was a reasonable explanation for her lack of feeling; also a motivation for murder. 'Not like the pregnancy with Genevieve.'

'How did you feel when Genevieve died?'

'I knew immediately she was dead. She was blue and cold.'

'How did you *feel*?'

'I watched her; I've no idea for how long. Then I called Paul. He was out at the shops. I wasn't sure if I should call an ambulance or not, given she was dead.'

'Georgia, I'm wondering how you *felt*?' Natalie repeated.

'I...I don't know. Stunned I think. It really didn't sink in.'

'And Paul?'

'Devastated. Kind, supportive. Though...'

'Though...?'

'Though...?' Georgia looked blank. 'I, well I can't really recall that period very well.' She looked down, rubbing her hands on her legs. 'I just remember feeling afraid.'

'Afraid of what?'

Georgia looked up, eyes widened. 'Of...nothing in particular.' Natalie was sure the smile was staged; but why? It broadened when Natalie said her time was up. Georgia almost skipped out of the office.

Natalie reflected on statements she had read from Georgia's friends. When her children died, Georgia had seemed disconnected, emotionless. Dissociation? Because she didn't have any emotions? Or because it was her lifelong pattern, learned at the hands of abusive or unavailable caregivers, where it was safer to hide your emotions rather than be vulnerable?

Neither quite fitted with Georgia's departing words. Her mention of feeling afraid didn't ring true for someone getting in touch with their inner demons; it was too *easy*. Was she afraid of Paul?

'Your weekly present has arrived.'

Natalie took the red envelope from Beverley's hand and

realised her own hand was shaking.

This time it said, *I'm watching you. Taking your mood stabilisers are you?* She felt nauseous.

No one knew about her illness except a handful of health professionals, Tom and her family. She didn't talk about it, didn't like to think about it. She hated being reduced to a diagnosis and hated, too, the powerless rage that it caused to sweep through her. Now someone else knew. Who? And how?

She thought of the car outside her house, the noise on the roof. Of Travis and his two dead babies and what he stood to lose. Of some of the psychopaths she had interviewed over the years and how little regard they had for the lives of others. Just *who* was watching her do *what*? She wondered what the cops would make of this, imagined them looking at her, asking about her mental illness, forming their judgments. She was going to file this message away too. Just as the stalker probably thought she would. What else did he know about her and what did he intend to do with that knowledge?

'How's everyone?' Natalie asked as she came into the office.

Kirsty raised an eyebrow. 'I have two nurses off sick and no one wants an extra shift. I have a hangover, Wadhwa thinks the hospital should fund his research and Corinne has gone ballistic over the KPIs. Next question?'

Normal day at the office. 'The patients?'

Kirsty grinned. 'Pretty good, thank God. It's a lot quieter here now Georgia Latimer has gone.'

'Georgia? She created unrest?' Natalie asked. 'What do you mean?'

'We had more acting out over the two weeks she was here;

three patients slashed up and Corinne gave us a serve about how much sedation we were using. Place was a madhouse.'

Natalie groaned at the quip. 'And you think Georgia was behind it?'

'Hard to say.' Kirsty shrugged. 'She was always nice as pie to us, and I never saw her be anything else to patients either. But there's something off-centre about her. I think they sensed it.'

Natalie nodded. Maybe that was it, the same unease she felt. The patients were fragile enough for that kind of feeling to throw them.

Celeste was much brighter than last week. Her brother, Joe, heavily tattooed and sporting a large septum ring, was visiting her.

'She's okay today, Doc,' he said with a grin that showed missing teeth.

'That's great to hear,' said Natalie. 'Look ahead, not back?'

'I reckon,' Celeste said. 'Would be nice to have a future without the bastard about.'

'We don't have to talk about him; future, remember?'

'Suits me fine. I just want to forget.'

Her brother nodded and his eyes followed Natalie all the way to the door. Natalie met them as she turned and she saw a knowing quality that unsettled her. Was there some meaning there? Or was she being oversensitive?

'I have no doubt Georgia is damaged,' Natalie said, sipping her glass of wine. 'I feel there's something I'm missing from her story. I'm trying very hard not to be judgmental but if I hear about her shopping trips again I swear I'll gag her with her Gucci scarf.'

'Is it possible you're a snob?' asked Declan.

'That's a new one. Not something many people would call me.'

Declan laughed, measured and contained. She was pretty sure he timed things for effect; longer smiles and more nods if he wanted to reel her in, opening a space for her to feel safe, to reveal things about herself. Shorter, abrupt looks and words, threatening the withdrawal of approval if she didn't think about the point he was making. 'Snobbery works in both directions. I'm not suggesting Georgia hasn't done it hard but she sounds like she wears her middle-class status like a badge.'

'Like my mother?'

Declan's expression didn't reveal anything; it didn't have to. Here was something else to consider in the countertransference.

'It's not just Georgia,' Natalie continued. 'I have this bad vibe about Paul. I mean, if she is so damaged, what was he doing married to her for all that time? Why didn't he suspect something? I've seen hundreds of shitty marriages and mutual psychopathology, but in this relationship children kept dying. Wouldn't that be enough to shake an innocent man into wondering what was going on?'

'Perhaps it did, when she was pregnant with the last child. Could you ask him?'

'It had occurred to me. I'd have to get Georgia's permission...'

'You could try. It seems to have quite a hold on you. What about your other case?'

Natalie shifted uncomfortably, allowing herself to be distracted by the front door opening and the sounds of someone walking down the corridor, then the thud of shopping bags being dropped on the bench. His wife presumably.

She filled him in on the interview with Tiphanie. 'My gut feeling is that she's covering up.'

Declan frowned. 'You've told me nothing about her partner.'

'I didn't interview him.'

Declan didn't respond.

'The O.P.P. and the police thinks he did it. Angry, immature. He didn't have much to do with Chloe; Tiphanie was the stay-at-home mother.'

'Will you be interviewing her partner?'

'The police already have, there isn't a need for me to.'

Declan paused. 'If you want to understand Tiphanie, you'll need to look at her family. Including her partner.'

Liam was waiting outside in the shadows of the Collingwood lane, takeaway food containers in hand, when she arrived. Better than a stalker. Maybe next time she'd find someone who could cook; this much junk food couldn't be good for her. She had thought about getting Liam to meet her at one of the restaurants near Declan's rooms, but only for a second. Her warehouse offered the best after-dinner options. Which meant, she acknowledged, that she wanted to keep fucking him, and so what? It didn't have to mean a capital-R relationship, just mutual convenience.

The Lotus was in the cul-de-sac off the lane. Liam was still in a suit, although he had pocketed the tie. He followed her and her bike into the basement entrance.

'This place is something else,' he said, looking around.

'Could have been the star,' Bob called from upstairs.

Liam raised an eyebrow. 'What the hell was that?'

'Bob reciting a parody of "Hurricane" I believe.'

Liam laughed. 'Bob as in Dylan? Parrot's got the better voice.'

Upstairs Natalie grabbed two beers, shoved all the paperwork off the table onto the floor and started dipping naan into the beef vindaloo.

'Bring me up to date with Chloe's case,' she said.

Liam shook his head, mouth full, and made her wait until he had finished his curry and beer.

'Okay. You were right.' He wiped his fingers on the tea towel she'd thrown him. She wasn't sure that this was something she wanted to be right about. 'We've got a statement from Tiphanie's GP.'

'And?' Who had told him? Not Damian, she was sure. His boss, who Liam liaised with, maybe.

'Seems that despite Travis's claims that she wasn't a nutter like Amber'—Natalie cringed—'she's been on antidepressants for several months. Pops the odd Valium too.'

'So do many new mothers. Particularly if they have to live with a deadshit like Travis.'

But why had she lied when Natalie had asked her about mood and medication? Because she didn't want Travis to know? Or the cops?

'Maybe, but more to the point, how does it fit in with the case?'

'I guess it adds weight to the she-did-it theory,' said Natalie. Like Amber.

'Forget it, Natalie. Travis ties this and Amber's case together. He's just good at getting women to cover up for him. Use your psychiatry skills to help explain how he does that.'

'You think that if Chloe is dead, I don't want to see Travis go down for it? But wishing for it to be him doesn't mean it is.'

'No, but if it quacks like a duck...'

Natalie ignored him. 'The medication increases the chance she could have dropped the kid accidentally. But dropping her wouldn't kill her unless it was down a flight of stairs onto concrete. She was nearly one.'

'Travis wouldn't cover for her.'

'No, I agree. You might like this more. If she was sedated, she might not have heard Chloe wake up in the night; Travis kills her when she won't settle. She wouldn't have heard anyone in the morning either.'

They spent a few moments thinking in silence.

'Fancy another visit to see her?' asked Liam.

'I've already organised one on Thursday. With Damian.' She thought of Declan. Wondered how long before he found out about this case's connection to Amber, and what it would cost her.

Their eyes met over the remnants of dinner. Natalie drained the rest of her beer, stood up and wordlessly started to undress. Liam's eyes never wavered, drinking every bit of her in. Despite being slight with a narrow waist and muscles taut from the workouts that were essential for her sanity, she had retained the fullness of breasts and hips. It was the first time Liam had seen her naked in the light, and he seemed to be enjoying the view. He moved closer, his hands tracing over the scars across her lower abdomen and pelvis, eyes meeting hers with concern.

'Don't worry,' said Natalie. 'I was a passenger. I've never caused an accident.'

'God, you are....' Liam laughed. But it was the knowing

amusement in his eyes that made her want him. 'I can't get enough of you,' he said. He stood, still fully clothed, and pulled her towards him. She felt his belt buckle cold and hard against her stomach as his hands came over her butt and their lips met. Natalie pulled at his shirt, flesh on flesh sending tingles through her. She started to undo his belt but Liam stopped her, pulled it off himself, then grabbed her hands.

'Perhaps I'll try to tame you a bit,' he said. 'I still owe you for that debacle on the courtroom steps.' Natalie saw that he meant to use the belt to tie her up and laughed.

'You and who else?' She was more than twenty kilos lighter, but she twisted effortlessly out of his grip. Liam wasn't about to be deterred. Grabbing an arm he pulled her roughly and spun her into the wall behind, almost knocking the breath out of her. He was kissing her before she had a chance to move, using his weight to keep her from shifting.

Natalie kissed him hard in return. For a moment he eased his body back, decreasing the pressure as his hands moved over her breasts. Natalie used the moment to push him off balance. A second push sent him over the back of the sofa. Natalie laughed and grabbed his trousers, which were now around his knees.

Once they were both naked, he lay watching her as she arched her back and lowered herself over him, staring into his eyes. If he felt the flash of connection as strongly as she did, he reacted against it just as quickly, almost immediately flipping her over. It was an hour before they were sated. They fell back on the sofa, a mess of scattered fast-food containers and paperwork around them. Bob's stand was horizontal; he'd moved to the banister.

'I presume you need to go home?' Natalie asked,

returning from her bedroom wearing a white wrap she'd forgotten she even owned. It was undoubtedly a present from her mother.

Liam was collecting clothes. 'I guess so.'

'Where are you meant to be? Actually, no, don't answer that, I don't want to know. How many kids?'

'Two. James is twelve and in his first year of high school. He wants to be prime minister. Megan is ten and probably will be the prime minister, straight after she's finished writing her Booker-winning novel.' He spoke with warmth.

'Sounds like you're giving them the childhood you didn't have.'

Liam paused, reflecting. 'You're a shrink, so I guess that's pretty obvious. I don't want to be the sort of father my da' was. We'd never have any idea if he was staying or going and if he stayed, whether we wanted him to. I want my kids to know I'm always there, and it's a safe place to be: them first, no matter what.'

'It's none of my business,' she said. 'Does your wife care?'

'She doesn't know or want to know,' said Liam, avoiding her eyes.

'I meant does she care about you? The whole package? The part of you I see?'

Liam buttoned up his shirt and smiled. 'That bit I'm sure she'd happily give you.'

Natalie figured as much. The perfect wife for a corporate lawyer would have to be...respectable, she supposed.

'So you allow yourself to be tamed most of the time, and just permit the occasional breakout.'

Liam, now dressed, walked over to her and pulled her up, kissing her gently. 'Thank you.'

Natalie laughed. 'Nothing to do with you,' she said. 'I'm looking after my own needs, pure and simple.' She walked him down the stairs, musing that his motives for seeing her had shifted; revenge or bruised ego had been overtaken by pure lust.

'Then I hope you stay...needy,' said Liam. He kissed her again. 'See you Thursday night in Welbury?'

She nodded with a half-shrug.

'Oh wait.' Liam stopped. 'I found this under your door.'

He produced a red envelope from his jacket, handed it to Natalie and turned away too quickly to see her look of shock.

A few moments later at her computer she slotted in the USB, and read the single Word file saying what was now obvious: *I know where you live.*

Natalie felt she no longer had a choice. Stalking of the more malignant variety had the potential for escalation; her man was already well on the way. She took the USB sticks into the Fitzroy police station. Waited impatiently in a claustrophobic foyer with missing persons posters and a 'We know you are there and will be with you soon' sign staring at her. The duty constable, when he appeared, looked resigned to a day of lost cats. He was hardly able to contain his enthusiasm when Natalie explained why she was there, and handed him a printed list of the threats she had received. He took a long time getting details; enjoying the time away from the cats, perhaps.

'Could it be a patient?'

'I have no idea.'

'You mean none of them or all of them?'

'I have no idea.'

'So tell me about your patients.'

'I can't.'

The constable sighed. Natalie almost felt sorry for him. He reread the printout she had given him. 'What does this mean here about mood stabilisers?'

'Not relevant.'

'Do you want to be helped or not?'

'I can't breach confidentiality.' Her stalker knew that. He'd warned her about it from the start. Not that she had any names of patients, or anyone else for that matter, she could give the constable as likely candidates. Apart from Travis. She felt she was grasping at straws casting him as the stalker. Surely he had more to worry about than terrorising her? Would he have driven to Melbourne to deliver the first letter and, if so, what was he worried about?

If it was Travis, however unlikely, this was Damian's investigation. He'd hardly thank her for bringing in any more interference. Liam hovering on the edges was bad enough.

The constable stopped writing. 'Get someone to stay with you for a while. Make sure your locks are good. I'll put your residence on the cruise-past list.'

Jessie was subdued. She arrived with a huge bag, and seemed distracted. Natalie figured she'd get to the issue bothering her when she felt safe.

For the first half of the session she went over mindfulness techniques and added some relaxation and distraction to the repertoire: temporary scaffolding, while Jessie took the months or years to process what was driving her emotions and to manage it effectively.

The underlying problem surfaced suddenly, when Natalie was encouraging Jessie to close her eyes and take deep breaths.

Jessie opened her eyes and sat up straight, squirming before saying, 'I've been packing up Dad's stuff. The doctors don't think he'll ever be able to go back home.'

'Too many memories?'

Jessie managed a wry smile. 'You didn't give me a big enough box.'

Natalie met her smile and encouraged Jessie to continue.

'Jay—my stepbrother's—helping though, which is good.'

'How much are you seeing of Jay?'

'He keeps in touch. Without him I probably wouldn't have coped with Hannah being in prison.'

'Is he working? Married?'

'No. Not married. Works for…' She frowned then named one of the big consulting firms. 'Does something to do with computers for them. He's smart,' she added.

Sounded promising. Jessie hadn't held a job at any one place longer than six months.

'Would he come and see me? As your main support, he might benefit from knowing your crisis plan. I'd see you both together.'

'Jay? Here? I guess I can ask.'

Jessie rummaged around in her bag and pulled out a notebook computer. There were stickers all over it. Mostly Japanese cartoon figures. One looked like the figure tattooed on her arm.

'Found this in Dad's stuff.' Jessie looked down at it, picking at one of the stickers that was peeling off. 'It won't fit in the box.'

'Would you like me to keep it here until you're ready to look at it?'

Jessie nodded. She looked relieved but also…scared.

'We can go there when you're ready.' Natalie put the computer into the desk drawer.

Georgia was late. Natalie used the time to check her mail. No red envelope. Rather than being reassured, she felt tense.

Would the next one be under her door at home again?

Georgia arrived twenty minutes into her appointment time. 'I'm so sorry. The tram hit a motor bike and I ended up having to walk most of the way.'

'Right.' Natalie took a breath. 'How have you been feeling?'

'Good, actually. I've been painting the living room. It was that awful mushroom off-white. Drab. It was getting me down.'

Natalie drummed her pen on Georgia's file.

'I'd never painted a whole room before and—'

'Tell me about Olivia.'

Georgia didn't appear to hear the question. She rummaged in her bag and found a Dulux paint chart. 'It's that one now.' She pointed to a pale lilac. Natalie kept looking at her until she put it away, zipped up the bag and put it on the floor. 'It probably wasn't the smartest thing,' she said. 'I got pregnant not long after Genevieve. I hadn't been on contraception because we wanted a big family. I just didn't think about it.'

Repetition compulsion? Was Georgia driven by a need to create the perfect family—the one she had not had as a child—but destined never to succeed? Everyone was compelled to repeat patterns. It was only when the patterns were pathological that anyone noticed.

'We were both so delighted when we found out. It seemed like it was meant to be, that this child was going to help make things right again.' Georgia stared out of the window.

Natalie forced herself to stay still. A minute passed. She shifted slightly to see Georgia more clearly, wondering if she was dissociating or just remembering. She was startled to see a tear run down Georgia's cheek.

'Did it? For a while?' asked Natalie gently.

Georgia turned slowly and looked at Natalie with a blank expression.

'Make it better?'

'Oh.' Georgia took a breath. 'Yes. Paul and I could still plan our life together. The pregnancy was relatively easy which helped. And I was interested in sex again. I was able to keep Paul happy.' Natalie circled the word *happy* and added a question mark. 'Labour was okay. Olivia was even easier than Genevieve. Placid. Everyone loved her. She loved being dressed up.' Georgia unzipped the bag and pulled a photo from her wallet, a child in a ballet tutu. It must have been taken shortly before Olivia died. She looked about two years old.

'It was just fancy dress,' Georgia explained. 'She would have done ballet classes the next year.' Natalie stared at the photo; Olivia was the perfect pretty extension of her mother. Had this been Georgia's fantasy? If so, what had gone wrong to alter it? Cried once too often? Too needy and demanding?

'What was her health like?'

'Oh, she had the usual colds and things.'

Natalie looked at the general practitioner's summary that had finally arrived. Georgia had been in to see him weekly with Olivia, sometimes more often. A battery of tests, well outside the usual range, had been ordered. A normal reaction from both GP and Georgia after an earlier SIDS? Or was it Munchausen's; in this case, Munchausen's by proxy? As a nurse, Georgia would have known exactly how to fake illnesses to ensure particular tests were done. She could have given her children medications that would have induced vomiting, taken their blood to make them anaemic, ensured that faecal material contaminated collections or caused urinary tract infections. Natalie had looked hard at the tests and the results. It was hard to see them as anything more than anxiety driven. Nothing too invasive and no recurring theme.

Georgia started to say something then stopped, still staring at the photo. Her face again seemed devoid of emotion.

'Georgia?'

She continued to stare blankly. Natalie started timing. Five excruciating minutes passed. Natalie got up and knelt down beside her, putting her hand gently on the other woman's arm. 'Georgia?'

Georgia looked at Natalie dreamily. 'Sorry, what?'

'Where have you just been? What were you thinking about?'

'Uh, I don't know,' said Georgia, looking confused. 'We were talking about Olivia weren't we?'

'Yes.' Lost time? She cringed at the thought of eating humble pie with Wadhwa.

'Tell me more about Olivia. What was her relationship with Paul like?' Because Natalie still had a hand on Georgia's arm, she felt rather than saw the stiffening. It was so fleeting she wondered if she had imagined it; Georgia was smiling broadly.

'Oh he was wonderful with Olivia. Called her his little monkey.'

Natalie stared at her. Georgia's sudden brightness was patently excessive and completely at odds with the preceding fifteen minutes. Still, the overly bright Georgia had her uses. She gave her permission to contact Paul, as well as her Aunt Virginia.

'How can I tell if it's real?' Natalie watched as Declan finished arranging his desk. The file in the corner was now exactly square.

'The only way you'll ever be certain is if she tells you. And even then?' Declan shrugged. 'You can look for inconsistencies, lies over unimportant things, maybe an overall gut feeling. Just don't draw conclusions too soon.'

'Do you believe in dissociative identity disorder?'

'I understand it's popular with our American colleagues.' The expression suggested he wasn't going to add a bust of any American analyst to his mantelpiece in the near future. '*The United States of Tara* was very good, I hear.'

'You can't disregard the diagnosis on the grounds of it being dramatised on television.'

'No, but it may be a culturally based—in this case American—phenomenon.'

'So you're saying it can exist?'

'The human brain is very complex. Rather than ask yourself if you believe in some disorder that is an artificial construct, ask yourself if you believe in dissociation as a phenomenon.'

'I've had it. A reaction to antihistamines. I felt like I was separate from what I was actually experiencing. But I knew what was going on. And I didn't kill anyone.'

'You've been depressed and not tried to kill yourself too.'

Suitably chastised, Natalie thought for a moment. 'One of my borderline patients used to feel she was hovering around the ceiling watching as her stepfather raped her.'

'Analytical theory aside, what's the point? Does it help?'

'It's a survival technique. It helped my patient separate herself from the terror of the experience. It develops young.'

'Because that's when it's most needed. How does a child of five or even ten make sense of furtive behaviour, threats and pain from an adult they want and need to trust?'

'Okay. But dissociation isn't the same as D.I.D.'

'I agree. But is it a first step? What would it take to explain the subconscious taking refuge in different personalities?'

'Wadhwa would say a ton of abuse, perhaps specific abuse creating conflict in the child: "I love my father, I hate my father". The different personalities are supposedly a way of managing the contradiction.'

'And you've already established Georgia represses emotions. Can you conceive a way that other personalities would resolve it?'

'Gut feeling? It just seems too convenient. What I've seen could still be borderline and besides...'

Declan raised his eyebrows.

'Perhaps the police have this one right; the most obvious simple explanation rather than the deeper psychological one. A jury are going to take on board that she got angry and killed them more readily than Wadhwa waxing lyrical on separate personalities developing, one for rage, and others for fear and shame.'

'The jury is not your concern. She may have D.I.D. She may have a personality disorder. Or it may be something else.' Declan considered her gravely. 'But whatever Georgia's diagnosis, this is not about you and Wadhwa.'

'Urgent message to ring Dr Cortini at the prison,' said Beverley, handing her, at the same time, a note from Jacqueline Barrett suggesting a time to meet to discuss Georgia. Beverley had outdone herself today, dressed in the full array of rainbow colours, and her mood seemed to be in line with it. Natalie left her to organise the meeting with the barrister.

'Amber has just heard about Travis's second child going missing.' Lucia Cortini's voice was always gravel and strine. Today it sounded like it was coming around a cigarette parked in the corner of her mouth.

'She's taking it hard?'

'She's coming up for her parole hearing. I don't want another fuck-up like with her bail.'

'You think the parole board will see her as still unstable?'

'Yes. Someone put it in her head that it's her fault.'

'She isn't to blame.'

'Yeah. I get that. But she's not listening. She wants to see you.'

'I can't.'

'You mean won't.'

Shit.

Declan had been clear. 'You are going to cause more harm than good. You're over-involved and not seeing things clearly. It's affecting your judgment. You shouldn't be seeing her.'

'I can't stop,' Natalie had protested. 'She trusts me. She still has a lot to work through.'

'This is a directive,' said Declan. 'Explain, and then hand her over.' The threat of him reporting her and her losing her ability to practise gave her no choice.

Amber had been understanding and accepting, but only because she considered herself unworthy. Now, over a year later, Amber was asking for help and there was no one else who understood what she needed.

'No,' Natalie said to Lucia. It wouldn't be fair to Amber to drop in and then out of her life again. 'Give her my best wishes but there are professional reasons I can't see her.'

'Of course. Professional reasons. You just look after yourself.' There was a sound akin to a snort and Lucia hung up.

When Natalie got home she found herself looking into the shadows, thinking she'd seen something. The only movement was at the end of the lane near the brothel. A man disappeared into the door below the red light. *No.* She would not be intimidated. She opened the door tentatively. No envelope.

Bob flew around the warehouse and swooped down past her.

'Bob, you're an idiot!' The bird seemed to sense her displeasure and sat up on a rafter and refused to come up to the kitchen with her.

'Suit yourself,' said Natalie. She was tired. She wanted to run a bath and get an early night.

She wasn't about to get to bed in a hurry. At the top of the stairs sitting on the kitchen bench was a red envelope.

'Have you touched anything?'

'I live here,' said Natalie to the green constable the police station had sent, the same one who had taken her initial statement about the notes.

They had deduced that the uninvited guest had entered via one of the high windows in the garage. They were old and would have been easy to push in. The window that the intruder had chosen was next to a telegraph pole and an indent in the brickwork; both would have helped him manoeuvre in and out. She'd been lucky Bob hadn't escaped.

'I meant, have you touched the envelope? We need to get the crime scene team in.'

'Just the edge where I got the USB out.' She had needed to know what it said.

Constable-wet-behind-the-ears and his female colleague frowned but she didn't care what they thought. Her mind was still preoccupied with the contents: *You won't win. They belong to me.* There was also a scanned photograph. A gravestone, and one she recognised: Eoin's. Under his name her stalker had overlaid another: hers.

*

'So which rule do you think this refers to?'

At the police station the next morning—after she had watched new locks being put on all the windows and door of her warehouse—Senior Constable Tony Hudson, a tall cadaverous-looking man with a South African accent, was taking things seriously, meticulously repeating the words of each note in turn. 'Do you have a problem with your mental health?' he asked after the third.

'No.'

'What's this about mood stabilisers?' was inevitable after the fourth.

'Medication.'

'What for?'

Jaw set, she stared at him. 'Not relevant. The medication works.'

Senior Constable Hudson leaned forward. 'Seems to me he knows a lot about you.'

She knew that, felt it.

'He knows your friend had an accident. Did Eoin have family that'd blame you?'

That was a laugh. They had cut him off before he died. It had been *her* mother that had wanted to hold *them* responsible for her injuries.

'He knows about your mental health problem.' Senior Constable Hudson paused. 'Any chance it could be a health professional?'

The suggestion jolted her. 'No.' She'd answered without thinking and his expression suggested he was going to sit there until she did consider it. 'My doctor is hardly going to stalk me.' She looked quickly at him and sighed. 'There would be others, from when I was admitted. But that was seven years ago.'

'So how does he know?'

'It has to be a patient.'

'Any thoughts as to who?'

'I have no idea. All my current patients are female. A lot of them are incarcerated.'

'The notes say *they belong to me*. Any thoughts about who "they" might be?'

'I don't have any patients who are from the same family. Partner and child perhaps? I've helped women leave violent partners with their children, but as often as not they go back.' Maybe it wasn't about her patients at all, but as fast as the thought came to her she dismissed it.

Senior Constable Hudson could angle one eyebrow well into his forehead so that it disappeared under a thick brown fringe.

'Personal life? Ex-partners? Gay?'

'No. Nor have I turned down any would-be lover of either gender recently. Last boyfriend was a cop.' This wasn't the work of the rejected lover, and it was too organised, too intentionally threatening, to be the incompetent-suitor or intimacy-seeker type of stalker. Shit, she knew more than the cops.

Senior Constable Hudson frowned. Maybe he didn't approve of cops dating shrinks. 'I need you to go through anyone you are currently seeing at work or socially or who you've seen in...say the last year, who has a record of violence, stalking or threats. Include the incarcerated ones. They may have boyfriends. Anyone who has been angry, who you've given evidence against.'

She did need to make this list but she wasn't about to give it to him—not the full set of names anyway.

'There is an issue with confidentiality. Particularly for

my patients without convictions,' said Natalie. 'I can't have you guys turning up on their doorsteps.'

'My team will approach this sensitively.'

Yeah, sure.

'You need to take this seriously,' the senior constable said. 'Either move out or have someone move in with you.'

Let the arsehole win? Never. She had replaced locks and secured windows. She was smarter than her stalker; she just needed to work out who he was.

There turned out to be less than a dozen names, and she could even cross some of those off. Someone with chronic schizophrenia wouldn't have the planning skills, and others didn't have stable partnerships. Celeste had a brother, Joe. She thought of his toothless grin and his eyes following her but she couldn't think of any reason why he would be stalking her.

There was Travis. But as much as he niggled at the back of her mind, the timing wasn't quite right and she didn't think he could have worked out where she lived. A patient who was also a health professional might have access to health records...that took her to Georgia. She might qualify for the list if her court case was to go badly, but currently there was nothing in their interactions for her to be concerned about.

None of the others were anything more than business as usual. From the past there was one who had schizophrenia and had been charged for stalking a childhood sweetheart, a couple of murderers, and three women with borderline personality disorders who hadn't lasted in therapy. As the stalker had reminded her so compellingly, she couldn't give any of these last names up to the police. But if he was worried about confidentiality, then he or his partner or relative had to have been a patient. That meant she'd find him eventually. Then she could decide what to do.

Tiphanie was looking neither jubilant nor truculent.

They watched her through the one-way screen where she was sitting in a featureless room, biting her nails and looking at her feet.

'So what has she said to you so far?' Natalie asked Damian, who had loosened up considerably. Even greeted her with a smile.

'Not much. We haven't pushed her.'

'But Travis knows she was popping pills?'

Andie Grimbank grinned but there was an edge to her mirth. 'He does now.'

Damian and Andie had gone to see them at their home for an 'informal chat'. The place looked immaculate, but Tiphanie had been nervous and edgy, perhaps because she wasn't currently using anything. Travis was full of himself as usual.

Andie had taken them back over the day before the disappearance. Then Damian asked how Tiphanie woke up for the baby, given the pills she was on.

'We could have heard a pin drop,' said Damian. 'Tiphanie looked like she was going to pass out.'

Travis had launched into an angry spiel at the cops but then, realising Tiphanie had gone quiet, stopped and stared at her. 'Tell 'em Tiph. I know you don't do drugs. You don't even drink.'

Tiphanie had eventually said, no, she didn't do drugs. When Damian said, 'What about prescription ones?' there was another silence, not broken by Travis this time.

Natalie tensed as she listened to Damian's account. She knew from Amber what Travis was capable of. Knew from Kay's version what more Travis might have been capable of, none of which she could share.

Damian caught her glance. 'We took Tiphanie to her mother's after the interview.'

Natalie took a breath. This cop was one of the smart guys.

Tiphanie was now here alone, without Travis hanging off her and raging about their rights—which didn't mean he wasn't venting his anger elsewhere.

Natalie thought about the notes.

Breaking the rules.

That could mean the dressing-down she gave him before Amber's court case.

Then in the latest note. *They belong to me.* Amber and Tiphanie? Tiphanie and Chloe?

Tiphanie was still staying with her parents. Whatever rift had occurred with them previously had presumably been resolved.

'I think we'll be able to do this gently,' said Natalie. Andie looked noncommittal. Damian's expression suggested that he was happy to give her some extra rope and see what happened.

'Hi Tiphanie,' Natalie said, sitting opposite her as the other two took chairs to the side.

Tiphanie looked up briefly. Her eyes were puffy, her skin sallow.

'I understand you didn't exactly tell me the truth last time we talked.'

Tiphanie didn't respond, apart from a sniffle.

'Which is okay. There are a whole lot of reasons why

people don't want to talk about things.' Natalie paused, then added, 'We're trying to work out what happened to Chloe. Maybe you can help us find her. Whatever the answer is, you want to know the truth don't you?'

No response.

'So tell me why your doctor prescribed the antidepressant and the sedative.' Natalie let the silence sit this time. Finally Tiphanie raised her head.

'I wasn't coping all that well.' Natalie watched her, monitoring her affect and her level of eye contact.

'Chloe wasn't a problem. I loved her straight away. Soon as I saw her on the ultrasound.' There was a depth of emotion in Tiphanie's voice, at odds with the whisper in which she'd uttered the first statement.

'Yes, I know. Having postnatal depression doesn't mean you don't love your child.'

'I couldn't get out of bed, didn't want to do anything. I thought maybe I had glandular fever or something.'

'Were you sleeping?'

'Yes. Too much. But I was always exhausted.'

'Did the antidepressants help?'

'A bit. I guess. The Valium was better. For a while, anyway.'

'Are you taking them now?'

Tiphanie shook her head and tears welled in her eyes.

'Why not?' asked Natalie.

Tiphanie whispered something.

'Tiphanie?'

'It's all my fault.'

'What do you mean, Tiphanie?' Natalie held up her hand to stop Damian, who had sat forward in his chair, from intervening.

'I took a Valium that morning. Two. One when I got up and another when I went back to bed.'

'Okay,' said Natalie. 'Why did you do that?'

'I was stressed out.'

'About...?'

'Everything. I was so useless and I was afraid.'

'Of?'

Tiphanie looked down. 'Nothing. I...I wouldn't have heard her, you know.' As if a thought had come to her suddenly she looked up, eyes wide in fear. 'I mean I was out of it. I don't really remember the morning. I could have even—'

'Could have what?'

It took a few moments for her to pull herself together. She looked so lost and vulnerable that Natalie wanted to hug her.

'I don't...well...maybe I left the door open,' she mumbled.

'So is that the whole truth?' Andie asked after they finished the interview. 'People should get licences before they have kids.'

'I think she's still hiding something,' said Natalie. She had been certain that at the end of interview, Tiphanie had been going to say something else, and stopped herself.

Andie drummed her fingers impatiently. 'Can't you hypnotise her or something?'

Natalie stopped herself from rolling her eyes. 'Not that simple. Psychiatrists aren't mind readers, and even under hypnosis people can exert free will.'

'Then what can you do?'

Not as much as she'd like. Natalie's gut instinct was strong but what was it that didn't ring true? 'Try and put the pieces together, making sense of who she is and therefore why she is saying some things...and not others. Tiphanie couldn't maintain eye contact. I had...a sense of her knowing I knew she was hiding something.'

'Still protecting our mate Travis?' Damian leaned forward.

'Probably,' said Natalie. *He did it.* 'She's certainly feeling guilty, but is it for not saving Chloe from Travis, or for bombing herself out and not being there for her child? Or for not taking Chloe and moving to her parents' months earlier?' Amber had asked repeatedly, 'Why didn't I just take Bella-Kaye and walk?'

'She didn't say anything about Chloe having breakfast,' Natalie added, half to herself.

'Meaning?' Damian asked.

'If Travis is intimidating her to stick to the story, that's where it will come unstuck,' said Natalie. 'The morning. When Chloe may not have been there.'

'I'm thinking she's still scared of Travis,' said Andie.

Was she? 'Is she scared of her father too?'

'More likely her mother. I know the Murchisons.'

Of course she did. It was the advantage of small towns. Andie was older than Tiphanie—even if she'd grown up here they wouldn't have gone to school together—but still Natalie and Damian looked at her expectantly.

'A Welbury special,' said Andie. 'Parents both got kids from previous relationships. There's a much older half-brother who isn't around, a half-sister and a brother. Tiphanie's the baby.'

'So what are the parents like?'

'Dad runs the petrol station heading east out of town. Nice enough bloke, bit beige.' Andie wrinkled her nose.

Natalie warmed to her. 'And her mother?'

'A piece of work,' said Andie.

'Care to expand?' Damian asked.

Andie looked grim. 'Let's just say Kiara—her stepsister; no, half-sister...whatever—showed off some ugly bruises in the change room at school.'

Liam was waiting in the foyer of the police station. Natalie sensed Damian tensing up.

'Thinking of moving down here?' he said to Liam. 'I can introduce you to the real estate agent.'

'I'm starting to like the drive. Your boss tells me there's been a new development.'

Damian looked at him then Natalie and turned around without replying.

The late winter fog was descending as they walked back to the hotel and Natalie appreciated the protection of her leather jacket.

'You seem more on edge than normal,' Liam said. 'This case getting to you?'

It wasn't just the case getting to her, nor was it the games he was playing with Damian. And the stalker wasn't Liam's problem.

'I want to find Chloe; and whoever caused her disappearance. Don't you?'

They went out for pizza. The meal was purely fuel and afterwards Natalie would have been at a loss to say what topping was on it, apart from cheese, which she had played with, stretching the long melting strands between her mouth and the pizza slice, as Liam looked on. Wanting her and not the food. She made him wait though, lingering over her drink, enjoying teasing him, enjoying her own anticipation.

This time she let him tie her up; the brass bed seemed to ask for it, and she was curious to know how inventive he was. She was confident she could escape the ties if she wanted to. So why not lie back and enjoy?

She was naked as she watched him strip, slowly, eyes locked with hers. She imagined him debating exactly what he wanted to do with her and allowed herself to give in to it: the idea of her pleasure being in his hands. She had never allowed anyone, not even Tom, this much power. She didn't count Eoin, a lifetime of experience ago.

He didn't abuse the trust. She'd known instinctively he wouldn't. He lingered briefly over the tattoo that wrapped around her arm, the one she'd left to remind herself that when she was high she did really stupid things, but Liam knew better than to ask about it. His smile conveyed desire, but also made her want to believe that his need was and would only ever be for her. In her moment of climax her eyes were locked on his, and the vulnerability provided a connection she had never experienced before.

The experience for him must have been one of absolute power. For her it was a realisation that an abdication of responsibility contained the potential for ecstasy. And the feeling of safety she hadn't even realised was missing.

She felt good and wanted to hold onto her sense of peace without the dullness induced by medication; she hadn't taken her meds the previous night, in anticipation. And she wasn't going to let them take the feeling away now.

Natalie tried to organise her thoughts as she opened up the throttle on her bike. After leaving Welbury early, she had stayed on the ring road rather than heading home and turned northwest through the newer suburbs with cheap prefab housing estates. Taking the exit onto the long road to the prison, Natalie hoped there were no speed cameras. The speedo hit one sixty and it felt like she was barely moving. It would be just a one-off. Declan didn't need to know. Maybe she'd tell him afterwards and get absolution.

The first impression of Dame Phyllis Frost Centre was of well-tended garden beds and neat concrete paths, but beyond their formal cheer, it was bleak. Even the spindly gum trees looked as though they were struggling to make it. She tried to concentrate but her thoughts were leapfrogging over each other as though in a race to the finish. Declan kept popping into her mind and she shoved him aside. One visit to see Amber wouldn't hurt anyone, and anyway he'd never know. Amber would be released and her recovery could really start. Her family would welcome her back and, while she would never be the innocent young girl who had married Travis, she would heal.

There was the usual rigmarole getting through security.

'You're not on our list.' Fake smile from the big-boned one. 'Sorry.'

'Fuck you,' she muttered.

'What was that?'

'I said you must be able to find it. I'm a psychiatrist.'

'Really? Hear that Jen? We've got ourselves a *psychiatrist* here. Very impressive.' From the other side of the glass the two women crossed their arms and smirked. Natalie felt like strangling them. Might have even given it a go if the cowards hadn't been protected.

'I need to get in. Ask Lucia.'

'Lucia? Do you know a Lucia, Jen?'

'Actress, isn't there, called Lucia, or is that Lucy?'

Fuck. Her mind was moving at such a pace now she felt she was watching four television stations at once. It was starting to shoot coloured signals in the guards' direction. Like laser beams. Excellent, that should do it. She smiled and let them laugh, watching all the while as their brains started to fragment into green and gold filaments. Ten minutes later—silence from her and laughter that sounded like thunder from them—they let her through. She didn't suppose there was much hope for them. Still, they weren't her problem. Amber was. She shook her head, tried to block the barrage of thoughts. Later, when there was time to consider the cosmos.

Amber had put on a little weight and it suited her, though her anguished look took Natalie back to when they first met. They had the visiting area to themselves, sitting on fixed plastic chairs in the corner furthest from the wardens.

'Hi, fancy seeing you here. Mind if I drop in?'

'You came!' Amber smiled. 'I was hoping the next time

I saw you it would be in your office.'

'Yes, soon.' Natalie tried to focus on Amber. *Soon, tune, bloom.* Concentrate. 'You'll be coming up for parole, there's a hearing, you need to be careful, Lucia tells me there isn't any reason for you not to be approved. You don't want to mess it up again, got to think of yourself for once and of course your family and everything they've been through.'

Was she talking too fast?

'Did your mother tell you about Chloe?' said Natalie, deliberately spacing out her words.

Amber shook her head. 'No, one of the other girls told me.'

One of the girls. Natalie nodded, Liam's words about the paedophile ring were suddenly in her ears and she forgot why she was there.

'It's tough being here. I guess you hear horrendous stories.'

Amber nodded, taking a breath. 'Enough to…well I didn't realise how sheltered I was.'

'The women here tend to come from disturbed backgrounds.'

'Yes.'

'Have any of them ever talked to you about their abuse as children? Seems like there's some shithead men enticing girls with pink bunny rabbits. Pink of course. Little girls like pink.' *Shit.* Where had that come from? Hadn't she told Liam there was no way she'd ask around for him? Still, she couldn't see how it would hurt.

Amber looked a little startled, then shook her head. 'I'm kept separate from them most of the time. Except for other women with charges like mine. Tiphanie…she won't end up here will she?'

'You need to focus on yourself.' *Focus, hocus pocus.* No, just focus, yes, she needed to as well. 'There isn't anything you can do for her.'

Amber didn't seem to have heard her. 'Mum says that the papers only mentioned me briefly, and not my name.' Amber blushed. 'Oh that was awful. I didn't mean to be. It's far worse for poor Tiphanie.'

'Do you know Tiphanie?'

'Oh no, no...it's just...'

'You've been there.'

'Thanks,' said Amber. 'My family...' She looked down and twisted her tissue around in her lap. 'It's awful. I will never forget Bella-Kaye.' She looked up. There were tears in her eyes. 'I think of her all the time, on her birthday, Mothers' Day, the day—' She took a breath and looked hard at Natalie. 'I can't *bear* the thought another child died because—' She started crying.

Natalie put her hand over Amber's. 'You couldn't have prevented whatever happened to Chloe. Do you really think Tiphanie would have listened to you? She would have been defensive, never admitted she'd made a mistake. Believe me.'

Amber gave a faint smile.

'People are responsible for their own decisions,' said Natalie. 'You suffered for your mistakes. Maybe Tiphanie will have to for hers.' Her mind was heading her in another direction. *Focus.*

Amber continued to pull at the tissue. It was soon in shreds in her hands.

'I know...'

'What living with Travis was like.'

Amber nodded. 'There were things I could never bring myself to tell you.'

144

Natalie felt tiny icicles sprouting from her skin. She rubbed her arms, bemused that her skin didn't look any different. She forced a smile and nodded. Amber's mind was still closed to her. No green and gold filaments for her; must be just prison wardens' day for brain disintegration.

'I was so ashamed,' said Amber.

'You were also very confused.'

'Yes.'

Natalie looked at her critically and tried to define what was different but couldn't put her finger on it. More self-assured perhaps, even in the current circumstances? Her fingernails cut into her palm as she tried to listen and make sense of what Amber was saying.

'I think back and remember...how it felt and things he said.'

'And...?'

Amber bit her lip, looking down. 'He...he wanted me to do it.'

For a moment this meant nothing to Natalie other than a confirmation of what she had come to realise a year earlier; Travis was a controlling bastard. Then, as the silence reached out and encompassed her, Natalie knew for certain that this was something she had known, that it was part of the couple's dynamic but not something she had ever interpreted to her patient.

'How did you know that?'

'He told me,' said Amber, her voice strangely robotic. 'He said to me that one of us had to die.'

In the back of Natalie's mind a thought seemed to form words without her even knowing what was coming. 'Tell your mother that?'

Amber stiffened. 'No, I never told her anything.'

Thoughts seemed to ricochet inside her head. 'I heard about your father. I'm so sorry.' Natalie closed her eyes, fingernails carving out deeper furrows in her palm.

Amber sniffed. Natalie opened her eyes to see Amber was crying, large tears rolling down one cheek. 'I never got to see him.'

'I guess it all happened too fast for your lawyer to get you to the hospital.'

Amber nodded, took a breath. 'Wouldn't have mattered. He never woke up.'

'After the second attack.'

'There was only one. Massive. They were in town and the ambulance got there real quick but he never came out of the coma.'

Amber's words were reverberating in her head like ice cubes in a blender. Natalie felt she was drowning in the mix; so much so she almost forgot that she had intended to make the most of the visit and see Jessie's partner, Hannah. Older than Jessie, probably in her late twenties or early thirties, Hannah looked unexpectedly wholesome with only a hint of mascara and hair in plaits. She even had a sense of humour; shrugging good-naturedly when Natalie told her that no, she was not going to prescribe her anything.

'Had to give it a try. Look after Jessie won't you? She isn't as tough as she makes out.'

'I figured that.'

'Doubt she's got anywhere close to telling it all to you. Do you know about her family?'

'Some.' There were lights shimmering on the edge of the building. What did they signify?

'She has shocking nightmares she can't make sense of,'

said Hannah. 'But I can tell you, they happened. Something like them anyway.'

'How do you know?' Natalie was distracted. What were those lights? There was a subtle blue hue to them. What did blue mean?

'Too weird for a kid to think up; she's been having the same dreams for years.'

There was an awkward pause before Natalie realised Hannah was expecting another question. 'Um. Can you tell me about her stepmother and stepbrother?'

'She's got no time for the wicked witch, but Jay's always looked out for her I guess. I've only met him once. He was cool about her being gay. More than I can say for my family. I don't think he was big on me using. But he was there supporting Jessie straight after I got nicked.'

Natalie watched Hannah's eyes. They were trying to tell her something. About the cosmos or was about Jessie? Hannah was right; Jessie didn't trust her enough to share the really scary stuff with her. 'Other women in here have that sort of background?'

Hannah looked at her suspiciously. Liam owed her big time.

'Not asking you to rat,' said Natalie. 'Just wondering if anyone here talks about being abused. Seems like there's been a paedophile network targeting girls in Melbourne for years. They use pink bunny rabbits.'

Hannah dropped her cigarette butt and ground it on the cement. One of the wardens banged the window. Why didn't this one look like her head was going to explode? Was she a plant? Natalie felt on edge, unable to sit still. Hannah picked the butt up and flicked it onto the nearby bin. 'Last stuffed toy I heard about was for one of the kids here with their mum. Had dope in it. Screws found it and didn't even give the teddy back.'

'So how about you? Another five years isn't it?' Natalie snuck a look at the wardens. No green filaments. That must mean something. She'd have to wait for the cosmos to disclose.

Hannah shrugged. 'Less now. I'll manage. No choice really.'

'Do you think Jessie will be there for you?'

'I'd like her to be but I don't expect it. No one else ever has been. Do you think we could be parents, me and Jessie?' she asked suddenly.

'Stranger things have happened,' said Natalie. She giggled. Like green and gold brain fragmentation. Maybe she should write it up. It could make her famous. 'So long as you can find a donor.'

'That's the easy bit,' said Hannah, shrugging.

'So is there a hard bit?' More giggles.

'Not having the kid turn out like us,' said Hannah. 'I mean not fucked up.'

'I'd refer you to a good parenting program.' Natalie had to leave. 'Take it easy Hannah,' she said, and by way of farewell, added, 'I'll do my best with Jessie; she's trying hard.'

As she was dressing for Shaun's wedding band gig—not in fact a wedding but some corporate function—she knew that this was meant to be. Of course it was. The cosmos had a reason for everything. She'd agreed to have Tom pick her up because drinking didn't go well with a motorbike. Nor did a dress. She refused to do conservative, but she felt she owed it to Shaun to wear a dress. More goth than business world—black and red leather corset, with a tulle and lace skirt and fingerless gloves—but still. She'd probably overdone the makeup. She didn't normally drink much when she was working but tonight the alcohol was going to be essential to cope with some of the awful songs Shaun would expect her to sing.

When they arrived at the Grand Hyatt, rather than following Tom to where the band was setting up, she intercepted the drink waiter who was holding a tray of champagne in long-stemmed glasses for the first of the guests. It was a twenties theme. Men were in standard dinner suits with the odd cravat or scarf channelling Scott Fitzgerald. The women were shimmering in jewelled and feathered flapper outfits with headbands and unlit cocktail cigarettes in holders.

'I don't think we've met.' A woman smiled tightly at Natalie as she took a glass.

'No, we haven't.'

The woman, in her late fifties, looked a little startled. 'I'm Maureen Hoffman.'

Natalie tried not to giggle. This was clearly supposed to mean something to her. 'Really?'

'And you would be?' Maureen was fixated on Natalie's corset motif but in the dim light it was almost impossible to make out that it said 'Bite Me'.

Before Natalie could answer, Tom grabbed her elbow and steered her away. 'We're the band, Natalie, remember?'

'Just chatting.' Natalie waved her hands, forgetting that she had champagne in one. A suited man ducked.

Tom dragged her over to the band.

'Please tell me I don't have to do "I Will Survive".'

'They always like it.'

149

Natalie grimaced, her concentration wandering. There was a lot of glitter in the air. It was congregating around a group of people in their forties. While Tom was busy with his drums, she wandered over to the table. There was a spare seat and she sat down.

'I'm Natalie,' she said to a man with a scarlet scarf.

'Boris,' he said, introducing his partner, a woman with a black bob whose name Natalie didn't catch. 'I don't know anyone here.'

'Me neither,' said Natalie. Boris's work involved something to do with spark plugs.

'Don't you find it boring?'

'No,' said Boris.

'Bet your wife does. She's probably on the lookout for someone more prestigious. Women are like that; they want to trade up.'

A waiter placed an entrée on the mat in front of her. It was something strangely stacked to look artistic and she wasn't entirely sure if it was all edible. The other women at the table seemed impressed. Getting excited about food stacks was not normally Natalie's thing but this one captured her imagination. She started building it higher with the bread and butter container, wondering if the flowers in the table decoration might work too. No one would mind, surely.

'Ah,' said Boris, 'I think you're meant to eat it.'

Tom appeared from nowhere and whispered in her ear, 'Natalie, up. And I mean *now*.'

Natalie started to protest but Tom put his bulk to good use, smiling at Boris as he hoisted her up and over to the stage.

'Here's the list,' Shaun said. He looked terribly dull tonight. Maybe she could find him a cravat.

'Make sure you stick to it,' Tom added.

The band played all the favourites from the seventies and eighties—minus 'I Will Survive'. The crowd of five hundred or so started to warm up. She was sure that her challenges to them to flap their arses off helped, though every time she introduced some light patter Tom kept hitting the drums. He seemed unusually agitated. In the break after the first set she felt like he was glued to her. But she really did have to go back and talk to Boris, whose glitter halo was now red. It seemed ominous.

She ducked away from her minder the first moment she could. On the way back to Boris's table, Natalie caught sight of a familiar figure two tables away and not looking in her direction. Liam. Didn't he belong somewhere else? In a James Bond movie?

She stopped still and was unaware of anything else until Tom bowled straight into her. Only quick manoeuvring on her part prevented her falling into Boris's lap. Then she threw herself there anyway. It was worth it for the look from his wife.

'Who is this function for?' Natalie said, as Tom apologised to Boris. Liam was looking good but it was his partner she was focusing on. She knew her from somewhere. Pussy Galore?

'Some law association function,' Tom said as he yanked her back towards the stage.

Of course. Natalie sat down and started giggling. 'I believe I shall sing "I Will Survive" after all,' she announced to the band. Shaun shrugged but he was looking at Tom.

Wow. She suddenly worked it out. She had picked Liam's wife completely wrong. It unsettled her. Fuck, she knew this woman. Did Liam know that? He must have wondered.

Natalie hadn't thought about his wife much at all. If anyone had asked she'd have given a glib answer. Blonde airhead from Toorak money, devoted herself to their children. School committees, maybe charity.

Natalie laughed out loud. Shaun and Tom looked at each other again.

Lauren Oldham might be blonde, but that was where Natalie's imagination and Liam's reality diverged. A bimbo she was not. Her blonde hair wasn't styled into soft waves, but spiked, like the wig Natalie wore when she fronted The Styx. Not gorgeous, but tall—surely as tall as her husband and maybe taller in heels—and striking. Unlike the other female guests, she was in neither ball gown nor flapper outfit. She was in a suit, probably on call, because she was one of the city's, if not the country's, most eminent infectious diseases specialists. With a towering reputation as a ball-breaker. About as far removed from the picture of airhead social climber as you could imagine. She was probably out of the country most of the time juggling WHO meetings and Ebola outbreaks. No wonder Liam could get away. Assuming they had live-in help, which they would.

They started the next set with 'I Will Survive'. She wished she could see Liam's eyes on her. She wondered what he had been thinking when he saw her, if he had planned to ignore her all evening. She had no intention of ignoring him.

She got the first couple of lines out through gritted teeth. Afraid? Petrified? Not fucking likely; but then Liam would get that. She started getting into it as the song went on, surprised the band with a few of her own variations to the lyrics. A girl had to have some fun.

She had even more fun with the next song, Melissa Etheridge's 'Similar Features'. About imagining a woman other than the one you're with. Lauren might have been taller than her and blonde, but their facial features weren't so different, and the fact they were both doctors was too delicious to overlook. As the song ended she caught Lauren's eyes and for a moment thought she must know. Everything.

Tom dragged her out of the ballroom before the final bracket so she didn't get a chance to introduce herself to Lauren. Later perhaps, before she left.

'Never quite heard the song done like that,' Maureen Hoffman sniffed as she sailed past.

Natalie ended the night unenlightened as to Liam's reaction, or whether he'd heard the subtle lyric change that identified her and Lauren. As soon as they finished, Tom insisted it was time to go home.

'Tom, you're being a spoilsport. I'm just warming up.'

Tom didn't seem to care. He frog-marched her out without a word.

'The green filaments will eat your brain,' said Natalie. Tom might have a different colour. She liked Tom: maybe it was only the wardens that had green brains and Boris the red halo. Them and her stalker, hopefully.

'Do you think he'll be there?' she asked suddenly.

Tom took her inside. There were no more notes. He stayed until she took her medication: in front of him.

'Enough green and gold filaments for one night,' he said.

Natalie was awake an hour later. The silence seemed to have a colour. A red, ominous presence sitting on her bedhead. She lay still. Somewhere downstairs there was a noise. Not the noise of the red that now was singing in her bones, electrifying them, making her buzz so loudly surely it would be heard, but a scratching.

At first she thought it was outside on her balcony, but then it seemed to move. An attack would be the obvious next step in the stalker's campaign. All her thoughts led her in circles. Frozen and powerless, she remained in her bed, listening and waiting.

How much time passed? Still the scratching. Had she dropped off? Had it gone? She willed herself to focus. Rolled off the bed, grabbed the cricket bat from beneath it.

She crept over to the door, watching the shadows, sure they were full of red noise. She was certain now; there was an outline in the corner of the patio. She opened the door cautiously then raced forward. Half aware that if the bat connected she might kill him, she felt unable to judge her strength. Fear and exhilaration mingled into red and green and gold.

She took one stride and swung hard, screaming as she did. The bat sliced through the air, swinging her around with its momentum and sending her flying back into the roof tiles of the factory next door. The tiles cracked and crumbled as she hit them, and they cascaded down with her onto her porch. *Fuck*. She pulled herself up and heard the scratching again. *Fuck*. It came from downstairs. Screaming she hurtled down the stairs, brandishing the bat.

Bob, who she'd forgotten to clip to his stand, had been digging up her dead pot plant. He flew to the rails screeching in alarm.

Natalie watched him as she caught her breath. Watched green and gold and red in the soil she had heard him scratching in, and shakily made her way to the phone.

Declan doubled her dose and had her come to see him on Sunday night. She was fortunate it was the weekend.

'How many doses had you missed?' He wasn't critical, more concerned.

'A few.'

'You've been bordering on hypomania for a couple of weeks. The over-involvement with patients, the increased libido—they're warning signs, Natalie.'

'Okay, maybe irregular,' Natalie said. 'I know, I know. I can't afford to not take them. I just got caught up in things and lost sight of the balance.'

'If you insist on taking on a large caseload, you can't afford to slip up with your meds.'

Natalie nodded, eyes averted.

'It would be in your best interest to cut your work back.'

'I can't.'

'You mean won't.'

'Okay, won't. At least not at the moment.'

'Did you do any damage?'

Natalie thought about the prison and cringed. Every time she got those wardens again her life would be hell. She'd kept it together more or less with Amber and Hannah. The ball? Shit, she didn't want to think about it.

'Natalie,' said Declan, patting her hand. 'I'm not the enemy.'

She met with Jacqueline Barrett for breakfast in a small cafe full of wigged and cloaked barristers at the court end of Lonsdale Street. Early had suited them both when she made the appointment. Now with a double dose of quetiapine in her system she felt as if her head was in a jar of treacle.

Ms Barrett was just as she would have predicted. In her late thirties, slim with a pencil-line navy skirt and tailored jacket, discreet makeup and the perfect coiffure—a sleek dark bob. She was easy to identify and not just because she was the only woman in the café. They had met before: Boris's wife. The one she had suggested was looking to trade up. *Shit.*

'Ms Barrett?'

Natalie watched the recognition briefly rob the lawyer of her perfect smile. 'I'm Natalie King and I would like to apologise for Friday night.'

Ms Barrett, who had started to rise, sat down with a thud. 'You certainly know how to create an impression.'

'So I've been told.'

They sat in silence while Natalie waved down a waitress and ordered a coffee.

'So then,' said Jacqueline. 'What do you think of my client?'

'Complex.'

'I would have to agree with you there. This is one of my more interesting cases.'

'From a psychiatric perspective not straightforward either.'

'If you think it's out of your range...'

'Not at all. Not much in psychiatry is straightforward.'

Jacqueline—she was definitely not a Jackie—let out a long breath. 'Do you know why we got another bail hearing?'

'Initially she was thought to be a risk to her unborn baby, and that risk no longer pertains. And the possibility of a Dissociative Identity Disorder diagnosis was brought up.'

'Yes, but unless it's very clear, it won't be enough at her trial to sustain an insanity defence. And by "clear" I mean distinct personalities. A number of people need to have observed, and preferably videoed, them. Even then, it is unlikely to be enough for an insanity defence.' Jacqueline looked at her. 'Your thoughts?'

'I'm still keeping my mind open.' Natalie wondered how much of what she reported to the lawyer made it back to her client. She didn't want to admit that Wadhwa might be right; not yet anyway. 'There was something else?'

Counsel looked like she'd have preferred to visit the dentist than sit and chat cordially with Natalie. 'Have you heard of Meadow's Law?'

Natalie forced herself to think through the fog. 'Lady Bracknell's Law. "To lose one parent is unfortunate; to lose two is careless." A child in this case.'

Jacqueline managed a polite laugh. 'One is a tragedy, two is suspicious and three is murder unless proven to the contrary.'

'If you know nothing about medicine or statistics. Meadow didn't factor in the possibility that multiple deaths might have a common underlying cause—genetic in the case of the same family.'

Barrett nodded. 'The British cases convicted on Meadow's principle have now largely been overturned.'

'So why would it even be raised in a current case?'

'You'd be surprised what a prosecutor can slip into the jurors' minds before the objection is heard. And let's face it, it probably makes sense to most people. In a lot of the UK cases there was nothing to suggest an underlying cause—the autopsy results were inconclusive.' She shrugged. 'Same with Georgia Latimer's children.'

'Really?' Natalie's mind still felt like someone had a finger on the slow-motion button. 'I haven't seen the autopsy documents.'

Jacqueline slowly pushed over a file. 'Genevieve was thought to be SIDS. They were holidaying way up north at the time, so the autopsy was done locally. The prosecution are going to argue that the coroner was not experienced in forensics.'

'Olivia?'

'Asphyxiation secondary to asthma. There's a problem though.' She put on reading glasses and shuffled through the pages. 'See there.'

'*A small bruise on the bridge of her nose, almost certainly occurring close to the time of death,*' Natalie read aloud.

'The prosecutor will try to get the pathologist and experts to say that it occurred when she was smothered. She was getting too old for SIDS and while she had asthma and a current infection...well, there is doubt.'

'Enough to convict Georgia?'

'It shouldn't be, not by itself. But it adds to the prosecution case. Obviously.'

Natalie let it go. 'And Jonah?'

'It was deemed SIDS. But of course there's no specific pathology finding that identifies SIDS. It's a finding of exclusion—when nothing else turns up on autopsy. So it's open slather. Who knows what some quack doctor will get up and say?'

Natalie flicked through Jonah's autopsy. Petechial haemorrhages—tiny capillary bleeds—suggestive of trauma were present. They could be found in SIDS; but they were also found in asphyxiation.

'So do you think the prosecution is going for her being essentially psychopathic?'

'D.I.D. or not, I'm hoping they might get interested in an alternative.'

Natalie felt the coffee hit her system but she still had no idea what the lawyer was hinting at. For one awful moment she thought Jacqueline was asking her to engage in pillow talk with Liam. She took another sip of coffee. 'Munchausen's by proxy maybe?'

Jacqueline frowned. 'You think?'

'As I said, I'm keeping my mind open.'

'Good, because I'd be interested in your thoughts as you see more of her. Particularly...any role her husband might have had.'

Natalie felt her skin prickle with déjà vu. Amber and Travis all over again?

'Such as?'

'Influence. Coercion.'

'Surely that wouldn't be enough to fight a murder charge?'

Jacqueline patted the froth off her lip with a napkin, being careful with her lipstick.

'Maybe not,' she said, 'but it might knock it down to infanticide. Then even if she's convicted she probably won't do time.'

'Olivia was two,' said Natalie. Genevieve and Jonah had been younger. Infanticide laws varied, but twelve months was the accepted cut-off age.

'She was one year and three hundred and sixty days. In Victoria, the age changed to two years in 2005. The year Olivia died.'

Natalie stared at her. She had thought the state law change was more recent; certainly in her forensic psychiatry lectures it had still been the subject of debate. Had Georgia known at the time about the law? Then she realised that if Jacqueline was wondering about the children's father, there was another thing to worry about.

'So,' said Natalie slowly. 'What about the youngest child?' Paul had her in his care. 'Has anyone thought about Miranda?'

Natalie was still thinking of her meeting with Jacqueline when she was checking the *Welbury Leader* online, waiting for Georgia to arrive. The journalists had finally let loose; a two-page feature headed *Tragedy Strikes Twice*. They had resurrected some old photos of Amber and her family and quotes from sources that were unclear which wife and child were being referred to. The subtext was clear: tragedy might strike twice but lightning sure as hell didn't.

Amber's words suddenly popped into her head: *one attack. Never came out of the coma.* Kay had lied. Made the whole thing up—but why? She thought of Kay's tears when she had talked about Travis not letting Glen die thinking his daughter was a murderer. Travis confessing was what Kay had *wished* happened. Like Liam and Damian, Kay wanted Travis to be guilty. It didn't mean he was. The Meadow's Law fallacy.

The photo of Travis managed to capture a mix of slimy self-satisfaction and poor-little-me. Natalie's first thoughts were for Amber, but then she wondered when the mainstream papers would pick it up and Declan would find out. She switched her iPad off angrily. Why weren't they concentrating on finding Chloe?

'You guys didn't encourage the arsehole reporter did you?' she asked Damian.

'Hardly.'

'I'm sorry, just...I know Chloe's got to be dead but somehow...it would be nice to find her one way or another.'

'We followed up on what you said.'

Natalie frowned. 'What?'

'The morning.' Damian's tone suggested a degree of respect; one she had yet to win from Liam regarding her involvement on the case.

'And?'

There was a pause. 'She said she couldn't remember. That she got her mornings mixed up, that it was all the meds, that she was bombed out and maybe she hadn't even given Chloe breakfast.'

'And Travis had?'

'No. It was clearly bullshit.'

'And you're thinking what?'

'She was scared. Told us Travis has been hounding her to go home to him.'

'So,' said Natalie slowly, 'you still thinking she's covering up for Travis?'

'Yes. We're putting the screws on. She'll crack soon.'

Georgia arrived flustered and on edge, dressed in a slimline pink and black tracksuit ensemble. On the way to the gym, presumably. Rather than sitting down, she walked to the window and stared out. Natalie tried not to let her frustration show. There were too many unanswered questions and even if she asked them she couldn't be sure the response would be genuine. How to even attempt therapy when she was still struggling with diagnosis?

'He sent another card.'

'Paul?'

'Yes.'

'Did he say anything on this one?'

'No. I mean, yes. A message.'

'Why don't you sit down and tell me about it.'

Georgia turned around, putting her hands in the pockets of her jacket, head down.

'He doesn't write anything,' she said. 'He wouldn't want to incriminate himself.'

'So the message was conveyed how?'

Georgia looked up. She sighed, walked over and sat in the armchair opposite Natalie.

'I told you he was attentive. We had an extremely close relationship. He always made me feel special. Right from the start he sent me bunny cards.'

For once Natalie was grateful for the medication slowing her thoughts. It took a few moments to formulate a neutral response. 'Why bunny cards?'

Georgia shrugged.

'What was the message this card gave then?'

'The last one was an Easter one. Just meant he was thinking about me, knew I'd been released, knew where I was.'

'What about this one?'

Georgia picked up her bag. Hands shaking slightly, she pulled out a card and handed it to Natalie.

It was blank: no printed or handwritten message. The picture was a scene from what looked like an eighteenth-century painting. A hunter with a shotgun in one hand and three dead rabbits in the other.

Natalie struggled to concentrate for the rest of the day. Was she seeing connections that didn't exist? Rabbits were commonplace, including on mass-produced greeting cards. She shifted her attention to trying to make sense of Georgia. Was this the Amber nightmare all over again? Or was Georgia working an angle, responding to conscious or unconscious prompts from the lawyer? Even if Paul was toxic to Georgia, already vulnerable from her background, would it matter in court? Would Natalie even be allowed to mention it? Just what did Jacqueline Barrett think would be 'helpful'?

She looked at her appointment book, counting down the time before she could leave. Tiphanie's parents had an appointment for Wednesday, but it was the message stuck to the page that drew her attention.

'From Liam O'Shea,' Beverley informed her. *Please direct any questions re the Chloe Hardy case to my colleague Carol Karnell.*

'What do I make of the cards?' Natalie wasn't sitting. Holding her glass in one hand, she paced around Declan's office, knowing she needed to demonstrate that she was well and not quite able to achieve it. 'I left a message with Paul and his lawyer got back to me and said bugger off. So all I have to go on is secondhand information.'

Declan viewed her with his usual level of calm. 'Look at it as a fascinating array of possibilities,' he said.

Natalie paused. 'Such as?'

'My dear, there is a fundamental problem here.' He paused and in the silence made it clear she needed to sit down. How did he do that? She sat down.

'You are being seduced,' Declan explained. 'By the dark side.'

Natalie suppressed a laugh, a picture of Liam naked in bed flashing into her thoughts.

'By that,' Declan continued, 'I don't mean the criminal element of your patients. I mean the law.'

Now he had her attention.

Declan leaned forward, hands as expressive as his face and voice. 'In law, everything is black and white. You think the decision is between good and evil, but it is a far more basic duality. Win, lose. Ms Barrett has a client she is representing and she needs to find a way for her to be innocent. She has less interest, if any, in whether she *is* innocent. A narrative will emerge in court. It may or may not resemble what actually happened but it will be the basis of the judgment.'

'Fine; I get that sometimes criminals get away with it. But there's an innocent child in all of this. What if Miranda is actually in the care of a murderer?'

Declan shook his head. 'When you're my age you will know there are degrees of justice and they don't always bear much relationship to the truth. We can only do our best.'

'That's what we must do isn't it? Find the truth. Protect the innocent?'

Again Declan shook his head. 'Truth? You know people

can have very different recollections of exactly the same event. We filter our memories, see things as we want to through our own lenses.'

'I know all that,' said Natalie, 'but there's still facts. Either Georgia and Tiphanie killed their children or they didn't.'

Declan took a sip of wine. 'Are you sure it's that simple? What about intent? Society is often unsympathetic and sees the woman as Medea. Is that really what infanticide is?'

'Medea,' said Natalie, trying to remember the Greek classic. 'Killed her children to save them? Like Andrea Yates?'

'You're referring to the Texan woman who drowned her five children during a psychotic episode?'

'She believed she was saving them from the devil.'

'*Let it never be said that I have left my children for my foes to trample on.* But I suspect Euripides had a lawyer's mind, not a physician's. Medea killed her children to punish her husband.'

'That's usually more the male thing,' said Natalie. The classic murder–suicide associated with family breakdown: sporadic weekend access and new de facto replacing the father in the home. *If I can't have them, nor will you.* 'I don't think that fits most of the cases I see.' It could fit this one, though.

'Think about Amber Hardy,' said Declan.

Natalie started at the mention of Amber's name. He couldn't possibly know that she had seen Amber, could he? She willed herself to calmness, not breaking eye contact.

'She was technically responsible.' Natalie was starting to feel weary with the angst of these women and the weight of their cases. 'Certainly guilty from a legal point of view.'

'As far as we know. But was Travis innocent?'

'No. Most definitely not. He's a weak bully. Leeches his strength from those more vulnerable. She did it for him as much as if it had been his hand, yet he got off scot free. She didn't do it out of vengeance.'

'No,' agreed Declan. He was looking at her carefully. Natalie looked away. 'I wonder what he then takes with him through the rest of his life. Into other relationships.'

'Whatever.'

'Natalie.' There was a warning edge to Declan's tone.

'Yes?' said Natalie willing herself to stand up, not able to meet his eyes.

'Take your medication.'

Natalie didn't bother with the speed limit. Her mind was ahead of her, already wondering if someone would be outside her house. She cut the Ducati's engine half a block before she got there. The street loomed before her, eerily silent, the shadows holding nothing but a couple of cats that were as startled as she was when they leapt off a bin and sent it teetering and falling, rubbish spilling out across the road. Her doors and windows were intact. The new locks were un-breached. She went back, got the bike and resolved to put aside the niggling anxiety. She wasn't paranoid, she told herself. She was normal, felt fine. Maybe he'd achieved what he wanted, getting under her skin, and now would give up.

She didn't believe it. She was alone and isolated. The cops couldn't help her without her telling them everything, and even then she had more faith in her own abilities. She knew she could call Tom but hated the weakness that would impute. Declan couldn't be told the whole story; Liam had ditched her as too much trouble. There was only her, at the end of the day, same as always. She looked at her pills. Thought of the green and gold filaments and Declan, and took the full dose. But it wasn't enough to stop the wind across the rooftops interrupting her sleep.

Tiphanie's parents were fifteen minutes early for their appointment. Natalie watched them from the doorway, wondering why they were there. To help Tiphanie? To help them deal with the loss of their grandchild? Or to defend themselves?

Sandra Murchison was probably mid-forties. She looked uncomfortable in a brown jacket and skirt that didn't fit. Her hand went under the waist band to try and ease the squeeze, exposing the pantyhose beneath. She made a striking contrast with Beverley, who today was in a spectacular leopard-skin pantsuit.

Her husband, Jim, looked equally lost. Long skinny legs, a beer-gut and rounded shoulders, jeans with shirt half tucked in and a sense that life weighed heavily on him.

'She spells her daughter's name with a *ph*,' said Beverley to Natalie in a loud whisper. 'And an *ie*. I'm surprised there isn't an *h* in *Sandra*.'

Natalie met their smiles as she introduced herself, and hoped they didn't think she was laughing at Beverley's take on bogan spelling. The Murchison's smiles were markers of a social code that stipulated politeness to doctors you didn't want to see and a pretence that all was well, no matter how bad things actually were. Australian country folk at their stoic best. Through a decade of drought, the men had done what they always did, not asking for help, drowning their sorrows at the local pub. And in epidemic numbers ending their lives with a rope or a gun.

They wanted to come in together, which was fine by Natalie, at least to begin with.

'Things must be pretty difficult,' said Natalie.

'Impossible,' Sandra replied, sitting on the edge of the chair. 'This has been going on for over two months now. We're all under enormous pressure and the police seem to be no closer to finding our Chloe.'

Our. Interesting.

'Poor Tiph's beside herself,' Jim added, patting his wife's hand. She didn't seem to notice.

'If they'd listened to me none of this would have happened.'

Jim looked like he had heard this spiel before. 'Now, Sandra, we don't know—'

'Yes, we do. As much as the police and probably more.' Sandra was unstoppable and Jim gave up trying. 'Travis is a piece of shit and his friends are no better. Do you know he got thrown out of school?'

Natalie tried to look neutral. 'So you think Travis was somehow responsible for Chloe's disappearance?'

'Of course. Him or his dim-witted mates.'

'This would be...the night before?'

'Yes,' said Sandra. 'Last I saw her before all this, Tiphanie was exhausted. I'd lay bets that Travis took Chloe with him to his mate's place.'

Natalie frowned. 'What makes you think that?'

'Because he had before. Not that I thought it was a good idea, mind. He usually made Tiphanie drop him and pick him up so he and his mates could drink. And when Travis said jump she'd ask how high.'

'This night Tiphanie was home in bed.'

Sandra made a dismissive gesture with her hand. 'As I said, just before all this she was behaving like one child was too hard to manage. As if.'

'Now Sandy that isn't—' said Jim. Andie's Mr Beige.

'We need to be honest here,' Sandra said. 'Tiphanie has always avoided arguments and doing the hard yards. The pills for instance.'

Natalie didn't think taking medication for an illness was an easy way out but this wasn't the moment to defend Tiphanie nor to explain a possible depressive disorder.

'So tell me about Tiphanie,' said Natalie. 'What was she like as a child?'

'Tiphanie was the baby and always spoilt.' If there was any motherly love underpinning Sandra's words, it wasn't apparent. 'She was a cute kid, don't get me wrong, but being cute she thought she could get things easily. Her teachers liked her, always gave her good marks and she thought that made her special. They encouraged her to do *Japanese* for God's sake. By *correspondence*.' She sniffed loudly. 'What use was that going to be to her?' Glancing at her husband she added, 'Had him around her little finger.'

'Jeez, Sandra,' said Jim, 'she liked helping out at the service station, that's all.'

Probably to escape her mother.

'What about her brothers and sisters?'

'Kiara is twenty-seven. She was always looking out for Tiphanie, you know, at school and the like.' Kiara, according to Andie, was Sandra's daughter, not Jim's.

'She's a nurse,' Jim added, straightening up in the chair. 'Works on the children's ward at the base hospital.'

'Married?'

'She lives at home with us,' said Sandra.

'And your son?'

'William has cerebral palsy,' said Sandra. 'He needs around-the-clock care.'

'Sandra's wonderful with him, but it's not always easy,' Jim added. 'The girls do what they can.'

Sandra sniffed. 'Kiara does. She was helping when I went into premature labour with him and no one else was around.' The look at Jim was unmistakable: Sandra blamed him for whatever had gone wrong with their son.

Natalie drew her thoughts back to Kiara. Kiara with the bruises in the school change room. 'Did she rebel at all as a teenager, Kiara?'

'Just the usual. We got that under control pretty quickly.'

'Did you believe in smacking in your family?'

'There were rules and consequences. The girls knew what happened if they played up.'

Rules and consequences were important, but for healthy development there had to be an underpinning of unconditional love. Tiphanie had tried to find the love she craved by escaping, but lurched, as so often happened, from one abusive relationship to another—in this case from her mother to Travis. Maybe Travis's weakness had reminded her initially of her father's passivity. Instead, Tiphanie's low self-esteem had been fuel for Travis's abuse. If Tiphanie had been like her mother, perhaps Travis would have become like her father.

'What I'd like to do now,' said Natalie, 'is to ask Jim

to step outside. Then after speaking to you, Sandra, have a word with him alone.' Before Sandra could object, Natalie continued, voice firm. 'I can see how much you want to protect each other and I want you both to be able to be blunt.'

Sandra's jaw slackened. Jim patted her hand then made a dash.

'Tiphanie needs to start taking some responsibility for herself.' Sandra had recovered. 'She left once before, you know; at fifteen I caught her reading filthy magazines. Well, not in my house. I had enough of that from the deadbeats my mother used to bring home.'

'What did you do?'

'More like what did Tiphanie do. She went to stay with Jim's mother. Took her *Cleo*s with her.'

Cleo? Jesus, the male centrefold wore a fig leaf. Natalie found it hard not to stare in disbelief. Sandra should have seen what Natalie had been reading—and doing— at fifteen. Her own mother had hung in there despite her disapproval of Eoin, nights out drinking and a request from one headmistress to remove her because 'she didn't fit in with the values of the school community'. It sounded like Sandra, reacting against the negatives of her own troubled childhood, had taken it way too far in the other direction.

'She had to eat humble pie the next year though,' Sandra said. 'Her grandmother died.'

'Did she keep going to school?'

'Yes, finished that year, her final year, and then moved out with *him*. No gratitude.'

Beverley ushered in Jim and offered to get Sandra a coffee. Sandra was too flabbergasted by the leopard print to do more than nod.

Jim didn't have much to add about Tiphanie's childhood. She was a 'good kid'. He was sweating and his shirt was now completely untucked.

'How does she get on with Kiara and William?'

'Kiara? I guess not that close, age difference and all. Kiara's a little bossy but her heart is in the right place. Tiph is good with Will; it can be hard at home.'

'You have another son too, don't you?' Natalie asked, remembering Andie's run down on the configuration of children from three different relationships.

'He lived with his mother,' said Jim. 'Tiph saw him a bit when she was younger, but he's grown up now.'

'How's Tiphanie faring?'

'Pretty well,' said Jim. 'She's a tough kid.'

'She might need to be.'

Jim nodded. 'You know, once when she was eight she broke her arm at school. Never told anyone. Came home, didn't tell us either. Kiara noticed the next day her arm was black and blue.'

'When do you think she realised Travis was a loser?'

Jim scratched his chin. 'I don't really know. Perhaps we can ask Sandra?'

'No,' said Natalie. 'I'm interested in *your* opinion.'

They sat in awkward silence for a few moments until Jim caved. 'Pretty early on, when Tiphanie was pregnant, she was really excited. We...well to be honest we weren't all that happy about the father being Travis, him being married and all the rest.'

'All the rest' seemed to include the fact that Travis's first wife was in gaol for killing their baby.

'Was she happy when he cut ties with Amber and they moved in together?'

'No, not really,' said Jim. 'Tiphanie...I think she was more...keen on having a baby than being a wife, to be honest. She knew she was always going to be a great mother. Used to talk to me about it, all her plans. The things she did and didn't want to do.'

'Did she ever talk to you about leaving Travis?'

'No. She said she wanted her baby to have a father. That was after we knew the first wife was going to stay in gaol.' Jim cleared his throat. 'I gather Travis didn't like the "image", you know, being married to a murderer. Tiph was a bit sorry for him—and scared about being alone.'

'How about after Chloe was born, did she ever talk about leaving him then?'

'She said Travis would never let her and Chloe go. Not because he loved them, but because of image. Image, she said, was all he cared about. Sounded to me like she wanted to leave but she was stuck.'

'Did you suggest she could come back home?'

Jim moved in the chair. At least he had the fortitude to look up and face Natalie directly. 'I think we were both afraid Sandra might not think that was such a good idea.'

'How were Tiphanie and Travis getting on, before Chloe disappeared?'

Jim yanked at the collar of his shirt. 'She and Sandra had a big barney about six weeks before so we hadn't seen them.'

'You kept in touch though, right?'

Jim looked to the door. 'I rang her a couple of times a week.'

'And?'

'She was doing fine, wouldn't have ever let anything happen to Chloe. That kid was her life.'

Until something happened.

'So what did they fight about?'

Jim frowned. 'Tiph and Sandra, you mean? No idea.' He paused. 'Tiph winding Sandra up. First time for a while. Guess she must've been having a bad day.'

Natalie had resisted revisiting the media coverage around Georgia because she hadn't wanted it to affect her judgment. But the journalists might have spoken to people Natalie hadn't. Right now she was keen to know what the people around Georgia thought of her. Who were the girlfriends she shopped with? Were there friends who really knew her, who didn't believe her guilty?

Natalie knew from her work in the mother-baby unit that women did have fleeting thoughts of not wanting their child, or of harming it. It wasn't unusual. She also knew these thoughts caused enormous guilt. Women felt that, to be good mothers, they must always love their baby and if they didn't, they were either mad or bad. Did Georgia's friends prefer to think she had been, temporarily, mad?

A search turned up several articles, including a feature piece. The police had first been alerted by the coroner after the death of the third baby, Jonah. They had interviewed her and Paul, checked the autopsy findings on Olivia, and noted the unclear source of the bruise on her nose.

'She was always bumping into things,' Georgia was quoted as saying to them. The inquest concluded that Jonah had died as a result of SIDS and that no ongoing police investigation was warranted.

They were involved again during Georgia's pregnancy with Miranda. A Facebook 'friend' of Georgia's alerted them to some concerning entries. The journalist interviewed the maternal child health centre sister from five years earlier. There was a picture of her accompanying the article. She looked about sixty. The sort who'd tell you that all babies cried and postnatal depression was a load of Gen-X nonsense.

'There's something not right about someone with a family history of SIDS not wanting to breastfeed,' she had said.

The journalist quoted an unnamed friend—it wasn't clear if this was the dobber from Facebook—who'd thought Georgia was behaving oddly. What had she meant by oddly? Behaviour that showed Georgia was terrified of losing another child, or D.I.D. odd? If Wadhwa's diagnosis was correct, there should have been periods of time when she either went missing, or was behaving in a manner very different from normal.

The papers had interviewed Paul several times. Seen in a fuzzy photo with Georgia, arm around her, head turned away from the cameras, he had been supportive—at least initially. This had changed; perhaps when he found the bloodied knitting needles behind the toilet. The O.P.P. decided this apparent attempt to induce an abortion shifted the balance of probability. They went ahead with charges.

Georgia's first psychiatric assessment deemed her fit to stand trial and she was denied bail because of the unacceptable risk to the unborn child. Her baby, born at the Women's Hospital while she was under guard, was immediately removed and Georgia had not seen her since.

Miranda, now eight months old, was in Paul's care.

When Georgia was eight months old her parents were still together, but a year later her mother was imprisoned for murdering her father and Georgia had gone to live with her mother's half-sister.

In all the press photos Georgia was smiling, patently at ease with the camera. In one she was holding Olivia. The friends initially expressed disbelief that she could be guilty; less so in the later articles. Her aunt, Virginia, was quoted as saying she had done well at school and never caused any problems. In the most recent article, Paul said he loved his daughter and they just wanted to get on with their lives. They had moved interstate.

Natalie googled his firm. It was still based in Melbourne but had a Sydney office. Paul was listed as the CEO. The internet search didn't give her anything she didn't already have except that he'd gone to Scotch College. She knew he was early forties, a little older than Liam. She googled Liam, something she probably should have done earlier. Plenty about cases he had been involved in, including a mention of the paedophile ring with his comments, and a few social page snaps with Lauren. He was a Xavier boy. No surprises there.

Natalie wasn't entirely sure what she was looking for in Paul's history, but if the marital relationship was part of Georgia's pathology, surely he would have shown earlier form? Georgia's teenage pregnancy loss certainly told her something about Georgia; maybe a previous girlfriend would fill in some blanks on Paul.

Having exhausted all avenues she could think of, she double-checked the windows and doors and took her meds. The original, lower dose. She needed to be more alert.

The weekend was busy. They had the Bendigo gig on the Friday night, the Halfpenny on Saturday night and practice Sunday.

Monday morning, Jessie was on time. And she wasn't alone.

'This is Jay.' The man with her smiled tentatively. Blond, tallish—maybe just short of one eight five—he had a wiry frame and looked at her from behind large black-rimmed glasses. Category geek, subcategory non-cute. And not ponytail man, Jessie's occasional lift.

Natalie took the lead. 'Thanks for coming.' Jay hesitated before taking her outstretched hand. His skin felt cool against hers. 'I understand you've been a great support to Jessie.'

'It's been hard for her since Hannah went to prison.' Jay glanced at his stepsister but she was looking around the room.

Natalie spoke to Jessie. 'Did Hannah tell you I visited?'

'Yes, um, thanks,' she said. 'It meant a lot to us both.'

She seemed to mean it, so at least Natalie hadn't been manic enough to put Hannah off.

'I try to visit and ring as much as I can,' said Jay. He patted Jessie's hand, little fingers entwining. Was this a habit from supporting each other through their adolescence? Jessie made a visible, unsuccessful, attempt to use it to stabilise herself as Jay talked about how he worried about her.

'Jessie, is there anything you'd like to say to Jay while he's here? Or have me talk to him about?' Natalie tried to make sense of the emotions that passed across her face: it was always going to be about trust. The people she had loved had failed her before. Even Hannah, by going to gaol, had fulfilled Jessie's expectation of abandonment.

Jessie shook her head.

'Is there anything I can do to help?' asked Jay. He looked at Natalie and then Jessie.

'Jessie, maybe you'd like to answer that?'

Jessie shrugged.

'Maybe just knowing you're there helps,' said Natalie. 'Part of therapy is to help Jessie be more independent.'

'Do you think I could look after a baby?' Jessie asked.

Jay quickly covered up his look of disbelief.

'I think one thing at a time, don't you?' said Natalie.

'Meaning?' Jessie's face clouded. Rejection.

'Meaning it would be great to be able to talk to you and Hannah about this, together.' Jessie managed a hint of a smile. 'I know four more years sounds like a long time,' said Natalie, 'but you're still young. The work we do in that time can help you be prepared, be a better mother.'

'Hannah wants us to be good mothers,' Jessie agreed. 'Not like the trash Hannah has to deal with.'

Natalie raised her eyebrows.

'Saw her yesterday and there's another baby killer in.'

'They are often mentally ill,' Natalie said.

'Yeah well, maybe. Don't think this one is. They're just plain shitheads down in Gippsland.'

The tightening of Natalie's muscles was hard and sharp enough to stop her breathing for several seconds. As soon as Jessie and Jay were out the door she went to the coffee room and found a paper. Page three. Tiphanie had been arrested.

Natalie read every word of the *Herald-Sun* report and then searched the net. Travis and Tiphanie's neighbours had finally decided it was their civic obligation to cough up what they knew. Or more likely, it was time for payback over something, or for their fifteen minutes of fame. Amber was mentioned. Would Declan see the article? The *Age* report was brief, with no photos or reference to the death of Bella-Kaye by name.

According to one report, Tiphanie had been seen the night before—when Travis was at his mate's—carrying a screaming child to a car. Another suggested that it was a 'bundle'; the implication being that Tiphanie had silenced the child, perhaps fatally. Tiphanie was now the last person to be seen with the child. She had clearly lied earlier. Natalie's judgment had been right but it didn't make her feel any better. And Tiphanie had been charged with murder, not infanticide. Chloe was less than a year old. What were they thinking?

She rang Damian in Welbury and spent several minutes on hold before being connected.

'Why did it take these neighbours so damn long to talk to you guys?'

'Let's say they weren't falling over themselves in their attempts to be helpful,' said Damian. 'One side have history with Travis, they've got an AVO out against him. The other's a friend of Tiphanie.'

Some friend.

'You believe them?'

Damian hesitated. 'Yes. The media exaggerated the differences between the stories.'

'Timing?'

'Vague, but definitely that night, while the football was on. The Collingwood–Essendon match locks in the timing.'

'She took Chloe in her car?'

'They only have one car.'

'So what car was she carrying the child to?'

'We're investigating.'

Natalie wasn't going to let him off the hook that easily. 'Investigating what?'

'She lied, Natalie, has lied from the beginning.'

'What else do you have then?'

There was a brief silence. 'The screaming baby wasn't that night, but the bundle was. The screaming was in the back garden during the day. They'd mentioned this to us before; but they'd played it down, hadn't wanted to get Tiphanie into trouble. Now they've said they heard more. Something might have happened then.'

Which would mean Travis was helping *Tiphanie* cover it up. Or that she alone had been responsible for the death and the cover-up. Natalie shook her head in disbelief. 'Why murder? You saw her. She was a mess, she was on pills. Mental state unbalanced by childbirth.'

'I just did what I was told, Natalie. We had a request from the O.P.P. to put it past them before proceeding and he wouldn't listen to me.'

'He?' asked Natalie through gritted teeth.

'Your friend O'Shea.'

Georgia had cancelled because of a meeting with her lawyer, giving a welcome break as Natalie counted down to when her work day was over. She wove her bike through the peak-hour traffic and parked outside Liam's office.

Natalie put her helmet through the scanner and went straight to the tenth floor. Liam O'Shea and maybe half a dozen other lawyers occupied this half of the floor, protected by the rottweiler secretary at the front desk.

'I need to see Liam O'Shea.'

'Mr O'Shea is leaving for the day. Would you like to make an appointment?' She showed her teeth. Less rottweiler, more toothpaste ad.

'Tell him Dr King is here and it's urgent.' She put one of her cards down to underline her status, one that Toothpaste Grin was clearly struggling to believe.

'I'm afraid he can't possibly—'

'It's okay, Carol,' Liam said from behind her. 'This won't take long.'

Natalie didn't look at him as she pushed past into his office. It was big and messy and the view was obstructed by the next building. Liam clicked the door shut behind them. He walked over to his desk and sat behind it.

'You were wanting to see me, Dr King?'

Liam's look was so cold it almost took her breath away. She had never known him, not really. If he thought he could scare her off he was mistaken. There was a flicker in his look. Natalie was too fired up to stop and wonder where he was coming from.

'Why the fuck didn't you tell me?'

Liam looked at her for a long time. She stared hard at him without wavering.

Liam leaned forward on the desk. 'You were the one who didn't want to know about my wife.'

'What?' Natalie kept her voice hard as she tried to make sense of what was going on.

She hadn't seen him since the law association gig. She started laughing. 'Oh shit, you dickhead. This isn't about Lauren. Or you.'

Seeing Liam was now confused, she stopped. Admittedly some of the new lyrics she'd extemporised were a bit over the top, a little risky, but Lauren couldn't have known she was directing them at her husband. But that was beside the point; she'd come to see him about Tiphanie.

'Look Liam, I've always known you were married and I don't give a fuck. When I saw you there with Lauren Oldham, of all people, I couldn't help but tease you with that song, but that's all it was.'

Now she was looking for it, she realised how tense he had been. His shoulders slumped slightly. She almost felt sorry for him. He had been afraid she was going to turn into a bunny boiler.

'So it's business, and I'm seriously pissed off.' She took a breath. 'Why didn't you tell me you were arresting Tiphanie, and why murder, not infanticide? You know she'll get a custodial sentence if she gets convicted, she might not even get bail. Was all that caring and sharing of information and cases just so I could set her up for you? I know that as far as you're concerned my involvement in the case was purely a means to get into my pants, but like it or not, I have been involved.'

Liam nodded to a chair. 'Why don't you sit down? Coffee?'

'No, I don't want us to sit and have coffee like a couple of lawyers,' said Natalie. 'I care what happens to Tiphanie even if it's just another case to you.'

'You might be surprised.'

Liam stood up and went to a fridge in the corner of his office and got himself a beer. He offered her one and she ignored him, glaring at him, arms folded. He sat down in one of the lounge chairs by the window and pointed to the other. Natalie remained on her feet.

'I didn't know they were going to arrest her,' he said. 'I was in Hong Kong.'

'And the murder charge?'

'It's complicated.'

'I'm sure it is,' said Natalie. 'Trouble is that won't be how Tiphanie's seeing it, whether she did it or not. She'll be terrified.'

'Good.'

'Good?' Natalie stared at him. 'You really are a complete arsehole.'

She turned to leave but he was at the door before her, hand over her shoulder ensuring it stayed shut. She could feel his breath on the back of her neck. She wanted to screw him as much as she wanted to slug him.

'I know she didn't do it,' he whispered into her ear.

All the anger drained from her. She turned around; their faces were only centimetres apart.

'You want to scare her into dishing Travis up.'

Liam stood back. His eyes confirmed her guess.

Natalie shook her head. 'I sure as hell hope you know what you're doing.'

Justice Christina Stavrou delivered a coruscating lecture to the O.P.P. regarding their insistence that Tiphanie go to the Dame Phyllis Frost Centre, and sent her to Yarra Bend for a psychiatric assessment. Natalie knew about it from the morning paper before arriving on the ward.

Before she could see Tiphanie, Natalie's mobile rang: Amber calling from Lucia Cortini's office at the gaol. Almost hysterical over Tiphanie's arrest. *Shit.* She'd have to see her again. Surely even Declan would concede she had to put her patient first.

Tiphanie looked better than Natalie had expected. She reminded herself of the girl who had taken off to her grandmother's with the pile of *Cleo*s. There was backbone in there somewhere.

'How are you feeling?'

Tiphanie forced a smile. 'Crap.'

'Want to tell me about it? What really happened?'

Tiphanie looked away. 'I have.'

'Yeah, well, we both know you haven't told me everything. Maybe it's time for the truth now. It can't get you in any more trouble than you're already in.' This wasn't entirely accurate, but then, Natalie wasn't the police.

'I didn't carry Chloe anywhere screaming,' Tiphanie said, her knuckles white. 'And she didn't scream in the backyard. They're bloody liars.' In a softer voice she added, 'Chloe knew she was safe with me.'

Meaning Chloe *would* scream with Travis? Was Tiphanie denying carrying the child, or just denying that she had been crying?

'So what did the neighbours see?'

'They're liars.'

'May well be, but they aren't lying about this, are they Tiphanie? They saw something.'

Tiphanie stared at the floor. 'Do you think they'll change the charge? To infanticide?'

Her lawyer would surely be working on it. Natalie knew she had to make a choice. Focus on her patient, or consider the bigger picture? Fulfil her responsibility as Tiphanie's treating doctor, or buy into Liam's scheme and scare her, which might also help Amber.

Natalie kept her tone even; she was just conveying the facts. 'You can get five years for infanticide, more for murder.'

Tears started to trickle down Tiphanie's cheek. 'I didn't kill her.'

'Then tell the truth. But what you tell me, I want to be able to tell the police. Understand?'

Tiphanie looked up. 'She played like she always did in the backyard that day. We make a lot of noise when we play; she hides—well pretends to—and I play animals tracking her down. She was laughing, yelling, we both were. We were having *fun*.'

Natalie didn't have time to consider the likelihood of

this scenario; wasn't Chloe put in the front of the television all day? Wasn't Tiphanie being treated for depression?

'That night she wouldn't sleep,' Tiphanie continued. 'I wasn't coping. I...let her go with Travis.' She was sobbing now. 'I thought she'd sleep in the car...It's worked before. He...he's her father.'

The neighbours had said the bundle was packed into the car during the football match. But according to Damian, Travis had been at his mate's place, with witnesses, for the entire game. Maybe the neighbours got the time wrong. Made sense; football supporters would be glued to the box, not monitoring the activity next door.

'You're feeling guilty that you didn't protect her.' Natalie deliberately softened her tone.

'I love her!' Tiphanie was screaming, loud enough that a nurse came running. Natalie waved her away.

'I'm prepared to believe you didn't kill her, Tiphanie,' Natalie said, 'but you might get charged as an accessory.' She might have added that, like Amber, she would have to learn to live with the fact that she didn't save her daughter by leaving long before the crisis point.

But it was too early for that. Her denial, the first stage of grief, was falling away and her feelings of guilt would now warrant Tiphanie being put on suicide watch. She relayed what she had been told to Damian before heading out to see Tiphanie's parents.

The Murchisons were in the waiting area beyond security.

'How is she?' Jim asked.

'Feeling guilty.'

'She didn't do it,' said Sandra.

'No,' agreed Natalie looking at Sandra. 'But sometimes

188

people feel guilty for the things they should have done, and didn't.'

Sandra looked away.

By 6 p.m. all Natalie felt like was a bad television show and bed, but she had her appointment with Declan, as well as one with Georgia's aunt. It was the only time they'd been able to agree on. Virginia's husband had died three years earlier, and she liked to keep herself busy.

Virginia Parker would have been in her late sixties. Her long grey hair was pulled into a plait and she was dressed neatly in the alternative clothing of an earlier time: loose trousers and a long top, slippers and a necklace of bright beads. More California than Melbourne. Her smile was tight as Natalie ushered her into her consulting suite.

Natalie settled into a comfortable chair opposite Virginia, both with cups of herbal tea in hand. 'Tell me about Georgia.'

'God.' Virginia's sigh bordered on theatrical. 'Do you know how many times I've been asked that? I suppose this is going to continue until the court case is finished.'

'Only since the legal proceedings? Or earlier?'

'Dr King, I, and everyone around Georgia, have been trying to understand her for the last thirty-seven years. I gave up. Perhaps you'll do better.'

'So let's start from the beginning, when you first took her in. She was not quite three, is that right?'

'Yes. We felt it was our duty. Understand, I barely knew Lee,' said Virginia. 'It was my father's second marriage. He died. And after Lee did what she did, killed her husband, her mother wouldn't take the child.'

'So you were strangers to Georgia?'

'Yes. We knew it would be hard. We thought, maybe

tantrums? Bed wetting or stealing food? We read all the books. We were convinced that as long as we stayed steady, we'd get through.'

'Did you?'

Virginia looped the beads through her fingers. 'There wasn't anything to get through. At least not the sort of things we'd read about and been told to expect. She was an angel. A delightful little girl who was placid and obliging.'

Natalie sensed the 'but' before they got there.

'We thought we were tremendously fortunate. We hadn't ever wanted to be parents, you understand.'

'Until?' Natalie prompted.

'When we first took her the...blandness was a relief,' said Virginia ignoring the question. 'I mean, it wasn't like we had to take her.' She paused, Natalie felt, to emphasise her civic-mindedness. 'We never could understand what the earlier issues were about. She did well at school, she had friends. And then she got married and cut us off as though we didn't exist.'

'As a child, there was nothing that worried you about her?'

'I guess we mostly saw what we wanted to see. That's what Vernon told me. She was hard to be close to I suppose, but we were private people. It didn't seem strange to us.'

'How did she get on with Vernon?'

'The same. He worked of course, but he helped her with her homework as she got older.'

'So what problems did other people have with her?'

'Nothing really...no more than any other teenager.' Virginia looked at Natalie, perhaps looking for signs of agreement. Natalie kept her expression neutral. Virginia reprised the dramatic sigh and continued. 'She was accused of bullying once, but the other family were so obviously jealous. Their daughter wasn't getting anything like Georgia's grades, and was, to say the least, *plain*.'

'Other things? Even little things?'

'The teachers thought the other girls were friends with Georgia because they were scared of her. I suppose she changed friends a bit, but really? We're talking teenage girls.' Virginia looked at Natalie defiantly. 'What would you make of that if it was your daughter? She was pretty, got A's, went to parties. Perhaps she was a bit full of herself, but I thought she was covering up her insecurity about what Lee did. We wanted her to feel confident enough to make a place for herself in the world.'

'How about with boys?'

'I thought she was putting too much emphasis on them,' said Virginia. 'We fought. She could be quite vicious, but then I expect most teenagers can be.'

'And Vernon?'

'Left it to me. I think she scared him a bit. He was a quiet man, not fond of outbursts.'

'You know her better, or at least for longer than anyone else I've spoken to.' Natalie paused. 'Do you think she killed them?'

Virginia looked out the window. Her answer was clear and crisp. 'Yes.'

Natalie let out her breath. 'Mrs Parker, this may seem a strange question, but how did you *feel* towards Georgia? I'm finding it hard to get a real sense of her; perhaps because this was how she came across, I'm not sure. Was she affectionate, or more remote? Do you think she loved you?'

Virginia looked at her hands and rubbed her wedding ring.

'Have you seen the movie *We Need to Talk about Kevin*? Or read the book?'

Natalie had read it. A grim exploration of a pathological mother–son relationship that ended in mass murder.

'I couldn't bring myself to go to the movie,' Virginia continued. 'But reading the book I thought, for the first time in all the years I tried to be a mother to Georgia, that I wasn't alone.'

Natalie waited.

'Understand,' said Virginia, looking at Natalie with an unflinching gaze, 'that I read it before Georgia was charged.'

Natalie nodded.

'What struck me was the inability of the mother to love. In the book she was his biological mother, and I'd always put my problem down to the fact that Georgia came to us late. That whatever happens when you give birth hadn't happened for me and maybe three years old was too late for us both. After the book, I wondered if maybe it wasn't me. Is it possible, Dr King, that some children are just not lovable?'

Natalie wished she had the answer, but Virginia was no more lovable than Georgia had been. In the end, she had failed to rise to the occasion and remember that she was the adult. Georgia, at the age of three, had already learned not to ask for hugs. This woman hadn't thought to give them.

'Tonight is a two-glass night,' said Natalie.

'Work or personal?'

'Both. But believe me there's more than enough work shit to justify two glasses.'

Declan raised an eyebrow as he poured her first glass.

Virginia was freshest in her mind. 'Do you think children

can be unlovable?' She described her interview and then without a pause moved on to Sandra. Eventually Declan put a hand up.

'Time to take a breath.'

Natalie stopped mid-sentence and took a gulp of wine. *No*, not manic.

'You need to take some time out to think.'

'About whether Georgia is the female version of Kevin?'

'No, about the dynamics,' said Declan. He was sounding irritable. 'When Georgia was young her mother didn't measure up. You also need to look at the child's contribution.'

He caught Natalie's look.

'I don't mean the child was responsible, just that a relationship is a two-way thing. Some children who have abusive childhoods survive without turning into monsters or becoming psychiatrically unstable. So why? What resilience does the child have or not have? It seems to me that both Tiphanie and Georgia have some survival skills. Both left mothers who perhaps couldn't nurture. Tiphanie's sister is still there. Why? How does it help inform you where Tiphanie and Georgia are now, or were at some point in the past?'

Natalie mulled over Declan's take on her patients and their maternal figures. 'What really matters,' she said, 'is whether the abused daughter—or son—repeats the pattern or can shift the intergenerational repetition.'

'So where does that take you?'

'Doesn't seem Tiphanie and Georgia have shifted far.'

'Can they? Or others like them?'

Natalie thought of John Steinbeck's *East of Eden*. Cathy was the mother from hell. Worse than Sandra or Virginia, wilfully malicious and self-serving. But one of her sons had come to the realisation that he could make choices about his own destiny. She didn't think Georgia or Tiphanie were quite at this level of contemplation. Repetition was driven by a deep psychological need to master the emotions, and insight was needed for that mastery to actually be achieved.

She wondered for a moment about Lee, Georgia's biological mother. Lee's mother—Georgia's grandmother—sounded as cold as Virginia, given she had not supported Lee or taken in Georgia. Lee must have gone to prison in New South Wales, where Georgia was born, but she would be out by now. Natalie was going to be in Sydney in a couple of weeks for a forensic conference; she made a mental note to ring one of her colleagues there, to see if they knew where she was.

Declan topped up his glass. 'I feel you still have a mindset against Georgia.'

'I just want to know the truth.'

'Natalie, you know better than that. I'm talking about your unconscious motivations. Georgia has had to use a range of tactics to survive. I wonder if you recognise having done some of the same things yourself?'

'Hardly.' What was he getting at? It wasn't as if she'd had any babies to kill. Her motorbike accident? Completely different. Her relationships, perhaps? No, she was in control of those—she kept them strictly at a distance. Not enmeshed like Georgia and Paul seemed to be. Repetition? She squashed the thought almost before it was formed.

She didn't need her second glass in the end. She was tempted to have it just to worry Declan, though the way he was lining the pens up on the desk suggested he needed it more than she did. Then she might be tempted to discuss her social situation and she didn't need to hear 'I told you so', however nicely Declan framed it. She liked playing with fire and if it meant she got burnt occasionally, what the hell. Worse though, she might let out Tiphanie's connection to Amber, or reveal that she had seen Amber again and had another prison visit planned. Her recent hypomanic episode, even though she had got onto it quickly, had put Declan on alert. But she had no intention of pulling out of this case.

Amber was crying so hard that Natalie broke confidentiality —albeit in a minor way—and assured her Tiphanie was coping and the police were looking at a new angle. This mollified her a little.

'I should have told her. I should have made sure she knew.'

'There's no "should have done" anything.'

'But *murder*,' she said, arms around herself and rocking.

Natalie recognised the problem. Amber was reliving her own early days in prison.

'It's Travis that should be in prison,' said Amber, still rocking.

'Why?' The question was as much about Bella-Kaye as Chloe; she hadn't entirely dismissed Kay's claim about Travis.

'I bet he…drove her to it. You know what he was like.'

'Tiphanie's case is different to yours. Try not to read or think about it. You can't change anything.'

'My family's falling apart. Mum had to stop Cam from going and beating Travis up.'

'Your mother is tough, Amber.'

Amber shook her head. 'First me, then Dad. The farm is a struggle and she does a lot of care for the kids. I should be there to help.'

'Kids? Cam had another one?'

Amber put her head in her hands as she nodded. 'Jed's two and a half now. Bella-Kaye would have turned two a few weeks ago.'

Poor Amber; the anniversary undoubtedly had added to her distress.

'I haven't even met their youngest,' Amber continued between sobs. 'At first they didn't want to upset me, then I couldn't bear the thought of them bringing Sam into the gaol to see me. The two of them run my mother ragged. Cam's wife works full time.'

Both she and Amber knew that this was the sort of exhaustion Kay Long had dreamed of. It had been denied her with Bella-Kaye, but it sounded like she was making up for it with Jed and Sam.

'You'll be there to help out soon,' said Natalie. 'When is your parole hearing?'

'Next week.'

'Just focus on the questions you get asked. Your record here is clean, so the board should regard the application favourably.'

Amber hesitated, then gave Natalie a quick hug. Natalie could feel her body trembling.

As Natalie manoeuvred her bike into the garage she became aware that she wasn't alone. She tensed, ready to hit out with full force. Then she saw it was Liam, standing in the doorway.

Had he been there the other night, or was she just getting unnecessarily jittery? *No, I am not getting sick.*

'You're not coming in,' she said.

'You'd best close the door, else Bob may disappear.'

'I will. With you on the other side of it.'

She sensed his hesitation and uncertainty, and admonished herself only a little for revelling in it. She'd never let him know how vulnerable he made her feel.

'I need to talk to you.'

'Hey,' said Natalie turning, 'I remember that line. The answer's the same. I have no need to talk to you.'

'I'm sorry I jumped to conclusions.'

'Okay, apology accepted.'

'There's something more.'

'Not interested.'

'I need your help to get justice for Chloe.'

She hesitated. She had to put Tiphanie ahead of her personal feelings. And her behaviour at the ball had been appalling. 'I'll meet you in fifteen minutes at the Halfpenny.' She swung the door shut in his face.

It was a busy night. Benny and Maggie at the bar had no time for more than a cursory greeting and Vince just glared. Liam had obviously arrived.

'Just for the record,' said Natalie, accepting the Corona Liam thrust at her, 'I think you're a shit. I mean regarding Tiphanie, not your wife, okay?'

'If the murder charge works, will you still say that?'

'It's unethical.'

'It's where the evidence lies.'

'I hope Damian gets in there quickly. She's coughed up that Travis took Chloe in the car that night.'

Liam brightened. 'You've spoken to McBride? He should be able to come down on Travis's mates.'

'This was a regular thing, Travis's paternal contribution to childcare. Chloe, who would go off to sleep in the car. Damian's going to talk to Tiphanie's family as well.'

'Except this time.'

'Except this time,' agreed Natalie.

'Probably wanted her mum, wouldn't shut up. Maybe before they get to the mate's house, he hits her. Maybe doesn't know how much damage he's done. Maybe she dies then, maybe later. He gets rid of the body and convinces Tiphanie it was her fault for not being a good enough mother to settle her own child.'

'If you say so. I thought it was the cops' job to put the story together.'

'Sure.' Liam accepted the reproach without the expected enmity. He even sounded convincing when he added, 'Thanks. That's great.'

'Now I have a question for you,' said Natalie. Liam flinched. Jesus, he was still worried about Lauren. 'Look, you stupid dick. I'll say this once and once only. I wouldn't tell your wife I'd been fucking you if my life depended on it. With her reputation, she could probably make sure I never saw a patient again. But you know what? That isn't why I wouldn't tell her. There's no way I would let her think I made do with her leftovers.'

She couldn't tell what Liam was thinking, and was annoyed to find she cared.

'Which, incidentally, is not how I see it,' said Natalie, 'but I know she would. The fact that you and I have screwed each other has nothing to do with her as far as I'm concerned. Maybe it does for you. It probably should, but that's your problem, not mine.'

She took a breath. 'So can we do business now?'

Liam opened his hands out towards her.

'You told me you were investigating a paedophile ring, right?'

198

Liam nodded.

'Tell me more.' Natalie's second Corona had arrived and she focused on the bite of the lime for a moment.

Liam drained his pint. 'I can't. Professional ethics I think you called it?'

'Bullshit. You want me to help? I need to know more.'

Liam looked at her. She could see he was weighing up what the best strategy was and whether she had anything to actually tell him.

'You first.'

Natalie shook her head. 'Forget it then.'

'All right, but I can't tell you much.'

Natalie grinned at him. He thought he was so fucking tough and smart but at the end of the day he was still a private school boy with a trophy car.

'There is a large-scale operation,' said Liam, putting on that supercilious air that undoubtedly made Carol in the office wet and probably bored Lauren senseless.

'It involves a number of players, some big ones. Hence the secrecy.'

Which told her fuck all. 'The bunny rabbit?'

'In the videos, or at least some of them. Pink. The little girls are...often clutching them.'

Natalie finished her drink and Liam went to the bar.

'You must have more than that,' said Natalie when he returned. 'Every little girl has got a pink bunny rabbit at Easter.'

'We thought we had the guy behind it.' Liam's tone was measured and he wasn't looking at her. 'We couldn't nail him.'

'You still think it's the same person?'

Liam nodded, looking at her hard. 'Don't even think of

asking. I can't and won't tell you his name.'

'Tell me about him then. Must be more to him than a storage unit full of stuffed toys.'

'He's smart, keeps his nose clean. No steady girlfriend but has a regular job, people he works with think he's average but maybe a bit remote. Goes to Friday drinks, doesn't get drunk or act inappropriately.'

'Well that really narrows the field. Not.' But it told her what she needed to know: it wasn't Paul.

'He has a tattoo.'

'So do I.'

'This one may be a motif that is used by members of the ring.'

A motif? He didn't seriously believe he was going to get away with that did he? 'What sort of motif, Liam? Where? On their penises?'

Liam sighed. 'A signature on the videos and chat rooms.'

'The signature and motif? What does it look like?'

Liam looked at her and she could see him deliberating. He was asking himself whether he could trust her, which of course he couldn't. Or shouldn't. He wanted to, though. 'Guess.'

'A rabbit.'

'See, I didn't tell you. A kind of Playboy bunny. Two actually.' Liam spread out a serviette and drew ears and a head, but with a superimposed circle, presumably the tail. In the second half-overlapping bunny the circle was an oval. Male and female? There was a split second where Natalie was sure she recognised it, but just as quickly as the picture flashed into her mind it disappeared. If she had seen it before, she had no idea where.

Natalie nearly didn't answer the call. It was a blocked number and there was a chance it might be Liam. She was still uncertain about how she was feeling about him. Avoiding him was easier. Her mania had given her the chance to end the affair; maybe she should go with that. It wasn't as if there was any future in it.

But it could be about Tiphanie. Nothing seemed to have happened in the last week, with Tiphanie still sitting in Yarra Bend.

She hit the answer key.

'I wanted you to know the latest,' a male voice said. No Irish accent, just reason and calm. Damian.

'Yes?'

'We're stuck.' Damian sounded apologetic. 'The evidence is slanted towards Tiphanie acting alone. Travis is denying he took Chloe and his car is clean. For the moment we can't touch the charges.' There was a pause. 'I want to get the bastard as much as you, but we have nothing.'

Georgia was back to her middle-class groomed look.

'I met Virginia last week,' said Natalie after Georgia had

settled into the armchair.

Georgia moved around in the chair and crossed her legs, smile meeting Natalie's gaze. 'No cards this week.'

Was Georgia avoiding talking about her aunt, or were the cards—and Paul—overwhelming everything else? Natalie went with the latter. 'What do you make of that?'

Georgia shrugged. 'I suppose his way of saying our relationship is over.' There was an evenness to the delivery, smile never wavering, that made Natalie wonder if Georgia had practised in front of the mirror. Her hands gave her away; as Natalie waited, she fidgeted with her blazer, and smoothed out her dress. Not dissociation, more like disbelief. Unwilling to accept that Paul was not coming back.

'He isn't allowed to see me anyway.'

'And that worries you?'

'He isn't *allowed*.' Georgia folded her arms and averted her eyes. 'I know you think I don't care about losing my children. But Virginia used to hit me if I cried. She couldn't tolerate weakness. So I learned to smile instead.' She appeared to force herself to look at Natalie. 'It doesn't mean I don't feel. Okay, not so much about the pregnancy I lost, I concede that. But my girls? Jonah? They were my flesh and blood. For a while I had three, three pieces of me that just...' She bit her lip and looked out the window. 'They just slipped through my fingers.'

In Georgia's quavering words Natalie visualised the children, hazy images melting and disappearing into the oblivion of her patient's carefully segregated memories.

'You spoke last week,' said Natalie after a moment, 'about how close Paul was to you and your girls. Did that ever worry you? His closeness to his daughters?'

'Surely every mother worries?'

No. Their eyes met, and Georgia was first to look away. Natalie wondered if what she was seeing was the denial breaking down; the denial that her husband controlled her and abused her daughters. So many of her patients had, as children, told their mothers of the abuse and not been believed. Had Georgia at least subconsciously been aware of it and killed her children to save them from Paul, rather than confronting him? Or was her motive that she wanted Paul to herself?

'What sort of father was he?'

'Wonderful.'

'Tell me more about that,' said Natalie when the silence had stretched to nearly a minute.

'He used to give the girls their baths when he wasn't away. Olivia loved it when he poured water over them both.'

'Just the girls? What about Jonah?'

'I had to bathe him; he was difficult.'

'So Paul was *in* the bath with Olivia?'

'Oh yes, it was easier that way.'

There was distance in Georgia's voice as she reminisced about her girls, but something approached disdain when talking about Jonah. Because he was a boy? Because he was difficult, and made her feel rejected rather than adored? Or because of Paul's attitude?

She wondered about Georgia's mention of Virginia, right after she had appeared to ignore the fact of the visit. Maybe Georgia's real mother would be able to provide something more. Her colleague had tracked down the address and Natalie had arranged to see her on the Friday afternoon of the conference.

The next blocked call was Lucia Cortini ringing on Amber's behalf.

'Amber has her hearing tomorrow,' said Lucia. 'What the fuck is going on with Tiphanie?'

'I'm trying to keep her here until she gets bail,' said Natalie. 'Tell Amber I'm pushing.'

Lucia started coughing up what sounded like a lifetime of tar and hung up.

Tiphanie herself was in shock, repeating that she'd never harm Chloe and that she didn't want to talk to the police.

'How can she be so stupid?' Natalie asked Declan that evening. 'I don't trust her not to change her story again; how does she expect the police to believe her? She may just be adding a perjury charge to the list.'

'Maybe it's as well that the police have taken their time,' said Declan. 'Stories, as we know, seldom reveal themselves in their entirety in the first telling.'

'I've spoken to the police. They're stuck. They don't think there's any more to find. The neighbours heard screams earlier in the day but Tiphanie says it was play and either is possible.'

Declan, sipping his wine, waited for her to continue.

'They searched the car and found nothing. Signs of Chloe, but that was to be expected. Tiphanie was probably bombed out when her partner came home. And the next morning?' She shrugged. 'That was when she was intimidated and I guess took a shitload of Valium to block out any thoughts at all.'

'Her partner...must be very persuasive. Violent?'

'Yes. No doubt Tiphanie was under'—Natalie stopped herself saying Travis's name just in time—'her partner's influence, but I'm equally certain she wanted and loved this baby.'

'Not enough to protect her. A bit like Amber.' Declan looked at her intently.

Natalie willed her gaze to remain steady. Had Declan dropped Amber's name intentionally? There had only been that one article in each of the main city papers. Surely he wouldn't have taken any note of it, particularly given Amber wasn't mentioned by name in the *Age*? She couldn't see Declan as a *Herald-Sun* reader. He might have googled it. But Declan was upfront about his technophobia.

'Tiphanie didn't have a great maternal role model,' she said.

'It's hard to give affection to a child when you're empty inside, though some people manage it.'

'She tried, I think,' said Natalie. 'Seems like her grandmother might have been a bright light in her childhood. Father's mother. He's okay too—just needs to grow a backbone.'

Natalie took a sip of wine and changed tack. 'Georgia actually showed emotion this week. I even felt like it might have been real.'

'Grief for her three dead children?'

'Possibly. Even probably; but it's complicated. It's also about losing Paul. I'm not sure which is stronger.'

'It's good that you are questioning her reactions, and your own.'

'Because I recognise something in her? A conflict I've faced myself?'

Declan smiled; the smile he saved for his star student, accompanied by a twinkle in his eyes. 'Now what would that be do you think?'

Natalie took a deep breath. Just sometimes, supervision seemed very like the therapy she had had years earlier and ceased, according to Declan, prematurely. 'As a teenager I found myself facing a choice. Conform—at least in most ways—or live on the outer. In sorting out the answer I found a "me" I could live with.'

'And Georgia?'

'Georgia had the same choice, but was driven by the need to be accepted by men. Work gives me who I am and fills my, if you like, narcissistic needs. Georgia is wholly dependent on her relationships to tell her who she is.'

'So where does her relationship with her children versus her husband fit?'

'Paul, I think, was who centred her. But did he manipulate that for his own needs? I don't know. It's possible. He could have pulled the strings and sent her off into dissociative episodes. Georgia loved her children when she could see them as extensions of herself. But when her children had their own needs, she would see it as rejection, right?'

Declan nodded. 'The narcissist needs to think of himself—or in this case herself—as one with the child, unique and special. Anything that interferes with that perception creates a risk that reality will come crashing down around them. They have buried feelings of chaos and rejection from their own childhood that threaten to bubble to the surface.'

Declan launching into lecture mode meant he'd forgotten about her near-slip. Or so Natalie hoped.

'What about the psychopath's relation with their child?' she said.

'The psychopath, of course, feels no empathy or remorse. Their connections are determined by how useful other people are to them.'

'Which really colours my relationship with Georgia, given I'm going to be called to court to give evidence.'

'Stick with her,' said Declan. 'Remember it took a long while for Amber to disclose the truth to you.'

The Halfpenny was having another busy night. The evenings were getting warmer and Vince had opened up the back section, and it looked to be full of students.

Gil was running late. His wife had had the baby the day before. They were still in hospital and he'd told the band he'd be there after a stint of proud fatherhood.

'Any special requests tonight?' Shaun was looking at Natalie.

'Yes,' she said. 'That under no circumstances do we do that fucking awful Gloria Gaynor number.' Shaun laughed. Tom didn't.

'Let's do the Dixie Chicks one while it's still fresh.'

They did mostly their own songs. The students ignored them but that wasn't unusual, particularly for the first set. By the end of the night the crowd was as loud as the music but at least some of the noise was appreciative. They seemed to enjoy Natalie's sassy angry version of *Not Ready to Make Nice* with Shaun and Gil playing the background vocals and expressions added for comedy. Natalie didn't do nice, on the whole, but she allowed herself to be a little whimsical about time improving things.

Vince grabbed her before she went out front for her routine Jack Daniels.

'I know it's none of my business,' he said, 'but he's out there. I don't like him.'

Liam's testosterone had got the better of him then. She grinned. She'd figured another week before he caved. 'What you don't like, Vince, is his wedding ring.'

'So? What's so wrong about that? Man's got a wife, kids

too probably; that's where he should be.'

'I'm not about to defend either of us Vince. I note your concern.'

'If you were my daughter—'

'But I'm not,' said Natalie, and turned to go to the bar.

'And who's the other bloke that's been nosing around after you?' she heard Vince say to her back. She was already out the door before it had registered.

Liam had her bourbon ready. She took it and looked at him. 'Publican thinks you need to go home.' She sipped. 'To your doting wife and brood.'

'I kind of got that impression,' said Liam. 'Do you bring out the protective instinct in many men?'

'Just the father figures.'

'I'm relieved you haven't put me in that group, then.'

Natalie's expression eliminated the need for words.

Tom joined them, standing with his back to Liam. 'Still want me to walk you home?'

Natalie hesitated. As she left her warehouse tonight she'd had that uncomfortable feeling again that someone was watching her.

'No, Tom that's fine, thanks.'

Tom glared at Liam. She wondered if Vince had worded him up.

'So was that fatherly concern?' asked Liam.

'TLC. Maybe a bit of lust.'

Liam smiled.

'I have a bone to pick with you,' she said. 'Why the hell is Tiphanie still sitting in Yarra Bend?'

'Better than prison.'

'That's not an answer.'

'I'm kind of here to apologise for that, and to explain.'

'It had better be good.'

They adjourned to the courtyard area, which was slowly being deserted by the students. Natalie was still hot from singing so she threw her jacket over her chair and put her feet on another.

'Start talking.'

'We can't get him. We have nothing.'

'I know that. This is fucked up, Liam. It should at least be infanticide. What do you need?'

'Something that ties Chloe to Travis that night. I understand he's now saying he isn't even sure he saw Chloe at all that night, that maybe he'd mixed nights up, which feeds into the screaming going quiet in the afternoon.'

'Like he's a credible witness?'

'And Tiphanie is any better?'

Natalie drained the remainder of her drink and stood up. 'I'm going home.'

Liam remained seated. Their eyes connected. 'You know I'd come if you invited me.'

'I wasn't sure actually, so thank you for letting me know. But you're not invited.'

'I haven't slept with her for five years.'

'Your problem.' Except why did it make her feel so much better?

'Not ready to make nice, or will never be ready?'

Natalie smiled and walked away. In the doorway she turned and replied, 'Time is a healer, I'm told.'

It was only when she got home that she remembered Vince's comment about the other man.

*

She wasn't sleeping. Tiphanie's case was going around and around in her head—better than thinking about her stalker. Rather than wait until Tuesday to talk to Tiphanie, she made time to see her on Sunday afternoon. It was a good excuse to escape the house, even if the Sunday traffic on the cycle path was slow. Immersed in thought, she nearly ran into an elderly couple and their dog on a ludicrously long leash.

Kirsty waved at her as she passed the nurses' station but she kept going. Celeste's brother Joe flashed his usual toothless grin.

'Meds doing somethin' right,' he said, hand on his sister's arm and eyes on Natalie.

'Can I have some more?' Celeste asked. 'Them Qs?'

Natalie deflected the question, and wondered if Joe had put her up to it. Qs had street value. She couldn't understand why anyone would take mood stabilisers voluntarily.

'Tiphanie,' said Natalie as soon as they were alone, 'I'm going to make this really simple. You have a choice. You either tell the truth now, and consistently to the cops, or you're going to go down. And not here, you'll be in prison, where child killers mostly have to stay alone in single cells or else they get murdered.'

'I didn't hurt her! I would *never* hurt Chloe.'

'Look, Tiphanie. Time to grow up. If you did it, fess up. You've been lying since the beginning. You've said you were depressed; the right lawyer should be able to get you out on a community treatment order for infanticide.'

Tiphanie started to tremble.

Natalie was on a roll. 'And if you didn't? Tell the cops what happened. So you were doped up, so you were too tired to close the door properly or settle her. So you covered up for Travis. Whatever. We can deal with your own guilt some other time. Don't punish yourself by letting him get away with it.'

'I don't know what happened,' she whispered.

'You know something.' Natalie said. 'You took her out and put her in the car with Travis, when he went to his mate's, yes?' She figured that the neighbours got the day right, timing wrong.

Tiphanie paused.

Natalie waited, until Tiphanie nodded. 'You were out to it when he got home, right?'

Tiphanie nodded again.

'And in the morning...?'

Tiphanie was shaking. 'She wasn't there.'

'So what did you think?'

'He told me...' Tears started to trickle down her face. 'I, that is, that she hit her head. He said we could both get away with it, that it wasn't anyone's fault and we shouldn't go to prison for an accident.'

'So who came up with the story that she wandered off?' said Natalie. It was Amber all over again, though this time he had done it himself. Was he that charismatic, this man that had cowered before her?

'Both of us.' Pause. 'Travis.'

'The car was clean, no blood,' said Natalie.

'Which car?' Tiphanie didn't look like she was concentrating.

'Travis's,' Natalie replied. 'There was no sign of her having been hurt.'

Tiphanie nodded, not looking at Natalie.

'It wasn't Travis's.'

Natalie frowned.

'Travis's car broke down that night,' Tiphanie continued.

'At Rick's. He drove Rick's car home.'

Natalie didn't hesitate in ringing Damian; she had made it clear to Tiphanie that she would share information with the police.

'Broke down? Jesus, you mean that's what he told Tiphanie,' said Damian.

'Yeah?'

'Yeah. I can't believe his mate has kept quiet; we've had him in twice. I'll go pick him up again now.' A pause. 'Thanks. You've been a big help.'

When Natalie got back to her warehouse there was another red envelope stuck to the door. Outside, at least. The locks were working. She steeled herself and refused to give any external sign of reacting in case whoever was responsible was lurking in the shadows as dusk was settling. He was dangerous, she was certain. She could feel the menace as if he was there with her. At the moment he was still playing, but she had no doubt he would pounce eventually. Her hand trembled as she bolted the door.

She put the envelope by the television, got Bob his food and sat down with a beer. She would have to ring Senior Constable Hudson but it was the solid reliable sound of Damian McBride she would have preferred, or Liam, who would have been aggressive and proactive. Perhaps it was time *she* was. She'd relied on the police to date and it hadn't stopped things escalating. She couldn't, in all fairness, see what they could do. There had been no direct threat. A break-in was illegal but he—or she—hadn't trashed the place, and the reality was they wouldn't do time for it if they were caught.

Natalie felt the threat just as the sender had intended.

She was sure Senior Constable Hudson was going to get nowhere with the list, reduced as it was. She needed to work out if it was Travis. So she could predict what he might do and how far he might go. So she could be ready.

She shook the USB out of the envelope, picked it up using a tea towel and put it in her computer. This time it contained a video file. She stared at the icon, steeling herself, focusing on keeping her hand steady as she hit the play button.

The first clip was her arriving at Punt Road on her Ducati. It was taken from within the gardens of her rooms, among the trees at the fence line. The second was of her arriving by bicycle at Yarra Bend, from the Yarra River path. She saw herself narrowly missing an elderly couple, dog barking loudly. She knew immediately it had been taken earlier that day. She tried to imagine someone in the place he must have been standing but failed. He had conveyed exactly the message he wanted to. He was watching her, waiting. And getting closer.

Jessie was early, pacing the waiting room. Whatever was causing her agitation could be a turning point in therapy. If they were lucky.

'He's dead.'

The words exploded out of Jessie before Natalie could sit down, a mixture of anger and hatred, as well as the fear and desperation of a child who still wanted her father's love.

'I wasn't there! They didn't ring me until it was too late.'

'You'd been there for him recently.'

'He died alone!' Jessie paced, hands rubbing up and down her arms, scratching at her right shoulder where her tattoos were densest. No sunglasses though.

Natalie let Jessie vent for ten minutes. She ranted about her father's medical condition, then jumped to a diatribe on the nurses at the hospice and about how she hadn't been able to talk to Hannah. As the spiel wound down she announced through sobs, with a sense of hopelessness, 'And now I'm an orphan.' She dropped, exhausted, into a chair—a comfortable one, not the stiff-backed upright one she had chosen in recent sessions, and between gulps of air said, 'Daddy I don't want you to go.'

Natalie moved to sit next to her and put a hand on her arm.

'I'm sorry, I'm sorry.' She rocked herself in the chair, alternating between mumbling things Natalie couldn't make out and singing a song with no recognisable tune. Five minutes passed before she opened her eyes and looked at Natalie. 'Do you think he forgave me?'

'For what, Jessie?'

'I was only young. I'm so, so, sorry—'

'Jessie,' said Natalie. 'You were a child. He knew that. He was responsible, not you.'

'No, no, you don't understand.'

Natalie sat with her, in the silence.

After several minutes Jessie seemed to pull herself together. 'I need the computer back.'

'I'm not sure now is a good time, Jess,' said Natalie. She opened the drawer to show her it was still there. Jessie leaned forward and Natalie rolled her chair slightly to sit between her patient and the drawer. 'You're very emotional, and have a lot to deal with. Why don't you leave it here and we can talk about it next session?'

For a moment Natalie thought Jessie was going to push her and grab it, and she leaned back to show that she wouldn't prevent her. Jessie stood, hesitated.

'If you understand it, maybe you can save me,' she whispered.

At the end of the session, after the door closed behind Jessie, Natalie pulled out the computer and looked at it. There was something on it Jessie was ambivalent about. Should she look? Did Jessie hope she would?

*

Beverley caught Natalie before she took Georgia in.

'The Prosecutor's office rang,' she said.

Natalie wondered if Beverley and Carol hit it off. Maybe they swapped dentist details or nail specialists. Beverley's latest nails were impressive. 'Very patriotic,' Natalie remarked, noting the green and gold.

'What? Thanks. I said you were busy until Thursday and then in Sydney.'

'Did they say what they wanted me for? Do I need to ring back?' Had they found something in the car Travis had borrowed from Rick?

'Don't know,' said Beverley.

Natalie handed her Jessie's computer. 'When you get a chance can you back the files up?' Beverley started listing the things she had to do but Natalie was already collecting Georgia from the waiting room.

Georgia looked like she wanted to be anywhere but where she was. Her clothes, all black, seemed to have been chosen to fit her mood. She denied she was feeling anything other than 'fine' when Natalie made the observation, but her statements were terse until Natalie asked her to talk about Jonah.

'Why? It's just all the same stuff again and again,' said Georgia. 'I can't see it's getting me anywhere or what it's achieving.' She gave an exaggerated sigh. 'We waited three years before getting pregnant again.' Georgia was staring out the window as she spoke. Natalie took notes.

'It had been horrible. I can't tell you how horrible. People saying how sorry they were was almost as bad as when they didn't know what to say. People saying how brave we were to try again...We felt we'd had our bad luck.'

'You were a nurse. Did you ever consider it might have been a genetic problem?'

'Not really. I mean, the children all looked perfect. The pregnancy was difficult. I was tired, I threw up a lot. Paul was very worried about me.'

Georgia was still looking out the window. 'Jonah came a week early. He seemed fine, though. A good feeder, better than the girls. Hungrier, at least.'

'Did you breastfeed?'

'I didn't make enough milk. Jonah was a very unsettled baby. I wonder sometimes if my being anxious through the pregnancy affected him somehow. That's possible isn't it?'

Natalie nodded.

'He was always hungry but he gulped, you know, then he'd get wind and throw up. We took him to the GP and the paediatrician. We tried different formulas and medicines. They said he'd grow out of it. Of course that never happened.'

'What happened the night he died?'

'Nothing,' said Georgia. 'He fed at eleven and then three in the morning, and I went back to bed. Paul checked him at seven and couldn't wake him.'

Natalie and Georgia looked at each other. Georgia's coldness was back: a form of self-protection or was it how she really felt about the loss of a third child? And a boy that perhaps neither of them wanted? Was there any significance of it being Paul who'd found the child?

'What about the next pregnancy? Tell me about the knitting needles.'

Georgia turned her head slowly and stared. Natalie had to work hard at keeping her expression neutral. 'You read the papers.'

'Yes.'

'There were no knitting needles.' Georgia crossed her arms.

Natalie made a note to ask her lawyer. Any inconsistency needed consideration: as much as she didn't want Wadhwa to be right, ensuring Georgia was properly diagnosed and treated was more important than their point-scoring, as Declan had reminded her.

'I got another card,' Georgia said suddenly. She tossed it onto the desk.

'Where's the envelope? Did you recognise the writing?'

'I threw it away. It was typed.'

Natalie picked up the card. On the surface it was less concerning than the last one. One large rabbit and a smaller one: a scene from Peter Rabbit.

'It's him and Miranda,' said Georgia in a voice barely more than a whisper. But Natalie wasn't paying much attention. Her focus was on the small hand-drawn logo on the back. Had it been on the last one too? It looked just like the one Liam had sketched for her on the napkin.

Amber, finally out on parole after two years, was booked to see her next. She needed to tell Declan. He couldn't blame her for Amber making the appointment but he would insist Natalie not see her again. Given the connection Amber had with Tiphanie, this did make sense. But it was hard to deny the strong sense of responsibility she felt towards Amber. No one she referred her to would care as much.

When Natalie walked into the waiting room, Amber stood then hesitated. Natalie took the initiative and stepped forward and hugged her. 'You're out.'

Amber nodded. She was crying. 'It's all so strange.'

In Natalie's office Amber was no more settled. She

looked like she hadn't been sleeping.

'Tiphanie's still in prison.' Amber sat in the chair but moved almost immediately to perch on the armrest.

'She's in hospital.'

'She can't leave,' said Amber, dropping back into the chair. 'I can't bear this. Isn't there *anything* you can do?'

'A lot is being done, Amber. She isn't you.'

'I could have stopped it if I'd told the truth.'

'Talking about the threats wouldn't have changed anything,' said Natalie. Amber knew as well as she did that the lawyers believed that bringing in the battered wife argument would have undermined the infanticide defence.

'That wasn't what I meant.' Amber didn't look at her. Natalie was conscious of holding her breath.

Amber whispered something that Natalie didn't catch.

'Sorry?'

'It didn't happen the way I said it did.' Amber was looking directly at her.

'All right.' Natalie kept her voice low and even. 'Tell me what did happen.'

Was Kay right after all? Amber had tried to tell her something in the prison, but she'd been too high to hear, interrupting rather than listening. She was listening now.

'We'd been arguing. Like always. Bella-Kaye had kept us up the night before and she'd been unsettled all day. I was tired and I was crying. He said things to me.' She sniffed, fishing in her bag for a tissue. 'Like *you can't do anything right, you cow*, and *what sort of mother are you?*'

'Did you respond?'

Amber shook her head. 'I had dinner ready for him.' Her voice was faint and flat. 'Bella-Kaye started crying while I was finishing it off and I froze. I couldn't settle her or finish

219

dinner. I just stood there watching it sticking to the bottom of the pan and Travis threw it over me.' Tears had started to trickle down her cheeks. A full minute passed before she continued. 'I was just standing there covered in potato. Carrots in my hair. It had splashed on my face and it burned me, but I don't remember feeling anything.'

Natalie remembered her face on the police video and how flushed Amber had looked. Not flushed; scalded. In the version of the story that had gone to court, Travis hadn't been there, had yet to arrive home from work.

'Travis was laughing. He said how stupid I looked. He told me I had better clean myself up, said I looked pathetic.'

Amber grasped the edge of the chair tightly. 'I *was* pathetic. I can't believe—'

'Amber,' said Natalie, 'you had put up with months of abuse; he'd made you believe it. You were acting how he was telling you to.' No worse than the psychology students in those prisoner and guard experiments. In Amber's case there had been a long lead-up, a concerted campaign on Travis's part, to belittle her. Not many people could withstand a constant barrage of being told they were worthless and not start to believe it.

'I went to the bathroom, like a robot,' Amber continued. 'I had run a bath for Bella-Kaye but I had forgotten about it and the water had gone cold. She started screaming, you know, in her bassinet. I think she was hungry, but Travis yelling scared her. Her eyes used to go wide and...and her bottom lip would tremble.' Amber looked up at Natalie through her tears. 'She was only six weeks old.'

Natalie kept her hand on Amber's. They were both there, one reliving it and the other picturing it so clearly that she had to swallow to stop bile filling her mouth.

'He started yelling even louder, calling Bella-Kaye...
a...a...cunt just like me. I, I didn't know what to do. So I...I
went out to get her and I thought I could give her a bath.
I mean, I was washing myself, and I guess I knew baths
soothed her and she hadn't had one.'

Amber's body was racked with her sobs. She had never
told the full story, even to her family. Even through the
therapy with Natalie, her shame—the deeper belief that she
was everything Travis had called her—had made her hold
this back.

'He followed me. He was still yelling and Bella-Kaye
was screaming and I...I just couldn't think straight. I put
her in the bath. She...she even had her clothes still on. It was
cold by then so of course she cried even more. Then...then...'

Natalie waited, not wanting to hear but knowing she
had to. Had to allow Amber to tell the truth so she could
get on with her life. Not guilt-free. But perhaps, eventually,
she could forgive herself.

'Travis yanked me back and wouldn't let go,' said
Amber, now a whisper again. 'He...oh my God, he laughed.
I can still hear him laughing.' She shivered. 'I saw Bella-Kaye
disappear under the water and the look of surprise on her
face, but she...she was quiet and it seemed, seemed...easier.'

'He was holding you.'

'Yes.' Amber bit her lip. 'But he wasn't holding me that
hard.'

Natalie put her arm around Amber, fighting her
repugnance, knowing that what Amber said was the truth
but that there had been no malice in her action—or rather
inaction. It had been a desperate and hopeless acquiescence
to the peace she'd craved. Respite from the confusion, the
fatigue; the overwhelming inability to think rationally. But

by giving in, she had failed to save her much-loved and wanted child.

'It's why I didn't ask for bail,' she said after a moment of silence. 'Travis did it but I let him, I didn't fight him. He had said one of us needed to die and I let it be her and it should have been me. He wanted to kill me too; after she was dead he said it was my fault and I had to do exactly what he said, how he didn't deserve to have such a useless wife who couldn't even protect her own child. So instead of dying, I'm living in hell.'

It all finally made sense. By the time of the plea Amber had wanted to leave prison. Natalie had thought it was the reality of prison life setting in, but she had also broken up with Travis, and had gained some insight into how he had manipulated her. Natalie broke the silence.

'Amber, you need to tell this to the police.'

Amber looked up. 'No.'

'You can talk to your lawyer first,' said Natalie. 'You've already been convicted so it won't affect your charges in any negative way. You need to do this for Tiphanie.'

'I can't go through it again, I just can't. I don't want to ever see Travis again.' The diffidence had vanished. 'I've already killed my father; it would be the last straw for Mum.'

'I don't think she'd be...surprised to find Travis did it.' Had Travis really confessed to Amber's father or to someone Kay didn't want to implicate? Or had Kay simply guessed?

'It doesn't matter. She had to sell part of the farm to pay for my lawyer. We can't afford to do it again. You can't make me, and you can't tell anyone what I've said.'

Amber was right. But if Damian and Liam knew, they could use the information to help Tiphanie.

'Tiphanie will get out anyway won't she?' Amber asked.

'What if she doesn't?' Natalie pushed her harder, for Tiphanie's sake. Damian and Liam were both slower than she would like. And there was the neighbours' testimony to complicate matters, information she couldn't share with Amber.

'I can't,' Amber repeated, starting to shake. 'You promise, don't you?'

Amber was her patient too. If she had come clean earlier, things could have been so different. Had she closed Amber down too soon? Been too ready to let her accept the blame?

Natalie knew that the confession had taken strength. It would take more to face a charge of perjury or, perhaps worse, face her mother, brother and friends and help them make sense of what had really happened. Amber and her family had already been through hell. If Amber told the truth now it would be all rehashed; she'd be back in the papers. The police or courts might well not believe her.

'I promise,' said Natalie.

'Senior Constable Hudson here. Tony.'

'News?'

'Possibly.' Senior Constable Hudson's tone didn't fill Natalie with hope her stalker had been charged and locked away. But ringing this early in the morning meant something.

'Are you going into your rooms today?'

'No.' She had finished there for the week.

'I'd like you to.'

'Care to expand on that?'

'There was a break-in. I want to know if they were after you.'

She felt a wave of nausea. He seemed to be taking her

little problem very seriously, but she wasn't sure that she found that comforting.

When Natalie arrived at the Punt Road rooms, the police were long gone. Glass shards were pushed to one side of the door; Victorian mansions weren't built as fortresses and the broken glass panels gave easy access to the door handle. The thief would have been eyeball to eyeball with the small sign saying *No drugs kept on the premises.*

'Anything missing?' she asked Beverley.

'Not that we've found.'

Her two colleagues in the coffee room said their rooms were untouched; so not a random vandal. She walked into her room, which she shared with another psychiatrist who used it on her days at Yarra Bend, and hadn't arrived yet.

Natalie looked at the filing cabinets and opened the drawers. She only kept her current files here, the rest were in the storage room. Nothing missing; but she could feel the intruder's fingerprints. The files were still in alphabetical order—but backwards, as if he had taken them all out to go through them. If there was one that he was after, he had read it. He was making sure she knew.

Natalie stood in the middle of the room and closed her eyes. She knew her imagination was being fuelled by fear but she couldn't shake the feeling that someone was in the room with her. There was nothing obvious. No papers thrown over the floor or vase smashed on the hearth of the fireplace. She sat in her chair, aware of the sweat of her palms against the leather. Closing her eyes she tried to picture the room as she had left it. Opening them she stared at her desk. Then saw it. Or rather, saw what was not there.

The photo had always been a bit of a joke. Psychiatrists

weren't meant to have anything personal in their rooms, no family photos or things that identified them as anything other than the neutral holding container that the patient could use as they needed. Not that Natalie would have put up family photos even if she had been allowed. But a photo Tom had taken of Bob reminded her to keep a sense of humour. Now it was missing. The thief had already been in her home, knew Bob was her housemate. It was a direct threat.

The cheapest fare to Sydney for the annual forensic conference was first thing on Friday morning. Tom was taking Bob to his house. The theft of the photo had made her jumpy.

Bob greeted her with 'How do you feel!', landed on her shoulder and bit her ear. 'Ouch, Bob!' said Natalie. 'Keep doing that and I'll let the stalker have you.'

He nestled on her shoulder, oblivious to any threat.

Natalie was halfway through a beer when Bob began flapping his wings and jumping up and down. It was the door, but Natalie wasn't expecting Tom for an hour.

Not Tom; Liam. He looked good. Annoyingly. He'd either changed at the office or been home first. His suit had been replaced with casual black trousers and a dark polo shirt.

'I thought we could share some travel time.' He leaned against the doorway, looking her up and down. Natalie was wearing shorts and a tight top that accentuated her nipples.

'Meaning?'

'I was hoping I could give you a lift.'

Natalie raised an eyebrow and waited.

'I have a car waiting.'

'Let me guess, a limo with champagne in the fridge.' Natalie tried not to smile.

'Haven't looked. But there'll definitely be some bubbly in the Qantas lounge.'

'Qantas lounge?'

'I believe you have to be in Sydney tomorrow.'

'My flight is in the morning.'

He shrugged. 'Change it. You'd just be going a night early. Live dangerously. '

Beverley had a lot to answer for.

'Carol is doing an investigator course to enhance her role with us,' said Liam. 'Though I don't think your secretary put up a fight.'

'Just totally by coincidence you happen to be going to Sydney?' There was no reason she couldn't go tonight, besides the cost of an extra night's accommodation, but Liam probably intended that she would share his room. His arrogance had gone up a notch. Or was this his idea of making up?

'Not exactly. I have to meet someone and tomorrow is as good a day as any.'

'You're that sure of me?'

Liam laughed. 'That stupid I ain't. Jaysus woman...' Shit, she loved it when he laid the accent on. 'I can enjoy a dinner in Sydney by myself, but it seems a waste. I thought spontaneity might be your style.'

It only took her a few minutes to throw some clothes together. She remembered to grab Georgia's file to read before seeing her mother, as well as her conference presentation, which had yet to progress beyond headings. *Live dangerously.* She could almost hear Eoin's laughter as she changed and packed her bag. It took five minutes. Tom had his own key; she'd ring him from the cab.

Liam burst out laughing.

'What?'

'I think you just achieved the impossible. Don't women need at least two hours?'

With the slam of the door, and Bob letting out a screech, Natalie slid into the limo next to Liam.

Liam took her straight through security to the business lounge. The receptionist greeted him by name. Liam had her ticket changed without any apparent penalty.

'Drink?'

'Don't need anything.'

Liam flipped open his laptop.

'You might be interested in this. I warn you, it's hard to watch.'

Liam showed her fifteen seconds of a video clip. She was grateful for its brevity. A little girl no more than five: blonde with blue eyes who reminded Natalie uncomfortably of Chloe. With the child was a pink bunny, fluffy and new-looking. And a man in a face mask holding her hand.

'Let me assure you the rest is unpleasant. There's just one other thing you need to see.' Liam went to the end, to the logo: bunny ears on a circle, with a smaller circle in the centre, the second bunny's oval more clearly phallic.

'You need to tell me more about your suspect,' said Natalie.

'You know I can't.'

Natalie pulled out Georgia's file. In it was a photocopy of Georgia's card, complete with logo.

Liam took it from her. 'Where did you get this?'

228

'Seems we have a stalemate. I can't tell you either.'

'My suspect is in his late twenties, very smart.'

So he had been telling her the truth last time she'd asked. Natalie let out her breath and took the card back. 'Different person. This one maybe just downloads the videos.'

'Whoa up. I still want—'

'No can do, Liam,' said Natalie. 'I told my patient to tell her lawyer. She'll be in touch.'

Liam leaned in. 'This isn't a game, Natalie. We're talking about lots of kids. The video I just showed you is old, the one we thought was our chief suspect. The crime techies couldn't do a definite match and in later videos he got smart, used lots of other perps. We're just this far'—he held up his thumb and index finger a millimetre apart—'from getting him. I need to know where this card came from.'

'You will,' said Natalie. 'Just not from me.'

When Liam handed her the second key to his room, she just looked at it. 'I never said I'd stay. Come to think of it, I can't recall being asked.'

'Think about it over dinner.'

Dinner was very good Chinese. The spicy salt and pepper squid was the best she had ever tasted and they'd ordered a second serve. A layer of tension had disappeared with the knowledge that she wouldn't be under surveillance. Until she felt it roll off her shoulders she hadn't realised how much of a burden it had been.

'Does Carol the Dental Queen know you're fucking me? Or at least were,' asked Natalie through a mouthful of squid, 'and still want to?'

Liam grinned. 'If she was a betting woman her money would be in the right place.'

'Does Lauren know?'

'I thought we didn't discuss exes or wives,' he said as he called for the bill.

When he opened the door to the suite—*their* suite, she thought, with a shiver that was unreasonably, unconscionably erotic—they didn't speak. They stood for a moment, just looking at each other, then, item by item, pulled each other's clothing off. She sensed in him a need that went deeper than just the sex, but right now it was the physical sensations that dominated her own thoughts, and she gave into them as his hands moved all over her.

When she had come three times they climaxed together on the table.

'Think about this when you're meeting the suits here tomorrow,' she whispered in his ear before pushing him off her.

They adjourned to the spa tub. She added a whole bottle of bubble-bath and the bubbles frothed up and over the edge as they sank into it.

They had drunk only Chinese tea at dinner, so Liam opened champagne.

'Okay, you've got me captive,' said Natalie, wishing her words had less truth than they did. 'So tell me about your life.'

Liam nibbled on her ear. 'What would you like to hear?'

'Meaning what lie or what topic?'

'Take your pick. Honesty is easier.'

Natalie held her breath. Did she really want to know anything? She probably already knew too much.

'Favourite song?'

Liam laughed. 'All time or current?'

'All time of course.'

'"Hungry Heart".'

Natalie burst out laughing. 'You have got to be joking.' Seeing his expression she added, 'Okay, okay, everyone can have a Springsteen moment.'

'Your turn.'

'I've already sung them to you.'

'How about films?'

'*Four Minutes*,' replied Natalie without hesitation.

'Don't know it.'

'It's a German movie. Culminates in a piano recital of classical music, in handcuffs.'

Liam laughed. 'I'll watch it some time.'

'Your movie?'

'*Sound of Music*.' He was so deadpan she almost believed him; until he was laughing at her for being so gullible. '*Life is Beautiful*.'

'The one in the concentration camp?'

Liam nodded.

'Where the father looks after his son?'

The simple interpretation stopped him short. Then the wit took over again. 'The one where the father gets shot.' He paused again. 'How about you—a movie you liked but you wouldn't ever tell anyone about.' Except him, obviously.

Natalie thought for a moment. 'Okay, this is like you are *so* dead if you tell anyone.'

Liam rubbed her leg affectionately.

'*Flashdance*. I was confined to bed for four months when I was sixteen. My mother felt helpless and kept finding me old movies. I think she thought it would inspire me to do my physio; trouble was I wanted to be a singer not a dancer, but it was…Well it had some good music and dancing in it.'

'That'll not be why you liked it.'

It wasn't hard to figure it out; the heroine was from the wrong side of the tracks and had to do everything the hard way. In the end she had changed the establishment's ideas rather than having to compromise her own. Not what happened in real life.

'Nick was rich, a working-class guy made good, who'd left his wife,' said Natalie, conscious of the significance as the words left her mouth. 'And he drove a Porsche.' She grinned. 'You'd enjoy the scene where she takes off her jacket in the restaurant.'

Liam let the marriage reference slide. 'How important to you is the band?'

'It's a good outlet.'

'And the tattoo?'

Natalie had seen him looking at the band of initials around her arm. *PRANZCP*: President of the Royal Australian and New Zealand College of Psychiatrists. She'd been manic.

'Overexcitement at my qualifications and a bad tattooist.' she said. 'Did a *P* instead of an *F*.'

They got out of the spa with champagne still left in the bottle, and sat on the balcony in hotel robes looking out across Sydney Harbour.

'This is the best,' said Liam.

The lights on the bridge, the convex shapes of the Opera House and the buildings around them, the boats bustling around the port made Circular Quay look like a fairyland. She didn't even know she was going to ask it until she did.

'What went wrong with you and Lauren?'

Liam didn't look fussed. 'We both got exactly what we wanted.'

Natalie looked at him.

'What you want in your early twenties is not necessarily what you need in the long term. Then, she needed a husband who looked good both physically and professionally. I wanted a smart, pretty and interesting wife. What was not to like? She's great. A very smart and capable woman.'

Natalie was reminded uncomfortably of a conversation she had had with Declan about a patient.

'There is, you see, a fundamental dilemma for the single woman having an affair with the married man,' he had said.

'What? Whether he'll leave or not?'

'I'm talking about a deeper level. What she really wants is not him, but rather to know what it is to be *her*.'

She didn't want to be Lauren: she didn't want the job that was probably more about committees than patients; the two kids with the nannies and the private schools; and for that matter the husband who had grown bored and was screwing another woman.

But she thought of Liam tying her up and wondered where else he could take her. Where she could lead him. To explore that, there needed to be a relationship. She was beginning to think that might be what she wanted.

After the keynote presentation on the unreliability of memory and a workshop on assessing dangerousness, Natalie slipped out of the conference and hailed a cab to take her south of Cronulla, where Georgia's mother lived. Damian rang while the driver was still negotiating city traffic.

'I thought I'd let you know Tiphanie made bail.'

'About time. Anything new on Travis?'

'I was right. They were too plastered to recall that the car didn't start, until we jogged their memory. Travis borrowed Rick's car and gave him a ride to work the next morning.'

If Travis had left Chloe in his car while he was watching football, he would have needed to transfer her. Or her body.

'Have they found anything?'

'Nothing on Rick's car yet. It didn't look like it had been cleaned. A couple of samples are with the lab.'

'Did Travis or his mate come up with anything else?'

'Mate still saying he didn't see anything, just threw the keys at Travis so he could go to bed. Travis still denying he had Chloe.'

'Can I ask you for a favour, Damian?'

'If I can.'

'Can you get me a copy of an old police file, a Welbury one? Amber Hardy's.'

'Can I ask why?'

'No,' said Natalie, thinking he might work it out anyway. Half-hoping he would.

Georgia's biological mother, Lee Draper, was sixty. She had served fifteen years of a twenty-year term. Georgia would have been in her late teens when Lee was released. Natalie wondered if she had been informed at the time or if Lee had ever tried to contact her. Natalie wasn't certain what she hoped to achieve by seeing Lee, only that she was looking for anything that would shed light on Georgia's case. She wanted to be able to make a clear cut assessment of Lee: either a monster or a domestic-violence victim who had done the best she could for her baby in the circumstances.

The journey took more than an hour. Lee's house was a compact weatherboard with a well-kept garden and an early model Corolla in the drive.

A thin woman in jeans and T-shirt, short grey hair tucked behind her ears, looked Natalie up and down from behind the screen door. She clicked the lock and opened it.

'You can come in but you'll have to put up with me smoking. Else we can sit out the back.'

The smell of stale smoke was strong and the weather mild, so Natalie chose the backyard option. Lee looked older than sixty, her skin dry and taut as if she had been drained of life. There was a suggestion of Georgia in the bones of her face. Mother and daughter shared the same clear blue eyes but in Lee they were more focused and self-aware.

'Does Georgia know you're here?' Lee asked, stubbing

her cigarette in a beer can on the ground beside her chair.

Natalie hesitated. She had asked Georgia's permission to see her mother. But she'd never specified which one.

'Didn't think so,' said Lee. 'I'm an embarrassment. Certainly to Virginia. My half-sister.'

'Have you ever spoken to Georgia?' Natalie noted a child's plastic bike and wondered who it belonged to.

Lee had seen her look. 'The screws told me it was a bad idea and I figured she'd find me if she wanted to. I'm still her mother; I'd always help her if she asked. The bike's for my bloke's grandkid when she visits.'

'You must have...been curious,' said Natalie, mindful that Lee had evaded the question.

Lee leaned back, head against the weatherboard wall. 'Hard not to be. I watched her for a whole week. Sat in the coffee shop at the hospital and watched her come off her shifts. Never said a word to her.'

Too embarrassed? Afraid? Natalie had no idea what this woman was thinking. If she had been mentally ill once, she wasn't now.

Lee lit another cigarette. 'So what do you want to know?'

'Tell me about Georgia's early years.'

Lee inhaled and watched the smoke as she blew out. 'It was a long time ago.'

'Yes, but it was an important time for Georgia. She lost you, then had to move in with her aunt and uncle who were strangers.'

'Losing me wouldn't have fussed her. It would have been losing her father.'

Natalie watched her. This wasn't the time for a lecture on the importance of the primary attachment figure.

'She wasn't planned, you understand,' said Lee. 'I was a

good Catholic girl and even if I hadn't been I wouldn't have thought to get the pill. Wouldn't have an abortion; still had hopes.' She coughed and the mucus sounded heavy on her lungs. 'We weren't married, but Cliff was older; he had a house. My parents cut me off; holier than thou. It was all right that my mother fucked a married man, but me? I was a tart. Virginia must've thought I was getting my just deserts.'

'You knew Virginia?'

'Met her once. Her mother dragged her to our house when I was a kid. Must have been when my old man's annulment came through. I was only young and the language was pretty colourful, I can tell you.'

'You and Cliff?' Natalie prompted Lee to return to her own story.

Lee was on a roll. It sounded like she had been waiting a long time to tell this story.

'Cliff was a cunt. A bully. Weighed probably a hundred kilos and I was about the same size then as I am now. He used to tell his mates that he'd put me on top and give me a spin. Offered me to them as well more than once.' Lee took another drag and briefly seemed lost in thought. 'He was violent, but you probably know that. Didn't help me in court though. Male jury, mostly. He broke my nose once.'

There was still a slight bump.

'But fuck me dead, he loved Georgia like there was no other creature on the planet as pretty or as smart. I swear, from the time she was three months old she knew his voice and was always looking out for him. Her whole face lit up whenever he was around.'

'How did you feel about this relationship with Cliff?' Natalie wondered if Lee saw it as another rejection. Maybe as Georgia had when Paul had loved his 'girls' so openly.

'I liked being a mother. At first, anyway. It made me feel, I dunno, like I could do something, you know what I mean?'

Natalie nodded. She had heard the same thing often from new mothers, particularly younger ones whose motivation for having a baby was to have someone who would love them exclusively. Except that children need other people in their lives, and that need could be easily misconstrued by these vulnerable young women.

'She wasn't a difficult baby but I wasn't doing it easy. We were living way out of town in the middle of nowhere and we only had Cliff's car. He used to go to work and leave me behind. It was a way of keeping me dependent. I had no one. He sometimes came back with mates and they'd get wasted. Mostly beer and dope, but whatever they could get their hands on.'

'Did you use?' asked Natalie, thinking it would be hard not to if drugs were the only escape on offer.

'No.' There was a proud edge to Lee's tone. 'A bit of weed but pretty much nothing. I wanted to stay clean to keep Georgia safe.' She paused. 'It's one thing Georgia probably should know, but I guess it doesn't matter now.'

'That you stayed clean for her?'

'No,' said Lee. 'That I killed him for her.'

Natalie tried not to react, but it didn't matter. Lee wasn't looking at her.

'Cliff had been drinking all day. He was a big man and could drink more than most and still look okay.' She looked at Natalie. 'Georgia needed to go to bed; it was hot and she was cranky. Cliff wanted her to stay up and we fought. It must have been ten o'clock before he said he'd put her to bed.' Lee took a longer pause, lips pursed. 'They were there a long time. I went to find out why and Georgia was lying in her cot, naked. It had been a hot night and she used to pull her clothes off. Cliff thought it was funny having her parade around nude.'

Lee lit another cigarette and they both watched the glow of the tobacco and the smoke that whirled around her face as she spoke.

'He wasn't touching her. She wouldn't have understood. But I did. I'd been played with...*abused*...by...it doesn't matter. I knew where it would go, what it would do to her later, and I knew then without a doubt.'

The cigarette smoke hung in the air. Natalie wondered how much Lee's story was a rationalisation that she had murdered her partner for Georgia rather than for herself. It would have made her a hero in the women's prison. For some reason it hadn't moved the jury.

'He had his dick out,' Lee said, no emotion in her voice. 'He was coming. Globs of cum shooting into the air and over Georgia's blanket. I turned and went to the kitchen. I knew exactly what I was going to do and I knew it wasn't wrong. I'd do it again in an instant.'

She had sharpened the carving knife.

'I remember how it sounded on the steel. It was like I was getting my strength from it. I knew I had only one chance. Like I told you, he was a big man; a big, angry man. If he got the knife I'd be dead and there would be no one to save Georgia.

'He was turning around as I came back into Georgia's room. He'd been drinking and he had that mellowness you get after sex. He saw me and saw the knife but I don't think it ever occurred to him I was going to use it.'

She had. Five times.

'That's why I got a long sentence,' Lee said without

emotion. 'Made no difference that he was wanking himself over his baby daughter.'

'Why not?'

Lee looked at Natalie. 'Because I never told anyone.'

Like Amber. Shame? Because she felt she deserved to go to gaol or because she didn't think she'd be believed?

'It must be hard then to make sense of what's happened with Georgia,' said Natalie.

'I've come to realise that women just have shit lives mostly. It's a man's world and women get the short end of every deal.'

Natalie nodded, not in agreement but in empathy.

'She was always a man's woman,' said Lee. 'So she was lucky there. Found herself a better husband than I did.'

Natalie raised an eyebrow.

'There's a few good uns,' said Lee laughing. 'Paul came to see me, you know.'

No, Natalie didn't know.

'Brought Olivia with him. He was curious about me, I think. I suppose he wanted to play happy families; they'd already lost the older girl by then. Georgia didn't know; they were here for a holiday. He said he was gonna tell her when the time was right.'

'Then Olivia died.'

'Yes. Paul came to see me and cried. I never saw him again, never met the others.'

'So how do you feel towards Georgia?'

'Georgia is my daughter. My only child. A daughter I never wanted and who loved her father more than me. We all make mistakes. I was able to give her a life that she couldn't have had with me. Cliff would never have left us alone. Never have left her alone. Single mothers were still a bit on the outer back then and I would have had no support. I did the right thing.'

The self-justification didn't really answer the question.

'What do you think happened to her children?'

'SIDS runs in families,' said Lee. 'Maybe it was in Paul's. I read Olivia had a history of asthma. Kids die of asthma. It's on the increase, did you know? More than doubled in the last few years. Looked it up on the net.'

'So you believe Georgia is innocent?'

Georgia's cool blue eyes looked at her out of Lee's wrinkled face. 'I *know* she's innocent. She's my daughter. The police thought that made her a murderer. But I was the one standing watching that cunt abuse her. A mother protects her child at any cost.'

Natalie rang Jacqueline Barrett from the cab as it slowed into the peak hour crush.

'Can you tell me about the knitting needles?'

'Reporters got it wrong.'

'So Georgia didn't try to induce an abortion?'

'I don't know what she did or didn't do, I only have the facts.'

'So what facts did the reporters embellish?'

'A scalpel.'

'A *scalpel*?'

'Yes, a scalpel. With her blood on it.'

Natalie stood in the garden drinking sparkling wine, watching the boats in the harbour. Her head was crowded with thoughts of murder and abuse. The forensic psychiatrists milling around her must have had similar experiences, but they were probably smart enough not to go to cocktail receptions when they did. She decided she couldn't manage small talk and started walking towards Paddington. She found a funky restaurant that served Thai with an Australian twist, and ate alone, but with thoughts of Georgia, Paul and Lee, as well as the three lost children and the dead Cliff keeping her company. She didn't notice the food.

Natalie went back to her room and flicked on the television. It was 10 p.m. and she wondered what Liam was doing. Did she want to see him again? Annoyingly, yes. Maybe it was stupid not to make the most of the opportunity. It wasn't like he was this free all that often.

She was playing with her phone when the message came up. *Fancy a fuck?*

She typed *Bar in 20*. The walk took her thirty minutes and he was there waiting.

'No drink already ordered?' she asked in mock surprise.

'Not sure what your post work-function drink is.'

'Guess.'

She waited for him to joke about cocksucking cowboys but he didn't. 'Bourbon, neat?'

They lingered over a second drink. Liam looked more relaxed than she'd seen him before.

Back in the suite there were papers scattered over the table from Liam's meeting. She couldn't resist a cursory look, but nothing related to either Tiphanie's case or the paedophile ring.

Liam started to undress her, stopping her doing it herself, kissing each part of her, tongue lingering over her scars. She struggled to stand still but he insisted, saying he wanted to take his time and enjoy her. He carried her effortlessly to the bed then worked her over with his tongue until she was desperate for him, but he still made her wait. Finally she couldn't bear the exquisite touch on her clit any longer and she let herself come, with him still fully clothed and watching her.

'Your turn now,' she said, undressing him. As she sucked him he was touching her and she came again.

When he entered her, she had the clear thought that this was the best sex she had ever had. As an image of Eoin tumbled through her mind, she wondered if she would always be doomed to want men that she had to let go of. Her own repetition-compulsion.

Bob was predictably put out when Tom brought him home late on Sunday. She spent an hour chasing him around the garage and putting up with him asking how she felt.

When she finally had him clipped to his perch she looked at the time. Nine p.m.

'Declan, I'm really sorry to disturb you.'

'Not at all, my dear. Are you all right?'

'I was wondering if I could run something past you.'

There was a pause. 'I was just about to have a tipple at my local. Would you like to join me?'

The bar was close to Declan's home office in Northcote. Before leaving her warehouse she paused to reflect on the feeling that she was being watched, but standing in the shadows scanning the rooftops and doorways revealed nothing apart from a stray cat.

The barman pulled a cap off a craft beer and directed her out the back.

'So, tell all,' Declan said.

'Jesus, how long have you got?' Natalie smiled. 'The main thing I actually can't tell you about, so we'll do a hypothetical, okay?'

Declan nodded.

'Let's say I have a patient who knew about a crime. The person who committed it has done the same thing again, but isn't currently a danger to anyone.'

Declan wasn't about to give anything away, hard as she was looking for it.

'My patient refuses to go to the police and refuses to let me tell them. I have *another* patient who may go to gaol, and this information could make all the difference.'

Declan nodded. 'I see your dilemma. Though of course it isn't a dilemma at all, or at least not yours.'

Natalie looked at him hopefully.

'Imagine you were only seeing patient A, the one with the information and knew nothing about patient B. What would you do?'

'Same as I am now. Try to convince her to go to the police.' She bit her lip. 'But not too hard because if this comes out it will be detrimental for her.'

'So you have your answer.'

'But—'

'There is no "but". Your duty to patient B is the same, with complete disregard to the information you have from patient A. Chinese walls.'

'What if someone else worked it out and—'

'You are in dangerous territory,' said Declan with a firmness that was unusual for him. 'If you are in any way involved, however peripherally, you have a legal and moral obligation to patient A. It is not your information. She trusted you. Break that trust and you break her, your relationship with her, and any good so far achieved.' He added, patting her hand, 'Natalie, you are not God. We can only be what we are.'

Natalie didn't think she was God, but she was more than just a psychiatrist. Every other part of her was screaming at the injustice.

'Okay,' she said, knowing he was right, but wondering how to reconcile the part of her that wanted to see Travis brought to account.

'Is there more you want to talk about?' asked Declan.

Natalie shook her head. 'No, thanks. It'll wait until Tuesday.'

She rode home knowing he was worried about her.

On the door of her warehouse was another red envelope, with another USB. While she was able to reassure herself that the locks were keeping the stalker out, the content rocked her. And gave her cause to completely rethink just who her stalker might be.

Jessie was in the waiting room: good. Sunglasses on: not so good. She followed Natalie into the office, sat in the upright chair and said nothing.

'How was the funeral?' Natalie asked. Might as well deal with the elephant in the room.

'How do you reckon?'

'Funerals are for the living. So it depends what you and the others there were looking for.'

'They were there.'

'They?'

'The bitch—my stepmother, with my half-sister. And Jay. The bitch only came because she thinks she'll get money.'

'Is there any money?'

'Not that I know of. She was so sweet it made me want to puke. At least I had someone with me.'

Jessie had said she didn't do 'alone'; like many people with borderline personality styles she mostly felt empty and the feeling of abandonment was accentuated when she was by herself.

'How was your half-sister?'

'She's a brat. Nine going on eighteen.'

'Jay?'

'He's doing good.'

'Have you talked much with him since your father died?'

'A bit. At the funeral Kyle was with me. We all talked. He filmed it, the funeral. Said he'd send me a copy.'

'Kyle is a friend?'

'From school,' said Jessie. She went into a long and confusing explanation of how she'd run into Kyle again.

'So Kyle is the ex-boyfriend of your high-school girl-friend?'

'Yeah, and a mate of Jay's when they were at school, not so much since. When I ran away I stayed with him a while. He used to kind of look after me. Before Hannah.'

'You're seeing him again?'

Jessie shrugged. 'A bit. He brings me here sometimes.'

Ponytail man. 'Does Hannah know?'

'No, but it's not like she's here helping is it?'

'Be careful,' Natalie said, pretty sure that Jessie wouldn't be. At least she wasn't asking for the computer back.

The next patient cancelled. Natalie found her mind drifting. Drifting, she told herself, *not racing.* She hadn't had much sleep the previous night. When she had fallen asleep, she had jerked awake after only minutes, heart racing, sure she was being watched. *Not paranoid.* This was real. The USB from the last envelope left on her door was still in her laptop on the bedroom floor. This wasn't someone having a lark. It wasn't a patient acting impulsively.

She needed to keep both well and alert, so she had reduced her dose of quetiapine to 200mg. A little less than usual, but it had been enough in the past.

She pulled her mind back to the present and opened the

drawer in her desk. No computer. Shit. The break-in. Or did Beverley have it? She couldn't recall.

'Did you ever copy the files on that computer?'

Beverley pushed her shoulders back. 'I've been very busy.'

'Could you do it today?'

Beverley made huffing sounds as she opened her drawer and retrieved Jessie's computer.

This was one of Georgia's well-dressed 'I'm like any normal housewife' days. Unprompted, she started talking about Miranda, her fourth and only surviving child, currently in Paul's care.

'We weren't going to have any more. I knew we should have waited, but I wasn't getting any younger and already had to have extra tests because of my age. Paul wasn't happy. He was irritable; I felt it came between us, that pregnancy. He fussed over me a lot but he also stopped having sex with me.'

'Why?'

'He said he didn't want anything to go wrong. He spent his time on the computer.'

'Doing?'

'What do you think?'

Natalie felt mildly irritated. Georgia was making her work for it—and it felt deliberate. Was this Natalie's countertransference again, driven by Natalie's issues with her own mother, or some sounder instinct? She couldn't decide. 'I'd rather know what you think—or know.'

'It was just the usual porn.'

'The "usual" porn?'

'Yes.' Georgia's eyes were disconcertingly like her mother's.

'There are different types of porn. What did Paul like?'

Georgia shrugged.

'Women with big breasts? Violence? Bodily functions?'

'Paul wasn't a breast man. He liked women skinny. There might have been young girls, I really just didn't pay much attention.'

Natalie leaned back in her chair. As a therapist she should ask *how do you feel about that?* Or even *you seem to want to deny Paul's use of porn affected you?* Had they been together in this dance longer, she might even have risked an interpretation: *you seem angry.* But the connection wasn't there. Georgia was not ready to expose her vulnerability. If she wanted to blame Paul then Natalie might as well try and work out how much blame he deserved. At least that was how she would explain her interrogation to Declan.

'What about that bunny sign he does on his cards? How long have you guys been doing that?'

'Ages,' said Georgia. She frowned. 'Actually I'm not sure. A few years maybe.'

'When you were arrested, did anyone look at his computer?'

Georgia shook her head.

'So when and how did he find out about the Facebook page?'

'No one believes me when I tell the truth.'

'Try me.'

'He always knew.'

'Okay,' said Natalie. 'Take me through this. He always knew what?'

'He told me I should put the kids' pictures on Facebook. When Olivia was alive. I put up Genevieve too. She was still our little girl, part of our family.'

'This wasn't just photos.'

'I know.' Georgia played with the wedding ring she still wore. 'But those things...well he thought them too. We'd laugh about it, how hard it was sometimes. It didn't mean we didn't love our children. Surely all parents get frustrated with sleepless nights, the never-ending needs.' She grimaced. 'The nappies. The milk and vomit smell.'

'Georgia, there was a lot more on your Facebook page than normal frustrations. What was written suggested a deep anger.'

'That's just it. I wrote it down to get rid of those angry feelings. So when I was with them I could be the mother I wanted to be. Not cold and unfeeling like Virginia, or murderous like my mother. It was because I didn't want to be them.'

For the first time in all of their sessions, Georgia was showing something close to anger.

I know she is innocent, Lee had said. Georgia's eyes were focused like her mother's had been, her jaw firm. Jacqueline Barrett thought there was doubt; maybe Georgia had been unlucky, with SIDS in two children and asthma in the third. So Olivia had a bruise; she'd hardly be the first two-year-old to have one. Experts had been wrong before and statistics could be manipulated in court like anything else.

'I was in prison when Miranda was born,' said Georgia, 'or at least when I went into labour. Paul met me at the hospital and stayed with me.' Her voice choked and Natalie realised she was crying. 'He said sorry.'

Sorry for what? Natalie tried to put herself in Paul's shoes but there were too many unknowns. Perhaps he encouraged her to write on Facebook but was horrified when he read it. He might be feeling guilty for not supporting her enough and for his own failure to protect his children. All she could be sure of was that his emotions were likely to be complicated and full of contradictions. Perhaps he was still unsure, but was cutting himself off to survive emotionally, for Miranda's sake.

'As soon as they cut the umbilical cord, the nurse handed Miranda to him,' said Georgia. 'I haven't seen either of them since.'

'Has he told you how she's doing? Does he put her photos on Facebook?'

'I don't know. Perhaps it's better she never knows me. At least until...this is all sorted.'

Georgia hadn't wanted to meet Lee as an adult.

'Do you worry about Miranda?'

'Oh no, I'm sure Paul will look after her. As long as she's amusing.'

Amusing.

'You used that word before; what does it mean?'

'Nothing really. Just that Paul likes to be amused. I always had to keep him happy.'

'I don't think that's a role for a one-year-old,' said Natalie.

'No, no, I suppose not.' Georgia looked flustered. Natalie bided her time. She'd seen Georgia like this before, just prior to dissociating. On that occasion, Georgia had been looking at a photo of Olivia. Was that what destabilised her? Things that took her back to her own childhood vulnerability?

'It's hard when you're little,' said Natalie slowly, visualising the picture Lee had painted for her. 'Hard when someone you love is also scary. Terrifying even.'

The steeliness disappeared from Georgia's gaze.

'I'm a good girl.'

Natalie nearly dropped her notes. The voice was not Georgia's. Or rather, it was a childlike version.

'Yes, Georgia, you are a good girl. Who are you a good girl for?'

'Daddy loves me.'

'Yes he does,' said Natalie wishing she could get to her iPhone and record this. Her bag was in the drawer and it would create too much noise. 'Tell me about your daddy, Georgia.'

'I'm his special little girl,' said Georgia in a singsong voice. She giggled. '*Round and round the garden, like a teddy bear, one step, two step...*' The giggles exploded.

'Where are you, Georgia?' asked Natalie. Was the Daddy she was referring to her biological father Cliff? Her uncle, Vernon? Or even Paul? 'On Daddy's knee? In bed?' When Georgia just kept giggling Natalie added, 'In the bath?'

The giggling stopped. Georgia looked confused and started shaking. She looked around her and grabbed her bag, which tipped, spilling out the contents: an array of lipsticks, coins from the purse that had burst open, tampons, a small pink rabbit, several envelopes and a mobile phone. Georgia grabbed the rabbit, but it was the envelope on top that drew Natalie's attention.

As quickly as Georgia had regressed, she returned to her normal self. She looked at the mess on the floor and asked: 'Did I do that?' Then she leaned forward and began to scoop her things into her handbag.

When she had finished, Natalie looked into the eyes of the ostentatiously overbright coping housewife.

'Do you recall what just happened?'

'When?'

'Just then. Georgia, where did the rabbit come from?'

Georgia looked down into her hand at the fluffy figure. 'This? Just something I bought.'

'Why?'

Georgia shrugged her shoulders. 'I guess a bit of nostalgia.'

Nostalgia, or was it the child version of Georgia, one of Wadhwa's 'other personalities', who'd gone into the shop to purchase it?

'How many do you have at home?'

Georgia frowned. 'Funny you should ask. I keep finding them. I forget I've got them.' She laughed. 'Maybe I have OCD.'

No, but maybe she did have Dissociative Identity Disorder. As far as Natalie could judge, she had just witnessed a dissociative episode.

'What about the letter in your bag?'

Georgia drew out an envelope. 'This was in the post this morning. I took it out of the letter box and I wasn't sure if I should open it.' She put it down on the table between them.

'Why shouldn't you open it?' Natalie asked.

'Well, you seemed to be interested in these letters and so was my lawyer.'

'You think it's from Paul?'

'Yes. It's addressed to my maiden name: Ms Parker, not Mrs Latimer. He's telling me he wants to be rid of me.'

'Why don't you open it and see,' Natalie suggested. 'Then if it is from him, take it to your lawyer.'

Georgia fingered the letter and opened it gingerly. She tipped the contents onto the table. It may have once been a card with rabbits on it; maybe several cards. The rabbits had been cut up. Beheaded.

Georgia gasped, her hand going to her mouth as she

paled. She stood up and backed away from the table before rocking slightly and fainting, hitting her head on the seat of the chair as she fell.

Natalie called Jacqueline and dispatched a recovered Georgia to her office in a cab.

'I'm sending the envelope and contents with her. O'Shea knows about them, right?'

Jacqueline assured her that the prosecutor had been notified of the previous letter.

'Another question.'

'Yes?'

'Whose idea was it for Georgia to see me? I mean did you suggest it or did she?'

There was a pause. 'Georgia was adamant she wanted to see you.' From her tone it sounded like there had been an attempt to dissuade her.

Beverley had got the message that Natalie was less than happy with her after the disclosures she'd made to Liam's secretary, so she disappeared into the filing room for the rest of the day. Natalie checked her emails. Damian had scanned the pages she'd requested from Amber's file.

Natalie usually found police reports unhelpful. Cops wrote as little as possible and it was often hard to see what they meant through the stilted jargon. Not that her notes would have been any better; she'd had to learn to stop using her own abbreviations so other people could make sense of her comments.

The police had been called to the home of Amber and Travis Hardy after being alerted by the emergency services operator. The file included a copy of the excruciating call transcript. Amber had frozen and resisted any attempts to make her go back into the bathroom. With Amber's recent confession, it made sense. Bella-Kaye was already dead. She'd waited long enough for Travis to leave unobserved, so he could then cruise home via the pub. The police and ambulance were at the house when he returned.

Natalie scoured the notes. One of the police in attendance was DS McBride. This made it even more likely that Damian would go back over the notes. Could she be blamed if he saw what he had missed last time? What was the worst that could happen? She wasn't worried about herself so much as Amber.

She didn't know what she was looking for until she found it: two pieces of information buried in the report.

The first was the state of the kitchen. The pots were in the sink, not on the stove where they would have been if Travis hadn't yet got home for dinner.

The second was a single word in the detailed description of the 'crime scene' room. *Wet* children's clothes on the floor. Travis must have removed them when he came up with the cover story for her to tell.

This time, Amber had told the truth. The whole truth.

Liam met her at the Halfpenny. She had texted him first thing in the morning after her restless night. Vince and Benny were watching to see if Liam was followed. A man had asked after her recently; nondescript, late forties. Not Travis. A private investigator? Her stalker?

Benny brought Liam to the back room.

'Why do I have bad vibes?' Liam asked. 'Is this where you tell me you don't want to see me again and they—' he tossed his head in the direction of Vince and Benny '—beat me up and throw me out?'

'We may get to that.' Natalie stood up and shut the door. 'You need to see this.'

Her laptop was on the table.

They watched the clips from the previous night's USB in silence. There were several, of varying quality. All were of Natalie and Liam drinking champagne on the Sydney hotel balcony, bare-legged in robes.

'Fuck,' Liam said, echoing Natalie's thoughts.

'This isn't the first video clip,' said Natalie, 'and there have been notes delivered on a USB.' Looking at him directly she added, 'Could it be Lauren?'

There was a long silence and Natalie felt her heart pounding. If she was honest, it was the most likely scenario. Lauren was no fool, and much smarter than Travis. Men, particularly arrogant ones who thought they owned the world, weren't that observant; Liam wouldn't have noticed if he was being followed, as he could have been that day he had come to her rooms, the day of the first note. Lauren would have the resources and more than enough cause. She wouldn't need the video for a divorce but it might give her some extra leverage with the financial settlement or the children.

Liam pulled his chair back from the table, one foot across his knee. Defensive. 'Tell me about the notes.'

Natalie outlined the history of her red-envelope stalker, minus the references to her mental health. 'I presume you don't want me giving this to the police.'

There was only a second's hesitation. 'No. It'd be a tad awkward. But if you're in danger, obviously that's far more important.'

'Right now I think I—we—have a better chance of working it out than the police.'

Liam dropped his leg and smiled. 'It isn't Lauren.' He sounded unconvinced by his own words.

'From my perspective, he—or she—is more resourceful than my patients. The film shows Sydney, not just Melbourne.' This had been the first thing that had occurred to her. It had left her feeling vulnerable and powerless. And alone.

'So who is doing it and why?' Liam appeared to be over the initial shock.

'This is the list I gave the police,' said Natalie, smoothing out a folded piece of paper. 'It doesn't make sense. Not when you add the Sydney angle. This person either got on a plane after us or hired a PI. Both options would take money and motivation. A patient doesn't fit, particularly a psychotic one; they don't have the focus. And the antisocial patients I've seen haven't got the resources.'

Then there was the fact that the room was booked in Liam's name, not hers. The night before she was even meant to be there. Back to Lauren.

Liam was reading the list. 'Two murderers?'

'Both antisocial personality disorders. One I saw as a once-off. He was a nasty piece of work and thought he could con me into supporting a sleepwalking defence I told him was crap—'

She saw Liam's expression and despite herself she laughed. 'I didn't exactly say it was rubbish, but that was the general tenor of my report. Two other psychiatrists said the same. It wasn't like there was really any hope of the defence working.'

'So he's in prison?'

'Yes, but he has lots of friends. Friends with money.'

'Given we're grasping at straws, you'd better give me the names of the other psychiatrists in case they're being targeted as well.' Liam jotted the names down. 'The other murderer?'

'Luke Wheeler,' said Natalie. 'I looked after him for two weeks at Yarra Bend when I started there. Plain bad with a big dose of weak, and I sent him back to Port Phillip Prison. He got parole a few months ago.' She only knew this because Senior Constable Hudson had checked it out. Wheeler had been at Yarra Bend at the same time as Bob's owner but the theft of Bob's photo could have been opportunistic.

Liam was looking at her. Natalie shook her head.

'I really can't see why he'd bother,' she said. 'He used

to enjoy creeping me out, making sexual suggestions and getting off on my response.' He'd stopped when on the third occasion she'd turned to him, smiled sweetly, and told him that if he tried it again she'd have his balls fried for breakfast.

'Who did he murder?'

'Technically it was manslaughter. One of the last people to use provocation as a defence,' said Natalie. 'He caught his girlfriend in bed with his best friend.'

'What happened to the best friend?' asked Liam.

'Survived the bullet. Girlfriend didn't.'

Liam wrote his name down with a star next to it. 'Anyone else?'

'Three women with borderline personalities. They were all angry, but the most recent was six months ago. They'll have redirected their anger to someone else. Only one had a history of violence to anyone other than herself, and that was road rage.' She thought for a second. 'I suppose I should include Celeste. A current inpatient at Yarra Bend, in for attempted murder of her pimp husband. I guess he's still around. And she has a brother.'

Liam looked at her thoughtfully. 'She got a history of abuse?'

'They all do, Liam.'

'Okay. Who else should be on this list that you didn't tell the good senior constable about?'

Natalie looked at him. She'd thought about this most nights, alone in bed and not sleeping.

'There's really only two. First is Travis,' said Natalie, 'but I wouldn't have thought he had the brains or the money. Plus, the timing is a bit early. I got the first letter the week before he saw me at the police station in Welbury. That said, he didn't look surprised to see me there.'

Liam shook his head. 'No one would have told Travis.'

'Think again. Amber's mother knew I was involved two days after we met for dinner; the day after you booked the room. It's a country town.'

Liam shook his head. 'Would anyone help Travis? Who's the other?'

'Paul Latimer. The husband of my patient. He sent the card with the bunny logo; Georgia's lawyer would've spoken to you about it, right?'

Liam nodded. 'Jacqueline Barrett. She did.' He wasn't giving anything away.

'So have you found anything?'

'We're looking.'

She could play that game too. 'I can't and won't tell you anything about Georgia other than what you can find out for yourself. She was already in my care when it started. But maybe he had more to do with the death of his children than the police thought, and thinks Georgia has told me.' She added: 'And he lives in Sydney.'

Corinne was in her office at 8 a.m. The woman needed a life as much as Natalie did.

Natalie hovered in the doorway. 'I wanted to let you know I'm starting to write a report on Georgia.'

Corinne looked up. 'And?'

Natalie took a deep breath. 'I think Wadhwa is right.'

'Good to know we're paying him well for a reason.' Her tone was dry but Natalie sensed something else.

'He's still an incompetent jerk.'

'Seems the feeling is mutual.'

'Maybe you'd like my resignation?' Natalie suggested, only half-joking.

'Christ, don't you start. No, that wasn't what I meant. Never mind. You do a good job. Just try not to push his buttons if you can avoid it.'

'The registrar's with Celeste,' said Kirsty. 'She's been cutting again.'

Natalie stuck her head into the examination room. Celeste's slashes looked superficial and the registrar was finishing dabbing them with mercurochrome. It wasn't the cuts that drew her attention. As Celeste turned around to get her T-shirt, Natalie caught sight of a tattoo. 'Haven't seen one like that before.' Natalie smiled faintly. 'What does it signify?'

Celeste stared at the floor. She ignored the question when it was repeated.

Natalie went closer to be certain. Yes, it was Liam's porno-ring rabbits.

Celeste mumbled something, several times, that sounded like 'angel'. Delusional.

Natalie went back to Celeste's file and reviewed the admission notes. Okay, not delusional. Her husband's name was Angelo. She was wondering about the implications, when Wadhwa made a grand entrance with a television crew and began to parade them around the unit. Natalie thought of Corinne's comments and went home early.

'I'm not exactly feeling on top of my patient load,' Natalie confessed to Declan, not adding that she had more than enough other things to worry about.

'Patient A and patient B?'

'Yes, as well as Georgia and Jessie. It's like I started to look for dissociation and now I see it everywhere.'

She brought Declan up to date with her visit to Lee, finishing with the unnerving similarities between mother and daughter. 'Who's to say that a murderous impulse, directed to a husband in Lee's case, couldn't be directed towards a child in Georgia's, maybe even through one of these other "personalities"?'

'The unleashing of the primitive id. We all have murderous impulses, but most of us don't act on them.'

'Then there's Saint Paul who likes cutting up rabbits on cards for fun. As well as being kept amused, whatever that means. Why did he go to see Georgia's mother without telling her? A fascination with murderers?'

'It's hard to know without talking to him. Try to place yourself in his position. Maybe he really did love her. There could be some truth in what she says about him knowing, but it may be subconscious. If he then feels he was duped into colluding in the murder of his children, anger would be understandable.'

'Why not just leave her alone? The court is taking care of her.'

'They've just let her out on bail, so maybe not. Perhaps her release rekindled his anger and he doesn't know what to do with it.'

'That describes where I feel I'm at.'

Declan raised an eyebrow. She took a deep breath and gave him a potted summary of her stalker, minus the possibility that it could be Travis.

'I assure you,' Natalie concluded, 'that this is real. The police have the notes and videos.' Well, one of them.

'It sounds very real and quite frightening. Do they think you're in danger?'

'They're not specific threats. I think the purpose is to

scare me off, but I'm not sure what from. I've a feeling he likes to play with me, maybe see or imagine me being scared.'

'Are you?'

She let Declan read it in her face.

'Have you thought of taking some time off? Moving home to your family?'

Natalie shook her head. 'I'd sit around worrying. My mother would make me feel worse. Besides, it could be related to my private life rather than work.'

'Ah. The married man?'

Natalie nodded. At least Lauren was unlikely to murder her. Too smart, and without the psychopathology of the predatory stalker.

'Hell hath no fury...' Declan caught her expression. 'Have you considered taking a break from that?'

Yes, but she couldn't do it; she needed Liam too much. Something else she wouldn't admit.

'You have suggested to me before,' said Natalie, 'that women who have affairs with married men have more curiosity about what it is to be the other woman than actually wanting to be with the man. Is that an accurate summary?'

'You have the essence.'

'Why?'

'Because their curiosity is about how to be a wife, their internal conflict about how such a relationship could work.' Declan's eyes never left her.

'Surely that's what they get from their parents?'

'We don't always have the parental role model we want. For whatever reason there is a need to reject or question it, look for an alternative.'

Her mother versus Lauren; Craig, her stepfather; the real

father that was at the tip of her memory…Or Liam. *Shit.* 'So what's the man's role in this?'

'They have a role,' said Declan with a smile. 'Beyond the obvious. Perhaps the fantasy of what a husband should be, but without the risk associated with commitment.' He paused then added, 'Perhaps part of a past they are stuck in.'

Natalie took a breath. *Repetition-compulsion.* Declan knew too much about her, had too many dots joined. She wasn't ready. Yet she needed to work out a different ending.

'I saw Amber,' she blurted out.

Declan took a sharp breath.

'She'd just got parole,' said Natalie with more care, 'and wanted to let me know. Before you say anything, I've said I can't keep seeing her.'

Declan nodded, face very still. 'You are treading on dangerous ground, Natalie.'

'She's out, she's fine. It's good to know that she can get on with her life.'

'And close the chapter?'

'Yes. Thanks.' She stood up abruptly and kissed Declan lightly on the cheek before leaving. She didn't normally do that and wondered what he would make of it.

She rode home feeling strangely settled within herself. Relieved, perhaps because she'd come clean to Declan. So relieved that the danger seemed to recede. She felt back in control, though objectively she knew this was far from the reality of her situation.

She could just imagine what the tae kwon do teacher would have said, if she had still been doing classes. He'd told her on the fifth week she was unsuitable and to come back to formal lessons when she was ready to learn. She'd dismissed his advice, hadn't been all that interested anyway, or so she rationalised. She liked being on the edge, liked living dangerously. To be good at any martial art you had to overcome that impulse. You had to run first, negotiate second and fight only as a last option.

In the end she settled for a balanced fitness regime that used a punching bag for boxing. And leg-sweep manoeuvres she hadn't ever intended to use, although they'd worked effectively enough on the court steps.

She'd never been in a physical fight. The bikie thing— she had been on the periphery of the whole scene. Something that had made life exciting, if only briefly, still stirred inside her. A need to prove herself, even if it put her in danger. A death wish, Declan had called it. The survivor's guilt that was aroused every time she visited Eoin's grave. And perhaps when she got too close to anyone.

Her confidence faltered as soon as she reached the top of the stairs. Something was wrong. She stood perfectly still, the thumping of her heart and Bob fussing on his stand the only noise. What was it? She looked around. There was the usual state of chaos; it would take an intruder with OCD to create any oddity here. Had she left that glass on the counter? Stepping forward, she saw it contained the dregs of the morning's juice and dropped it quietly in the sink. Something else?

From where she stood now it jumped out at her. The television was on, sound muted. The picture flickering between scenes sent shadows across the room, all the more eerie in the silence.

Hand shaking, she found the remote on top of a pile of papers and clicked it off. She looked more closely at the papers; she didn't recognise them. She picked up them up and peered at the top sheet. Spun around as the papers fell around her in disarray, feelings of terror surging through her, certain he was still there, looking over her shoulder.

Nothing. She dropped to her haunches, on full alert, sensitive to every sound that Bob made. Another sound in the distance made her turn but it was outside, too far off. It was minutes before she could bring herself to pick the papers up.

They were case notes. *Her* case notes, from the one time she'd been admitted while manic. Seven years ago.

'Could he be a health professional?' Senior Constable Hudson had asked.

Jesus. It looked like it had to be, and suddenly the net seemed a whole lot wider. A nurse she'd pissed off? The intern who had been her friend until her manic behaviour had driven a wedge between them? Or...? Lauren. Lauren was based at the hospital where Natalie had been admitted years earlier. Her case notes would be archived there. She longed for Liam, but was not going to show this to anyone, least of all him. Instead she found where he had got in— this time he had smashed a back window in the garage— boarded it up as best she could, and rang Tom. Then she waited. Unable to rid herself of the feeling she was being watched, her response scrutinised.

A piece of plastic in the garage below flapped in the breeze from the broken window. She sat perfectly still as she listened.

Beverley had booked Tiphanie to see her Wednesday morning in a slot that didn't exist. Then she'd gone off sick. Natalie wondered what revenge she could exact. Maybe banning false nails on hygiene grounds? It took twenty minutes of rearranging appointments to make her day manageable.

Tiphanie arrived with her father Jim and headed straight to the consulting room.

'How's she going?' Natalie asked him.

'When the going gets tough...' He shrugged.

Tiphanie was already seated, not looking at all tough. 'It's nice being out.' The bags under her eyes had almost disappeared.

'I wasn't expecting to see you.' Natalie was curious; her contact with Tiphanie had been for assessment, not therapy.

'It's okay isn't it?' Tiphanie looked younger than her twenty years. 'I just...I can't talk about it with Mum and Dad.'

'Family members often grieve in different ways. Helping each other can be hard.'

'I think about her all the time.' Tiphanie pulled her

phone from her bag and thrust it at Natalie. There was a photo of Chloe filling the screen. 'Just swipe.'

Natalie scrolled, watching Chloe's life from the newborn photos to those of a month earlier. Her brief life had been well documented. Tiphanie provided a running commentary.

'I called her my little Eskimo,' she said, as she pointed to Chloe dressed like a giant snowball. 'She hated being cold.'

Despite the past tense, and the tears in her eyes, Tiphanie was still talking about Chloe as if she was part of her life. She had yet to come to terms with the reality that her child wasn't coming home.

'Do the police...keep in touch?' Natalie finally asked as the session came to an end.

'Yes. Andie mostly. The cops...' Tiphanie bit her lip. 'They're looking for blood.'

'They may not find anything,' said Natalie.

'If he...they will get him won't they?' Tiphanie looked at Natalie, desperate for reassurance. 'I mean she was only... yesterday was her birthday.'

Natalie hugged her. Reassured her, without knowing if it was the case, that the police would find evidence to charge Travis, and that she would do anything she could to help.

Natalie fought back the way she always did: music and exercise. The Styx played Friday and Saturday night in Bendigo and she did two workouts in a local gym to blow off the last of the steam. She felt relaxed enough afterwards to buy a pair of earrings that looked like handcuffs, and flirt with one of the barmen. On Sunday she managed a ten kilometre run. Tom arrived for takeaway on Sunday evening. Bob's serenade capped a return to some approximation of normality.

She felt in control, and refused to allow herself to obsess about who was watching her. She could feel the anger working its way into her system. *Worm.* A little demeaning name for a pathetic little person who was hiding and thought he could get to her. She pictured him as small in every way. A *worm* that she could feed to Bob. Most of the time it worked.

She kept an eye out for the worm, but told herself it was only for the opportunity to vent her anger on him. She had a security firm install a camera underneath her Bridge of Sighs, bars over the garage windows and, in the living area, an alarm that alerted the local police. She asked Vince and Benny to use their own security cameras if the man who had asked after her turned up.

Liam dropped into her rooms to bring her up to date.

'Spoke with your Senior Constable Hudson.'

'And?'

'Not Wheeler; he's back in gaol, and has been since prior to our Sydney trip. Assaulted the new girlfriend.'

No surprise there.

'The other psychs involved with your sleepwalker haven't received any USBs or red envelopes,' Liam continued, 'and Angelo is an alcoholic and rarely leaves the boarding house.'

'So we're no closer.'

'They're still looking at Celeste's brother Joe. Has a record for assault—pub brawl and a robbery. Suspended sentence.'

'What if Celeste's husband was part of your network?' said Natalie. 'As well as her brother. Then they'd be concerned about her telling us, or specifically me, what she knew.'

'Is this just guesswork?'

'Not entirely.' Liam raised an eyebrow but she shook her head. Mentioning the tattoo on Celeste's arm would expose her to interrogation she wasn't stable enough to deal with.

'I'll have the locals keep an eye on Joe.'

'If it's not him, that takes us back to Paul.'

Or Lauren and a private detective. In which case Liam had more to fear than she did.

Liam was still dealing with interstate police politics so Paul had yet to be questioned.

'We have to tread very carefully. We don't want to alert him that he's a suspect in the paedophile ring because if it is him he's smart enough to have a back-up plan where all the evidence gets destroyed.'

'Do you think it's him? My stalker, or your paedophile, or both?'

'He was in Sydney when we were there,' said Liam, toying with his coffee cup. 'My Mr Big? To be honest, no. Carol managed to get his secretary to give out some details of his diary. We've confirmed he was overseas at the one time we are certain this guy was in Melbourne. He has had business trips to Asian countries, as we are sure the perp we are looking for has, but half of Australia travels to Asia regularly. Doesn't mean he isn't part of the ring though.'

Paul wouldn't have been able to access her health records. Did this mean he'd got help from other members? The thought was daunting.

'You'll go after him hard?'

'If we have enough evidence.'

'A prosecutor with a conscience?' said Natalie, forcing a laugh.

Liam didn't smile. 'I like putting the bad guys away. But only if they did it.' The Hadden legacy.

'What about Tiphanie?'

'She's still lying; but in any case I haven't taken her to

court. You know I've thought it was Travis all along.'

'Someone I knew once'—Tom had interesting friends—'was put away for a burglary he didn't do. He figured it was payback for the ones he didn't get caught for.'

'His choice to take that attitude, and maybe a good one for a career criminal. But not for a prosecutor. My rule is that if we miss some of the bad guys, so be it. We only prosecute if I'm sure. I'm not God.' He grinned. 'I don't want to be responsible for anyone spending time in prison unless it's for a crime they did.'

'Then you'd better get Tiphanie's charges dropped.'

'They were only ever an attempt to get Travis. But we can't arrest him until we're certain. Completely.'

Jessie was late and upset. It was hard to draw her out. One-word answers to questions and comments were separated by long silences. Natalie decided to push things. She was grateful to be feeling on top of things. Walking the line between maintaining the therapeutic alliance and making a patient work with their conflicts was hard work.

'Your father's illness, his death, his belongings. Brought up memories, I'm guessing.'

Jessie mumbled something indistinct.

'There's stuff in your head that must be hard to make sense of. Why don't you try to pick something and let me help? Is there anything you want to put in your box?'

'I want to die.'

'Why?'

'Because I'm a fat useless piece of shit.'

Something she had been told as a kid? Or something she was telling herself now because the memories were stripping her of any self-respect?

'Hannah doesn't think so.'

'Yeah, well, she's not here is she?'

'I don't think so either.'

'Doesn't matter. I just want to die.'

Jessie pulled a knife from under her sleeve. It was a flick knife; illegal, shiny and dangerous. Natalie had seen one used in a fight. The victim had died while her hand was buried in the sinews of his neck in a futile effort to hold his carotid artery together.

'You have a choice, Jessie. You either give me that knife right now, or you get up and leave and never come back. You want to kill yourself? Your call. But not in my office.'

Jessie hesitated; her eyes went to her shoulder and the hand with the knife started in that direction. Natalie knew she was taking a gamble but she was pretty sure Jessie didn't want to die. She wanted boundaries, to feel safe. 'Now, Jessie.'

The arm came down. Jessie looked at the knife. She dragged a finger over the blade and small globules of blood formed on her fingertip.

'The knife.' Natalie put her hand out, calculating whether a kick would dislodge the weapon from Jessie's hand. She shifted slightly so the angle was better. Not that she rated her chances of success as high. Five tae kwon do lessons didn't make her Bruce Lee.

Jessie, still fixated on the knife, flicked it closed and threw it on the floor. Natalie started to breathe again. She picked it up and put it on the far side of her desk.

'I want you to talk. Really talk.'

Natalie had either passed a test or Jessie was so desperate that she had to grasp at whatever was offered. It was the turning point in any therapy. Jessie spilled out the horror stories of her childhood. Most of them were more dream than clear memory, disjointed and made little sense: stories about spiders and snakes and dead babies. But woven through the narrative were obvious allusions to penetrative sex. A uniting theme of frank abuse at multiple levels; physical, sexual and emotional.

Even after Jessie had left home at sixteen, things hadn't improved.

'Lived on the streets for a while,' said Jessie. 'Slept under a bridge for a few months, till I woke up and found a guy with his hand in my pants.'

'You must have felt very vulnerable.'

Jessie's expression moved from blank to fearful and when she spoke her voice had dropped to a whisper. 'I'm being watched.' Natalie wasn't sure if she was referring to her childhood, or current life. Or both. 'I was filmed.'

Amber looked brighter. Natalie hadn't lied to Declan. She had told Amber she couldn't be her psychiatrist. But she had agreed to one last appointment.

'I probably didn't need to come,' Amber said, 'now Tiphanie is back home with her parents.'

'That doesn't mean that she won't go to prison,' said Natalie. 'The police are still investigating.'

'I know.' Amber looked...smug? Or was it just relief?

'How do you know?' asked Natalie.

'Everyone in Welbury knows.'

'Amber, who have you been talking to?'

Amber blushed. 'Kiara; I used to go to school with her.' And Detective Constable Andie Grimbank presumably. Small towns.

'They're looking at Rick's car. I'm sure they'll find

273

something...' Her voice trailed off. As sweet as it might be for her to see Travis gaoled, if it represented the final confirmation that Chloe was dead then the victory would be pyrrhic.

As Amber left, Natalie wondered again if Travis had known that Liam was going to invite her to Welbury. All it needed was one person at the police station to have known. At that point Travis would have had a motivation to deter her from being involved. It would surely make him the prime suspect as her stalker. She felt, for a moment, powerless at the thought of him in her home, sitting in her chair, lying on her bed while she wasn't there, opening the bottles in her bathroom. He would have done all that and what else? Spat on her food? Ejaculated...

She tried not to think about it but could not free her mind of the feeling that she was surrounded by his invisible traces. Travis was a coward, but cowards were dangerous.

She was still turning it over in her mind when she got home. There were no more notes or USB sticks, but she was unable to stop herself from looking in her drawers, imagining he had moved things just to freak her out, even though her house was all but a fortress. She checked the camera and alarm. Maybe Travis would leave her alone if he thought the police were monitoring him.

Natalie's faith in professionals was not helped by seeing Wadhwa on the evening news.

'My study is opening up exciting possibilities about how personality and criminality can be interlinked.' Natalie hit the off button and went up to bed. Bob's photo from her office was sitting by her bedside table.

The Halfpenny was filling early; it would have been nice to think it was the band drawing them in but the Magpies had annihilated the Blues, and the customers were more interested in celebrating football results than hearing music.

'I'm thinking more overnighters, guys,' Gil said as he tuned his bass.

'Jesus,' said Natalie. 'Your wife needs you with her.'

'Believe me, I'm more use to her for the rest of the week if I have one good night's sleep.'

Shaun pulled out his diary. 'Focus, guys. What do we think about Albury-Wodonga?'

'Bloody long way. And more car-scratchers,' Tom said, without sounding as if he meant it. The others were keen to go.

'Done. Warrnambool have given us another date too.'

Busy was good; less time to think. If being away meant giving her stalker the run-around, all the better. Even the new lock on her bedroom balcony door and the camera on the roof were not enough to make her feel safe.

Vince stuck his head in and gestured to Natalie. She

followed him into the corridor, taking her beer with her.

'We've got trouble.'

She felt the adrenaline surge, took a breath and welcomed the tingle of energy.

'There's a guy out there.'

'The one Benny saw before?'

Vince nodded his head.

'And?'

'Tonight he asked Maggie if The Styx was the band with a shrink singer.'

'To which she replied?'

'I answered for her. Something like, why did he want to know?' The grin suggested there'd been some additional descriptive language.

'Point him out,' she said. From the doorway to the bar, she followed the direction of Vince's nod. He was hovering behind a group of revellers, trying to blend in. Most of the crowd was twenty to thirty and he was the wrong side of forty, and wearing a blazer, so he wasn't succeeding. Medium height, brown hair on the longish side, glasses. Nondescript.

'Never seen him before,' said Natalie as another wave of adrenaline hit her. She fought to calm herself. 'Could he be a private investigator?' Vince had a pretty good nose for the law in all its guises.

Vince narrowed his eyes. 'Do you want to tell me a bit more about what shit you've got yourself into?'

Natalie shrugged.

'The jerk's wife?'

'Maybe.'

'Okay, I'll watch him. We'll have him on our security camera. And regardless,' he went on, still glowering, 'tonight, one of us walks you home.'

Natalie kissed him on the cheek. 'Thanks, Dad.'

It was one of their better gigs. Maybe it wasn't obvious to the audience but the band always knew when they were on fire. Tonight there was an extra vitality in Natalie's performance. Partly perhaps from not having a full dose of medication on board, but also a frisson of anticipation. Maybe she'd have her answer tomorrow when the police saw him on video and she could stop feeling like a paralysed insect waiting to be eaten.

They didn't do many covers in the end. The crowd were right behind them, loving what Natalie did with the raw sexuality of Shaun's lyrics.

Vince was backstage when they took a break.

'The jerk is here too,' said Vince. 'Can I throw him out?'

Natalie sculled a bottle of water. Who was following whom, she wondered? Her stomach turned at the thought of confronting Lauren. Would she be satisfied with venting her anger at Liam, or would she turn up on Natalie's doorstep with pictures of the children? Children in person, even? She steeled herself. If she had to, she could handle Lauren. At the end of the day, it was Liam that had broken trust, not her. And it would be a better scenario than a predatory stalker with sexual motivations and an interest in escalating her distress to add to his excitement.

'Don't chuck him out. Let's see if we can resolve the issue after the next bracket.'

They didn't let up in the second half. If anything, they played louder and edgier. The Collingwood locals seemed to love it; a good result at the footy always helped. In the final song Natalie had her tongue in Tom's mouth and later her hands down Shaun's pants. Knowing Liam was watching might have spurred the bad behaviour. He had shied away from her mania at the ball; she wanted to know if he could cope with the real her.

She was so fired up she contemplated going up to Mr Nondescript and asking him directly what he was up to but restrained herself. Give Liam a chance to sort the mystery out first. As she slid onto the stool next to him at the bar, she noticed Mr Nondescript watching and wondered if Liam had too.

She didn't speak to him, didn't even acknowledge him. Just took the glass of the bourbon from the bar and downed half of it.

'Don't look now, but we're being watched. Wearing glasses near the door. Brown hair, your age or older.'

Liam kept drinking, never looking at her. After a minute he knocked the coaster that had been stuck to the bottom of his Guinness glass to the floor, and glanced around the room as he picked it up.

'Never met him, but he looks familiar.'

Natalie slugged down the remaining bourbon. 'I still think there's a chance this is about you.'

There was a long pause. Wondering where he had seen the stalker before? 'No. I have thought about it.'

'I think the first note was spontaneous, maybe outraged over something, hence the handwriting, which I unfortunately threw out. It arrived the day I ran you into the flower bed. Let's suppose Lauren was already having you followed.' Natalie paused. 'Maybe because of a previous indiscretion?' Liam's expression was impossible to read, so Natalie continued. 'Maybe she came to my rooms in person after she got the report that first day, thinking I was the latest woman but not sure, but then sent the USBs after that.

Once she found out we really were…involved, then she got the PI to do more serious surveillance.'

Liam remained silent.

'Could Lauren have found another man and want to dump you? Maybe she wants your children to think it's your fault with the bonus of giving me a hard time in the meantime?'

Liam managed a half-laugh. 'You seem to have the hang of Lauren's style. But the language in the notes isn't like her. And all the notes were about you.'

'The Sydney video was both of us.'

'Lauren doesn't fit with the "they belong to me" note.'

'Sorry to remind you that you aren't the centre of the world, but don't you have two children?'

'Shit.' For a moment Liam looked unnerved.

'Any suggestions from here?'

'I'm on it,' said Liam. He got up, wandered closer to Mr Nondescript and fiddled with his phone before rejoining her. Natalie watched as he sent the photos he had taken. Vince glared at Liam from behind the bar.

Liam caught Vince's eye. 'I don't intend her any harm, if that helps.'

Vince banged down a glass and froth spilled down the sides.

'What if it is Lauren? Or if she does find out?' Natalie asked quietly.

'She's tough. We'll cope.'

The similarity between herself and his wife was suddenly obvious. Natalie had thought she shared nothing with the blonde beyond being a doctor. But they were both tough women. Liam was one of the few men she knew who revelled in taking it up to her; maybe Lauren had lost her appetite for the fight.

'So can I go up and ask our admirer who he is and tell him to bugger off?'

Liam shook his head. 'Not yet.' Liam's phone rang. He spoke briefly and smiled.

'It's not Lauren. You were right on your other guess. Your stalker is Paul Latimer.'

Natalie felt a sense of anti-climax. This she could deal with. Easily. *They* meant Georgia and his children. He wanted to control the court case, but he had no reason to cause Natalie any real harm. It validated everything Georgia had said about him.

'I'm going to talk to him then go home,' said Natalie.

'Love your plan. But I don't want him knowing that he's a suspect in the paedophile ring.'

'Why would he think that?'

'He might be worried Georgia has told you something.'

'I'm just going let him know I know what he's been doing, put a stop to it. Afterwards you can help me celebrate.'

Paul Latimer saw her coming. He hesitated, then looked to the door. Out of the corner of her eye she saw Benny positioned there, ready. Vince tensed and bent slightly, arm going below the bar where he kept a cricket bat.

'This conversation is going to be short and not so sweet, Mr Latimer,' said Natalie, looking Paul right in the eye.

Paul took a step backwards but she continued before he could attempt to deny anything.

'You been checking me out?'

'You rang me. I just thought—' Paul looked embarrassed, like most bullies she had confronted. He must have checked her out when he knew she was Georgia's psychiatrist at Yarra Bend, hence the first hand-written note. After that he'd sent USB sticks and either he or some douchebag he hired tried to scare her off when Natalie had taken Georgia on privately. Fleetingly she wondered why he was back.

'This is how it's going to be. If you want to speak to me you're going to ring my rooms and make an appointment. You are going to stop the terror campaign and refrain, either you or anyone else, from following me, filming me, sending me notes on USBs, breaking into my house or anything else you can think up.'

'Look I—' Paul took a step backwards, but Natalie hadn't finished.

'No negotiations on this,' said Natalie. 'And don't think for a moment'—she paused and looked at him coldly—'that just because I'm a doctor I will play by the rules if you cross me.'

Without waiting for an answer, Natalie walked back to her stool, grabbed her leather jacket and walked out, leaving Liam to scramble after her.

Perhaps her death wish was receding. Maybe she wanted to build on the reprieve from confronting Lauren. She directed Liam to the connected building's street entrance rather than the front door. He was standing in a darkened stairwell when she opened the electronic door at the end of her Bridge of Sighs and let him in. Liam was impressed.

As she led Liam to her bedroom she wondered if it was he who had the death wish—the death of his marriage at least. In Sydney there had been no attempt to hide her. He didn't know her that well. She had always been trouble, and he surely knew that instinctively. Yet he was prepared to give her a room key, have his secretary know about her, have the receptionist and bar staff in Sydney remember her. It wasn't like she had tickets on herself. But a conservative-looking lawyer with a younger woman wearing an ear full of silver and distinctive attire? It was the kind of thing people remembered.

Right now it was hard to think about it in any rational way. She hadn't had much to drink, but she was tired, emotionally as well as physically. It was the downside of living on the edge.

It occurred to her that confronting Paul might have the opposite effect to what she'd intended; pity she hadn't considered that before she'd taken him on. This worm liked to play with women. Paul still liked to play with Georgia's head. He wouldn't enjoy being challenged any more than Travis had. Even if he wasn't Liam's Mr Big, the logo on the card was a strong tie to the network and he would still be worried Georgia might tell her something about it. It might lead to a raising of the stakes; and it might not be just him, because at the very least he'd had to enlist help to get her case notes. Her instincts were still on full alert.

They had sex without ceremony, one quick release enough for them both. He was probably as emotionally on edge as she was. Paul knew who Liam was. He could send the film to Lauren out of spite, or even try to blackmail Liam.

Afterwards, Natalie sat up in bed and wrapped her arms around her legs, pulling them into her chest. 'Promise me,' she said, 'that if by some chance Latimer sends the film anywhere that Lauren sees it, or she finds out about us some other way, you will do everything humanly possible to repair your marriage.'

There was a long silence where the panic welling in her seemed to underline every interpretation Declan had ever made. However illogical it was, part of her wanted Liam to have the perfect marriage.

'Why?' asked Liam.

'Because she deserves it. Because fifteen years ago it was like this with her. Right?'

She looked into his eyes but the wall had gone up. She had lost him. At least his children wouldn't get hurt. Jesus, she did have a conscience.

Liam sat up and kissed her gently. 'I don't have to go. Lauren is in Geneva.'

'The kids?' Her voice caught and she hated herself for the weakness. She didn't feel safe yet.

'James is at school camp and Megan's at a friend's.'

Natalie hugged her knees tighter. She wished he hadn't used their names. She had to let him go, that was given. Did it have to be tonight? Seemed no one else needed him. 'You haven't promised me.'

'My marriage, my kids, my problem.' He caught her recoil at his tone and softened. 'You don't know everything.'

'Possibly. I mean, I'm sure I don't know everything, but that doesn't mean I'm not right.'

'Still my problem.'

'Okay Liam, I'm not your psychiatrist and I know I've always been clear that this was just for fun. I just don't want all this...you and me, all the stuff we're doing together...to wreck your marriage.'

Liam dropped his guard; he suddenly looked younger. 'I got caught. She knows how much it means to me to have our kids grow up with two parents under the same roof. My Achilles heel.' He paused and Natalie waited. 'We agreed, no more playing around. Either of us.'

'So if she does find out?'

'I'm fucked.'

Jessie had visited Hannah in prison on the weekend. 'She thinks I need to work out what really happened.' Jessie sounded ambivalent.

'There's no "really" with memories. They're never exact.' Natalie leaned forward. 'Sometimes delving back into memories makes things worse, at least at first. Sitting with that can be tough. But it gets easier.'

'I want this to stop. My nightmares are weird, but they feel so real. And scary.'

She pulled out her memory box from her canvas bag; it had been painted black with red streaks. From it she retrieved a collection of drawings and paintings and spread them out on the table. One look told Natalie she had talent. The largest used heavy oil paint in swirls that reminded Natalie of a dark moment from Van Gogh. It showed a small child at the bottom of a pit with a snake; coiled, fangs bared. The other pictures, maybe ten in all, were small; some no bigger than a business card. Tiny intricate images and heavy charcoal sketches depicted ferocious animals and again a small child, presumably Jessie. No rabid bunny rabbits at least.

'When did you do these?' Natalie asked, picking them up one after another.

'That one,' Jessie said, pointing to the biggest, 'years ago. After a nightmare. They're what I see. The rest I did in the last few weeks.'

'Is it possible,' Natalie asked, 'that when you were young you were still pretty unclear about what was happening? A mix of terror and...' She stopped, thinking of the video clip she had seen on Liam's computer, of what she knew about child abuse, how the child might, at first, be a willing but naive participant, 'and wanting to be grown up. When the situation overwhelmed you, your mind tried to make sense of it in other ways. Scary things like spiders and snakes would have been frightening, but understandable. Something your mind could grasp.' Natalie didn't think Jessie needed the Freudian interpretation of the snake.

Jessie shrugged. 'I guess. They seem very real though.'

'Are there people in the dream too?'

'I—' She stopped and frowned. 'I don't know. Sometimes it's just fear.'

'Which shows how complicated and compartmentalised your memory is.'

'Seeing my father...' Jessie faltered. 'My nightmares are way worse.'

'You said last week that you remember being filmed. What were you doing when you recalled that?'

Jessie shrugged. 'Nothing really. Just...' She stopped dead. 'None of it matters anyhow, not really. Kyle...' She looked away.

'Does Kyle ever intimidate you?'

'No, of course not. He's my friend, he looks after me. It was when I found the computer.'

Natalie paused. Was Jessie ready? It was always going to be difficult, but Jessie had opened the door. Natalie pulled the computer out of the drawer and put it on the table in front of Jessie. 'Did you find anything on this before you gave it to me?'

Jessie shrank into the chair, hugging herself, fingernails digging into her arms. 'I didn't look.'

Natalie let the silence grow. The clock on the mantelpiece ticked. Jessie's expression slowly changed from fear to confusion.

'It was my computer. I remember my father confiscating it. There was a huge shit fight with my stepmother, but it was maybe the only time my father didn't wimp out. I somehow, I felt he was doing it for me. Now *that's* weird.' Jessie managed a forced laugh.

How was her computer linked to Jessie's state of mind, either then or now? Surely if her father had filmed her he would have transferred it to his own PC? If he had, for some reason, put something on Jessie's computer, why hadn't he just deleted whatever he was concerned about and given it back?

'A few months after that they broke up, and I went to Kyle's. I came back to Dad's a few times but he was drinking all the time. I was pretty pissed off at him over everything.'

'Didn't you ever ask for the computer?'

'Dad said he'd thrown it out.'

So why had he kept it? 'Would you like me to look at what's on it?'

Jessie shook her head. 'No, no you mustn't do that.' She looked around her as if someone might be there listening. 'I mustn't ever—' Her voice sounded regressed, childlike. 'Not ever. He said...' Her eyes widened and breath quickened. 'I shouldn't be here,' she said suddenly, firmly. 'It's making things worse.'

'I warned you that bringing up memories would do that to start with. You couldn't deal with what happened as a child, but you're an adult now. Facing your fears is going to help you move on.'

'No!' She stood up and gathered her drawings. 'You can't help me. No one can.' She bolted, taking her computer with her.

Georgia was having a bad day.

'There weren't any fingerprints. Jacqueline gave the letter to the police.' Georgia didn't look at Natalie, a fatuous smile on the edge of her lips. 'Do you think Paul really has stopped loving me?'

On the face of the evidence, the answer seemed obvious, but in Georgia's fragmented early life no one had been there to give unconditional love. Paul had provided what her fragile narcissism needed to maintain equilibrium and consequently Georgia's sense of self was tied in with her estranged husband. What internal dialogue kept her from falling apart now? She seemed to be on the verge. Her eyes were glazed and her speech vague, yet there was an edginess as well. The need to be seen as good, the smile she'd learned to produce for Virginia, came at a cost. What did Georgia do with her anger? If there was a 'personality' that killed her children then it was surely the angry one. Neither the over-bright fifties housewife nor the giggling two-year-old were going to suffocate their children.

'I keep thinking about Facebook,' Georgia said. 'I remember Paul picking photos to put up. We laughed over some of them.'

Georgia looked out of the window. 'He wanted to put up one of Olivia in the bath,' she said abruptly, her voice loud, as if she was giving a speech. She stood up, and Natalie noticed her hands were trembling. She dropped her voice to a whisper—theatrically?—and added, 'He liked to see her naked.'

Natalie wasn't sure Georgia could handle a direct question about abuse. When Natalie had tried it in the past she had always denied it. Was it worth trying again now when she was more vulnerable? Natalie didn't feel the rapport between them was enough to hold her; the trust had still to develop. She went gently.

'What are you thinking, Georgia?'

Instead of answering the question, Georgia put her arms around herself and started to sing a nursery rhyme. 'Rock-a-Bye Baby'. When she got to the last line, *Down will come baby, cradle and all,* she sat down in the chair and looked down.

'He wanted my girls,' she said. 'They were so little. I saw how he looked at them. I could see...I knew what he wanted to do to them. I didn't know how to protect them.' Looking at Natalie, she added, incongruously, 'I knew he loved me too.'

'What did he want to do, Georgia?' Natalie kept her voice soft and even, eyes fixed on her patient.

'He liked seeing them there, those pictures, and it made me so angry, knowing what he was really thinking. The anger...I don't know why, but I wrote...I was angry at *him*, not my children. Angry at myself for not knowing what to do.'

'How did they die, Georgia?' Natalie asked.

'God did it to punish me. Punish me because I didn't

know how to save them.' Not vague, but not thoughtful either. More stilted, as if she was reciting something.

'God, Georgia? Or part of your own anger that you directed to them instead of Paul or yourself?'

Natalie flipped open her file and started reading to Georgia from the Facebook printouts the police had found. *'She thinks she's smarter than me but she isn't. I'm the one with the power, not her.'* The anger was there, she could feel it; could she get Georgia to show it? Digging for the truth would come at a cost to their therapeutic relationship but it would give her a clearer idea of what to target in treatment.

Georgia looked down, hands shaking.

'Jonah is so demanding, it's never-ending. Unless I end it, of course.'

'I put him in the cot. I walked away.'

'It is so much more peaceful without him. The angry part of you soothed by silencing him,' said Natalie. 'Was that what happened?'

'No!'

'Then what do you do with all that anger Georgia?'

Georgia stood up. Natalie should have been worried; she had pushed far too hard, too fast. The angry personality, if it was a separate one, would act without restraint. But as Georgia rose there was nothing aggressive in the stance. She was in control. Natalie watched as Georgia pulled up her skirt. She wasn't wearing underwear. It took Natalie a moment to work out what she was looking at. Her registrar had physically examined Georgia and reported no self-harm marks; but she wouldn't have examined the mutilated genitalia that Natalie was now viewing.

Her pubic area was shaved or waxed. Carved across her mons pubis were letters, mostly scars. One was recent and had crusts of blood—the one that spelt the T of *cunt*. Along the edges of her outer labia were hints of what could be seen were she to open herself up. Gnarled scars formed from repeated trauma.

The bloodied scalpel in the toilet.

'Are you happy? I would never have harmed them, they were *mine*,' said Georgia. 'I was their mother.'

'I was...stunned,' Natalie admitted to Declan, still feeling much the same a day later. She felt contained in his office. Partly by him, partly by his orderliness. For the first time she appreciated the obsessive positioning of his three coloured pens and the stack of files on his otherwise empty desk. 'I can't tell how much is performance. Why didn't she have underwear on? Did she plan that before coming to see me, or does she just not wear underwear? Did she need to show me because she wants help and doesn't know how to ask? Every time I see her I end up going around in circles.'

'She sounds very complex,' Declan agreed. The bottle of wine sat on the side table unopened. 'But I think you are still looking for some ultimate truth.'

'The court—a jury—is going to have to make a decision. If I can't, how can I expect them to? If I'm called to court, and I will be, I'm not sure I can explain what I think. Treating her is like trying to bandage someone in the middle of a switchblade fight. New cuts keep on opening up.'

'Literally. Let's try and get your thoughts clear. Start at the beginning, with a formulation of how she got to be how she is.'

Natalie tried to construct a timeline in her head. 'Georgia's genetic heritage: possible character traits inherited from both parents, who had impulse control difficulties. Complicated by attachment difficulties: her mother was isolated and unsupported and probably emotionally unavailable, but there was some positive input from her father. So she learned to look to men for affirmation, underpinning her defence style which is a mix of Cluster B personality traits: antisocial, narcissistic and borderline. Enter man number one: she sees him as an escape from her cold aunt, someone to finally love her. He gets her pregnant and dumps her. She loses the pregnancy, with or without intervention—my guess is with—then she meets Mr Right. Paul adores her and gives her a stable base.'

'Until she has children.'

'Having children destabilises her in two ways. One, it reminds her of her own childhood vulnerability when her needs were never met and she learned to pretend. The crying child takes her back subconsciously to the moments of terror, being alone and unheard. Two, it puts her in competition with them for Paul's affection, which is the one thing that has helped her be stable and live relatively normally.' Natalie took a breath. This much was fairly clear in her mind. The rest of the explanation was not.

'Hypothesis One. She has a personality disorder. With dissociation but without multiple identities. She kills her children because she can't control her anger, which originated from her unmet needs in childhood. Virginia and Lee only ever taught her to hide it, not resolve it. In this hypothesis she knows what she did, is legally responsible and is, at least in part, lying or acting.' She had said *they were mine*: to do with as she pleased? It resonated uneasily in Natalie's mind with Paul's note.

'Hypothesis Two?'

'Wadhwa's option. She has Dissociative Identity

Disorder. She is still destabilised in the same way but her subconscious copes with the emotions she can't deal with by drawing on different parts of her that manifest themselves as other personalities. One of these personalities unleashed the anger at her children, and as such, she—the real Georgia—isn't responsible. Her mental illness is.'

'Is there a Hypothesis Three?'

Definitely.

'Paul is a psychopathic, narcissistic paedophile and manipulator. His wife and children are extensions of himself; his playthings. In her destabilised state—possibly both D.I.D. and a personality disorder—Georgia is vulnerable. She still kills them, but in a dissociated state in which she may believe she is protecting them. Paul is pushing the buttons of her vulnerability because he likes the power and isn't fussed about the consequences. There is a possibility'—the thought was articulating itself for the first time—'that he killed Jonah. He was there and the dynamic was different with a boy. In this scenario, Miranda, his daughter, is at risk.'

'Too much conjecture even for the psychiatrist's office,' said Declan. 'What do you know about Paul?'

'He's an only child and a successful businessman. Georgia's lawyers have been told by the police and social service that there is no reason for them to be concerned about Miranda.' *But they don't know he stalks me.* Even as she spoke Natalie was thinking about their recent encounter and beginning to favour Hypothesis Three.

'The police will not intervene unless you have something a great deal more substantial,' Jacqueline Barrett had told her in their most recent phone conversation. 'The social services loved Paul. Unfortunately for us.'

But it wasn't just Miranda being killed that Natalie was worried about. Georgia had hinted at abuse and it was hard to get the word *amused*—along with a picture of Paul naked in the bath with his daughters—out of her head. And him walking around her apartment.

Despite Natalie's best attempts to avoid him, Wadhwa put himself everywhere she was until he had a chance to corner her.

'Dr King, I am keen to hear about your impressions of Mrs Latimer.'

'Georgia is doing as well as can be expected.'

'She hasn't completed the last research form I sent. Could you be so kind as to remind her?'

'She might not be in the best mindset for filling out forms at the moment,' said Natalie. Wadhwa would be in Corinne's office in ten minutes to complain she was obstructing his research.

'So your therapy is not working?'

'She's very disturbed, as I'm sure you'd agree.'

'If you do not have the right diagnosis you will not be giving her the right treatment.'

'At the moment,' said Natalie, working hard to keep her voice steady, 'I'm trying to keep her alive and as stable as possible.'

'Of course,' said Wadhwa. 'In court it will only be the diagnosis that matters. I am being retained as the expert witness.'

'And I'm her therapist who actually knows her and deals with her.' As Natalie made an exit, she added: 'And the one who worries about her.'

Jacqueline Barrett had finally emailed her the three-page PI report on Paul Latimer.

Paul had finished school, gone to university and completed an engineering degree. He had a number of good mates. After school he had travelled to southeast Asia and Europe for the traditional Australian backpacker tour, returned three months later and started university while working part time in his father's scrap metal business. He met Georgia, got married, enrolled in an MBA and his father died. He now owned the business and a black Porsche and had a full-time nanny caring for Miranda.

The report was so bland and superficial it could also have been the exterior world of half of the US's serial killers. She wondered why no other relationships, either before or after Georgia, were mentioned. Had the PI not bothered looking? Engineers, if her experience at university was anything to go by, tended to be socially awkward. Maybe he was the shy kind of awkward rather than the type that ran a nudie past your tutorial.

He had seemed benign in their brief encounter, but psychopaths were great con men, and he had been stalking and intimidating her. If he was such a successful manipulator, why had he made the mistake with the first note? Any pathology seemed within his family—it was Georgia and possibly his children he liked to control and manipulate. Why would he see Natalie as a threat? Did Georgia know what the bunnies meant?

Natalie met Liam at his request, this time at the Everleigh, a New York-style cocktail bar in Gertrude Street. It was more his style than hers.

'Friendlier security,' he noted, kissing her on the lips.

'Anything more on Latimer?' Natalie had picked up a beer at the bar but Liam, who had arrived before her, was halfway through a martini.

'Not yet. I got some interesting stuff on your support team. Not exactly Mr Squeaky Clean. Be grateful he likes you.'

'Who? Tom is—'

'Not your drummer. Your publican. Vince Castentella has done time.'

'I'm sure that will be incredibly useful information when he has you in a headlock, and you're flying into the street.'

Liam grinned. 'I figure I just need to stay on the right side of you to keep safe.'

'What? Hiding behind a woman?'

'Whatever it takes. You know he—'

'Stop. He's a friend. I don't want to know.'

Liam shrugged. 'Fair enough.'

'I presume that isn't why you called me.' Nor did she think it was just to get into her pants again, though that was probably on the agenda too.

'Tiphanie and Travis.'

Natalie waited.

'He hadn't had a chance to clean his mate's car, but it was clean anyway. I'm sorry, I know you think Tiphanie is innocent but we're having to look at her again.'

'Shit.' She took a sip of beer. 'I've been thinking about the videos. Of you and me.'

Liam sat very still. 'Have you had any more?'

'No,' said Natalie. 'But even before the video...ever since the card, I keeping getting stuck on why Georgia hasn't brought up the paedophile ring in therapy. That has to be what Paul is worried she's going to tell me. She's hinted other things, but nothing beyond how it applies to her situation.' Georgia's narcissism, her interest in Paul only as directly related to her? Yes, but the imperative to stay out of prison would make it all the more likely she'd use what she had. Which left a high level of dissociation or ignorance as the best level of explanation of Georgia's failing to mention whatever it was Paul thought she might, yet this didn't sit well with her either.

Natalie lay her head back against the booth and stretched her foot out under the table to rest over his groin. She was recreating a scene from *Flashdance*; Liam grinned. 'Have you found *anything* that links him to it?'

Liam didn't seem to be concentrating. Not on what she was saying at least. His hand ran up her leg. She didn't feel like concentrating on Paul either; but the missing jigsaw piece left her uneasy. 'No. Not even enough to bring him in for questioning. I'd love another drink,' he added, though his expression suggested it was more of the under the table activity he had in mind, 'but Lauren is just back from Geneva and tonight's one of those united parental front occasions.'

'Sure.' She pulled away her foot, smiled stiffly and only stayed long enough for him to brush her cheek. She stormed home, still trying to deny her vulnerability to the man and losing the fight when she rounded the cul de sac to her door.

At first she couldn't quite make sense of what she was seeing. There was another note. Only this one was pinned to something hanging from the door of her warehouse. From a distance it was white, about the size of a football. Or a...

She ran, remembering the stolen picture of Bob.

It was a dead rabbit.

She cut it down, feeling sick. She put the envelope in her bag and disposed of the carcass to the accompaniment of Bob's screeches.

'Lucky you're smart enough not talk to strangers,' she told him. 'Or else he might have tried that parrot au vin I've been threatening you with.'

She played the security-camera video. It revealed a figure in dark clothes, including a balaclava and gloves, almost certainly male. It could have been Paul but she felt it was someone younger, more agile. His hired help presumably. Or an associate from the bunny club.

The file on the USB was, as always, simple: *You've been meddling where you shouldn't have.* Then: *Mr O'Shea will find your hospital file interesting I should think.*

Natalie's Fridays had increasingly been taken up with Tiphanie's case. She figured losing another one to it would hardly matter. She had to get out of the warehouse. After a workout, shower and a coffee, she eased her bike out of the garage space and hit the road. It was another beautiful spring day, not yet warm enough for the leathers to be a problem. But it could have been pissing down rain and she wouldn't have noticed. Her body was tense and her mind on edge. The ride cleared her head and by the time she parked outside the Welbury police station she was able to put aside, for the moment, what had happened the previous night.

She hadn't bothered to ring ahead and the constable indicated that she could be in for a long wait to see Damian. But Andie Grimbank spotted her, took her through to the back of the station and made her a coffee.

'We're about to interview Tiphanie and Travis. I'll check with Damian but he'll probably appreciate you watching.'

Damian stuck his head around the door a few minutes later. He looked uncomfortable.

'Can I watch?'

Damian hesitated. 'I guess. But Natalie?'

'Yes?'

'I think...maybe she did do it. Accident, whatever.'

From behind the one-way screen, Tiphanie looked shell-shocked. She was pale and shaking, and seemed to struggle to understand the questions.

'You must have found something,' she mumbled, in response to a question about her neighbours. 'In the car. Rick's car. Are you sure?'

Natalie wanted to reach out and hug her. Would she feel that if Tiphanie was not genuine? But there was something else in her manner too. Something that reminded her of Georgia. She stared through the screen and tried to pinpoint it. She replayed in her head Tiphanie's initial disclosure about the car; the tone and expression had been uncannily like Georgia's when she had talked about the bunny cards. A superficial sweetness with an underlying wariness? Natalie felt herself go cold all over. Was Tiphanie still lying? If so, what about? Why was she so sure they would find something?

Still. Natalie thought of how long it had taken Amber to finally tell her everything. Of the twenty years Lee had served rather than face the shame of what she had allowed Cliff to do to Georgia.

Afterwards, she had another coffee with Damian.

'Can I ask you something? To help clarify things?'

'I'll help if I can.' Meaning he liked her but he wasn't going to tell her things he wasn't allowed to. Natalie figured he wouldn't have to.

'Take me through what happened on the day Chloe was reported missing.'

The call had come via triple zero at 11.23 a.m. Tiphanie had been hysterical, repeating 'My baby's gone' and little else. The operator traced the call and dispatched a police car, which arrived at 11.44 a.m. The police suggested she call Travis, which she did; he was at work. He had arrived at 12.32 p.m.

'How?'

Damian frowned. 'What do you mean how?'

'His car had been left broken down at his mate's place the night before.'

Damian looked at the police record. 'Must have been driven by his mate. He arrived accompanied by Rick Marshall. The guy we've questioned.'

Natalie nodded. 'So when did Travis pick his car up?'

Damian shrugged. 'No idea. Does it matter? He had it back by the time we impounded it. The mechanics confirmed they'd fixed it at Rick's the next day. He would have had plenty of time to get it cleaned.'

'Are you going to question him again?'

'He's here.'

'Can I watch?'

Damian hesitated but didn't come up with any reason why not.

'Can you humour me and ask about the car? Ask what was wrong with it?'

Damian paused. 'Does this have anything to do with the file you asked for?'

Natalie shifted uncomfortably. 'Not really.'

'You know I was one of the cops that turned up to that call. Bella-Kaye Hardy. It still haunts me. You don't forget the really nasty car crashes...or the kids.'

Natalie nodded.

'This has got a hold of you too, hasn't it?'

'I can't believe Travis doesn't have something to do with it. He's the common factor. Amber may have been the one to let the baby drop,' said Natalie, 'but he was sure as hell shaking that bough.'

She took the remainder of her coffee into the same cramped viewing room to watch Travis being interviewed.

'That bitch is lying to save her own skin. Must be fucking obvious,' Travis said sulkily.

Damian looked at Travis, giving nothing away.

Damian took him through his story again. No, he didn't take Chloe in the car to Rick's. Yes, he had sometimes in the past but there was no need to because she was asleep. Yes, he was sure. Tiphanie had been very sleepy and gone to bed. He'd gone to Rick and Alli's, as he often did. They drank, watched footy. He'd said goodbye and left them at the door. His car wouldn't start even though there had been no problems with it earlier. He'd gone back and banged on Rick's door. Rick had got the car keys and come out with him and seen the other guys off. He had tried his car one more time, then got into Rick's car and left.

'Rick's car was locked; he went back and got the keys and threw 'em at me.'

'Rick saw you leave?'

'Yeah.' So he would have had to come back to get Chloe's body if it had been in his own car.

'You drove Rick's car straight home?'

'Yeah,' said Travis drumming his fingers on the table top.

'You got home when?'

'I dunno. Takes about fifteen minutes, I guess.' Travis paused.

Damian asked about the car, only for her sake, Natalie was sure.

'I rang the mechanic first thing when I got to work. Why?'

'So they fixed it?'

'Yeah, cost two hundred and twenty fucking bucks. For nothing.'

'Nothing?'

'I didn't get it until the day after, with Chloe disappearing. They couldn't find anything wrong with it.'

Damian frowned. 'It just started up?'

'Yeah. Cunts still charged me. For turning the key.'

From behind the screen Natalie briefly caught Damian's glance as he looked up. He didn't like unexplained events any more than she did.

Tiphanie was in the waiting room when Natalie left. An older version of Tiphanie was sitting with her.

'You must be Kiara,' said Natalie, introducing herself.

Tiphanie looked surprised to see her. Natalie explained

that she had to come up to talk with the police.

'How are you?'

'Not great.' Tiphanie was in jeans and a shirt, perched uncomfortably on the edge of the chair. She looked very young. 'I can't believe—'

'Tiph would never have hurt Chloe.' Kiara sounded if she was forcing the upbeat tone.

'I just want to disappear somewhere,' said Tiphanie.

Kiara gave her a hug. 'When it's all over, Tiph. You'll see, it'll be fine and you can take that job and start again.'

'Job?' Natalie asked curiously. Tiphanie looked down at her hands.

'Of course she can't until the charges are dropped,' said Kiara, still forcing a smile. 'Mum isn't keen, but Dad and I think it would do her the world of good to get out of Welbury. Start again.'

Escape this town. Great idea. There was no hope here for Tiphanie. She'd be sucked into her mother's or the town's psychopathology and never emerge. It was what she should have done before she had Chloe. Now it might be too late.

'I want to have a service for Chloe,' Tiphanie said. 'I can't bear to...I mean I want to say goodbye.'

Kiara gave her another hug and they talked about the possibilities of a service and Natalie said she'd like to be there if it went ahead. Tiphanie looked ill and said she needed to lie down. But the police hadn't finished with her; Andie asked her to come back into the interview room.

Before Natalie left, she asked Kiara where the job offer had been from. The response was a surprise.

'Japan. Teaching English,' said Kiara. 'Like a private tutor. Tiph did really well in Japanese even though she had to do it by correspondence.'

302

Natalie was deep in thought when Damian interrupted to give her his mobile number.

'You free for a drink before you leave?'

'Ah, no, sorry. Got to go.' Natalie turned, but not before she caught the brief flash of disappointment. He was too nice for her.

Liam caught her on the phone just before she got back on the bike.

'Where are you?'

'Welbury.'

'Anything I should know about?'

'Damian was interviewing Travis and I wanted to know about the car breaking down.'

'Important?'

'Maybe.'

'I got your voicemail.'

He hadn't answered his phone the previous night and her message about the rabbit had been brief—curt even. 'When will you be back?'

'Two and a half hours.'

Liam said he'd meet her at her house, and hung up before she could reply.

'So the warning about meddling refers to Georgia?'

'I guess,' said Natalie, pacing. She couldn't sit still. She'd been over every part of her warehouse to be sure the worm hadn't been there, and found nothing. The absence of evidence hadn't convinced her.

'What about your hospital file? Why would I be interested in it?' Liam hadn't—yet—received anything.

'He's just playing with my head. To make me think he

knows things.' She thought of the pile of case notes she had burned, that she didn't ever want Liam to see. Unspoken between them sat the possibility of the video being sent to Lauren.

Liam let it go. 'You need to tell me more about him and his wife.'

Georgia had yet to go to trial. Natalie was professionally bound not to discuss details of a patient's therapy with anyone, let alone someone likely to be prosecuting them. But she wanted her stalker caught.

'Could Georgia and Paul be involved in the paedophile ring together?' asked Liam. He sounded frustrated.

Natalie shrugged. 'I don't know. But she hasn't said anything that would make me think that.'

'If Latimer is my Mr Big, he's damned good at hiding his tracks. More likely, he's just a member of the group. But that's still potentially very useful to us.'

'Natalie took a breath. 'The rabbit might have been a reference to *Fatal Attraction*. From Lauren. She could easily access hospital records.'

'Lauren?' Liam stiffened. 'She might nail one of us to the fence, but not a rabbit. And nobody's going to draw that logo randomly. It's not Lauren.'

'Okay, so Paul then I guess,' said Natalie. 'Initially he was just playing, maybe trying to get me so on edge that when he asked me to stop seeing Georgia I would. When he found out about my connection to you, I guess, that was when he really freaked. The video was meant to drive a wedge between us. But now...'

'Sending Lauren the video might be the next step in his strategy given he's now mentioned me.' The corner of Liam's eye twitched.

'You said you don't have enough cause to question him, but I do. Maybe it's time for Paul and me to talk.'

They had the quick urgent sex of distraction. Natalie willed herself to be in the moment.

As she watched him leave down the staircase from her bedroom, she hated that she had felt safer with him there, hated that she even wished he could be around for practical things too. There were little jobs she never got around to that it would be nice to share; the window that wouldn't open, the door hinge that squeaked and the mess from the tiles that crashed regularly off her neighbour's roof.

She stopped herself. She was wanting too much.

Jessie was patently nervous, barely holding it together. At least she had turned up.

'Have you had more memories? More nightmares?'

Jessie nodded.

'Try not to worry too much about what's real and what isn't. Your mind has blanked bits out, substituted things. Just talk about what you see.'

Jessie held her black box, lid closed, and stared out of the window. Natalie watched the flickering expressions of pain and remembered what it was like to be lost and alone. She had to trust Jessie to do the hard work. All she could do as a therapist was guide her; help her to access whatever resilience she had.

Jessie was no longer a child: the healing had to help the adult part of her reconcile all that had occurred in her childhood, and make up for the unconditional love and safe haven that she had never had.

'Did he love me?'

The question jolted Natalie. 'Love can mean different things to different people.'

'Did he?'

Natalie wasn't sure how to answer. Who was 'he'? Her father? Probably. He had also loved the feeling of power and perhaps of sexual gratification as well. But he had never loved or valued Jessie as a person in the way a child needed and deserved. Truth was going to be the best answer.

'Your father?'

Jessie gripped the box.

'Abuse isn't a way of showing love.'

Jessie bit her lip. 'None of this, these feelings, make sense. I just don't know what to do with them.'

'Give yourself time.'

Jessie nodded. She opened her box and retrieved another drawing, an anime character. It looked a little like her arm tattoo except in red; thick and reminiscent of blood.

'Who is it Jessie?'

'Aoi Sakuraba; she loved Kaoru.'

'You're going to have to explain that.'

Jessie's shrug said 'no point'.

So who was Kaoru in her childhood?

'Why draw her now?' And why in blood red?

Jessie picked up the picture and with both hands, scrunched and threw it across the room. 'Just fantasy.'

'Do you want to put it back in your box?'

Jessie thought for a moment, collected the ball of paper and did as Natalie suggested. Natalie found her eyes drawn to the tattoos on one shoulder, above the one she imagined to be Aoi Sakuraba, in the dense area where another had been partially and inexpertly removed.

'What was the tattoo there?' asked Natalie, pointing.

Jessie looked at her. Wondering. A child looking to a parent for guidance. Natalie was acutely aware of her responsibility. In an instant Jessie's expression changed. 'You watched it didn't you?' she said loudly. Without saying anything more, she turned and left, slamming the door behind her.

Natalie stared after her. She went to the window. Jessie strode out the front door, banging it behind her, and headed towards the car park. Natalie saw a car door open and a man step out: Kyle. He put his arm around Jessie and, as he ushered her into the car, turned around, looking back towards the house and directly at Natalie. She willed herself not to move, meeting the stare and reading in it all the malice that was intended.

When Natalie turned back to her desk, she saw that Jessie had left her box behind.

She pulled out the USB Beverley had given her and looked at it. She thought about the pathology between Georgia and Paul. She remembered how Amber had sacrificed herself for Travis and thought about how victims and their mothers so often protected their abusers. She thought of Jessie and her abuser, and, finally, of Tiphanie.

'I was in *Who Weekly*,' Georgia said. 'They had a picture.'

'A picture of you?'

'What? Yes, that too.' Georgia wasn't looking at Natalie as she picked at the chipped nail polish on her thumb.

'So who else did they have photos of?'

Georgia pulled her bag into her lap. She unfolded a few ripped-out pages. 'Look.'

The picture was of Miranda, the daughter she hadn't seen in nine months. It was not a posed shot. Paul was holding his daughter, trying to shield her from the camera.

'Tell me about Paul before he met you.' Natalie temporarily abandoned the therapeutic process. She needed information if she was going to deal with the worm and it would give her a better understanding of Georgia's enmeshment with him.

'What do you mean?'

'Had he had other girlfriends?'

'Nothing serious.'

'Any trouble with the police? Trouble at school?'

'What do you mean?'

Natalie shrugged, watching Georgia thinking. She seemed to be weighing her answer, choosing her words.

'He didn't have many friends. I thought that was…all we needed was each other. Then he was working and I had the children. We didn't go out much.'

'What about his trips? Was he travelling with people?'

'He met people, did deals. I'm sure he never had an affair, if that's what you mean.'

Natalie hadn't meant this. Georgia was good at picking up cues and giving what she thought you wanted. She was also adept at avoiding the questions she didn't want to, or couldn't, answer.

Lee Draper had painted Paul as caring and balanced, but she'd only seen the side he had presented to her, and if Georgia's father, Cliff, was representative of Lee's taste in men, she was probably not a good judge. Virginia hadn't mentioned meeting him. After the session, Natalie rang her.

'Paul?' asked Virginia. 'We went to the wedding of course. Vernon gave her away. She wanted everything to be right.'

'Before that?'

'After she started nursing we didn't see her much, and you know later she cut us off. We had dinner with them once. Paul was quiet. Georgia wanted to be the centre of attention and Paul seemed to be happy with that. We were just pleased she'd found someone.'

Natalie really had to meet him. His answering service picked up.

'Mr Latimer, this is Dr King. We spoke at the Halfpenny. I was perhaps a little hasty.' It had been Liam's suggestion to say this. 'I would very much like to hear your side of the

309

story if you're prepared to talk to me.' She left her mobile number.

Tiphanie was booked in to see her. Both she and her father looked like they hadn't slept in days.

Tiphanie paced the room, not speaking. Finally, she sat down on the edge of the chair.

'I'm your patient, right?'

Natalie nodded.

'So it's not like when I was in Yarra Bend? I'm not being assessed?'

'Yes and no. But my notes can be subpoenaed and used in court.' She held her pen up for a moment then purposefully laid it on the desk.

Tiphanie took a breath and looked straight at Natalie. 'Can you find a way to have the police ask if Rick or Allison removed a rug—like a blanket—from their car? He would have had to wrap...her up. It was cold.'

Only if she had still been alive.

Paul rang back. He was in Melbourne and could see her at 6.30 p.m. Liam arrived an hour earlier.

'This office is all yours,' she told him. She parked him next to door to where she'd be seeing Paul. At 6.25 p.m., both with mobiles in hand, she phoned him. With the communication link established she went to her own office and put her phone on the desk behind the stack of files.

Natalie recognised Paul immediately. He was less out of place than at the Halfpenny, but just as awkward.

'Thank you for coming,' said Natalie as they sat down. Her smile felt taut.

'Sure.' Paul shifted in his seat. 'Does Georgia know

you're seeing me?'

'She knows I tried to earlier.'

'So she really thinks I'm still on her side.'

'I'm not sure I'd say that.'

'What do you want to know?' Paul sounded weary. He looked harmless, but then so did most serial killers. Most murderers were weak rather than scary, but psychopaths were different. Paul might well be one.

'Your side of the story. Not so much about things related to the case but rather what Georgia was like. Why you got together.'

'I liked her, she was fun, confident.' Paul ran his hand through his hair. 'I was at a party with a mate and she and a girlfriend just started chatting to us. I thought they both liked him, but turned out Georgia fancied me. I just let it happen.' He shrugged his shoulders. 'I never saw any of this coming. Idiot bloke I guess.'

'Any girlfriends before her?'

'Isn't this about Georgia?'

'I want to know how her take on you tallies against reality.'

Paul shrugged. 'One girlfriend that was keener than I was. Didn't go anywhere. I was twenty-five when I got together with Georgia, and I have to say I was a bit of a nerd. But we both wanted kids.'

'What did you think of her parents?'

'I thought it was a bit strange she wanted to cut Virginia and Vernon off, but Virginia seemed pretty cold. I guess I thought it was her choice.'

If he was acting, he was doing a good job, but then Georgia was the accused, he the hard-done-by loving father and husband. All he had to do was play innocent.

'You took Olivia to see Lee.'

Paul looked surprised. In his look was a flicker of something else. 'Yes, I did. Lee is my children's grandmother whatever she did. I don't know, I just thought Georgia was missing something in her life. She'd cut her mother off for good reason of course. But I thought if I checked her out and found she was, well, human, Georgia might come around.'

'But she never did.'

'No. She had very firm ideas. I suppose that was the first time I saw the other side of her. On the subject of Lee, she couldn't be moved.'

Natalie let him talk more, sensing a fascination with Lee. Because she was his wife's mother—and a murderer?

Natalie tried to picture him as a monster, recalling a paedophile she had interviewed early in her career. He had genuinely convinced himself that he loved the little girls and that his initiating them into womanhood was as lovely for them as it had been for him. Georgia had always maintained Paul 'loved' his girls.

'Did you love her?'

'Yes,' said Paul. 'Stupidly and blindly it seems, but yes I loved her.'

'So much so that you still send her cards?'

Paul stared at her. 'What are you talking about?'

'The bunny cards.'

Paul shook his head. 'I have no idea what you mean.'

Natalie bit her lip. She probably shouldn't reveal any more.

'Did you have a pet name for her?'

'Not really. Georgy Girl occasionally. I sang that to her once. Badly.'

'Did your children ever have a toy rabbit?'

'Hell, I don't know. They had tons of stuffed toys. We got rid of them all after Olivia died.' He took a breath and looked down.

'What about Jonah?'

'We should never have had him. When we threw the toys out, I decided that we just weren't meant to be parents, that I couldn't handle the pain.'

'Then Georgia got pregnant again.'

'Hard to know how, it wasn't like we were having sex very often,' he said. 'When it was a boy I thought, well maybe this will be different. But—'

'So if you two weren't having sex much, did you find a substitute? Affairs? Porn?'

'No,' said Paul. If he was surprised by the question he didn't show it. 'I didn't have the energy for anything.'

'What about Miranda?'

There was a long silence. 'Georgia told me she was on the pill. She...worked hard on me, must have known the time was right.' He put his head in his hands.

Natalie waited.

'I started to have suspicions. I don't know what made me look at her Facebook page. I'm not into Facebook myself. I knew she put photos of the children there and I didn't want to revisit any of it. It was too hard.'

'So why did you look?'

Paul's gaze was steady. 'I've thought a lot about this and it doesn't make sense. Maybe because I knew about Lee? Lee isn't a monster, she's an ordinary person, yet she killed her husband. Maybe I was subconsciously worried, I honestly don't know. It was one look. Just one. It made me feel cold inside. A window into her soul is the way I've come to think of it.'

'It wasn't you that alerted the police.' One of her other Facebook 'friends' had.

Paul shifted in his chair. 'I probably would have eventually, because of Miranda. I was still processing it. Georgia was my wife.'

'So how do you understand what happened now?'

'Georgia is evil, pure and simple. Don't know if it's the genes or what happened after she was born, but she's evil.'

Natalie didn't believe in evil. People were complex products of their genes and experiences. Perhaps too many of Georgia's influences had been bad ones with nothing to compensate. Personal integrity came from a balance of these influences; you weren't born with it.

'Actually Mr Latimer, I'm not sure it's that simple. All of what you've been telling me is very interesting, but I'm really struggling with one thing.'

Paul looked at her blankly.

'Why you've been sending me notes and videos and having someone break into my house,' said Natalie, now coldly in control. She watched Paul struggle with his emotions. She searched in his face for lies, or the psychopathic self-confidence, but saw neither. There was just a sense of him wanting to please, to be liked, wanting all of this to be over. A normal response from someone in his position or the carefully constructed veneer of the psychopath who was a master at reading what the other person wanted?

'Look, you mentioned something about notes last time you saw me at the pub and it's really the reason I said I'd come.' Paul looked uncomfortable. 'Can I go back to the start? My lawyer found out you were seeing Georgia and he was worried you were a bit of an anti-man crusader. I wanted to know all I could about you.'

That solved the timing issue. His conversation with the lawyer could have been before the first letter.

'Meaning you checked me out.'

'Yes. You have to understand...' He was struggling for the right words. 'It's my daughter I have to think about.' He looked at Natalie. 'She can't ever see Georgia. She really is a monster.'

He was convincing. Very.

'So what was finding out about me going to achieve?'

Paul shrugged apologetically. 'It's your profession that got her out on bail.' There was a hint of anger in his tone. 'When you rang me the first time...I wanted to check you out before I agreed to see you. I hired someone. He gave me a list of cases you'd been to court with and it seemed to me that you believed in what you were doing. I thought maybe I could talk to you—convince you that she's guilty. That you needed to protect my daughter.'

'I'm Georgia's psychiatrist, not her jury,' said Natalie. She paused. 'The notes and the surveillance video were also just to help convince me?'

Paul looked puzzled. 'Why would he do that?'

'What about the dead rabbit?'

Now Paul gaped. 'What rabbit?' There was silence as Paul shook his head. Then he moaned, shaking his head. 'You asked me if I sent cards to Georgia?'

'Yes.'

'Well I didn't. Which means she really is totally fucked.'

Natalie stared at Paul, taking in the implication of what he was saying. Could Georgia be behind it all?

'Bunny cards. Like this one.' She showed him her photocopy.

Paul looked exhausted. There was no reaction.

'What did you think about having sex with someone who mutilates her genitals?' asked Natalie abruptly.

If she hadn't been looking she wouldn't have seen it, but for one microsecond she saw a different Paul, instantly replaced by the one who now frowned in bafflement.

'Whatever do you mean?'

'She takes a knife to her labia, mostly. Ever have oral sex with her?'

He shuddered. 'She must have started that after we separated.'

'We might have to wait for court to decide that.' The GP report had only one relevant line, easily missed. Years earlier the scars had been noted when Georgia had a postnatal check after Genevieve. They had been fresh then and were explained away. The later obstetric records had mostly not noted it, except for one record of the suturing of her episiotomy, which had mentioned 'unusual' scar tissue.

Liam came into her office as soon as Paul had left. 'He was very plausible.'

'I agree,' said Natalie. 'Very. But he lied. I caught him out on the genital mutilation. He wasn't ready for it and denied it before he could think it through. And he did it well.'

'That might have been for any number of reasons. Not comfortable talking about his sex life. Maybe they did it in the dark.'

'I think it's a male on the security camera tape, but not him. Paul's got broader shoulders.' Her intruder was more Travis's shape.

'So he hired someone? Or one of his paedophile mates?'

'Or,' said Natalie, 'it really isn't him.'

She replayed the interview in her mind after Liam left to play happy families again, but her mind kept taking her back to Travis. She rang Damian's mobile.

'Damian?'

'Nothing new, I'm afraid.'

Natalie took a breath. 'Did you find a rug in Rick's car?'

'Rug?'

'It was cold. Chloe would have been wrapped up while she was alive. Which probably means her body still is. But maybe the rug or whatever was left in the car and Allison and Rick removed it.'

There was a long pause. 'Is this to do with those files you asked for?'

'In a round-about way.' It wasn't a complete lie.

There was another long silence. 'Okay,' Damian said.

'Damian?'

'Yes?'

'Can you find out if there are any toys missing?' The toys that Tiphanie had told her were Chloe's favourites.

'I'll let you know.'

There were new shadows in the laneway, dark places that seemed more ominous than before. Natalie parked her bike and, cricket bat in hand, searched a fifty metre radius. Nothing. Shutting the door, she pulled the chain across and rattled it to test just how strong it felt. Fair. It would hold up long enough for her to hear someone forcing the door.

She threw her bag on the sofa and walked around the kitchen and living area. The alarm hadn't gone off but she couldn't reassure herself he hadn't found a way in. Had anything been moved? Was there a trace of anyone other than her? His fingerprint on half-closed curtains—she had left them like that hadn't she? —or the drawer that wasn't quite closed? She steadied her breathing and picked up her laptop. Time to take her mind off her stalker.

She began with a Google search of Japanese cartoon characters. It took her a couple of spelling variations to find the series Ai Yori Aoshi, first out when Jessie would have been eight. As described, Aoi Sakuruba was sweet and loyal, with short black hair just like Jessie's—minus the dye job. It was Kaoru, the love interest, who grabbed Natalie's attention; because his parents never married, his life was difficult—particularly in taking over his father's empire. Her fantasies about her stepbrother Jay saving her as a young teenager?

Pulling out the USB she decided not to spend too much time thinking about the ethics. Jessie had given it to her and all but asked her to look before changing her mind. Declan wouldn't be happy, but looking at Jessie's files wasn't a reportable offence. What she did with them might be.

Beverley had copied a dozen folders over. Natalie moved them onto her computer. She did a search for video files. Family Album had several. She clicked onto one. Knowing what she was looking at, Natalie could make out the younger Jessie. She was skinny with short, dark messy hair. There was a look of innocence captured in one or two of the clips—in one she was holding her baby sister; in the other, opening Christmas presents. An older man, presumably her father, and a woman with too much makeup were watching. Jay must have been filming. She checked the other clips. No Jay, no Kyle.

The School Assignments folder didn't look promising as a title, but she opened it anyway. Two videos.

The first was of a teenager with light-coloured hair. He was a willowy adolescent with a few pimples and a winning, slightly self-conscious smile, telling the camera about who were the hot chicks at school. No glasses, but it could have been Jay. If so he had filled out a lot since then. Jay's features but more Kyle's frame. He named a few teachers and made it clear his testosterone was dominating his thoughts about them. Nothing explicit. He cupped his groin at one point but it was within the range of normal adolescent behaviour. It was only at the very end that Natalie's stomach churned. He winked at the camera and said: 'Of course I get to do anything I like to my very own chick.'

Was he referring to Jessie? Had her father confiscated the computer because of what he feared was on it rather than because it incriminated him?

The next clip was twenty minutes long. Camera steady, fixed, she figured, on a tripod. The two actors moved out of frame and there was no alteration in the angle or focal length. She forced herself to watch every minute of it, then went to the bathroom and threw up.

Afterwards she washed her medication down with a full glass of bourbon and slept, and managed to struggle through the next day somehow. That night, neither her stomach nor her head were thinking bourbon was a good option. Natalie knew she couldn't keep the feelings buried. She had to think about the video, and eventually talk about it. Maybe with Declan, but it was Liam she wanted to ring. Perhaps because he had seen these things before. Maybe just because she needed a hug.

But before she could show Liam the video, she had to talk to Jessie. She found herself back in the Tiphanie–Amber dilemma. What she had seen needed to be in the hands of the police—whether or not Jessie was currently being abused, and whether or not she agreed. But the current or ongoing risks weren't clear. Ethically Natalie needed to maintain confidentiality, unless Jessie gave permission or there was a current risk of harm to others.

A wave of nausea gripped her stomach and she looked at the bourbon. *No.* She needed a clear head. Whatever shit she had been through in her past was nothing like what Jessie had been subjected to. She would be eternally grateful to Eoin not only for sharing his soul but ensuring that when they lost their virginity together it had been a normal human experience. Awkward and funny and finally a triumphant soaring into the adult world. Even Eoin's death, followed by the year in rehab and all the tensions with her mother, hadn't changed that. The adversity had made her stronger. And she needed that strength now, for Jessie.

Tiphanie and Georgia popped into her head again. Why? Natalie closed her eyes and pictured the girl in the video. Jessie. Sweet, giggling Jessie, who initially had been cooperative. A pre-teen, no more than twelve, breasts little more than tiny buds, with sexual feelings that were starting to awaken. Sometimes girls of that age thought they knew it all, hid their vulnerability. Jessie's innocence had been on full display. She was still essentially a child who had needed her father to tell her she was beautiful when she went on her first date, who needed to swoon over a safe, pretty boy at a distance, who needed time to be emotionally ready for the physical eventuality.

The physical acts themselves were nothing two adults wouldn't do in a consensual relationship. Penetrative vaginal sex, anal and oral sex. But the sinews in the perpetrators arm were taut as he forced Jessie's head over his cock and the fear in her eyes raw. Her terror when he entered her from behind, contrasted with his apparent immense satisfaction and disregard for the young girl, was stark.

Natalie started dry retching. Then she did something she hadn't done since her eighteenth birthday. She cried.

She didn't check herself. There was no one to know. Then she watched the video again. But when she finally went to bed, she still hadn't been able to put to rest a niggling sense that there was something she had missed.

'I know you think I shouldn't be looking for truth,' said Natalie. 'But right now I'm pretty sure that at least two people and maybe more are lying to me.'

'You do work in forensic,' Declan pointed out. 'Doesn't everyone say they're innocent?'

'Exactly.' Natalie was wandering around his office. 'Simplest explanations are usually best, right?' she added, more to herself.

'If you're talking about behaviour, then yes. People are complicated but their actions are usually self-serving and rarely thought through. And most of them are not good liars.'

Which was why they got caught: poorly equipped people making bad choices. Psychopaths, who manipulated and lied as a matter of course, had a chance of getting away with it. Liam would say it was better than incarcerating the innocent.

Natalie paused to look at a new bust Declan had put up on the mantelpiece; she wasn't sure who it was and didn't want to show her ignorance. She caught her reflection in the mirror. Could she lie too? Well enough to fool Declan and the police? If Declan worked out what she was doing, would he put it down to her bipolar or to poor judgment? He'd have to report her to the Medical Board either way.

Declan's forehead wrinkled into deep crevices as he watched her. She had no doubt he understood what drove her—some of the time; she was also pretty sure he had no idea what she was capable of.

Declan spoke to the back of her head. 'If you're trying to pick the lies, think about motive. People, even if they're not psychopaths, look after themselves.'

'Which means everyone is lying.' Natalie's laugh felt harsh in her throat.

'Then bring in your personality assessment. The psychopaths will lie more convincingly: remember they routinely pass lie detector tests. But they'll lie over even small things, which is where you may pick them up. Why they are late, how they got the stain on their shirt. Whether they masturbate.'

Declan laughed and added, 'If they say they don't you can be sure they're lying.'

Natalie was conscious that Declan had made his quip calculatedly but couldn't manage the groan that would have been her normal reaction.

Declan continued. 'In the person without frank psychopathy, emotions will ultimately show through. Particularly if you catch them unawares on the big things.' Travis.

She thought of some of the harder interviews she had done. The trouble wasn't that there were no emotions on display, it was deciding whether the emotions were a genuine response to the patient's situation or an attempt to manipulate the therapist. Georgia and Paul. Amber and

Travis. Tiphanie and Travis. All with complex motivations, some but not all self-serving.

'What if I decide they are lying? I have a responsibility to my patients, of course. But don't I have a responsibility to society as well?'

'If you're called to court, yes. Then you give your truth, whole truth and nothing but the truth. To the best of your professional judgment. Making it clear that's all it is.'

In Amber's case there had been no chance to tell the whole truth.

'Is this the missing child case?'

'Among others.'

Declan removed his reading glasses. 'Tiphanie's charges haven't been dropped?'

'No,' said Natalie.

'Even though Travis probably did it?'

'Murdered his child? Yes.' She thought about the wet clothes, the messy kitchen, Amber's scalded face. Oh yes, he murdered his child all right. Then she froze. *Travis.* She stared at Declan. 'You know.'

'Of course I do,' said Declan. 'I had hoped you would tell me.'

'I...I haven't interviewed Travis, just Tiphanie.'

'You knew you were too close to this case, too much baggage from Amber.'

'Yes, but that also gave me motivation to get it right this time.'

'Motivation and bias.'

'He did it!'

'It doesn't matter, Natalie.' Declan's voice was hard. 'I have to be able to trust you, and your patients have to know you are balanced.'

'I didn't lie, but I'm sorry.' She looked involuntarily at her handbag, where her USB stick was waiting for her to decide what to do about it.

'You're too close to this, Natalie.'

Even if he was right, it was too late now. Her mind was more focused. No matter what Declan said. Sometimes confidentiality wasn't the highest value.

The prison guards were more annoying than usual. She recognised one of them as Jen from the earlier visit. Natalie steeled herself and vowed to smile and not lose her temper. Yes, she should have rung. No, she wasn't Hannah Peterson's shrink. She wanted to see her anyway. Natalie waited.

It was nearly two hours before she sat down with Hannah in the empty visitors' area.

'Is there a problem with Jessie?' Hannah looked worried, lighting up a cigarette.

'No, well no more than usual,' said Natalie. 'We're talking about those nightmares though.'

Hannah nodded. 'I figured from last time I spoke with Jessie. You saw whatever that arsehole filmed?'

Natalie hesitated. 'I'd like her to give it to the police.'

Hannah looked at her grimly. 'I know people who might deal with him better.'

Tempting. Maybe the backup plan.

'That isn't why I'm here.'

Hannah drew on her cigarette.

'Remember I asked you about the paedophile network. The one that used pink bunny rabbits to entice the children?'

Hannah crossed her arms, dropping ash over her jeans.

'I know you know something.' Natalie had been manic

when she'd last seen Hannah; she hoped she had read her right. 'I need you to tell me.'

'Why?'

Natalie chose her words carefully. 'Because more than one person's life is involved here.'

'It won't hurt Jessie?'

'The paedophile ring is going to be busted anyway. I don't know what videos are out there, exactly what will come out or how it will affect her.' Natalie paused. 'Whatever happens, I can help her work through it.'

Hannah nodded and leaned forward. 'I won't stand up in court and say this.'

'That's okay. This is just for me.'

'One of the other women that was here. Her man was into little girls.'

Natalie nodded. It was one of several hypotheses she needed to test. 'The pink bunny rabbit?'

'She mentioned it. That's all.'

'Did he have the pink rabbits,' asked Natalie, 'or were they just like...logos. In videos?'

Hannah frowned. 'Not sure. Never asked really. This sick shit isn't my thing. Men aren't my thing.'

Natalie nodded, deep in thought. 'Hannah,' she said slowly, 'in Jessie's nightmares, did she ever mention a rabbit?'

'Jessie never like stuffed toys. She was into Japanese cartoons.' Hannah flicked her cigarette end towards the wardens. They weren't looking.

'Were they in her nightmares?'

'Not that I recall. It was pretty weird. She had a tattoo, kind of rabbits. She kept trying to cut it out herself. I made her get it removed. They stuffed it up and had to put another over the top.'

Natalie stared. Jessie's shoulder. *Fuck.* She could almost make it out in her memory. Jessie hadn't mentioned a rabbit in therapy. Ever. Nor had there been one in the video of her. Natalie figured it had started later. Maybe something Jessie had drawn for him and he'd fetishised it. It was an indicator that this early experience had been formative for him in the development of his sexual pathology. Encapsulated in the child-adult form of a rabbit.

'Who mentioned the pink bunny?'

'One of yours,' said Hannah. 'She had the rabbit tattoo as well.' She pulled out another cigarette and lit it off the previous one, inhaling and watching the smoke she blew into the air dissipate before she continued. 'Her old man got her young. Celeste.'

'Do you know if Celeste's brother was involved too?'

'No idea.'

Natalie took a breath. Now to test her next hypothesis. 'Did other women here listen to this story?'

Hannah snorted. 'Listen? We were cheering her on. You know she cut his dick off, right? Believe me, you want to get one of them sick fucks sorted out, just give me the word. We'll all be fighting over which one of us does it.' She dropped her butt and ground it under her heel, smearing ash over the concrete. 'Jessie's at least died.'

'Did she ever tell you it was her father?'

'Sure.' Hannah stopped. 'Actually I don't know. Her dreams never had any real person in them. I just presumed, I guess.'

'When you were all cheering,' said Natalie, 'what about those women that are segregated? Were they there?'

Hannah frowned. 'Some do-gooder group was here, they got us thinking about our pasts. Like that would help.'

She laughed. 'Sorry. It got a bit out of control. But yes, they had us all in together with extra screws to keep an eye on the special inmates.'

'Hannah,' Natalie asked. 'Why did Jessie come to see me?'

'I pushed her to. She wasn't doing well.'

'Why me?'

'Amber Hardy thinks you're God's gift to the underdog. The doc here thinks you get over-involved.' She grinned. 'Sounded like a good thing to me. We saw you take out the prosecutor on TV.'

Great. 'So, not Georgia?' Natalie was talking more to herself than Hannah. Maybe this was why Georgia had wanted to see her too: at Amber's recommendation. They would have been in the same unit. Amber had thought she was a hero for tackling Travis. Had Georgia thought she would do the same to Paul, only inside the courtroom?

Natalie squeezed Hannah's shoulder in farewell and was halfway to the door when she turned back. 'One last question.' Hannah hadn't moved, head down picking at her fingernails. 'How did the police catch you?'

Hannah frowned. 'No idea. Someone dobbed me in. The guy with me swears it wasn't him and he certainly didn't get any cosy deal. Longer sentence than me.'

'Jessie knew about...what you'd done?'

'No fucking way would she lag.' Hannah stood up abruptly.

'No,' agreed Natalie. 'She wouldn't.'

Natalie opened the locker to retrieve her belongings. She felt she was close to making sense of more than just Jessie's case, but the pieces of the puzzle wouldn't quite fit. She had resisted the idea that her cases were linked but the evidence was accumulating. It wasn't coincidence: they were tied together through the prison and Yarra Bend, through the patients' common histories of abuse that had made them vulnerable to mental illness, and to her through her specialisation and appearance on the infanticide documentary.

The guards weren't paying her any attention; she could hear them talking about a reality TV show. She tapped on the window. Jen rolled her eyes and let the other woman open it.

'Did you know Georgia Latimer when she was here?' she asked the guard that wasn't Jen.

'Sure. Model little psychopath.'

'She was studying, wasn't she?'

'Yeah.' The guard didn't sound overly impressed. 'Regular bookworm.'

'Is there a record of what she studied?'

'Yeah. Want to look?'

'Yes. And—'

The prison guard looked at her expectantly.

'Do you keep visitor records?'

Natalie jotted down some notes about Georgia's studies. But it was the visitor records that shook her.

D amian texted Natalie to say there was going to be a service for Chloe on Thursday afternoon. Tiphanie wanted to say goodbye, even though, without a body, it would be a long time before Chloe could be declared dead.

Natalie put in a half day with her ward patients, then headed southeast. The September day was windy, with intermittent rain pelting her visor. It fitted the occasion.

The church was full, with people standing at the back and along the sides. A huge photo of Chloe was propped on a chair at the front, soft toys surrounding it. She looked angelic. And the picture alone would have been enough to reduce everyone to tears, without Eric Clapton's 'Tears in Heaven' playing in the background.

Natalie recognised more people than she thought she would. Travis was with his family, standing awkwardly apart from Tiphanie and hers. There were a number of police, Damian and Andie included.

Damian spotted her and strolled over. 'You were right. Again.'

Natalie willed herself to look him in the eye. 'A blanket?'

Damian nodded. 'Allison was quite upfront. The blanket

was usually in the car. She'd brought it inside because her heating wasn't working.'

'And?'

'Forensics have identified blood. Is it going to be Chloe's?'

'I don't know,' said Natalie.

'You asked me about the toys too. Neither were missing.'

'Did you see them?'

'Yes.' He tipped his head. 'Tiphanie has them up there with the photos. What's this about, Natalie?'

Natalie looked across the heads to where she had seen the soft toys. Flanking the photo chair was a big pink and white rabbit that had fallen on its side and a version of Big Bird that would have been bigger than Chloe. 'I just wondered why they hadn't been with her that night; they were her favourites. But seems like they were too big, not the take-to-bed type of soft toys.'

Tiphanie and her family were sitting in the front row. She and Kiara gave awkward but touching eulogies. Jim and Sandra sat with a young man in a wheelchair, presumably Tiphanie's brother William. Amber kept towards the back with her brother Cam and his wife. Natalie saw no sign of Amber's mother; babysitting, presumably.

At the end of the ceremony, most of the mourners headed towards Tiphanie. Cam spoke with his sister and left. Amber looked unsure of what she should do. Natalie went up to her.

'She won't blame you,' she said.

'No, I know.' Amber replied. 'I just...Well it's an awful time and I don't want to intrude.'

'You appreciated your friends' support,' Natalie said. 'Are Rick and Allison here today?'

Amber seemed to know who she was talking about. She looked around and pointed to a couple heading out the door.

'Go wish her the best,' Natalie suggested, and as Amber went in one direction she went in the other, following Rick and Allison.

'I'm curious,' said Natalie after introducing herself. 'Do you have any idea what was wrong with Travis's car?'

Rick shrugged his shoulders. 'Would have looked at the time if I hadn't been smashed. Carport light wasn't working, which didn't help. Loose battery lead, I'd guess. Electrics were dead when Travis tried it.'

Natalie nodded. This much mechanics she could manage. 'Why didn't you drive him home, rather than let him borrow it?'

'No fucking way.' It was Allison who spoke this time. 'Next time he gets caught drink driving he goes to gaol.'

Rick looked sheepish.

Natalie made it back inside just in time to see Amber squeeze Tiphanie's hand and leave.

Natalie arrived home exhausted. Her mind hadn't let up for a second during the long journey but she had been unable to make sense of the recurring thoughts. Later, she blamed fatigue for her inattention. She was normally vigilant, but on this night she just wanted to grab a beer, sit on her terrace and space out watching the sunset.

Bob dive-bombed her. Natalie swiped at him and he retired to the rafter and refused to come upstairs. Natalie stared at him, her hand trembling on the banister. *Shit*, this stalker had her so on edge she was relying on a cockatoo instead of her expensive security system. She left the door up into the kitchen open. She figured loneliness and hunger would get the better of him.

She threw her bag on the sofa and took a beer from the

fridge, aware suddenly of how quiet it was. Something was different. She walked slowly around the room. No television turned on. Fridge empty as always. She wasn't obsessional enough to notice if he had switched anything around. Had he just walked through, touching things? Surely he couldn't have found a way of dismantling the alarm? Even if he had, her cameras would have caught him, maybe with a better angle this time. She walked over to the security unit and played the tapes. Nothing. She was letting this bastard get to her.

Natalie tightened her grip on the beer, aware from the churn of her stomach that instinct hadn't been subdued by her self-talk. She took a deep breath and cautiously went up the stairs to the deck. Stopped on the top step and looked ahead. More of the neighbour's tiles had landed on her patio. Because he had come in by the roof again? Would he have known that there was a second security unit, one in her bedroom? She felt a surge of hope. Maybe he'd missed it and she'd have captured him on it, and would finally get a good look at him.

She turned to go in and check.

He grabbed her from behind and pulled hard. Must have been hiding behind the outside door from the kitchen and followed her up the stairs. Spinning out of his grip, she slammed hard into the wall, the stubbie in her hand flying and spewing beer across the patio. He stepped towards her, stooping down to her level. A thought flashed through her mind almost as fast as the pain. In the end, all her intelligence and fitness were worth nothing. Brawn was going to win without her ever having a chance.

'Bitch,' he whispered through the balaclava that covered his head. His full weight was against her, the brickwork rough against her face as she turned away from him. 'I warned you.'

Natalie steeled herself. He was going to have to move; she just needed to be ready. He did move, but too quickly. He bunched up the front of her leather jacket and sent her sprawling across the patio again, into the other sidewall. She barely noticed the pain that shot through her right shoulder, her mind racing, trying to push down the rising panic. She staggered up, letting him think she was as weak as she felt, while she focused on her strength. She might only have one chance and every blow would weaken her further. As he stepped towards her she spun around on her left leg, lifted her right foot to knee height, and with all the power she could muster, lashed out in the groin kick she had practised a thousand times.

She missed. She connected with his upper thigh, but he was too slow to catch her leg and pull her over. It told her an important bit of information. He was relying on size, not skill. She felt a small ray of hope, and concentrated on the first and most important lesson of self-defence: getting out whatever way she could.

She made it to the second stair but he was right behind her. He grasped a full handful of hair and pulled and her scream echoed across the rooftops. She fell and the man pulled her backwards, dragging her across the patio, through the door into her bedroom, the pain in her head so intense she wondered whether her scalp was being ripped off. She kept screaming. The patio door was open and maybe someone would hear. Breathing heavily, he kicked her hard and she heard a rib crack before the pain caught up and tore through her.

'You took a copy, didn't you? Did you really think I

wouldn't know?' Did she know the voice? Maybe. Not Paul Latimer, not Travis Hardy. Full set of teeth, not Celeste's brother. He lashed out again, and Natalie had just enough time to move to protect her injured side, his foot connecting this time with her pelvis. Painful, but the bone, reinforced with metal from her bike accident, was solid enough to take it. She rolled over groaning, playing for time. He had no intention of leaving her alive after this encounter. If she survived it would only be because she saved herself.

'It's in my bag,' she managed to say. 'Downstairs.' She lay still, hoping he wouldn't notice her right arm edging below the bed where she'd stashed the cricket bat.

'You thought you'd take her away from me didn't you? The girls are mine.' *They.* Jessie and all the others he had filmed and abused. Or Jessie and the video he needed to get back.

'You're right,' said Natalie. 'She's never given you up.' Her fingers were only millimetres from the bat when he leaned down and pulled her up, throwing her on the bed as if she were a doll. She saw his eyes glistening behind the mask and knew he was evaluating her. A wave of fear rippled through her; she willed herself to glare back angrily as she thought furiously about her next move.

'I like them younger than you,' he said coldly. 'But at least you're small. I might just pretend. I rather like the idea of fucking her shrink.'

The predatory stalker, the psychopath that had no regard for anyone other than himself. Intellectually she had always known this was the most likely.

'The feeling, dickhead,' said Natalie, as her foot aimed again at his weakest point, 'is not mutual.'

Again she didn't connect, but in pulling back to protect

himself he gave her the split second she needed to roll over, off the bed, and grab the bat. He stepped towards her then stopped, grinning.

'I'll make you regret that.'

'You? You're not good enough.'

She'd practised the manoeuvre in one form or another countless times against her bag in the garage. This opponent was bigger, heavier and intent on causing injury. It took every ounce of her mental energy to sound calm. 'You never were good enough were you? It must have been a disappointment for your mother.'

His hesitation was all she needed. He caught the bat as she swung it, but this time her foot smashed hard into his balls. She didn't wait to see how much pain it caused. She was already running before he'd let out a groan.

Straight down the stairs, into the kitchen, grabbing a knife out of the block as she went past. Still running, she took the passage that crossed over the road, hoping her assailant would keep heading down to the garage. He was right behind and would have grabbed her if it hadn't been for Bob, swooping from above. As Natalie raced to the electronic door and turned to push the button to close it behind her, she saw a flurry of feathers as Bob channelled his inner eagle and took on her assailant with beak and claws.

The door slammed behind her and she kept running.

From the safety of the Halfpenny bar she called Liam and then the police. Vince watched grimly as the police interviewed her. He insisted on returning to the warehouse with them. The assailant was gone. So was her bag, and Bob, who had escaped either through the open door to the balcony or the garage door her attacker had left open. There were feathers all over the floor. She hoped he wasn't seriously injured and that he would enjoy his freedom. She'd miss him.

'You still have no idea who it was?' asked Senior Constable Hudson, clearly frustrated.

'No,' lied Natalie.

Liam looked at her hard. She shook her head and looked away. She wouldn't spend a night alone until her stalker was caught, but she was going to do it her way, and this at least ought to keep Declan happy. She would protect her patient.

Liam rang her the next morning.

'The charges were dropped against Tiphanie, and Travis was taken into custody an hour ago.'

'Will they get a conviction? Given there's no body?'

'It's a bloody brilliant bit of police work. Damian went back to Rick and Allison and asked if they'd removed anything from the car. He figured that Travis would have wanted to wrap the child or body in something. There was a rug. The lab confirmed it was Chloe's blood on it, or at least a child of her parents. It was his *mate's* blanket, from his car. Rick and Allison have made a statement that Chloe had never been in their car. At least not until Travis borrowed it that night.

'There was only a trace of blood on the blanket. Chloe was probably dead and wrapped up in something either on the backseat of Travis's car or in the boot. Afterwards Travis transferred her to the seat where Rick's blanket was. The crime scene analysts went over the car again, and they're pretty sure they've found more. They weren't looking hard enough the first time. I think we have a good case. I am well aware that Travis was threatening and physically violent towards Amber and Bella-Kaye. We'll use it to support Tiphanie if we have to.'

'I wasn't allowed to use it with Amber.'

'This time Travis's violence is what the case is about. Directly.'

Travis might finally have got his dues. Amber hadn't wanted to revisit Bella-Kaye's murder but she might be prepared to give evidence about the abuse. Tiphanie's family wouldn't get Chloe back, but they would at least have final closure.

'What about the neighbours?'

'They saw Tiphanie taking Chloe to the car which Travis then drove off in. They just got the timing wrong. Happens all the time with statements.'

'What about the mate and his girlfriend? Didn't they say he couldn't have moved her?'

'They said they saw him off, that he didn't have time to move Chloe. But they were all drinking. We have him on camera driving past the service station at 11.01 p.m., which is later than he should have been. He left his mates, then came back, got her body and put it into Rick's car; we're thinking he might have put it in a dumpster. They're searching the tip but who knows? We may never find her.'

Jessie arrived twenty minutes late. Natalie was surprised she had turned up at all.

'He said you copied the videos.' She was angry, but it was a cool, controlled anger.

Did Jessie know he had attacked her as well? 'Jay?'

'He just wanted the videos. They're ours.'

'Who wanted the video Jessie? Jay? Or Kyle?'

Jessie looked at her furtively. Natalie was antagonising

her and could ill afford to. Jessie had the answer to her stalker's identity but in order to protect her, Natalie needed to be sure it was Jay's voice she had heard. She took a different tack.

'Why did you give me the computer, Jessie?'

Jessie's façade had held up for less than a minute. 'I got… mixed up. I didn't want you to know…but…'

'Got mixed up or wanted to be free?' Natalie forced her voice to be softer, inviting of the confidence and building on the rapport they had already developed. 'Jay's been in contact a lot more since your father got sick, hasn't he?'

'He always rings to wish me happy birthday.'

Jay. Their very first appointment. Her birthday. And the first note, hand delivered after he hadn't been able to convince her not to see a psychiatrist, enraged that he was losing power over a possession. Once the appointments became regular he'd got smarter.

'He couldn't believe I was going to some bullshit head shrinker. Told me I didn't need it.' That would explain why Jessie hadn't come when she was referred a year ago. He was afraid of what she might reveal. So he'd played with Natalie, wanting to put her on edge, hoping if she did suspect anything she'd keep it to herself rather than risk incurring his wrath. But when Jessie gave her the computer the stakes had changed.

Jessie continued. 'Hannah was the one that wanted me to come. She was the one who got your name.'

From Amber.

'What he is doing is wrong, Jessie,' said Natalie. 'You know that.'

'No!' Jessie leapt out of her seat. 'He loves me. He's all I have left.'

'You know that isn't true. Hannah cares for you. So do I.'

'You? You want to show that video to the world. How's that going to help me? No one understands except us, can't you see?'

'I don't want to hurt you,' said Natalie, feeling Jessie slipping away from her. 'But he has to be stopped. Do you think he hasn't kept abusing little girls?'

'No!' Jessie screamed. 'He loves *me*. I'm the special one. It's *my* rabbit drawing.' She started walking towards the door then turned. 'He took me home after my father's funeral, cared for me,' she added, tears streaming down her face.

'Jessie,' said Natalie, standing and walking towards her. 'Let me help you. I can refer you to someone else if you want. Or you could come into hospital for a little while.'

'I don't need anyone to help me. I have all the help I need.' Jessie took a red USB stick out of her bag and tossed it at Natalie. 'Watch this, you'll see he loves me.'

Natalie let Jessie leave then put the USB into her computer. The video started at the funeral; she recognised Jessie as well as Kyle, who had his arm around her, then the two of them talking to the camera, or rather the camera operator. A woman who had to be the evil stepmother made a brief appearance with her son and the precocious stepsister, and then the shot moved to Kyle and Jay talking to each other. Jay, smiling, pulled Jessie into shot, intimacy and certainty in the action. Jessie's expression was difficult to interpret: in his thrall, intimidated but telling herself she was safe because he loved her.

Natalie rewound, paused in one spot. This was the man who had abused Jessie, a man who was still trying to control

341

her. And inadvertently, Jessie had provided what she needed to answer the critical question. Jay had a signature move. She had seen in her office when he had accompanied Jessie to her appointment. A gesture of support she had thought at the time, but it had heralded Jessie's deterioration. A message that said he was in control.

Liam was waiting for her at her warehouse. She took him upstairs to her bed and they made love. And it was making love, not just sex, a gentle prolonged enjoyment of each other's bodies into the early hours of the morning. Lauren was away again. Natalie intended to talk before they slept, so she could benefit from his mellow post-coital state of mind and the alcohol that had preceded it.

To enhance the effect she went downstairs, naked, letting him watch her breasts move as she returned with a bottle of cognac that someone had given to her once. The two large glasses weren't quite brandy balloons.

'I have something for you.'

'Mmm...just what did you have in mind?'

'It's work, I'm afraid. I thought you wouldn't be up for any more, you being an old man.'

'Now that's fighting talk.' Liam reached out lazily for her breast.

'I know who assaulted me.'

He sat up, immediately serious.

Natalie handed him a USB stick. 'I don't want to bring charges for the assault if you can get him for your paedophile ring. He's very computer savvy and the company he works for has done work for the health department, which I imagine is how he accessed my hospital files.'

It was an educated guess but it had been easy to find out;

the company listed their clients on their website, including the hospital where she had spent four weeks in the psychiatric ward during her intern year. 'Watch how he interlinks his little finger with the underage girl he's abusing on the first clip and the young woman on the second. It's the same as the masked man in the video you showed me with that little blonde girl.'

'Who are the girls?'

'Can't tell you. You can't see the young girl's face.' Thanks to some judicious editing. 'And the older one is just there to show you the gesture. But that's not what you really want to know is it?' She smiled.

'Who is he?'

'Jay—Jesse—Cadek.' The edge of Liam's mouth twitched. Bullseye. Liam knew the name. He was clearly Liam's original suspect.

There was one last thing she had to be sure of.

In the morning, after Liam had left, she got on her bike. The Princes Highway was becoming increasingly familiar. This time she took a turnoff a few kilometres past Welbury, and had to stop several times to get her bearings. At the end of a long dirt road she found the farm she was looking for.

The house was a large rambling weatherboard that hadn't seen paint in a long time. Behind it, a river wove between thickets of gum trees and scrub. Dairy cows on either side of the driveway looked up, curious, then put their heads back in the grass. Natalie turned off the bike, took out the camera she had brought and walked down the side of the driveway, among the trees. She was hoping not to be seen, afraid for them, not for herself. She heard voices and slipped behind a bushy tree.

She recognised the woman who came out onto the balcony, older than her forty-four years, but without the tension in her shoulders that Natalie associated with her. She called to a younger woman who was walking towards the house holding the hand of a small child. An older boy was running ahead. Natalie was too far away to make out what was being said, but her attention was focused on the smaller of the two children, a dark short-haired child of about twelve months who held a pink soft toy in her free hand. Natalie attached the long lens to Tom's camera and took a couple of photos. The toddler was walking, but only with recently acquired confidence. As the child fell, Kay Long walked down the steps and hoisted her upright and Natalie captured the moment when she was facing the camera.

Back on the bike, Natalie headed into Welbury.

Sandra opened the door.

'I need to see Tiphanie.'

Sandra stood firmly in the doorway. 'She's moving on. She doesn't need any shrink in her life. Leave her be.'

'Tell her I know about Japan.' Natalie's stance was just as determined.

'It's okay, Mum,' said Tiphanie from the end of the corridor. She came to the door. 'We're going out.'

They walked.

'So what do you think you know?' Tiphanie was cautious, still hopeful.

'I have a photo on my camera if you need to see it.' Natalie let it remain hanging in its case off her shoulder. 'It was you not telling anyone about the broken arm when you were a kid that got me thinking. That told me how tough you are. Then there was Amber squeezing your hand at the funeral.' It wasn't as if Amber wouldn't sympathise with

Tiphanie, but there had been a particular intimacy in that action.

Natalie paused. Tiphanie's rigid stance wasn't inviting empathy but she wanted to hug her all the same. 'Then you visited her in prison; they keep records you know. You two were more to each other than just women who had children to the same man. But,' said Natalie, 'Japan finally did it. Two reasons, I guess. It's a difficult language and to do it by correspondence you would have to be very motivated and work damned hard. Which means you're smart.'

They reached a public garden space and Natalie leaned over the fence, watching children playing in the distance. 'Then the toys, at the memorial service. They were too big. Little children like toys they can cuddle and hold close. The ones at the ceremony were not the ones you told me were her favourites. I saw one with her in the paper. I imagine the same one that goes to bed at night with her. Still.' Natalie paused. 'You provoked your mother because you needed to distance yourself and Chloe. The maternal child health nurse described you as an *exemplary* mother, which fitted with the story you told me of never leaving her. It fitted with how you missed her and worried about her, but only *if* you knew she was safe. I thought about the screaming the neighbours heard in the back garden that day, and about your explanation. I believed you. You were having fun. Because you knew you were going to have to separate for a while. Which was at odds with her watching cartoons all morning, and being left to fend for herself.'

There was a long silence as tears ran down Tiphanie's face. She made no attempt to wipe them.

'What's the second thing about Japan?'

'It's a damn long way away,' said Natalie.

'I'm not coming back. Ever.' Tiphanie looked at her hard. 'If you haven't told anyone I can still do it. We both can. Live happily ever after.' There was focus and a fierceness Natalie had never seen before. Her father was right. She was a survivor.

'My family don't know,' she added.

'Amber's family does.'

Tiphanie still wouldn't acknowledge it. 'If you tell Travis, he'll kill me.'

All things considered, Natalie doubted it.

'And, he'd have access to her,' Tiphanie said. Her eyes narrowed, letting Natalie reflect on the implications that Tiphanie had weighed up over weeks, if not months. 'I'll never go back to him, but the fucking courts will give him access. Custody, if I get put away for what I've done. Without me there to protect her, he'll kill her.' She turned on Natalie and hit her hard on the chest, pummelling her with all her strength. 'You fucking can't. He tried to kill her once already, just like I pretended it happened. He threw her and she hit her head. It was what made up my mind. I was going to make a better life for us both. Protect her no matter what. Because he'll do it again, I know he will.'

Natalie, who was much the same size as Tiphanie, was struggling to remain upright under the onslaught. In the end she swept her leg under Tiphanie's so the girl landed on her butt.

'This conversation never happened,' said Natalie.

'You look calmer than I have seen you in a while.' Declan observed.

'Thank you for not reporting me,' said Natalie. 'I wasn't manic and I'm out of those cases now.'

She wouldn't relax completely until Travis had been convicted but he had been refused bail which augured well. She was taking her pills again; full dose. 'I've made my mind up on Georgia,' Natalie added.

Declan raised an eyebrow. 'An absolute truth?'

'No.'

Declan waited.

'To be honest, I don't know what I'm going to say in court.'

'You have three options, as I recall,' said Declan. 'One: Bad—she had a personality disorder and acted in anger when killing her children. Two: Mad—she had D.I.D.'

'It might be a variation of the third one: grey and murky. Personality disorder *plus* external influence; there was pathology in the relationship, no doubt. Paul isn't the main driver if he's involved at all. But that's gut feeling, no real evidence.'

This wasn't black and white, it was real life with all its complexities. But Georgia was in control. And when she had worked out what Georgia had been doing, it had opened her eyes to Tiphanie.

'You'd better read it,' said Natalie, putting her report on Corinne's desk. 'Wadhwa will go mental.'

Corinne's eyebrows shot up. 'I thought you decided he was right.'

'She had me conned for a while.'

'I'm meeting with him at eleven o'clock. Make sure he has a copy before then and be here to defend it.'

'I don't know about the genetics,' Natalie began, feeling curiously detached and barely registering Wadhwa's look of simmering fury. 'Certainly the rejecting mother—both her real one and her aunt—and an affectionate but abusive father left their mark on her personality from an early age. She was a smart child who craved love and acceptance but saw that the love of a man was the kind that counted.'

'Not the love of a child?' Corinne rather than Wadhwa.

'I think she mostly felt her children were in competition with her. The first pregnancy was no use to her, and I imagine it was quite easy for her to separate herself from it. The others? There were probably times she had positive feelings, even love. Olivia probably lasted the longest because she was little trouble. But ultimately as a toddler she was becoming her own person, and Georgia couldn't tolerate that. She couldn't share Paul's affection.'

'She dissociates!' said Wadhwa.

'Yes, but not into complete personalities, and not enough to explain murder,' said Natalie.

Corinne looked at her curiously. 'What makes you think that?'

'She has a mixed Cluster B personality disorder—narcissistic, borderline and antisocial—and she's smart. She doesn't have well-defined personalities, nor shifts that last any length of time. She probably dissociates, but only briefly. And the time she did it in my office, at least, it was carefully orchestrated.' She thought about the toy rabbit and the envelope that just happened to fall out of her bag. 'She has had this planned for a long time; she planned it when she was in prison.'

Natalie wasn't sure about everything, but most things had fallen into place. The card with the Sydney postmark? All she needed was a friend in Sydney. It was not beyond the realms of possibility that she had enlisted her mother, Lee.

But this was where the evidence ran out and her intuition took over and where she'd have preferred to present her third hypothesis. There were things about Paul that didn't ring quite true. Why had he stayed in the marriage so long? The word *amused* rang in her ears; his word or hers? He had found Jonah, the boy, dead. He *could* have sent the cards.

But given the first pregnancy was before Paul, Georgia's pathology was still the common factor.

'She was in prison, a prison full of women from troubled pasts and not as smart as her on the whole. She just had to wait for the right one, with the right story.'

Wadhwa snorted. 'I think you are spending too much time with the police and lawyers.'

'Possibly,' agreed Natalie, 'though not for much longer.'

Corinne looked at her quizzically but said nothing.

'I think she decided to see me because I have a reputation for telling the court how it is, for getting...over-involved.

She thought I was a man-hater or at least a crusader against down-trodden women, from Amber, one of my patients in prison, and that she'd be able to use this to fool me.'

Georgia would have heard about the pink bunny rabbits from the prisoners, as well as directly from Celeste. Enough to allow her to frame Paul as a paedophile when she was afraid her D.I.D. diagnosis wasn't going to work. And do it slowly and subtly. Georgia had known from Barrett that the chances of D.I.D. getting her off were low—and that Natalie wasn't committed to it. Ironic in retrospect: when Barrett had asked, Natalie was on the verge of being convinced Georgia did have D.I.D.

'Georgia had enough to set up her husband Paul. And there was an element of luck. There was a connection with a serious paedophile I knew about, and she picked my reaction, my request for a photocopy of her bunny card, and went with it.' Natalie remembered staring at the logo on the card, Georgia watching her and then demurely agreeing to mention it to Jacqueline Barrett. Georgia must have thought she'd hit the mother lode.

Wadhwa looked as if he was going to explode. 'This is preposterous!'

Natalie ignored him.

'It's particularly critical because if Georgia can get the murder charges changed to infanticide she'll get a much lighter sentence. She may be able to do it because Olivia was one week short of her second birthday, and Olivia died in the year Victoria amended the act to extend infanticide up to the age of two. If I had to put money on it I'd say that had something to do with the timing of the death.'

'This is a very brilliant legal case,' said Wadhwa, 'but not a psychiatric one. What is your *evidence*?'

'Evidence?' Natalie thought better of reminding him he had told her psychiatrists should rely on history and mental state. 'I know about the link with Amber, which was her link to me. I think Georgia used to push the patients here for information too; all the abuse victims tended to get worse when they were here in Yarra Bend with her.'

Natalie took a breath. 'Then there's Paul, Georgia's husband. Paul denies sending the cards.' He had been convincing; maybe not totally innocent, maybe stupid, but thankfully for his daughter, Miranda, there was no evidence for him being a threat, beyond the line Georgia had spun.

'Anything more?' asked Corinne.

'This.' Natalie produced her notes from the prison.

Wadhwa grabbed at them. 'And this is?'

'Georgia was studying an arts course. These are the subjects she took.'

The three of them looked at the list: Freudian Analysis, Psychology and the Law, Mental Disorder and Criminal Responsibility.

'So she plans to use this as an entry into a degree in criminology,' suggested Corinne.

'Right.'

Wadhwa started to object. He looked confused by Natalie's sarcasm.

'Ultimately,' said Corinne slowly, 'it is not up to you to apportion blame. You only have to state what you have been told and observed, and what your conclusions are, based on this.'

'This is all nonsense,' said Wadhwa throwing Natalie's notes onto Corinne's desk. 'She has D.I.D. and she was *not responsible* for her actions.'

'Possibly,' agreed Natalie, 'but we don't *know* that do

we? I've seen her angry and she was very much in control.' She had turned the anger on herself. The self-harm had been occurring right after Genevieve was born. Mutilating her genitals was perhaps a way of punishing herself for failing as a mother, hurting herself initially, as the rage built, rather than hurting her children. Or perhaps hurting herself because of what she had done to them. With or without Paul pushing the buttons. She was damaged, of that there was no doubt. But she had the mental capacity to make choices and understand consequences. That was the difference, ultimately, between bad and mad.

'I know she has D.I.D.'

'Really, Associate Professor Wadhwa?' Natalie and Wadhwa both stared at Corinne. There was a tense silence.

'Are you questioning my judgment?'

Corinne looked at Wadhwa pointedly. 'You think there is no chance she knew what she was doing?'

'That is correct.'

'Your certainty is rather alarming Professor Wadhwa. Natalie has been seeing Georgia Latimer for some time, and psychiatry has its grey areas, don't you think?'

Wadhwa pulled out a well-used sheet of paper from his leather compendium. 'I am the senior clinician. You must accept my professional judgment or I have no choice but to resign.'

Corinne looked at it, then at Natalie, before stretching out her hand. 'Thank you, Professor Wadhwa. I'm sure we'll all miss you.'

Operation Bunny was on the front page of the Saturday papers. Jesse Cadek had been arrested. It seemed like there would be months of trawling through his computers and following up but the police were already questioning two other men. There was a small inset picture of Liam O'Shea, and interviews with him on the evening news. He looked pleased. Travis made page three of the same edition. Bail denied. The media had already convicted him and cast doubt over the police investigation into the death of his first child. Amber's family had declined to comment.

Damian came to Melbourne to have Sunday lunch with her. 'Our boy is shitting himself. Thinks he's going down for life without parole. Still saying he's innocent.' Damian looked at her hard. 'You don't seem surprised.'

'Just a lot to take in.'

Damian looked like he was contemplating asking her something, but then decided against it. 'Helped that we found out Travis was thrown out of school for downloading pornographic literature, among other things,' Damian added. 'When we impounded his computer Travis became convinced we were going to frame him for pornography. Probably more worried now if he's read the papers.'

'You deserve a promotion, Damian,' said Natalie. 'You got the bad guy put away.'

Damian just looked at her.

Natalie hadn't booked anyone into Jessie's appointment slot, though she didn't think Jessie would turn up. But people could surprise you. Beverley buzzed to say she was on her way in.

Jessie looked washed out, but managed a smile. It might have been a week since her hair had seen shampoo.

'They took him away.'

Natalie nodded. 'How are you feeling about that?'

Jessie looked out the window. Natalie watched Jessie use the silence that followed to feel contained, safe. Jessie had already shown great strength. Now she needed Natalie to believe in her: trust her to deal with whatever came up in the aftermath of her abuser's arrest. Not alone, but empowered as well as supported by Natalie and those around her.

'I don't know,' Jessie said. 'The first thing I thought was that I needed to do something. Like I was to blame, and somehow I had to help him.'

'And then?'

'Hannah said I was talking shit. Thinks he'll get what he deserves in prison. Kyle says he's an arsehole too.'

'Kyle?'

'He never liked Jay. He's being great. Better now he's got it straight that I'm gay'—she grinned—'and want to wait for Hannah.'

Natalie smiled. The beginnings of the support network she needed were in place.

'I think Jay shopped Hannah to the police.' Jessie looked to Natalie for confirmation.

Natalie nodded. The more she had thought about it, the more Jay's acceptance of Jessie's relationship didn't gel. But he'd been able to effectively remove Hannah from Jessie's life. Which meant he hadn't been as worried about Hannah as he had been about Natalie.

Jessie was picking at a sore on her arm, where the bunny motif had been. The sore started to bleed. It was going to take her internal pain a lot longer to heal, but the process had started.

Beverley buzzed her as she was packing up.

'There's another patient here,' she said sounding irritable. 'Did you book her in?'

Natalie hadn't. It was Amber Long, looking contained. Nervous perhaps, but she held herself very differently from the Amber Hardy whom Natalie had met two years ago. It was hard to believe they were the same person.

'He deserved to be locked up.' Her tone wasn't accusatory or angry, merely a statement of fact. 'I told him I'll tell the real story about Bella-Kaye if he doesn't plead guilty. He won't risk two murder charges.'

'He won't enjoy being in prison,' said Natalie. 'He'll get a lot longer than you did.'

Amber nodded. 'He thinks the cops framed him. He'll just try to get the best deal.'

'You could have all got into serious trouble,' said Natalie. 'Your family still could.'

'We'd all do it again,' said Amber, arms folded.

'I don't doubt it,' said Natalie. 'To satisfy my curiosity, just when did this scheme get dreamed up and by whom?'

'After the shock—you know, hearing he'd got Tiph pregnant—I started to worry for her. I talked to Mum and she said I should write to her. I sent the letter to Kiara.

'Tiph didn't do anything then. But later, Travis was doing the same stuff...he did with me. Chloe was less than a month old when Tiph called me.'

'Why did your mum come to see me?'

Amber stared hard, as if trying to make certain Natalie wasn't trying to trap her. Not as street smart as Tiphanie, but she'd learned. 'When?'

'As far as I can tell, as soon as she heard I was going to be involved.'

Amber nodded. 'Yeah, she might have panicked. Always thought you could see through people. Mum was right behind our plan from the start—well, Tiph's plan really. I think she wished it had been me that had done it. I guess we both wished that.'

'So it was Tiphanie's idea?'

'No way was she going to stay with him,' said Amber. 'She hadn't ever wanted him, just Chloe.' Amber's voice caught. Whatever the plan had achieved, it still hadn't given her Bella-Kaye back. 'Tiph thought, you know, that he'd stay with me. But when I went to prison...well she couldn't live with her mother, I mean her mother's a shocker, and she had no money and no car. And later, she knew she couldn't ever leave Travis alone with Chloe.'

'So you decided to frame him?'

'He did it!' said Amber angrily. 'He killed Bella-Kaye.' She took a breath. 'One time, he pulled Chloe off Tiph and threw her. She hit her head. She was okay, maybe because she was older than...'

'Why Rick's car?' This was what had made Natalie suspicious initially.

'We wanted the proof to be good enough without a body. Tiph thought if the blood was in Travis's car, they could say that it could have happened any time.' Amber paused. 'So it had to be another car. Tiph knew Allison wouldn't let Rick drive drunk, and they always drink. So Tiph said she was tired and wouldn't drop Travis off. After he'd left, Mum picked up Chloe and took her home.'

The neighbours had been spot on. They *had* seen Tiphanie with the bundled up child, *and* it had been later.

'My brother, Cam, disconnected the battery lead. He used the spare car key Tiph gave him; went back after and put the lead back on. So it'd look like Travis was just drunk and stupid. Tiph was sure Travis'd be too smashed to bother checking, but Cam took the light globe out in the garage as well.'

'How did the blood get on the blanket?'

'Tiph waited until Travis was asleep. Got the keys to Rick's car and...yeah. On the seat too, but there wasn't a lot of it.'

'So the first part of the plan went as hoped but then things went wrong.'

Amber shifted uncomfortably. 'We always thought Tiph should take the rap at first, then once the blood was found they'd know it was Travis. When Tiph was charged with murder instead of infanticide we freaked. It took them forever to work out he'd used Rick's car; Tiph didn't want to say anything. She thought it was important things were dragged out of her gradually. Then they didn't find the blood. I guess there wasn't enough. And someone had taken the blanket.'

Hence Tiphanie using Natalie as the messenger.

'I never asked,' said Natalie, 'about how Tiphanie plans to get Chloe to Japan. I get she has a job—but she needs a passport for Chloe.'

'She's using...' Her voice caught. 'Bella-Kaye had one for New Zealand,' she said softly. 'Same surname. Birth date was bit over a year apart but as long as she leaves before she's five she can have the same passport. Two, three years old. No one will notice.'

'Amber, they'll never let her travel with a different mother. Not a child of that age.'

'They won't have to,' said Amber. 'I'll go too. I just won't return with...I'll be alone.'

And after that? Maybe Tiphanie would have found some Japanese connections to change their nationalities. Maybe she wouldn't ever come home, as she had said.

'What about Georgia?' asked Natalie. 'Did you help her too?'

Amber frowned. 'What do you mean?'

'Ever talk about pink bunny rabbits?'

'I never understood why she kept on about it. Celeste must have hit some sort of nerve. Is it important?'

'Not anymore. Good luck, Amber,' said Natalie.

Amber looked at her sadly. 'It doesn't make up for everything, but it helps.'

Natalie went home via the pub and picked a bottle of the best champagne they had. She would have liked to share it with Liam but instead she headed her bike east.

Drinking Laurent Perrier straight from the bottle felt suitably anti-establishment. Eoin would have approved.

'I had to do it Eoin,' she said, sitting as she always did with her back resting on the gravestone. 'Because it was the right thing to do.'

And it was. Travis would get some approximation of justice, Amber and her family would have some closure, and, most importantly, Chloe would be safe.

She took another slug. 'This isn't bad but I'll go back to bourbon. More me. I just wanted to say goodbye to Liam with it even if he isn't here. So.' She took a drink. 'Farewell, Liam. And thank you.' Another. 'And sorry.'

The gig was in Brunswick, at a pub they'd played often in the past, and Natalie was grateful for the distraction. Music always helped. There was a song for every emotion and experience, any number for lost loves and love that was never meant to be.

She was singing a Pink song when she caught him watching her: saw the pain in his eyes. Damian had said something, then. She'd figured he would eventually. Damian was the one who had found Bella-Kaye and it had gnawed at him. When she had asked for the file, he wanted to know why; and if she could work out what happened, she guessed he could too. Damian was too straight not to tell Liam they'd messed up with the first child's death and conviction. More to the point, to tell Liam that she knew.

Liam was smart. He would have wondered why she hadn't told him. Would have wondered about patient confidentiality and what she was keeping back. He knew she had been the one asking about Rick's car—as did Damian—

and one or both would have gone over and over it until they worked it out.

She couldn't see his eyes as she sang, but she could feel his pain across the room. Soon it would be anger.

He came backstage, no Vince to stop him, no Benny to protect her, and she was glad. Not that the band wouldn't have rushed to her aid but she knew the danger wasn't physical. He stood in the doorway looking at her. She met his eyes.

'I just want to ask one question,' he said.

She didn't break from his gaze. She knew what the question would be. When she had decided on what she was going to do—decided to put herself outside the law and her profession—she'd had to ask herself how far she would go. Would she do something that, unlike allowing Travis to be framed, compromised a central personal value? And force Liam to do the same?

'You were happy to trash my integrity,' he said now. 'The one thing that you knew mattered to me, that kept me going in my job. After the fuck-up with Tim Hadden. You *knew* what it means to me to only ever put someone away if they're guilty of the crime for which they're charged. No exceptions.'

Natalie nodded.

'Amber shouldn't have gone down for the first charge; we could appeal her conviction if she wanted. But ultimately that was her choice—she pleaded guilty. And it doesn't mean Travis should go down now. I could still get the whole thing thrown out. Withdraw the charges. You know that.'

Natalie nodded again. 'But you won't.'

He paused. 'You'd do it then? You'd hold our affair over my head?'

Worse. Over his children's heads. Natalie knew how much he wanted his kids to have the security he hadn't.

She had said she would never tell Lauren, not even if her life depended on it, and she had meant it. But it wasn't her life that was at risk.

He stepped closer and she saw he had something in his hand. A thick post-pack envelope. 'Your case notes. Your *own* case notes. I could have played hardball too.'

So Jay had sent him the hospital records from her psychiatric admission after all. She wondered how long Liam had had them, whether he would have ever told her if the circumstances had been different.

He looked at her for one long last moment, before placing the envelope on the table in front of her. He turned and left without saying a word.

She couldn't sleep. Damian had left a message on her phone but she wasn't up to listening to it. She felt the pain of her loss and Liam's hatred; for a while it would outweigh her conviction that sacrificing Liam's and her own integrity had been the right thing to do.

Outside her door she heard the mournful sound of 'How do you *feel*!' Wiping a tear, she let Bob back in.

EPILOGUE

Travis took a deal for manslaughter and received an eight-year minimum sentence. Natalie would have missed it if Damian hadn't texted her to say it was on page five of the paper. A week later she got a postcard:

We both love it here. Thank you for letting my child have a future.

No signature. Postmark Tokyo.

ACKNOWLEDGMENTS

This book would not have been possible without the thousands of women whose stories I have been privileged to hear over a quarter of a century working in perinatal mental health. Every one of them has had a unique struggle that has helped me understand depression, personality disorder and an array of other conditions, and how the past impacts on the present.

I am indebted to the team at Text, in particular Michael Heyward, my editor Mandy Brett, Lea Antigny, Jane Novak and Kirsty Wilson.

Special thanks to my first editor, Ruth Wykes, and first readers: Dominique Simsion who encouraged me, saying *Medea's Curse* was up there with the thrillers she read; Sue Hughes—without her Bob would have been black, but apparently black cockatoos don't talk. Tania Chandler helped with structure; Karin Whitehead who also helped with Bob and encouraged me to believe this book could be put alongside some of my well-read heroes; Eamonn Cooke to whom I go for all things Declan and psychotherapy related; Sergeant Michael Brayley who helped with police procedure (any errors are mine not his!); Adrian McKinty who was of the right age and Irish background to help me with Liam's chat-up line (in a class, not delivered personally). Thanks also to Antoni Jach and his master class of dedicated writers whose feedback helped get the manuscript to a new level: Josh Lefers (I borrowed his outfit for Shaun), Erina Reddan, Emilie Collyer, Lisa Jacobson, Clive Wansbrough, Tasha Haines, Anna Dusk and Rocco Russo.

Final thanks, which can never be enough, to my husband Graeme. When we first got together he took it up to me: don't just talk about writing a book one day—do it! Life for us both has been a whirlwind since his novel became a bestseller. But he has made time to support me and be ruthless while trying to make my book better—despite my sometimes less than calm response to his suggestions (which are almost always right!)...he is my muse, sounding board and soul-mate, and I am indebted.